# Counterpoint

## Michelle Cook

"We can solve our problems, but it's not clear that we can solve our problems and get rich at the same time, and that is the current requirement for all solutions."

*Terence McKenna*

**www.darkstroke.com**

Discover us online:
**www.darkstroke.com**

Find us on instagram:
**www.instagram.com/darkstrokebooks**

Include **#darkstroke** in a photo of yourself
holding this book on Instagram and
**something nice will happen.**

*For Dad*

# Acknowledgements

First thanks, as always, go to the superb team at Darkstroke Books, particularly Laurence and my wonderful editor Steph. Their knowledge, support and open, collaborative approach is a gift for an author still bumbling their way through the publishing industry.

Thank you, too, to all the incredible and talented writers who have helped me keep faith, keep on and get this one over the line: Val Penny, Charlie Tyler, Kateri Stanley, Paula RC Readman, Alison Knight, Sue Barnard, Ted Bun, Morwenna Blackwood and Phil Price to name a handful. I hope you all know who you are because you're legends.

Thanks to my *very* understanding husband Daniel and to our two kids for helping me keep it real. Yeah, I really mean that. They don't care how many books I write, I'm still Mommy to them. Quite right.

Eternal gratitude is due to my readers, who have followed Essie through her heartbreak and trials. I hope you approve of how and where we leave her.

Finally, my parents. They've been my constant; the place I have always known I can come back to. I've been all grown up for a long time, but you're never too old to go home. Thank you for never asking me to return your door key.

# About the Author

Michelle Cook writes thrillers and dystopian fiction. She lives in Worcestershire, UK with her husband and their two young children.

Her first joyful steps into creative writing were at the age of ten, when the teacher read out her short story in class. A slapstick tale of two talking kangaroos breaking out of a zoo, the work was sadly lost to history. Still, Michelle never forgot the buzz of others enjoying her words.

More recently, she has had several flash pieces published, was long-listed for the Cambridge Prize for flash fiction, and placed first in the Writers' Forum competition with her short story The Truth About Cherry House.

Counterpoint is her second novel and sequel to the best-selling Tipping Point.

# SYNOPSIS OF BOOK I: TIPPING POINT

## England, 2035

The population, battered by the dual threats of climate change and religious terrorism, submits to a tyrannical government and a violent police force.

Beset by grief at the loss of her family, who died in a terrorist attack two years before, eighteen-year-old **Essie Glass** lives a meagre existence. She works as a waitress by day and spends her evenings arguing with strangers in online forums. Through this, she develops a friendship with a research chemist, **Jack**. Essie and her best friend, **Maya**, join a dissident group called *Change Here*, led by the charismatic **Gabe**, who begin a campaign of disobedience. Though she is initially reluctant, the group's activities inspire Essie to rebel further.

The two areas of her life collide when Essie meets Jack in person. He enlists Essie's help to expose a climate change conspiracy. He entrusts her with a high-tech prototype file—plans for new carbon capture technology that can produce free, clean energy. Jack believes that the technology is being suppressed to protect the profits of traditional power companies, which will endanger the entire planet.

Unbeknownst to either, their meeting is observed, propelling Essie into a maelstrom of deceit and danger. As the pressure on Essie intensifies, she seeks refuge with local cleric and *Change Here* collaborator, **Seth**.

Essie and Maya take the plans to *Change Here* members, appealing for help, but they are betrayed. A trusted ally snatches the file, and Gabe blackmails them into vandalising an unfamiliar private residence. Misdemeanour turns to disaster. Maya is left behind and goes missing.

Essie discovers the house belongs to a dangerous enemy: **Alex Langford**—Jack's employer. As she delves further, she learns that Langford has co-conspirators among the government, including local MP and Homeland Environment minister, **Kerry Tyler**. Langford has deeper connections to Essie's life than she could have imagined.

When Maya turns up dead, Essie's rage consumes her. She goes after Langford seeking revenge, but he turns the tables. She becomes a player in a dangerous power game and a fight to recover the prototype. In the final, brutal confrontation, it's not only Essie's future that hangs in the balance, but that of embattled planet Earth.

Surviving the clash, Essie begins a new life with Seth and their daughter, Willow. Her world is upended again as Kerry switches sides and makes an offer difficult to refuse. Essie is forced to make a choice. Should she leave her cherished new family and pursue a higher goal?

Reunited with Jack, whom she believed dead, Essie reveals she has made a secret copy of the file. As the story closes, Essie and Jack make their plans to build the model and redefine the future.

# Counterpoint

# Chapter One

## Essie

**31st October 2041**

"Mummy, look." Willow mounts the roof of the den and thrusts a jubilant fist in the air, her dark curls bobbing. "I'm at the top."

"Willow, hold on."

Before I can move towards her, Seth's at my side, a bag for life dangling from his arm. "She's fine."

"She's four. She'll break her neck."

"Who, monkey girl?" He flaps a dismissive hand.

"Neglectful father."

"Over-anxious mother." Seth's brown eyes fold into what Willow calls his tease-creases. "Oh, hey, I got us a treat." With a mischievous giggle, he pulls out a bottle of something bubbly from his bag with two glasses he must have grabbed from the caravan. He makes light work of popping the cork and pours. After handing a glass to me, he clinks his own against mine. "Happy birthday, Ess."

Twenty-five today. I feel older. When I look at the burnt sky, Seth's faded, checked shirt...everything feels older.

Willow has tired of climbing. She jumps down with Seth's easy grace and springs onto her bashed-up trike. Watching her across the trailer park playground is like staring into a bowl of syrup. That orange hue we've just got used to ever since Sherwood Forest went up in flames. Over a hundred miles away, but I can smell the sweet sharpness of charred pines.

Seth's hand, cool from the glass, is on my arm. "You haven't seen my costume yet. Wanna guess?"

Trick or treat is one of his and Willow's things. Like the baking.

I squint at his dark hair, imagine it slicked back from his widow's peak. "Vampire?"

"Nope."

"Sexy priest." An old joke.

"Too hot for dog collars."

"Yes, you are. Er…politician?"

"Christ, no. What do you take me for?" He chuckles, though there's a flicker in his eyes like there must be in mine. Memories of the time Alex Langford—OBE, and now beloved Prime Minister—tried to murder me in a locked room at his factory. I still dream about flashing light on concrete walls sometimes and wake up screaming.

I'll bet Seth is thinking about my appearance at his vicarage, soaked in blood and tears, after my escape.

"I got nothing else," I say, lips numb. "Tell me."

"Ah…wait and see, my beautiful assistant."

Willow crashes her trike into the railings behind the swings. Thank God they're there, or she'd have tipped herself into the river beyond by now. She's fearless, and that's not always a good thing.

A breeze swirls the skeleton leaves about as it grows darker under sweaty clouds.

"Come on," says Seth. "Looks like another storm's coming. And you've got a parcel waiting for you at home."

"Who from?"

Seth shrugs.

I can't think of anyone else who would remember my birthday. Nobody in a position to send me something. Brian gave me a bunch of flowers when I left the Braai yesterday, so it's not him. We quaff our fizz, gather our bags, and hustle Willow across the spit of waste ground home.

We've made the caravan cosy with cushions and pictures on the frail walls, but it makes me pine for my old flat. Even its damp smell was better than the burnt air that seeps in

4

through the cracks here. Willow loves this place, though. When we had to leave our cottage, she thought it was like a holiday. Six months later, the novelty hasn't worn off for her.

That's fortunate because Unity has commandeered the cottage for good. The new directive came out in April. Unity, our own 'harmonising coalition of faith and science', is now allowed to take possession of any property for 'authorised spiritual or scientific endeavours' as long as they provide a 'suitable alternative'. What kind of endeavour they needed our home for is beyond me. Are they training new clerics there? Indoctrinating new educators to enlighten the masses? Doubtful.

I bet they only took it because my name was top of a list somewhere, ear-marked for more hassle.

Seth hands me a brown package, about the size of a book. "And here's an official-looking letter." He plops a white envelope on top of it.

There's no contest. I chuck the letter on the little dining table and tear into the brown paper, revealing bubble wrap underneath. "Wills, I've got magic poppers for you later."

Willow giggles.

Inside is a picture frame and a pink envelope. It's a photo of Maya and me. She's tipping her head towards mine and sticking her tongue out at the camera. Looks like we're in a park. Heart pounding, I try to remember where the image was taken. We look about seventeen, so it must have been two years before Maya died.

Before she was murdered.

Another victim of Langford. Shot and suffocated because she was in the wrong place at the wrong time.

Who sent this? Are they screwing with me?

With cold, shaky fingers, I open the card. It's a print; an oil painting of a rainbow. Inside, a message straddles the two blank pages. I flop into the dining booth and read.

*Dear Essie,*
*Happy Birthday!*
*I found this picture when we were clearing out Maya's flat*

*back then. I always wanted you to have it, but it never seemed the right time. It looks like it was taken before she met that Lawrence.*

*Hope you're doing well, and Seth and little Willow. I'm sorry I haven't been in touch more. It's been six years, but it's still painful to think of Maya all alone down there. How scared she must have been of that man. Why did she move so far away? We have excellent colleges up here. She could have gone to LIPA; she was such a talented actress.*

*Sorry, I don't mean to mope. I hope I did the right thing by sending you the picture, and it doesn't make you sad.*

*Take care of your little family.*
*Much love*
*Alimah*

"Maya's mum."
Seth nods and takes the picture frame. "It's a lovely photo."

*That Lawrence.*

Alimah must still believe the lie they told her: Lawrence killed Maya. My eyes prickle with tears, but they're self-indulgent. I shake them away. "I never told her what really happened. How could I have kept it from her?"

Seth nudges me along the seat and squashes in next to me, taking my hand. "What choice did you have?"

I rest my head on his shoulder.

Much later, face still streaked green with trick or treat paint, Willow is tucked into her bottom bunk, listening to Seth's bedtime story. Remembering the letter, I scoop it up from the table and peel back the self-seal.

*Unity HMP Enlightenment*
*Hatcheton*
*Bedfordshire*
*England*
*Date as postmark.*
*Dear Ms Glass,*

*Permission has been granted for you to visit Mr Lawrence Cunningham at the facility above. Your appointment is Tuesday 5th November at 2.00pm. You must arrive 30 minutes before this time to enable security checks to be carried out. Please visit the web address below to confirm your attendance. Failure to do so will result in your slot being reallocated...*

Lawrence.

I gave up applying to see him over a year ago. There seemed no way, five years into a sham life sentence, they'd consent for us to meet. Not after all the trouble we caused them.

So why now?

\*\*\*

Kerry Tyler changes her office more often than I change my sheets. In her defence, she's had quite a few jobs in recent years. The sign on this latest door says she's a Public Relations Consultant.

Okay.

Filling my lungs with smoky morning air, I glance around the street. Nestled between a boarded-up bookie and a sex shop, the sign's gold lettering looks either classy or slutty. I can't decide which. Bit of a comedown from Homeland Environment Minister. She must have to skirt the sleeping bags under the bridge to get her coffee at the Worcester Spoon kiosk.

I check for patrol drones, then press the intercom.

The door buzzes. A silky, female voice says, "Come on up."

She meets me on the landing in a pinstripe dress and the usual French pleat. Despite the greying hair at her temples, her skin is as dark and smooth as the first time we met.

"Ess."

"Kez." I hate it when she shortens my name, and she knows it.

She gives me a tight-lipped smile. "Happy birthday for

7

yesterday. How are Seth and Willow?"

I should be nice. It's part of the game. Still, I can't stomach the chitchat about my family. Not with this woman who's been slithering around my life for years. Since she sniffed out her main chance, pinned her fortunes to me, Jack, and the carbon capture prototype he designed. "Jack on the call yet?"

"Not yet. I'm set up in the meeting room. Through here."

Cream carpets and lilac paint—fancy; aspirational. Like she's trying to recreate her heyday as an MP. Embedded in the far wall is a screen displaying a photo of a mountain scene.

With elegant, red-nailed fingers, Kerry gestures towards a leather chair facing us across a long, narrow desk. I fold into the seat, eyeing the pile of papers opposite as Kerry takes her place.

The mountains disappear and with no preamble I'm looking at Jack's tired brown eyes. His hair glints reddish in a sunbeam from the window beside him.

"Jack." Kerry leans forward, the chair squeaking.

"Hi, Kerry. Can you hear me?"

"Yep."

His eyes hold the weight of our secret as they switch to the side, presumably at the little version of me on his screen. "Essie. How are you doing? How's Willow?"

"Good. All good."

"New office, Kerry?"

"Uh huh. So, let's get started. You were going to give us a progress report."

My heart thuds. This is the part we must get right, or Kerry will know something's up. One wrong step and it'll all unravel: the copy of the file Seth made for me; that Jack's further into the build than Kerry imagines. Once it's finished, we can release it into the world, cut Kerry off from her meal ticket. She has no idea, believes Jack's building it from scratch, years away from completion.

At least, I hope she does.

"Well, we're doing okay," Jack's saying. "The physical absorbent is working."

"Which is?" Kerry purses her lips, clearly unhappy to be at

8

a disadvantage to Jack's expertise.

"The thing that's going to capture the $CO_2$. It's where the gas is stored until it's passed onto the chemical absorbent." Seeing Kerry's shoulders rise, he says, "Nickel. That's the thing that will convert the $CO_2$ to free energy."

Her posture relaxes a little. "Okay. That sounds promising. And when will the chemical absorbent be ready?"

Jack's chest rises, and he swallows. "Well, erm…that's going to take us longer."

"I see."

"I mean, I know it's possible. It's just tricky in practice. And we need to make it scalable. Also…"

"Also, what?" Her tone sharpens.

*Please, Jack, throw her some good news.*

But: "Well, it's kind of hard to buy large quantities of nickel in Cuba without raising eyebrows, you know? Are there any strings you can pull your end to get hold of some? I can give you the specifications."

I squash a grin. Jack knows as well as I do Kerry doesn't have strings to pull these days. He's cornered her.

She sighs. "Okay. Send me the info through and I'll see what I can do."

"Great. Thanks, Kerry. I guess that's it for now."

"Yep. Guess so. Jack?"

"Uh huh?"

"Next time set up for the call in your workshop. I want to see this tech in the flesh."

It's only a flicker, but I catch it in his eyes before he says, "Sure, no worries."

Jack disappears as quickly as he arrived. I'm staring at the mountain again, my mouth dry.

Kerry turns her gaze on me. "So."

"So."

"Don't suppose anyone bought you a truckload of nickel for your birthday?"

Willow's hair smells of herby shampoo and it tickles my nose as she leans in to kiss me.

"Can you read Rabbit Party, Mummy?"

"Didn't you have that one last night? And the night before that…"

She giggles and points at the days of the week poster on her wall. "Silly Mummy. This is *Friday* Rabbit Party. Last night was *Thursday* Rabbit Party."

"Oh, of course." I pluck the book from the top of the pile by her bunk, settle on my knees and open it to read about rabbits having a secret picnic in the woods with the gnomes and fairies and all the woodland creatures. Not for the first time, I wish I could go back to when my worst nightmare was Baby Bee getting stuck in the jam.

Willow knows Baby Bee's going to be all right. She's asleep before the rabbits mount their rescue with a daisy stem.

Seth's stretched out on the sofa with a beer. My laptop perches on a shelf next to him, playing old blues songs on low.

He swings his legs round to make room for me to sit. "She asleep?"

I nod, plucking the bottle from his fingers to take a swig. "Rabbit Party. Works every time."

"Boring as hell, isn't it?"

The beer goes up my nose as I laugh. Then the rain pinging off the caravan roof sobers me. There were landslides here in September. Across the park, nearest the river. Three families lost their vans. Thank God, everyone got out in time.

Seth squeezes my hand as he steals his bottle back. "What time's he calling?"

I check the burner phone. "Eight."

Ten minutes.

Seth smiles with closed lips. "I'll get you a beer. It's the only way to keep you from nicking mine."

There are no contacts stored on the phone, but when it

rings, I recognise the number as Jack. "Hi."

"Essie." As ever, he sounds relieved. Like each time he's wondering if someone else has swiped the burner.

"Jack. Well played today. Kerry seemed to swallow everything you fed her."

"Thanks. Yeah, think so. I've no clue what to do about next time. She's going to want something solid. I'll have to mock up a random bit of kit for her."

"Well, we've got two weeks. Will that be enough?"

Seth's staring at me, mouth set, like he's trying to discern Jack's words on my face.

"Should be," says Jack.

I swig my beer. "And what about the real thing? The nickel you need?"

"I've got shed loads of nickel, Ess." Jack chuckles. "D'you need any, 'cause I've got it to burn over here?"

"Yeah, well, don't burn it." A grin plays on my lips. "How?"

A brief pause. "You don't need to worry about that."

"Jack, have you done something illegal?" I ignore Seth's stare.

"You're kidding."

"You know what I mean. Did you steal it?"

Next to me on the sofa, Seth mutters, "Did he steal what?"

"Forget about the nickel. It's a non-issue." Jack's voice drops. "We're almost there. By the time we meet Kerry again, I'll have an operational $CO_2$ capture and conversion unit to release to the world. Once I share the spec, every mad inventor in the world will be able to build it."

"Every mad inventor with a heap of nickel in their garage." Still, my heart does a hop. After everything we went through to save this thing from Langford and his cronies. "Doesn't feel real."

"I know. I'll send you pics. You'll see for yourself." Jack's breath rattles in my ear. I imagine him doing a victory dance in his workshop. "We might still save the world, Ess. You, me and Seth."

Me, Jack and Seth. One of us doesn't seem like he's

celebrating.

When Jack's gone, he pings me a picture. It's out of focus, but in large concrete space looms an enormous cylinder of dark grey metal, maybe twenty feet long, propped on its side by struts of the same material. Wires and dials stud its surface here and there, but the rest of it gleams in the dim light.

Is this the thing that will save us?

Seth makes me jump with a hand on my arm. "What's he been stealing, Ess?"

# Chapter Two

## Essie

### 5th November 2041

Unity HMP Enlightenment is a dour, concrete block in the middle of a flat, brown wasteland, dismal even in the bright autumn sunlight. It took me forty minutes to walk from Hatcheton station, where the replacement bus service spat me out of its sweaty doors.

I ran out of water at Milton Keynes. Head pounding, I lick my salty lips and swallow what moisture remains as I approach the iron gate.

A drone swoops over the razor wire, hovering a foot from my face.

"State your name and display your Citizen ID," orders a toneless, female voice.

My face is numb, but I manage, "Essie Glass," while I fumble the little green card from my pocket.

She seems satisfied with my identity, because the drone launches back over the fence and skitters off to a sentry hut stranded in the no-man's-land between the perimeter and the prison. The gate buzzes open and a sallow-faced young guard steps out of the cabin, rifle strapped across his chest.

"Step inside, then halt."

I do as I'm told. He snatches the ID card from my hands and nods before returning it. "Papers?"

My hand shakes as I pass him the visitor permit.

"Come with me."

I glance behind. This is weird. I thought there'd be more

visitors, but no one else is here. As we pass the hut, another man, middle-aged and clad in the same dark jumpsuit as the first, looks up from his screen. "For Cunningham?"

"Yep," says the sallow one. "I'll take her in."

He marches me towards a pair of metal doors set in the concrete. Inside is more concrete, with only the occasional piece of dark wood furniture to break it up. Ahead of us, in a cluttered room behind Perspex, sits yet another guard, pale eyes in a broad, grim face. When Sallow hands him my permit through the gap, he buzzes us into a door on the right.

"Okay, thanks," says Grim. "I'll take it from here." He struts towards me, eyes flicking up and down. Assessing my purple dress and combat boots, maybe. Hopefully.

Sallow bangs the door closed as he leaves, and my pulse kicks up a gear. Uninspiring company though he was, I wish he hadn't gone.

"Bag," says Grim, whose real name, according to his badge, is Ashley Tanner.

"Huh?"

"Need to search your bag." He's donning a pair of blue plastic gloves.

When I hand it over, he dumps the contents onto his dusty, paper-strewn desk and rifles through them.

There's nothing interesting in there. He leaves me to put everything back.

"'Kay. Stand there." He points to a patch of dirty white plaster to the right of the Perspex window. "Face the wall, hands either side of your head, legs apart."

I swallow the lump in my throat. "Is there a female officer?"

He sneers and spreads his palms, looking around us with exaggerated raised eyebrows.

Stomach churning, I turn to the wall. My fingers press hard into the grubby paintwork while his hands skim and probe and his breath rasps in my ear. Cheap, sharp aftershave can't mask the stale sweat on his body.

"You're clean." He turns me around to face him. His name badge is skewwhiff.

"Can I see Lawrence now?" I strain to keep my voice even.

Face too close to mine, he murmurs, "What will you give me?"

My leg twitches, as it readies to knee him in the balls.

Grim presses against me, then grins. "Relax, ice princess. He's waiting for you."

It's just Lawrence in a large yet airless room filled with tables and chairs. I expected glass partitions and phones like in the old movies. He's lost so much weight the skin seems to drip off his cheekbones. His eyes are hollow, one sporting a fading bruise.

There don't appear to be any cameras in here, but Grim locks the only door and stands inside it, picking at his grubby nails.

"Essie." Standing to greet me, Lawrence tries to smile, but it's as though his lips are sticking to his teeth. He folds me in a gangly hug, hanging on me until I stagger. His ribs dig into my chest.

"Hey," barks Grim.

Lawrence flinches back, flopping into the chair, and I take the one opposite him across the metal table.

We look at each other for a while. Taking in each other's differences, maybe. Finally, he says, "It's fantastic to see you. You look great."

"I'm fat."

He looks down at himself and smiles. "You say that like it's a bad thing."

Instant shame warms my cheeks. "Lawrence." How to begin. "How have you been?"

He laughs without humour. "Oh, you know. It's fine. I mean, it's not great, but…they leave me alone now."

"Do they let your parents visit?"

He gives an awkward shrug. "Sometimes. But my mum… She can't deal, you know? It's been a while."

*Oh, God, Lawrence.*

I nod and blink away the tears. He doesn't need me going to pieces. His grooming done, Grim is idling against the door with a smirk.

When I check back at Lawrence, the dull mask of his expression, my eyes prickle again. "Oh, God, I'm so sorry. I should have done something. Shit, I don't know."

"There was nothing you could do. Langford…" He glances up at Grim. "Langford needed a scapegoat for what he did to Maya. If you'd raised your voice, you'd be dead. I can't believe you're still alive as it is."

"Me neither."

"Unless they think you'll lead them to the prototype one day."

It's like my ribs are crushing inwards. There's so much to say.

"I've told them over and over, it's gone." His eyes, so foggy before, focus on me, sharp as his voice. "I destroyed it, Ess. Panicked when I knew they were coming for me." He squints at the bare bulb on the ceiling. "Guess that's my contribution to history. Snatching our last hope from you; flushing it down the toilet."

I have to tell him. When I glance up at Grim, he's back to picking his fingers. "Not our last hope," I whisper.

Lawrence's head snaps up.

"We've got a copy of the file." I try not to grin, but my lips are stretching. "Seth copied it for me. We're building it now. Me and Jack. In Cuba, if you can believe that."

"No… Ess." He makes a tiny chopping motion with a flat hand.

"It's nearly finished, Lawrence. You didn't flush anything down the loo. Well, you did…but…"

Beads of sweat shine on his furrowed brow as he shakes his head. "Please don't…"

What's he stressing about? I glance around, looking for microphones or a camera. Nothing. And Grim's still flicking dirt from his nails. When I look back at Lawrence, he's performing a weird tic, pulling at the neck of his prison sweatshirt.

There's a wire peeking out of his top.

My face goes cold; my tongue freezes.

16

*Shit, shit, shit. You idiot, Ess.*

Lawrence's wide, wet eyes mirror my despair.

"They wired you." My voice is flat.

"I tried to warn you."

"I've screwed everything up." Too late, I think of back-tracking, pretending it was a joke. My legs unfreeze and I clamber to my feet. "I'm sorry. I have to…"

Grim glares at me as I crash into chairs and trip over a table leg. He doesn't move when I reach him.

"I need to leave, please."

Grim folds his arms across his chest. "In a hurry?"

"Family emergency."

A raised eyebrow.

Lawrence's chair scrapes behind me. "Let her go, Ashley. Please."

With a huff, he turns to unlock the door. "You'll need to submit to an exit search, of course."

I force down the lump of nausea. "Fine."

When I glance back, Lawrence lifts a shaky hand and my heart cramps. I may never see him again. Then I'm trotting down the grubby corridor back to Grim's lair.

*I'm sorry, Lawrence. So, so sorry.*

Grim's search seems to take longer this time, but I'm not thinking about him. My fingers twitch against the paintwork, and my toes wiggle inside my boots.

The second I'm beyond the gates, I speed dial Seth.

"I thought you'd be with Lawrence still."

"Seth. I've done something stupid." In the pause, I struggle to breathe. The forty minutes' walk back to the station feels like light years. I try to hurry my legs up, but they're so heavy.

"What's happened?"

"They wired him. They know." I hold in a sob.

"About the…?"

"Yes. I told him."

His breath catches. "Ess."

"I know. Don't say it." I screw my eyes up as the sun shoots from behind a cloud. "I'm so sorry."

"Will they come for us?"

My legs give up all at once. I flop onto a low wall behind me. "Yes."

That makes it real. Everything gone in one stupid act.

"Do you want me to call Jack?" Seth's saying.

"No. I will."

"Not on your phone, Ess."

"It hardly matters now, does it? You'll have to pick Willow up from school. Then stay at the caravan 'til I get back. Draw the curtains. Don't answer the door to anyone." God, why did they have to transfer Lawrence to bloody Bedfordshire? I'm too far from home.

"Is that necessary? I mean, do you think they'll come?"

"Seth. Why else was Lawrence wired, for God's sake? This is what they wanted."

*And I gave it to them.*

I lay my forehead in a shaking hand. "I'm sorry."

We say goodbye, and I know I have to move, but my legs seem glued to the wall. A haze of anxiety makes it so difficult to think I can't remember the way back. On my phone, I look up local taxi firms and dial one to pick me up. There's an emergency fund hidden at home in a tin. I can't imagine a more appropriate time to break into it.

Heart hammering, sweat trickling down my temple, I call Jack. He takes ages to answer.

He doesn't even say hello. "That's the wrong phone."

"Yeah, sorry. I'm not at home. It's urgent."

There's a loud buzzing at his end. "Hang on." The phone rustles, there's a click, and the noise stops. "What's urgent?"

It's like knowing I have to dive into ice water. My limbs ache with the cold already. "I—uh—I came to see Lawrence today."

"Lawrence in prison?"

18

"Yeah."

"After, what, six years? They let you see him after so long?"

"Yeah. He… They wired him." If I whisper, it won't be happening.

There's silence but for the rustle of space, then, "Ess?"

"Yes."

"Did you talk?"

I screw my eyes shut. "I'm sorry."

"You didn't think there was a *reason* they wanted you to visit?"

"I *did*. I didn't think wire."

"Why not? Jesus."

"I thought maybe camera or mic, but there wasn't. I reckoned it'd be safe to whisper."

"Jesus, Ess. What did you tell them?"

"You didn't see his face, Jack. He said he destroyed the original prototype. I had to tell him there was a copy; he was torturing himself."

"They'll come here." His breath roars on the line. "I'll have to clear out. Oh, God, Essie. And get rid of the entire unit. It took years."

"I know. I'm sorry."

"Shit. You'll have to run." He sounds like he's on the move.

"I know."


*All of us.*


He sighs. "Do you think Kerry's in this?"

"I thought that. Kerry, or Langford. Both?"

"Either way, it's back to square one."

I open my mouth to respond but close it in silence.

"I'd better shut down the workshop. Look after yourself, Ess. Call me tomorrow. Other phone." He doesn't say goodbye either.

The taxi draws up five minutes later. After a while, the driver gets the hint I don't want to chat and leaves me in peace to gaze out of the window, legs jiggling all the way home.

# Chapter Three

## Essie

### 5th November 2041

Seth's already packed our stuff in two dented suitcases. He darts about the caravan, fumbling stuff into a holdall, switching off mains sockets while Willow sits at the kitchen table, sort of colouring, sort of watching Seth buzz around.

He pays the taxi with money from the emergency tin. As I watch him trot back up the yellow-grassed incline, my stomach cramps at the conversation to come.

Picking up his bag, he says, "I had a word with Rich next door. He was scrapping his old petrol car before the ban, but he's given it to us instead. It's got a full tank. We can be at my parents' place by nine tonight. If the roads are still passable. Haven't been there in so long."

"Seth."

"I've packed us some sandwiches, so we don't have to stop. I know we can't stay long, but a day or two. They've never even met Willow in person. Mum will love that."

"I can't come with you." My voice cracks on the last word.

"Huh?" Seth blinks and glances at Willow, who's singing to herself as she scribbles with red crayon.

"You'll have to go without me."

"What the hell? No." He drops the bag and takes me firmly by the shoulders. "What are you talking about?"

"I've thought it through." Have I? "If I'm with you, you'll be in more danger."

"No. We're not doing that."

"Yes. Seth, I'm not risking you getting hurt. Think about it. They'll be coming for me. Kerry, Langford. Whoever. They let me live last time, but this time, I've screwed them over. And they'll use you and Willow to get to me; you know they will."

He grips my arms until they hurt, his eyes swelling with tears.

Because he knows I'm right.

"No." But there's no conviction in his tone.

"Mummy, what's wrong?" Willow closes her colouring book and switches her gaze between Seth and me.

I break free from Seth's grasp and crouch beside her as he turns away, sniffing.

"Nothing's wrong, Wills. Daddy and I were just saying you should visit his mummy and daddy in Yorkshire. Your nanny and grandad. They're dying to meet you. That'll be exciting, won't it?"

Frowning, she reaches up to stroke my tear away. "Then why are you crying?"

"I'm just happy for you. And sad I can't come, because I want to meet them too."

"Why can't you come?"

Oh, my chest hurts. Whatever's left in there has shattered into pieces. "I've got some things to do first. Then I'll join you."

I raise my eyes to Seth, who stands behind her, eyes wet, mouth frozen in a miserable twist. He stays out of Willow's eyeline, probably so she can't see his anguish.

Willow looks at the floor then back at me. "They won't take long, will they? The things you've got to do?"

"No, sweetheart." The lie crushes me, and I grab her in a hug so tight she squeaks. "I won't be long. You're going to have so much fun with Nanny and Grandad. I'm not going to miss out, am I?"

When she pulls away, I let her go, inhaling the herbal smell of her shampoo, as though I could hold on to her that way.

21

She grabs her little backpack from the table. "Bye, Mummy. Love you."

"I love you, Wills."

The moment passes before I take it in. She's gone.

Seth lifts her into the car, tucking the seat belt around her as I watch helplessly from the caravan's door. The sight of him as he returns, the thought that I might never see them again, rob my legs of their strength. I sag against the doorframe, and then against Seth as he nuzzles me, back inside the caravan.

He presses his lips hard against mine, his tears wetting my cheeks, then folds me in a hug.

My palms press against my temples. "I'm sorry, Seth. I'm sorry."

"No." He pulls back, hands on my shoulders. "Look at me. It'll be okay."

I wish I could believe that. "Yeah."

"Where will you go?"

I shake my head. Even if I knew, I couldn't tell him. "Please be careful."

"You, too. Call me when you can."

"Yep—" It turns into a sob. "I'll have to get rid of my phone and use the burner. Don't call me. I'll call you when it's safe. If they get to me..." He opens his mouth, but I grab his arms, still resting on my shoulders. "Please, Seth."

After a long look, he nods, then leaves.

Willow will be staring out of the window, waiting for me to come out and wave, but it's impossible. I fall to my knees and fumble the door closed as the engine revs, then fades...

I can't lose this family. I've lost too much already. My parents; my sisters; Maya. This isn't fair.

*Whose fault is it, though, Ess?*

How long have I been crying on the floor? Slow wheels scrape the rubble outside, and that pushes me to move. I crawl to the scratched plastic window and peer out. A dark blue van trundles past in the dusk.

Got to move.

Legs stiff with misery, I unfold myself and try to think straight. What do I need? Where do I go? Seth and Willow are all I have.

Brian could help me.

*Yeah, great idea. You're gonna get your boss trapped in this too?*

I have to go *somewhere*—away from here. Beyond that, there's no plan.

As quietly as I can, I grab my rucksack from the bedroom and cram in some clothes. From the shelf in the wardrobe, I root out the burner phone and shove that in too. On the way to the bathroom, I pass Willow's bedroom door. Something soft tangles in my feet and I stumble into the wall.

Boop.

Willow's green rabbit. She'll be inconsolable when she realises she left him.

Biting my lip, I stuff him in the bag then move on to the bathroom, sweeping random items on top of Boop's Marmite-crusted nose.

More scrapes on rubble. The blue van is back, pulling up at Rich's caravan next door. Two men peer through the windscreen. I duck below the window, breathing hard.

The engine dies. There's no time to think. Snatching the rucksack, I burst out of the door, turn away, and sprint into the dark.

A van door rasps open, a man shouts.

I won't get far. Any moment, they'll shoot me in the back.

I push my legs faster.

# Chapter Four

## Seth

**5th November 2041**

Fuck, fuck, *fuck*.

I grip the steering wheel so hard its plastic stitching burns my fingers. Sweat tickles my cheeks. My chest is heavy with the smoky air billowing in through the air con.

In the rear-view mirror, a black Lexus crawls behind us. When I switch lanes, the Lexus follows.

Willow's head sways against the back seat. She cried when she couldn't wave goodbye to Mummy, then fell quiet and dozed off half an hour ago, just after Ashby. Before the Lexus appeared—or before I noticed it. At least she can't see me freaking out. I squint at the car in the mirror, looking for a light bar or markings.

Nothing, but that doesn't mean anything.

Have they got to Essie? The thought freezes my breath. I imagine her mouthing off at some massive secret service guy; struggling; getting hurt. Heat sears my limbs, but there's no one to fight. A sign says it's half a mile to the Nottingham exit.

*Wait for it.*

Fighting my instincts, I accelerate and pull into the outside lane. The Lexus follows. There's only light traffic.

Three hundred yards. I floor the accelerator. Two hundred. One hundred.

I can see the slip road disappearing into the dark.

*Wait... NOW.*

I yank the steering wheel to the left. The tyres screech. We cut across the lanes. Any second, someone's going to plough into us. Willow's car seat is nearest the oncoming traffic. It'll hit her first.

What have I done? I turn towards glaring headlights. A horn blasts. Willow screams. The car scrapes something metal, but it's on my side.

Darkness closes in on the car as headlights pass. We're alone on the slip road, but for how long? The drones will be on the way.

Miraculously, the engine is still running. I slam the gear stick in first and pull forward. My door screeches as whatever I collided with tries to keep hold. The car rocks side to side as it thumps down on the tarmac.

"Daddy?" Willow's voice is uncertain, jagged with stalled dreams and sudden terror.

Hand pressed to my chest, I say, "Everything's fine, Wills. Go back to sleep."

Who am I kidding? Nonetheless, she flops back into the car seat and closes her eyes.

At the traffic island, I take the first exit, away from Nottingham. A few random turns later, we're out of the glare of streetlights. I open the window to gulp in the heat of the night, hardly believing we got away, certain the Lexus is waiting around the next bend. No other cars pass and gradually my chest slackens.

Willow must have felt some of the same relief, because her mouth is open, emitting little throaty snores. The air smells of petrol and the burnt pine trees that line the narrow lane. The wildfire has ripped through here and moved on. Above the canopy to the northwest, the sky glows red with it, like a second sunset. Thank God our destination is in the east.

I keep driving, praying like I haven't in a long time that the same good fortune will aid Essie.

And that it's not already too late.

No. Can't think like that. Have to focus on Willow. She's

my job now.

The road gets bumpier, the wheels are crunching on rubble. The pine tree carcasses and their charred stink dissipate, giving way to black fields, and then darkened windows. We cross a bridge over a brook. The dashboard clock says *19.05*. It feels like midnight. I grip the wheel, eyes staring beyond the lights, searching for things that aren't there.

A beep sounds from the dashboard. The fuel light flashes.

*Shit.*

I have to ditch the car, anyway. They'll be looking for it. An allotment tracks by on the left, a line of shed roofs picked out by a light somewhere in the row. We trundle by, taking the next right up a steep incline lined with stunted elms. Their bare branches grow twisted, swooping into the road as though trying to capture the beam of the headlights. Up we climb, the rushing air through the window echoing a wide landscape stretching in the dark.

The road bends to the left around a rock face. A passing place opens, and I pull in. Careful not to wake Willow, I ease out of the car. My boots crunch on the decaying tarmac as I approach the precipice. Clouds shift, revealing a bright three-quarter moon and a valley below—dark fields marked by silver-tipped hedgerows; an old farmhouse, its collapsed roof catching fractured moonbeams.

Bordering the road is a low, ragged steel barrier, collapsed in places among the rubble. I push my knee against it.

There's too much give.

I pitch into the dark scrub below. Heart pounding, I jerk backwards and skid in the dirt. Sharp stones graze my hands. A six-foot section of barrier disappears over the edge, landing with a muffled clank.

For a while, I'm stuck on the ground, my legs shaking. When my heart has slowed a little, I rise, wiping sore palms on my jeans, and shamble over to the car. Willow is shifting in her seat. My shrieking must've reached into her dream world.

Her door opens with a squeal of cold, rusty hinges. "Wills,

26

wake up. You have to get out now."

"Hmmp."

Releasing her seatbelt, I lift her out and keep hold of her arms as her sleepy legs fold under her. Her Minnie Mouse rucksack spills out of the car, and I grab it to place under her, lowering her to the floor. "You just sit here, okay? Don't move. Daddy's got to do something with the car."

Her eyelids droop as she leans against the rock face behind her. Satisfied she won't wander off, I jump in Rich's old banger, crank up the engine, and steer it to the breach in the barrier. It putters to a stop, dying before I kill the ignition. That fuel light was cutting it fine. I grab the holdall from the passenger seat and climb out, leaving the handbrake off. Not keen to risk the abyss, I move behind the car and push. With the silent grace of an ailing diva, the car passes through the gap and tips. It hangs for a couple of seconds, as if unsure if it's ready to end it. Then it's gone.

There's a cracking sound, a long, low rumble; then... silence. Clouds cloak the moon again and nothing is visible over the edge, so I can't tell how far it fell.

Willow's fingers close around mine. Her backpack swings loose and open in the other hand as she stares into the darkness.

She sniffs. "We left Boop in the car."

*Shit. Did we?*

"Oh, no. I'm sorry, Wills."

She nods and wipes her eyes. Her quiet acceptance is worse than all the screaming tantrums she could have mustered.

"Come on." I tug her hand.

After a final lingering gaze into the chasm, she capitulates. As we plod down the ruined slope of the road, I remember the torch I shoved in the holdall. The power cuts at Mum and Dad's are the worst, and they're always forgetting where their candles are, so it pays to be prepared. I shift the bag round on my shoulder and delve inside, pulling out the

27

flashlight in its black rubber housing. The beam bounces off stones.

"Where are we going, Daddy?"

"I saw some sheds back here. We can stay the night."

"In a shed?"

"We'll make it cosy. Like camping."

"Okaaaay."

I glance down at her and force a smile, remembering I left the blankets in the car, along with everything else. Some adventurer I'm turning out to be.

We settle into a silent rhythm. She doesn't cry or complain, only sniffs occasionally. As we plod on, I take mental stock of the contents of the holdall, the only things I salvaged from a carload of stuff. The emergency money tin, stuffed in after I paid Essie's taxi. I should have left her the remaining cash. Aside from that, there's string, scissors, spare batteries, a kitchen knife, matches, a flask, gardening gloves. Christ knows what all this junk is for.

I have my phone but…

Shit.

No charger. I packed that in the suitcase languishing in the boot of Rich's car, waiting to be discovered by whoever is pursuing us now.

Willow peers up at me as I halt and rifle through the bag for the phone. It's at the bottom. The display lights as I press the home button. Sixty-three percent, according to the battery icon. A day or so left for Essie to call. After that we're offline. I puff my cheeks and blow out.

"What's wrong, Daddy?"

"Nothing, sweetheart. Everything's good."

We set off again, following the torch's trail down the hill.

# Chapter Five

## Essie

**5th November 2041**

I hang back among the trees lining the dark lane.

There's been no sign of the blue van since I escaped the trailer park. When I got near to Bri's Braai earlier, the police were banging on the café door. Brian appeared in a red dressing gown, his scowl melting into a tense smile as he stepped aside to admit them. There was nowhere to hide on that stretch of Worcester Road. I ducked my head, turned away down Bank Lane, and dallied by the river for a while. From there, I couldn't be sure they'd gone, so I walked along the muddy path. In a spot that was unremarkable enough, I took out my phone, smashed it up with my boot, and threw it in the water. As it sank, visions taunted me of Seth being pulled over, arrested, and beaten; Willow ripped screaming from his arms.

I cut back onto the road after an hour. Now I've reached the section of Worcester Road that winds through a wood to the north of the Braai. Soaked in sweat, my dress clings to my back. My toes are numb, calves burning inside the boots. I long to call Seth, but it'll have to wait until I can tell him I'm safe.

Or until someone else calls to tell me they have them in custody.

When the burner phone rings, it's so on cue, my mind assumes that's the call coming in, until I see Jack's number.

I swipe to answer. "Risky. Calling me at random like this."

"I know. It's urgent. There's a storm on the way."

"No shit."

"I'm serious, Essie." There's shouting in the background. Where is he?

"Yeah, me too."

"A hurricane's going to hit Cuba. Julio. They reckon it could be the big one."

My hands go cold. They've been predicting a storm which would see Cuba go under, the way Fiji did. We thought we had more time. "Can you get out?"

"Not sure. The airport's rammed."

"Have you finished covering your tracks at the workshop?"

He laughs—a shrill, panicky wheeze. "I don't think that's going to be a problem in a few hours."

"No." There's nothing else to say.

"I, erm…just wanted to let someone know. In case." Another laugh. "What's the chances Langford's got an insurance gig riding on this one?"

It's not funny. The story broke a few months ago. Our beloved government has been shorting the island nations for years. Betting on when they're going under the ocean. Making a mint when they do. Of course, there were no reprisals, just a collective national shrug.

Except the journalist who ran the story disappeared.

"At least we tried." His tone is muffled, like he's crying.

Is this it? Am I going to lose him for real this time? "I'm sorry."

"Me too. Stay safe. Don't do anything daft. You have a family now."

No words will come out. Tears tickle my cheeks. I let them roll.

"I'll call you if I get out. Good luck, Ess." Then he's gone.

I'm on my knees in the dirt. The phone clatters to the ground. I want to check it for news of the storm, but I don't dare drain the battery any more. A few hours, Jack said.

I crouch there at the side of the road, weeping. Not just for Jack. The world is shrinking, drowning. Millions of people running for their lives on a planet trying to wash them off like fleas. We knew it would happen one day, but it's like losing someone after a long illness they caught from you. You're never quite prepared, they say.

Not that I know about that. My losses have been violent, immediate. All my family blown up; Maya murdered; Seth and Willow gone from me; and now, Jack.

My chest burns. Why me? I'm not up to this.

Headlights sweep the road, and that brings me back to tonight's problem. By now, the cops must have left Bri alone.

*Or they've taken him.*

No. Not possible. He's done nothing wrong.

*As if that matters.*

When I return, the Braai lies in darkness, and my heart thumps in my chest. Legs numb, I step up to the door and press the intercom that calls Bri's flat above the shop. I show my face to the security camera. If the cops are still there, it's already too late. Nobody speaks, but the door clicks open. With a shaky breath, I step inside. Whether towards help or death, I can't tell.

Tables loom in the dark. The hot air smells of cooking oil. As I pick my way across the room, a light turns on at the back, seeping under the door. Heavy footsteps clop on the tiled floor of the Braai's kitchen beyond.

This is it. I pull in a dense breath and wait.

The door opens, a bulky form silhouetted in the frame.

"Fuck's sake, Essie. What the hell, now?" His spiky Afrikaans accent never sounded sweeter.

"Bri." I bolt across the room, colliding with the back of an errant chair, and barrel into him. "They didn't take you."

"They didn't. No thanks to you. You are literally killing me, girl." His beard snags in my hair as he pulls back, eyes catching mine. He has a cut over one of them, and even in this dim light, it's obviously bruised. "You've been screwing

31

about again."

"No. Well… But—"

"Screw your buts. I could be in a cell right now. Or in the morgue."

I can't breathe. "What did they do? What did they say to you?"

"Nothing intelligible. Nasty threats. Smashed the flat up. Looking for you, they said, but they weren't really looking." He collapses into a chair and peers at me. "They took Kosta."

My legs give way. I flop into the chair opposite him, gripping the table between us. "Why?"

"Solicitation. Some other made-up shit." He explores his damaged eye with shaky fingers. "I loved that boy."

I squeeze his other hand. "They've got nothing on him, Bri. They'll let him go tomorrow, I'm sure of it."

Bri shakes his head. "He won't be back. They hate *poufs*." Bri's lips twist around the slur, and his voice cracks. "I know how this goes. He'll be dead tomorrow."

It took Bri so long to be honest about who he loves, and now he's lost him because of me. My stomach churns. "I'm so sorry."

Bri shrugs. It's a curious gesture; not dismissive. Perhaps hopeless, but his jaw is stiff. "We need to get these bastards, Ess."

*Tell me about it.*

"Well, we made a start. But now I've gone and screwed it up."

"Huh?"

Brian doesn't know about the arrangement with Kerry, or our double-crossing her. It all comes out in chaotic bits and bobs, but Brian pieces it together.

"Jesus. You've already built the prototype? Under her nose? That's smart."

"Not so much." I pick at a finger nail. "They know. They granted me access to see Lawrence today, but—"

"You saw Lawrence? God, how's he doing?"

32

"They wired him. I told him everything. And now they know."

"They wha—?"

A flash and a bang outside on the street fire my nerves. My head snaps round to the door as Bri grabs my hand. Two dark figures dash past the window, leaving behind a spewing fountain of light.

"Fireworks." Bri lets out a breath. "Bloody fireworks. Thought it was another raid. You English confuse the hell out of me. After everything that's happened, you're still celebrating some guy hundreds of years ago trying to blow up a bunch of shitty politicians and getting caught."

When I can speak again, I say, "We should get out of sight."

Bri nods and leads me to the Braai's familiar kitchen, through another door to a set of stairs beyond. In all the eight years I've worked for him, I've never been up here. Even in these last couple, when we get almost no business. And through all the days when we seem to be just cooking for ourselves and the odd vagrant, staring at each other across empty tables, he's never invited me into his flat.

I've sometimes wondered if it's because that's where he keeps the secret stash of blood diamonds that fund his illogical business. By rights, he should have closed long ago when most of the service sector collapsed.

The stairs carpet is dirty beige and sticky. At the top, the door hangs skewwhiff on a cracked frame.

Before they trashed it, Bri's flat must have been cosy. Throws and cushions decorate two couches. The same kind of pictures that adorn the Braai downstairs populate the walls. His home in South Africa; street scenes in black and white; close-up hands and faces of people I don't know. Some photos lie smashed on the floor. A small wooden desk in the corner lies naked of its drawers, their contents spilling across the nearby knock-off Persian rug.

In the kitchen, Bri has attempted a clean-up, but it's like someone dropped a bomb on his spice rack. Clouds of cumin and cinnamon tickle my nose. What the hell were they looking for in his *spice rack*?

"Bastards."

"Uh huh." Bri picks up a broken mug from the floor and drops it in the swing bin.

In the strip light, his eye looks much worse; swollen and purple, the white flooded red with broken capillaries.

"I'm sorry, Bri. This is my fault."

He screws up his face and waves a hand about. "You're not the one who kicked my door down and took the man I love."

It's not that simple. I'm sure we both know it, but I love him for his kindness.

He blows out his cheeks. "Well, I'm having a bloody whiskey. Want one?"

"Do I ever?"

When we're seated on one of his floppy sofas, large measures in hands, Bri takes a sharp breath. "Christ. Where are Seth and Willow? Are they safe?"

*God, I hope so.*

"I left them so they would be." My eyes prickle as the whiskey slips down. "They went—" I bite in the rest. The less Bri knows, the better for all of us.

Bri swigs his drink and flops his head back with a sigh. "What a mess."

Does he mean his flat or our situation? "I'll help you clean up."

Bri waves his free hand. "Ach. I'll just sell the place." His grin fades before it's truly there. "What will you do?"

"Shit, Bri. I don't know."

"You can stay here?" His questioning tone says he knows that's not possible.

"You should leave, too. They'll be back tomorrow." I drain my glass. "I might go to London. There must be a load of stuff happening there. I mean, *somebody's* got to be planning to bring down Langford and his band of bastards. Surely."

Bri's eyes go wide. "Oh, I forgot to tell you." Face flushed, he springs up from the sofa and darts into the kitchen, coming back with his phone.

"What? WHAT?"

Bri thrusts the screen at me. It displays a local news site from Birmingham. The top headline:

*Police seek local agitator.*

There's a picture of a young man with strawberry blond dreadlocks launching a blurry missile at a police officer. Looming dark behind, the fractured iron architecture around the ruin of New Street Station.

"Somebody *is* trying to bring them down. One copper at a time." He raises his eyebrows and peers at me. "Look familiar, this guy?"

I frown and shake my head. Then something clicks. The hairs on my arms rise as I grab the phone and zoom. "Is that… Gabe?"

"It appears so."

*Double-crossing bastard.*

"They said Gabe and Hallie killed themselves, blowing up Langford's factory."

Bri's mouth twitches at the corners. "Yes, they did. Looks like they lied. I never believed they'd done it. Hundred-to-one, Langford blew his own place up for the insurance."

"That's what Kerry said." I squint at the photo. The hair's different, but the angular jaw, the lean, tanned legs dangling from khaki shorts, have to be his. "Gabe sold me out. And Maya."

"He sold us all out."

Though it doesn't name him, the article claims the man pictured is wanted for attempted murder of a police officer and insurrection. They can add being an arsehole to that charge list. "I wouldn't mind a conversation with him."

"Ess, you've more pressing problems right now."

I take in a long breath. "You're right."

Still, twenty minutes in a room, just Gabe and me…

# Chapter Six

## Seth

**5th November 2041**

Willow is sniffling as we reach the allotment, but she doesn't complain. A ten-foot gate bars the way.

"Not far now, Wills. Just through here."

Willow nods. "It's locked."

A chunky padlock shines in my torch beam, fixing a thick chain in place. "We'll have to climb."

She gives a shaky sigh, her shoulders slumping.

"You can do it, monkey girl. Come on."

When she straightens and sticks her chin out, it's so like Essie, my throat aches. I sweep the torchlight higher. At the top, a menacing row of razor wire loops, its blades glinting.

A skittering buzz approaches. Willow collapses to the ground, arms over her head. My heart rages and breaks—that a child should know to hide like this. There's no time for bitterness. I take off my jacket and cover her, pressing us both into a nearby bush. There's a loose branch hanging low, and I pull it over us, holding my breath, pulse thudding in my ears. The drone hovers low over the allotment, then slithers off towards the city.

Willow lets out a breath at the same time as I do, and her muscles relax under my hands. She's four, and she understands her life isn't her own. I blink my stinging eyes as we move to the gate.

With the torch between my teeth, I shove my foot in the gap above the middle rail and haul myself up. The wire looks like steel, blades sprouting every few inches. There's no way Willow will make it over. Bracing my legs on the gate, I reach around into the holdall and pull out the scissors, but I already know they're useless against the metal. After a few vain attempts at sawing through the wire, I swap them for the gardening gloves and grab a loop. A razor punctures the padded finger of one glove, and its sting makes me hiss.

"Daddy?"

"I'm fine, sweetheart." I clutch my hand until the pain recedes.

But the steel is more pliable than it looks, and before long I've put a two-foot dent in the loops, leaving little droplets of blood behind on the metal. I delve into the bag and extract my jacket, laying it over the top of the wire before thumping to the ground beside Willow.

"Okay. You climb up. Skip over the top. Dangle over the other side and drop. Easy peasy."

She looks at the gate and back at me with a frown.

"It's okay. Here. I'll lift you."

My heart swoops as she rises, as if I've got vertigo from the ground. Fluid and graceful, she swings her legs over the jacket, then jerks, giving a yelp.

"Keep going, Wills."

Jutting her chin again, she bites her lip and swings her second leg. She lands with a thump and a cry, clutching her knee.

"Good girl. You did so well." Passing her the torch through the bars, I scramble over, rip my jacket from the wire, and land in the dirt beside her. "Let me see."

When I pry her hand away, it reveals a three-inch tear in her jeans just above the knee. Underneath, a jagged cut oozes blood. As my fingers brush it, she whimpers. Why didn't I bring any first aid stuff?

"Let's get settled somewhere, and I'll look for some water to clean it."

I shove my jacket in the holdall and take the torch back, illuminating a path that leads between vegetable patches. The smells of warm soil and polythene drift past as we approach the ramshackle row. Four doors face us. The first is green, or it used to be. Eczematous flakes come away with my hand when I touch it. The padlock holds firm. The door to the second shed stands ajar. A gas lamp throws out dim, flickering light from a bracket above the door, but no sound comes from behind it. I pull Willow behind me and reach out a stiff hand. The wood swings away. A bearded face, creased with age and fury, takes its place. "What the fuck d'you want?"

I pull back, hands aloft. "S-sorry. Just looking for a place —"

"Well, this is *my* place." The old man fumbles in a grubby pocket and comes out with a knife, thrusting it at me. "So, fuck off."

"Yeah, sure. Sorry, man." I reach behind me, taking Willow's trembling hand. She doesn't make a sound. We back away from the shed.

He pulls up a box and sits at his threshold. His knife wavers, tracking our retreat like his fervid, red-rimmed eyes.

"We should try the end one," whispers Willow.

"Agreed."

The old man's eyes weigh on my back as we approach the last door. This one is also ajar, and skewwhiff in its frame.

"Stay here, Wills." Heart hammering, I tiptoe the final few yards. The hinges rasp when I push, opening a dark space. I grab the torch and shine it inside.

Empty. No crazy old men with knives.

It smells of piss in here, and there's nothing to sit or lie on, but it'll do. I beckon Willow to follow, which she does, nose wrinkling.

"It's not much, but we can keep out of sight and get some sleep." I point to the far the corner, away from the window. "It looks pretty dry over there."

She nods.

With the jacket as padding, the holdall makes a decent pillow for her to lie on. I sit beside her, stroking her hair. She closes her eyes and gives a deep sigh. It's past her bedtime, and she's had a hell of a day.

Something scrapes against the shed's exterior.

Willow gasps. "What was that?"

"Just a branch or something." There are no trees beside the shed and Willow must know it. I grab the torch from beside me and fumble it on. "Stay here."

She doesn't move, but her eyes glow wide in the torch's beam. I switch it off as I head out the door.

It's profoundly dark. The old guy must have extinguished his lamp when we left him. A warm breeze tickles my sweaty face as I round the corner of the shed.

Something heavy hits the back of my neck. I stumble forward, dropping to my knees as the ground shifts around me. A chilly edge bites my neck. A knife.

The old man?

But the male voice that growls in my ear is young. "Move, and I'll slice your head off."

I keep still.

A bright light moves around before me. When my eyes adjust, I make out a figure, and a grubby, female hand attached to it. A face emerges—tight, brown ponytail, cleft chin, and sharp cheekbones. The light catches her belly, which bulges from the hem of a t-shirt that's too small. Six months gone, I'd guess. She peers at me while her companion presses the knife into my skin. Her eyes slide behind me. The knife retreats. A second later, she whips out her foot, connecting with my nose.

I yelp, can't help it. The pain is sharp and jagged, like broken bone.

*Stay inside, Wills. Don't make a sound.*

One of them kicks me in the stomach. I curl into a ball, mouth clamped closed against a cry. Blood drips from my chin.

The light recedes as the girl moves off towards the shed, and Willow. Panic rockets through me.

"Hey." My voice is wet with blood. "I don't want any trouble."

The boy straddles me, crushing my chest, and holds the knife to my eye. "Got any money in there, mate?"

"Dale." The girl; from the shed.

I twist my head away from the knife, squinting in that direction. She's in the doorway, one arm trailing behind her. When she yanks it, Willow appears, her hair twisted in the girl's fist. In the torchlight, my daughter's face is set, her lips caught in her teeth the way she does when she's trying not to cry.

"Well, now." The boy springs from my chest and prowls towards them. "How much would we fetch for you, I wonder?"

Willow returns his stare. "Piss off, freak."

Halfway to my feet, a moment of bitter pride hits me. Then there's a vicious crack as Dale slaps her.

"Hey!" My nerves burn. "Don't you dare *touch* her."

I launch at him. He's ready. The knife swoops, slicing into my hand. A roar of pain and fury bursts from me. Helpless, I back away.

He laughs and turns to his partner. "What you got?"

She lets go of Willow's hair and rifles through my holdall with the torch in her mouth. The emergency fund tin bounces on the ground. While they're both distracted, I gesture to Willow, who dives towards me, colliding with my legs. She buries her face in the fabric of my jeans, sobbing.

"Hey, Terra. This'll do." Dale holds up the tin, a grin stretching his thin face.

There's a bang and a flash. Terra screams and drops the torch. It flickers but stays alight, its beam skimming the ground. My mind is forming the word *firework* when the old man appears carrying a rifle.

He aims it at Dale and Terra. "I've had enough of you pair of degenerates. Why don't you just fuck off before I take your heads off?"

Dale sneers. "You're not gonna shoot us, you stupid old twat."

The old guy nods, drops his aim, and pulls the trigger. The report ricochets between the sheds as Dale darts back.

Willow jerks under my hands. Dust flies, clouds swirling in the torch beam.

"Shit. You mad old fuck." Dale's voice is ragged with panic.

The old man aims higher. "Get. The fuck. Off my land."

A glance passes between the two kids, then Terra drops my holdall. My knife falls out, but she ignores it. They scarper into the dark. With a minute of scraping and grunting, they're over the gate. None of us moves until the sounds of their retreat have fallen silent.

The old man looks from me to Willow. He lowers his rifle. "Good riddance. Boy's a psycho, and his sister's no better. Been hanging around here for weeks, bringing down the neighbourhood."

On autopilot, I grab the torch. "Sister? Not his baby, then."

"Oh, sure it is. Been at it like rabbits every night since they got here." I think he catches my glance at Willow because he clears his throat. "Sorry. Name's Nathan, by the way."

"S-Simon. And this is Ella." I enunciate the names, hoping Willow catches my drift.

"Nice to meet you both." He nods at my hand. "Might have something for that in the shed. Something for your stomachs too, if you're hungry."

A deep, throbbing cut runs the width of my palm, dripping blood into the dirt. It could do with attention, like Willow's leg, but I haven't forgotten this guy's earlier welcome.

Willow tugs the hem of my shirt. "Daddy, *I'm* hungry."

There aren't many options. What little food I packed went with the car. "Okay. Thanks." I scoop up the knife and holdall with my good hand. My chest loosens when I feel the outline of my phone inside the bag. Terra can't have seen it.

We trail Nathan into his shed as he lights a gas lamp. Inside is warm and larger than I expected. It smells better too —like mint and sage, and an umami smell like stock. The light flickers on a wooden table. Huddled nearby are a camping stove and an old-fashioned radio. A pile of hay and fleecy blankets occupies the rear half of the shed.

41

Nathan crouches at an orange crate by the door and delves into it, pulling out jars and boxes, squinting at the labels, then replacing them. "Sorry I was grumpy before. Get a lot of trespassers, you know? After the veg." He pulls out a roll of bandage. "That pair of brats sneaked in one night and took over the place. Swore I wouldn't let it happen again."

"I understand." In truth, I'm occupied trying not to drip over his floor. This place is cleaner than its resident, and my hand hasn't stopped bleeding.

Willow eyes it, frowning.

Nathan cups my elbow. "Come outside. There's a tap at the veg patch. Just about works. Until they shut it down, anyway."

"Shut it down?"

"That's what I heard. Free water, see? Can't have that, can we?"

The rusty crosshead squeals and Nathan grunts as he heaves on the tap. At his nod, I hold my shredded palm under the water. It's stings like hell but, conscious of Willow hovering at the shed door, I bite back the hiss of pain.

"Ella's cut her leg too."

Nathan nods and pulls the roll of bandage from his pocket. "Ella?"

When she doesn't move, I say, "Ells, it's okay. Come here."

Tearing off a swatch of dressing, Nathan wets it and hands it to me as Willow approaches. She stiffens and draws in breath but makes no sound as I dab at her already-scabbing cut.

Back in the shed, Nathan opens a jar of yellow waxy-looking stuff. "Elderflower and rosehip salve," he says at my raised eyebrows. "Antiseptic. Made it myself, so it's good shit."

It smells oily as I smear it on Willow's leg, and then my oozing hand. Nathan's ready with a bandage, which he winds around my cut, until I can't feel the pain.

"Should do the trick for a while," he says, tying the ends together at my knuckles. "Now for more important matters."

He smiles at Willow. "Parsnip soup okay?"

She nods, mouth clamped closed.

With fifteen minutes of clinking and savoury aromas, we're presented with huge steaming bowls of soup. It's warm and smooth, with an aftertaste of dill. Though she's never knowingly eaten a parsnip, Willow slurps with gusto.

"That was delicious, thank you," I say when we've emptied the bowls and filled our stomachs.

Nathan licks his lips and frowns. "Hmm…it's okay. Parsnips aren't what they used to be. No frost anymore, see?"

"Well, we appreciate your help. It's been a long day."

He blows out his cheeks. "All days are long now, Simon."

Essie's face appears in my mind, eyes sad and fearful. "Agreed."

Willow puts down her bowl and huddles into me as I stroke her hair. Nathan watches her for a while, then springs up and leaves the shed. There's a rustling behind the far wall, and a grunt. A moment later, he returns, swiping soil off a green bottle. From the crate, he pulls two camping mugs.

"Blackberry wine," he says, unscrewing the bottle and pouring. He holds out a cup to me and nods at Willow. "Will she?"

"Nope."

"No, no. Of course not. Got some purified water for you, poppet."

She wrinkles her nose but seems to recognise we're in no position to complain. The wine is fruity and strong, and I gulp it. It sends me woozy and blunts the pain in my hand even more. I put the mug, still half full, on the floor. Lovely as it is, I need to stay alert.

Nathan must feel it too—his eyes are misty as he drains his mug. "I don't know what we're doing here, Simon, I don't. Letting them poison the Earth. The air, the ground. The *minds* against each other. It's all of us…" He shakes his head and scratches his beard. "And now I hear Cuba's done."

"What?"

"Yeah." He nods at the radio. "They said on the six o'clock news. Be under the sea by tomorrow. Hurricane

43

Julio. That's a Latin alliteration for you. All over the news, like we couldn't see it coming."

*Shit.*

The prototype's gone, then. Not that it makes Essie safe. They'll still try to get to her. And… I'm not Jack's biggest fan, but I don't wish him drowned. "When?"

"Few hours."

Willow's gaze turns up to me. "Mummy's friend lives there."

"What's that?" Nathan raises his eyebrows, eyes glinting in the gaslight.

"So, tell me about yourself, Nathan. Where are you from?" It's not a subtle change of subject, but how many people have friends in Cuba? We can't afford to stand out like that.

He looks up at the cobwebby ceiling. "Oh, God. I'm from all over. Been to France and Scotland. Spend a year or two in Tibet. You know, before."

"Wow, Tibet?"

"I was a Buddhist. Figured I should do it properly, go to the horse's mouth. Couldn't get on with the reincarnation stuff, though. Faith's funny. Kind of all or nothing. No dabbling, know what I mean?"

I can't tell him what I used to do for a living. "Yes. I do."

Willow flops against me with a little snore. My limbs relax. At least if he's travelled the world he might forget the Cuba thing.

Nathan's eyes shine at Willow's lolling head. "Better get you settled for the night. You can sleep next door." He pulls a key out of his pocket. "Bit broken, but there're blankets in there, and spare straw. You'll be comfy enough."

Willow barely wakes when I lift her. She half-sleepwalks into the flaky-painted shed, lets me take off her shoes, and collapses on the warm straw. It throws up dust and a grassy aroma.

"Thanks, mate," I say to Nathan.

"My pleasure. Sleep well. Here, take this." He pushes a jar

of the elderflower salve into my hands. Then he's gone, leaving me to lock the door behind him.

Sighing, I lay a blanket over Willow. She stirs and smacks her lips. The covers are musty, but the straw is springy and fresh. I shove the salve into the holdall and curl up next to Willow. Despite the events of the day and the wine, I can't settle. Every time I close my eyes, Essie is there, crying, running, screaming for me with no voice.

# Chapter Seven

## Kerry

### 6th November 2041

"Say that again, Kerry?" Alex Langford smooths his non-existent hair, grey eyes glinting in the light of the banker's lamp on his oak desk.

It takes everything I have to trap the sigh behind pursed lips. "Of course, Prime Minister. I said I can be of assistance to you." The charm comes easier as I speak. "In an advisory capacity."

Langford's grin shows either side of the whiskey glass at his lips. "You want a job."

*Yes, you wanker. And you're gonna make me beg for it, aren't you?*

I take a large swig of my drink. A two-hour drive to his ostentatious Surrey constituency office for this? Dark wood and blood red carpets; beeswax and old cigar smoke pervade the air. All very country club, even without the family portrait looming behind him. Four sets of cruel, grey eyes glare at me from the gold filigree frame: our beloved Prime Minister gloats over the long-suffering Mrs Langford and Alex Junior. In the background glowers Daddy Langford—by all accounts, the bullying sociopath who shaped the soulless man sitting before me.

I should have met with him at parliament. At least that's not his absolute territory. Yet.

"You had a job with me, remember?" He makes a show of brushing something off a broad, pin-striped shoulder. "Minister for Homeland Environment. You quit."

*Did I hell? You all but fired me.*

"On a point of principle."
"Okay." He laughs. "Judging by the subsequent election results, I don't think the voters of Worcester saw it that way."

*Like you didn't rig the vote against me. Asshat.*

The nausea and fury grow into the silence. My humiliation drifts in the air between us and he lets it.

"Alex," I say eventually. "We've got a lot of history." I hold my hand up. "Not all of it good, I'll concede—"

"You think?"

"But we can help each other." I drain the dregs of whiskey, enjoying the fumes as they hit the back of my throat. "You might say we need each other."

Over his own glass, Langford's hard eyes narrow on me. "How so?"

"I can handle Foster-Pugh for you."

He snorts. "I don't need your help. Oliver's an old friend."

"Then you know he harbours his own ambitions for higher office."

A raised eyebrow is all I need.

"Oliver is happy serving as my Home Secretary, as he has faithfully for the last four years." His tells are firing everywhere; chin shoved out, he's trying to puff his chest, but it only accents the shallow breathing.

"And as the previous Prime Minister's Home Secretary for the four before that."

"Yes."

"You don't imagine Oliver might be bored?" I trail my fingers down the leather arms of the chair, letting my nails scrape its nap. "He let slip he was once. When I was one of his ministers. And that's a few years ago."

Leaning back in his chair, he nods. "I think he had a bit of a crush on you."

I give him a sly smile, still trying to decide if he believes me or not. "Useful. Potentially."

His eyes roam my top half. "You looked good back then."

*Back then? Asshat.*

I rise, the leather squeaking. "Well, you're a busy man. I won't keep you. Perhaps you could consider my offer and let me know. Don't leave it too long. I am exploring other avenues, and you don't want to miss the boat."

"Of course." He escorts me through the empty reception to the door, an arm hovering behind my back in a transparent show of chivalry. "Great to see you, Kerry. Keep in touch."

The door closes behind me, drowning the sound of my sigh as I step into the mid-afternoon air.

At a guess, Poulton High Street was once buzzing with overpriced boutiques and patisseries. Now, battered Tudor facades lean over me, exhaling the smells of old coffee and damp wood. The few shops still open sell essentials to anorak-clad pensioners. Where is everyone?

Then again, you could say the same about Worcester. It seems like these days the wealthy have gone to ground and all you see are the shuffling masses fighting over cut-price mop heads and cans of beans. Who knows how we get out of this mess. Or if.

I used to have a plan. We were going to save the world— Essie, Jack, and me. I'd stick it to all the smug elite wankers like Langford and get rich in the process. Didn't imagine the bitch double-crossing me. She didn't bargain on my connections in that hellhole jail they've got her mate in. Ashley Tanner's a sleazy git, but he knows the value of a good bribe.

What a waste of an opportunity. The only consolation is that Hurricane Julio probably drowned Jack and his poxy prototype, and good riddance. So it's back to the drawing board. Hence this nauseating visit to Langford. There's no way to win back my seat in parliament since they suspended elections last year, so I'll have to settle for being a political hack. If he calls.

Ed is waiting at the margin of the pedestrian section, the Range Rover puffing greasy fumes, tinted windows closed tight. One privilege of being a former government minister: you get to choke everyone else with internal combustion gases they're prohibited from producing. I'm not saying it's right, but who am I to turn down a rare perk?

"Any luck?" His eyes travel up my legs as I climb in.

"Who can say?"

He reaches out a palm and cups my cheek. Nestling into it, I twist my head, taking his thumb in my teeth. As he hisses in pain, Ed's other hand shoves up inside my skirt, hard fingers probing.

"Ow."

He withdraws without apology and grasps the steering wheel. "Want to go home to bed?"

"Yes. I do."

"You're the boss."

There's a tense, breathy silence in the car all the way back to Worcester.

\*\*\*

While I wait for the coffee to brew, I run my sore wrists under the cold tap. Ed's asleep upstairs, so when the coffee is steaming in my mug, I lower myself onto a chair at the kitchen table and boot up my laptop.

There's a message from Lenny in the secure mailbox. No sign of Essie since he lost her at the trailer park. Lying bitch got the better of him and my friendly police officers. I have little influence left, but I can still buy the odd bent cop. For all the use they are.

When I open my personal inbox, second line down is a message from Carlo. My heart thumps as I glance at the stairs, then I click the message.

*Mum*
*Hi.*
*Been a while, huh?*
*Wondering if we could meet sometime? No hassle, if not.*
*C*


My finger reaches out to the screen, tracing the shape of the C. He typed this. My son typed a message to me and then sent it. At—I check the stamp—three this morning.

"Not working now, are you?" Ed ambles down the stairs, lanky legs dressed only in boxers. As usual after sex, his abrupt, stiff air has gone, his dark hair swept forward, not back as he wears it for work. "I thought you'd be out of action." He slinks behind me, squeezing my shoulders and throat.

The laptop clicks as I close it, probably too late. "Funny boy." Though my heart's kicking off again, I push him away. Swigging my coffee, I wonder if I should say the next sentence at all. "Carlo emailed me."

"Carlo? That's good, isn't it?" Ed pours himself a cup and sits in the opposite chair. "I mean, that's what you want." His eyes flicker. "Ah. He didn't give you shit, did he?"

"No, no." I run a finger along the grain of the table. "He wants to meet."

"Great." He grins at me. "Right?"

"Well, yeah. It's just…" When I hold his gaze, it's clear he's not up to this, and I miss Carlo's dad. Only for an instant, then I hate myself for it, but there's no denying it. "Yeah."

The subject's history for Ed. He jumps up and rifles in the drawers, coming out with a bowl and a frying pan. "I'm going to make us pancakes."

"Ed, it's eight o'clock on a Wednesday evening, not Sunday morning."

"I don't give a shit. We're having pancakes."

I shrug. "Okay. I am hungry."

"Atta girl."

I open the laptop and peer back at my screen, stumbling to word a response to Carlo.

***

When Langford calls, Ed's gone home. It's late enough to remind me who's in control. "You start next Monday. That gives you a few days to find yourself a crash pad in Poulton. Not that you'll be crashing much."

"Poulton? Not London."

He sighs down the line. "Is there a problem?"

"No, I just—I thought I'd be with you in parliament."

"Let's not run before we can walk, Kerry." He's trying to sound benevolent, but he can't keep the smirk out of his voice. "You will join me for some meetings at Number Ten. After a period of settling in. Okay?"

My nails dig into my palms. "Sure, Alex. Thanks. I'll see you Monday."

I've no one to celebrate with. Celebrate. Langford's not doing me any favours. It'll be a shitty job, and he's got me where he can see me.

But it's a start.

***

The following afternoon, I'm waiting. He's late because he's trying to punish me. That's okay. I deserve it.

Carlo chose the venue. A grubby coffee kiosk huddled behind a tangle of outside furniture, playing strident, retro music. Called Grime, Carlo told me when we agreed the venue. Appropriate, judging by the mould on the counter. Sitting at one of the skewwhiff tables thrown about the place, I take a sip of rocket-fuel strength coffee and pinch the bridge of my nose. The caffeine will not help my headache, but I need it. Last night was a blurred cycle of sleeplessness and anxiety dreams. It's overcast today, but the dim light still hurts my eyes.

Twenty minutes after our agreed time, I'm still surprised when he's standing before me, his eyes shaded by a denim baseball cap.

"Carlo." I move to stand for a hug, but his stiff posture

51

prevents me. "It's so lovely to see you. Won't you sit down?"

He hesitates as though we haven't arranged this. Then he snatches the chair opposite me and drops into it, sitting at an angle to the table as if to keep his escape route open.

"Can I get you a drink?" I delve into my bag.

"Nah, I'm fine. The coffee's rank here."

"I thought this was a hangout of yours." And then it hits me. He chose this place because he never comes here. He doesn't want to be seen with me.

Carlo's legs are jiggling in his black tracksuit bottoms, his eyes searching the pavement. "Not really."

"It's so good to see you."

His eyes snap back to mine. There's something intense behind them but I can't tell what. Fear? Guilt? "Mum."

God help me, my heart swells to hear him call me that. I take some more rocket fuel to calm my nerves. "What is it, sweetheart?"

"The thing is… I'm moving away."

"Oh. I see." My heart thumps. Though I haven't seen him in over a year, knowing he's close by has been enough. Now his dad wants to uproot him just like that. "And your father didn't think to discuss it with me first."

"Not Dad, just me. I'm going to London."

"What? No. You're too young."

He straightens. "I'm eighteen."

"Exactly."

"For God's sake, Mum."

"What does your father think about this?"

He shrugs one shoulder, which tells me everything. James was a lousy husband, but he's not a complete moron.

"So you thought you'd ask me to back you up against him. Nice try, Carlo."

"It's not like that."

"So it's like what?"

"I have to do this, Mum. It's important." There's that intense look again.

"What's so important?"

"Don't worry about Dad. I'll square it with him. I just

need a favour." Then, much softer: "Quite a big one."

"Don't think I haven't noticed you're not answering any of my questions, kid."

"I will, I promise. It's just—"

"I can call James, you know. We can speak to each other briefly without resorting to violence."

"Mum."

"What favour?"

"I need some money. Just to set me up for a while. Dad said you had money put by for me, but he can't sign it over. It has to be you."

Nice one, James. Carlo wasn't supposed to know about that until the right time. "That's for your education. Not so you can flit off at random."

"It's not random. This *is* education. Sort of."

"You'd better clarify that statement."

His chest expands as he takes in a shaky breath. "I've met some people online. And they're doing some incredible stuff in London."

"What people? What stuff?"

"I can't tell you more than that. But it is important." He glances at the sky, where storm clouds are billowing. "Nothing is more important. Mum, I'm not going to college. You know that, don't you? With things the way they are, there's no point, is there?"

My turn to shrug. But I don't need to ask him what he means. Storms, floods and wildfires...this interminable heat. It feels like we're entering the end game. Can I expect him to spend three years in the library when the world is going to hell?

"So." He dips his head, trying to catch my eye. "I might as well have that money for something useful. These people are doing something that could help us all."

*Oh, God.*

"What does that mean?" Except I think I know what it means. I stare down at my cold coffee, fingers massaging my

53

forehead. Of course I should press him. There are questions I should ask, but I don't have the will. And I can't escape the suspicion he's on the right track. That whatever he's planning to do is more important than school. "Okay. I will pay a monthly allowance into your account. If…. *If* you call me weekly and let me know you're okay. Deal?"

His smile lights up the dark afternoon as the first thunder rumbles. "It's a total deal. Thanks, Mum."

"Starting this week, okay? Ring me this weekend and tell me when and where you're going. You need somewhere to live."

He waves a hand. "That's sorted."

"Then you need to give me your address." A fat raindrop plinks into my cup. More patter on the broken concrete around us. The couple of other customers pack up and scurry off as the kiosk owner shuts its hatch.

"Well, I haven't got it yet. I will, though. Soon as I know."

*Kerry, you're a fool.*

Maybe I am. "We'd better go before this storm breaks."

He springs up and bumps me with a tight, clumsy hug. "Love you, Mum," he says in my ear.

When we pull back, I'm glad for the rain streaming down my face that hides the tears.

"I'll be in touch." He's gone before I tell him I love him, too.

I sprint back to the car and speed out of town ahead of the floods.

\*\*\*

Four days later, I've achieved more than I imagined possible. Found myself an ugly little bedsit in Poulton. Bought some chic workwear-on-a-budget.

Not sure I'll ever get used to the contrast between the exterior and interior of Alex's office. It's just a blocky, concrete building, but he means the decor to make guests feel small.

He strides in with a smile dripping satisfaction from its down-turned corners. "Kerry. Good to see you."

I shake his proffered hand. "You too, Alex."

"So sorry I'm returning to London this morning, but I wanted to come in person to welcome you first. Get you settled."

"I appreciate that."

His eyes gleam as they skim over me, no doubt assessing the cheapness of my suit. "Well, there's plenty of work to do here. Come on, I'll show you."

He leads me into a room off his main office. The plush red Axminster doesn't venture in here, replaced by rough, rust-coloured carpet tiles. A beech effect desk takes up most of the space, leaving room only for a limp umbrella plant next to a filing cabinet in the far corner. Piles of papers cover every inch of the desk and half of the floor.

"My secretary retired last month. I'm afraid I've rather let constituency matters get out of hand." He sweeps his arm around. "As you can see."

"Hmm." What has this to do with me? I've a gnawing suspicion.

"There's some juicy stuff in there. Boundary disputes; complaints about bins. I need you to run with this stuff. Sort it all out." He peers at me. "What's up, Kerry?

"Well, it's not my skill set." My eyes rove the papers as my heart sinks further. "I was hoping for something a little more…big picture."

That smug not-quite smile slithers again. "Patience, Kerry. All in good time."

*Asshat.*

I smile and give myself virtue points for not smashing my fist into that mouth.

# Chapter Eight

## Essie

### 11th November 2041

I awake to the echo of a shout, my heart pounding. The zip grazes my cheek as I snatch my coat away. It's dark and cold, and I can't work out where I am. Rain splashes on the tracks beyond the crumbling concrete roof of the platform. As my eyes adjust to being open, my fellow station sleepers stir, too. I force my stiff limbs and sore shoulder to rasp against the concrete and pull me up. My aching head lolls back against the wall as I groan.

"Rough night?" Piper's sardonic, heavy-lidded eyes float into view above me.

"Is there any other kind round here?" My voice cracks with thirst.

Piper must have noticed because she hands me a bottle of dingy rainwater.

"Thanks." It tastes of dust but soothes my burning throat. Pity it can't do anything about the aching in my chest; the hole that's opened there the size and shape of Seth and Willow.

She flops down beside me and swigs from her own bottle. "What I wouldn't give for a bloody great sausage roll."

"Can't remember the last time I had any meat. We didn't all come from a line of Good Citizens, you know. Some of us aren't permitted."

She chuckles and wipes her nose on her sleeve. "My dad stole as much of it as he bought. But that's another story. What's your plan today?"

*Wish I knew.*

"Thought I'd nip into the Burlington for brunch, check out their sauna."

Piper spits out her water with a laugh. "Think I'll join you. Not sure the sauna's working, though. Probably clogged up with old piss."

That makes me chuckle, but I've no idea where to start with my stupid, hair-brained scheme to find Gabe. And God knows what I'm going to do if I find him. Talk. Smack him about.

I didn't think that far ahead when I borrowed Brian's rusty old bike and cycled the thirty miles north along the canal to Birmingham. After making it halfway that first night, I slept under a hedgerow that smelled like hay and wood. It was spiritual despite my anxiety, or perhaps because of it.

The next morning, while I dwelled on this idea, I reached the city with its hot, brown haze and splintered tarmac. Empty shops spewed shattered glass, which crunched under the feet of the passing gangs. The Queensway tunnel lay crumpled on the ground like a kicked dog. Corporation Street used to bustle with shoppers when I was a child. That morning it shuffled with people—young men, in the main— but none of the bonhomie. No one spoke or smiled. They just gave off a twin fug of rage and helplessness. You could almost smell it: dirty, angry people. They gathered in the mud around steaming puddles, and fought over discarded, rotting food scraps. The whine of drones was constant, but nobody reacted when they passed. Not like my hometown of Balmford, where that skittering buzz always elicits an anxious twitch of the brows or shoulders.

For sure they didn't care about the drones because I'd been in town around twenty minutes when something thumped into my front wheel, jolting the bike and tipping me over the handlebars. Heart frozen between beats, I landed with a grunt hard on my shoulder in the rubble. A second later, a knife pressed into my cheek and a male laugh released a cloud of rotten breath. By the time I could sit up, the knife, its owner, and the bike had gone.

"Scumbag," said a voice behind me. A grubby girl of about sixteen came around to crouch by me. She had blue eyes that measured the world from a wary distance, and that honey-blonde hair I always wanted instead of my bright red mop. "You okay, Bab?"

Bab. She looked ten years younger than me.

"Think so, yeah."

"Evil scumbag." She glared in the direction the guy must have escaped.

"What just happened?"

"You got mugged, that's what. Welcome to Brum Haven." She gave me a smile which was more of a weary pulling down of the lips, an old gesture on her youthful face. "Want me to look at your shoulder?"

It was stinging like hell and bleeding through my shirt. I didn't want to think about what was underneath yet. "I'm fine, thanks."

She frowned but must have decided against insistence. "I'm Piper, by the way."

"I'm Essie."

Her head tipped to one side. "Nice name."

"Thanks."

"Sorry about your bike."

"It was a friend's." I've no idea why I thought it was worth mentioning.

She nodded in sympathy. Bless her. "Well, let me prove to you we're not all savages. I'll show you around, if you like. Tell you safe places to sleep and that."

"I've been here before."

She gave a breathy laugh. "Not recently, or you'd have known better than to bring a bike into the city. Or anything else that could be nicked. Place is a den of criminals."

She had a point, but at least he didn't have time to search my bag and find the burner phone.

After only days, it's like I've known Piper for years, even though she was barely in secondary school when I became a mother. She's like I was at that age. Our stories aren't the same: her family weren't all blown up by terrorists, for a start. From what I understand, they're all still very much alive, for all the use they've been to her. She said little about them that first night, just that her dad used to hurt her. She told me in a spare, guarded tone that said *don't ask questions*.

God knows, I get that. She didn't quiz me on why I insisted on setting up for the night as far away from Platform 1A as possible. She just ushered me to the other end of the station, past the peeling, yellow *Welcome to Birmingham* sign with the thumbs up, under the ruined dome of Grand Central with its abandoned, aspirational boutiques and hand-spun shake kiosks, and down the steps to Platform 12. So I didn't ask for her story either, just stroked her hair until she drifted into a restless sleep.

All that night, I kept watch and guarded our stuff. It wasn't like I was getting any sleep anyway.

Drinking the water Piper brought, I turn my back on hateful Platform 1A and face the sooty terminal wall, but it is almost as if I can smell that bomb on the hot, fuggy air. Smell an eight-year-old explosion.

They never even cleared the debris. Once they found all the bodies they could, they just left it there—a mashup of steel and scorched concrete—and ran the trains around it. Until there were no more left on the timetable.

My family were trapped inside. Mum, Dad, and my sisters, Willow and Darya. How long did they lie there? Darya was still alive. She must have been terrified. Did she see their bodies before they took her to the hospital where, days later, she would die?

"Earth calling Essie." Piper peers at me, trying to smile through a frown.

I blink away the tears. "Sorry. Miles away."

"No kidding. Listen, we need to get out of town."

"What? I only just got here."

"I heard a rumour." She nods towards the exit. "When I went to fetch the water. There's gonna be trouble. A protest."

There's a jolt in my chest. "Protest? What about?"

"Dunno. Doesn't matter. It always ends the same. We've

59

got to go."

Could this be Gabe? There's no way I'm leaving if there's even a chance it might be. "I'm staying."

Piper dips her head to one side, her mouth slack as she stares at me. "You're joking. Essie, you haven't seen it when it kicks off. Believe me, you don't want to be here when it happens."

"You go. You should get out. I'm staying. I have something to do."

She snorts and spits on the platform. "Is this about finding your mate? What're you gonna do if you find him? What could be important enough to risk your life like that?"

*Oh, Piper, if I start talking…*

"For you, nothing. Have you got somewhere else you could go to?"

Eyes on the station wall, she shrugs. "Prob'ly. If I was going anywhere." She squints at me. "Can't leave you on your own, can I? You'd prob'ly get yourself killed."

"Piper, no. I'm not being responsible for—"

"Screw that." She springs to her feet, face flushed. "It's years since anyone's been responsible for me but me. You worry about yourself. Right, we'd better get sorted."

"Huh?"

"If we're gonna make it through a riot, we need some serious food in our bellies. Come on." She marches off down the platform, compelling me to scramble after her like a toddler.

As I catch up, we step out of the station and into a torrent. Water swells in the gutters and swirls around flooded drains. We're soaked through in minutes. Rain drips down my back and the sleeves of my thin coat. A few knots of people huddle in ruined doorways, but the streets are otherwise quiet. There are no coppers and no drones for once.

"I know a place where they hand out food parcels." She has to shout over the roar of the storm. "They're careful because the coppers will shut them down. They open when

60

they can."

"Shut them down?" I'm still trotting to keep up as we reach Hurst Street.

"They're 'encouraging congregation', or something."

"That figures. Congregation scares the shit out of them. People congregate, they talk. Enough talk, and one day someone might act."

Piper stops and bangs twice on a red, metal door.

An eye-level letterbox squeaks open, and a pair of dark eyes peep out. A female voice says, "Piper. How you doing?"

"Good, thanks." She giggles behind a hand. "Hungry. This is Essie."

The eyes switch to me, widen, then disappear as the letterbox clicks closed. A moment later, a hatch opens at the base of the door, like the world's widest cat flap. A large brown paper bag slides out.

"Thanks, chick."

"No worries," says a muffled voice behind the door.

Piper holds up the bag. It has *Made in HMP Unity Winson Green* stamped on it. She grins. "Cha-ching. Come on."

She leads me through the diminishing rain, along streets awakened with shuffling people, past ruined restaurants and shops. When we reach the corpse of a multi-story car park, she glances around, then yanks me through a gap in the wall.

When my eyes adjust, metal cabinets appear, squatting in the corner. Thick silver pipes crawl across the walls and ceiling. It smells of electricity and old pee, but it's cool and dry. Piper reaches behind one of the metal units and scoops up something. A second later, torchlight flares on the wall beside me.

"Let's have a look." Piper drops to her knees, slaps the torch down, and rips open the bag. "Bing-fucking-o," she says, holding up two sausage rolls wrapped in brown paper. She bites into her own packet and slides the other across the floor to me.

I waste no time. Oh God, it tastes good.

We finish them within a minute, and Piper throws me a juice box. "There's more in here. Bottles of water, apples, bananas…" She yelps in delight and a fleck of sausage roll flies from her mouth, catching the torchlight. "Flippin' Danish pastry."

"Let's save it for later, eh?" Shouldering my rucksack off, I yank open the zip. "Here."

She screws up her face, but must see the sense of it, because she stuffs the food into my bag.

Outside, the rain has stopped. The sun is hot on my scalp, and it turns the puddles to steam that drifts past the graffiti on the walls.

"We'll get that sauna after all." Piper closes her eyes and pokes her head into the vapour, breathing it.

We pass a six-foot concrete barrier displaying a faded Hands of Kinship sign. Someone has spray painted across it:

*UNITY*
*STOP DROWNING US!*

My heart kicks. That's what I used to think about that sign everywhere I passed it. The fierce grip of the fingers, meant to signify protection, always looked like assault to me. I shot a filthy look at the one opposite Bri's Braai every morning. The Drowning Hands of Unity, I called them. Somewhere along the line, I stopped noticing the hateful symbol. Perhaps because I was getting one over on them with the prototype. That's finished now.

There's a hum of tension. Instead of shuffling, the knots of people hanging around are stiff and watchful. As we pass one crowd, someone lights a firecracker and throws it through a broken shop window. Sparks fly as it bangs inside, and someone turns the volume up on heavy bass music.

"Come on." Piper takes my arm, and we scurry past, as a drone hovers into view.

It pauses for a second, then swoops down behind us, emitting a crackle like an echo of the fire inside the shop, then: *"POLICE. DISPERSE."*

We run.

In the heat and steam, my t-shirt sticks to my back and

chest as we pound along Corporation Street. When we reach the brow of the hill, I turn back. Flashes of light shoot from the drone. Someone in the crowd screams and a tangle of bodies drop to the floor.

"Never seen that before." Piper's voice wavers. "They've *weaponised* them things."

My arms prickle. "Let's go."

A police line blocks the way to the station. Dressed in black riot gear, they carry guns in belts and battens in hands, shields held up to their grim, red faces.

A bitter taste fills my mouth. "They're expecting trouble, then."

"Told you. Come on, this way." She pulls me to the right. We trot away up New Street. A hundreds-strong crowd in Victoria Square vibrates with expectation. People like us— grimy, weary, and stooped—mingle with bright-eyed young people who look ready to spring. There's music playing here, too—an old protest song that I remember from somewhere, all twangy guitars and harmony.

Yes. *Change Here*'s first meeting back in Balmford. When Maya dragged me along to the church hall.

*Gabe?*

Have I found him? A bit of a leap. Probably the tension. Still, my eyes dart around the crowd, up to the Council House and its stone pillars, the balcony. There's no sign of him.

More coppers turn up. They close in from all directions, alternating martial yells with the thump of battens against shields. It makes my insides vibrate. Within minutes, menacing throngs of riot police block all exits from the square. When I turn to Piper, her eyes are wide and pointed at the sky. A swarm of drones descends towards us, blocking out the sun. I can't catch my breath. It's like dark walls are closing in on all sides.

"Kettling," mutters an old man nearby.

"They're kettling," says a young woman next to him.

63

Everyone takes up the chant, the word tossed along the crowd.

A voice so deep it seems to reverberate from everywhere booms, "POLICE. GET DOWN ON THE GROUND. NOW."

"Everybody, sit down!" That voice. It's Gabe. He's hanging from a harness attached to the balcony of the Council House, megaphone in hand. A hundred yards away, his strawberry blond dreadlocks glow in the weird new twilight.

The crowd sits in waves from the front. Piper and I follow.

"Christ," says Piper. "Do they know about the drones being armed?"

Gazing up at them, I shake my head, unsure whether it's good if they do. They're bigger than the ones I'm used to seeing around Balmford. Up close, their guns are obvious, roaming the crowd's heads as they lower.

Everything stops. The police hold their lines, scuffing the ground with heavy boots, spitting on the tarmac. The drones keep formation twenty feet above, maddening with their low whines and clicks. Blood pumps in my ears and makes my fingers pulse.

Up at the Council House, Gabe is easing himself down inch by inch into the crowd. I stare at him, eyes narrowed, heart hammering with the desire to go after him, knowing I can't. Any sudden movement now would get me killed. Even if the drones aren't loaded, which I doubt, the police have rifles, and they look itchy about them.

"That your mate up there?" says Piper.

"Why do you ask?"

"'Cause you're staring at him like you're trying to drill holes in his head."

"Yeah, that's him."

"Well, then." She flaps her hands in a shooing motion. "Let's go."

"What? No. Not now."

She huffs out sausage roll-scented breath. "Bloody hell, Essie. We're only here because of him. *Now* you're gonna

64

lose your nerve?"

At the front, someone starts a chant of, "*Whose streets? OUR STREETS.*"

The police lines straighten and tense.

"No. We'll get shot."

She's already on the move, crouching, picking her way over the huddled limbs of the crowd. The whine of the drones notches up, melding with the ringing in my ears.

Three of them swoop. There's a crack and a flash above. Piper screams, blood flying.

"PIPER."

She crumples, landing on the space left behind as the crowd scrambles away.

"NOBODY MOVE," says the drone voice.

It's too late. Screams and bangs ricochet as people scramble. More bullets rain, chipping tarmac, puncturing limbs and chests. I struggle to my feet, only to be knocked flat again. My cheek scrapes on concrete. A fleeing protester stomps on my back, knocking the breath out of me. I curl up into a ball, then lift my head, peering through rushing legs, looking for Piper.

At a silent signal, the shooting stops. The running slows. Shrieks and sobs of injured, angry people dominate.

Gabe barks from the megaphone, but I can't make sense of his words. From the direction of his voice, he's still up front amongst the crowd.

Closer, on the left, I glimpse Piper on the ground, head bowed, a growing smudge of red on her top. A dark blur at the edge of my vision turns into police lines racing into the square. Two of them flank Piper, grab her arms, and drag her away. I squint in the gloom, trying to work out if she's still moving, but it's impossible to tell. Too late, I rise on numb legs and stumble towards her, but I won't make it.

"Piper." My heads spins as I sob. "No."

Mine's only one cry in a sea of pain. People bleeding, dying, already dead, litter the square, surrounded by others trying to help. Insinuating themselves amongst the devastation, the police drag more people away, some leaving trails of blood. I can smell it. A metallic tang mingled with the smoke. So much blood, my vision swims again. I drop to my knees and throw up on the slabs.

"Piper, what the hell did you do?" I wipe my mouth.

*She was only here because of you, Essie. You killed her. You kill everyone.*

The nausea hits again, and I retch. A foot jabs into me.

"Sorry. Hey, you okay?" A man with red-blond dreadlocks is peering down at me. At the same moment I recognise Gabe, his eyes pop wide. He turns away and sprints off towards the station.

"Wait." I mean to shout it, but it's only a gurgling whimper. My watery eyes can make out no sign of Piper. They must have taken her to one of the waiting vans that surround the square.

*Your fault, Ess.*

With the protest defeated, the police lines break up. They move to arrest as many as possible. I have to move, or I'm going to end up in one of those vans. Stiff with shock and fear, I make my legs support me and stagger in the direction Gabe ran.

As I emerge from the miasma of still-hovering drones, the light is barely less dim. Dark clouds have crowded out the sun. I hunch my shoulders and forge past the scuffles on Hill Street, keeping my eyes raised, searching the wreckage for Gabe. I reach the station without sight of him. My brain is racing with images of Piper in a police van, of Gabe getting away unscathed. Bile rises in my throat as I approach the smashed-up station entrance.

Dark figures break from the shadows to block my path. My instant thought is *police*, but these people aren't in riot gear. Three men and a woman stare with rage-filled eyes. Two of the men carry baseball bats, and they all have silver Unity badges on their lapels, its clasped hands glinting.

The biggest man leans forward, dark eyes on me. "You're one of the scum smashing up our city."

I step back. "N-no. I just—"

He grabs me by the collar and shoves me into a recess in the ruined station frontage. His sweaty hand clamps over my mouth and it tastes like vinegar. "Shut the fuck up. You don't get to speak now. It's my turn."

Behind his round, hairless head, the woman's sneering face appears.

He brings his baseball bat up and presses it into my throat. "I'm glad the cops killed half of you. We're here to clean up the other half."

# Chapter Nine

## Essie

"Do her, Jake." The woman's eyes are dewy with hate as her nostrils flare.

Something on the wall is digging into my shoulder blade. I try to shift away, earning a shove from him. The sharp thing punctures my skin and I cry out. Blood trickles down my back.

"Did that hurt? Get used to it." He pokes the scar around my left eye. "Looks like you already are. Good."

He yanks me from the wall and throws me to the floor face down. My teeth clank on the old tramline embedded in the tarmac and I taste more blood. There's no time to get my head straight before someone rips off my rucksack and jumps on top of me.

"You people'll think twice before you come here causing trouble again. These streets are ours, get it?" The baseball bat smashes between my shoulder blades, sending fireballs of pain up my spine. The woman crouches into view while the weight on me eases and the baseball bat hammers the back of my knees. I yelp as she peers at me, then grabs me by the hair and spits in my face. One of them pulls at my shirt, tearing it open from the neck, then jabs a foot into my side, kicking me over onto my back. They stand in a circle around me, laughing as I struggle to sit up and get to my knees. One of the other men is rifling through my bag, scattering food and clothes on the ground. There's a green flash as he tosses Boop behind him.

A gunshot makes me scream again. I can't stand. If one of them has a gun, I'm dead.

"Leave her alone, Unity freaks." The voice is familiar.

68

*Hallie?*

"I said get away from her."

When I turn, Hallie is striding towards us, pistol swinging by her side. She glances at me, a flicker of recognition in her eyes. Older and thinner than I remember, she flips her matted black hair. From ten yards away, she raises the gun and points it at the man who beat me. "I will shoot you in the head, Murray." Her tongue stud catches a ray of emerging sunlight.

Murray takes too long to react, so Hallie lowers her aim at his feet and shoots. The report stings my ears, echoing off the concrete walls. Hallie shudders, stepping back as her body absorbs the recoil.

"Bitch." Murray's face is flushed and warped with fear and rage. "You nearly hit me."

"Next time I will. Fuck off."

The four of them bunch together. They look like they're about to leave when Murray whips around and struts towards Hallie. Ignoring her raised gun, he bends his neck so his face is right in hers. "I know who you are. You'll keep."

With a final quartet of hate-filled stares, they march away. Murray stomps my bag on the way past, and I wince at the thought of the phone in there; my only lifeline to Seth and Willow.

Hallie turns sorrowful eyes on me while I huddle on my knees among the weed-strewn tramlines. "Shit, Essie." She springs to my side as I flail, helping me to my feet. "Is it bad?"

I shake my head, but my back feels like he cracked into it with that bat. My head swims, the vision in my left eye doubling. It still happens sometimes—since the encounter with Langford years ago. When I blink several times, hard, Hallie's face comes back into focus.

Half-crawling over to my bag, I plunge a hand into it. It seems empty, but then my fingers touch something smooth and come out with the phone. It looks intact. When I touch the screen, it remains dark.

"Come on." Hallie pulls my ripped shirt closed at the back

and squeezes my shoulder.

As I stand, the pain in my battered legs makes me hiss. "When did you learn to handle a gun like that?"

She gives me a tight-lipped smile. "After the first time I met Jake Murray. Long story. Let's get you somewhere safe."

Shoving Boop in the bag on top of my soiled clothes, I pause and shield my eyes from the late afternoon sun. Up the hill, the police occupy themselves with their victims in the square. "Somewhere safe. Where would that be?"

As it turns out, it's the place my family were murdered.

"It's okay, we're not stopping here," says Hallie, supporting me while I limp down the crumbling station stairs. "We just need to keep out of sight while they clear the streets."

"Won't they search the station?"

"Not the bit we're going." She slows for a second. "I hope."

"That's encouraging."

Letting go of me, Hallie springs from the platform onto the tracks, then turns and reaches up to me. I bite my lip and ease down on the platform to take her hands. My feet thump onto a steel rail, shooting bolts of burning pain through the backs of my knees.

Hallie grabs hold of me to keep me upright and waits while I catch my breath. "Okay? Come on." She leads me along the tracks into a tunnel with Unity graffiti scrawled on its decaying arch. We plunge into darkness and the murk of old diesel fumes. Fifty yards ahead, the light at the other end dims as the torrent starts again.

"Good." Hallie nods at the exit, now blurred by a curtain of rain. "It'll clear the streets quicker." She grabs my hand again and we pick our way ahead. Squeezing my fingers, she halts me halfway in and bends down. There's a scrape of metal and a pattering like an echo of gravel or rubble. How can she see what she's doing? Before I ask, she disappears. A soft thud sounds below me.

"You'll have to jump, Ess." Hallie's hoarse whisper spirals up. "Sorry, there's no ladder."

I feel for the lip of a grate or manhole and sit at the edge. "How far down is it?"

"Dunno. Six feet?"

Gravel scratches as I swing my legs into the hole and ease off the ledge into the void. The landing is brutal, my stomach turning over, legs buckling below me. I collapse onto the damp concrete floor.

Hallie catches my arm and pulls me up. With a click, a light springs from her hands and after a moment of confusion, I realise she's pointing a torch up at the hatch.

"I could have done with that light a minute ago."

Her shoulders catch the edge of the torch beam as she shrugs. "I didn't think you'd jump if you knew how long the drop was."

My cheeks grow hot. "Hallie."

"Sorry. But it's the only entrance apart from The Bank."

"Bank?"

She doesn't respond, moving away down a tunnel that doubles back under the platform. It smells of shit and stale water, and the arched brick walls glisten in the torchlight.

I force my aching body to catch up with her. "Is this a sewer?"

"Utility tunnel." She shines the light up and along the roof. "These up here are waste water pipes. Careful, they're a smidge leaky in places."

"Oh, great."

"At least it's not boiling down here."

She's joking, but it's not funny. I can hardly breathe in the heat and stench.

We pass several intersections, turning at random until I'm disorientated. I've no idea how Hallie is so sure of her route. Sweat soaks my clothes long before Hallie stops at a rusted ladder in the wall.

"Here we go." She hands the torch to me, pulls a bunch of thick iron keys from her jeans pocket, and climbs the rungs to a greasy-looking, black hatch in the roof. With clanking and grunting, the hatch squeaks open, and Hallie recedes through it, her face reappearing a moment later. "Come on."

My beaten knees complain when I flex them. I clamp my teeth together and mount each rung with a hiss. Taking my hand, Hallie helps me scramble through the hatch.

We're in a dirty, white porcelain-tiled corridor. There's a door behind us, and a flight of filthy stairs in front.

"This way." Hallie leads me up the steps to a metal door and retrieves the keys again. More clanking and squeaking reveal a dimly lit space.

The room smells of orange oil, although it will take a while to lose the memory-stink of shit from the tunnel. Naked plaster flakes onto the floorboards. Planks nailed to the frame obscure a small window, and an untreated wooden door stands ajar in the opposite wall. A gas lamp on the windowsill provides the only light. Its flicker, and the low note of its fumes, recall my old flat back in Balmford, a thousand years ago and a million miles away.

"Sit down. You must be shattered." Hallie grabs an oversized cushion from a pile next to the lamp and holds it out.

I take it and lower myself onto it. Now I can catch my breath, I give voice to the question on my mind. "Is Gabe here?"

She pauses at the opposite door. Her back is to me, so I can't see her expression, but her tone is careful. "He'll be back soon with some others."

*Others?*

She turns to face me. "Are you hungry? We've got leftovers from The Bank. Truckloads of Danish pastries."

And then it clicks. The dark eyes at the red door; the woman who served Piper the food parcel. That was Hallie. "We're on Hurst Street, aren't we?"

"Uh huh. And yes, I recognised you when you came here earlier. With Piper." She gazes at the floor, then back at me. "Did she get out of the Square?"

My head pulses when I shake it. "I think they shot her. They took her away."

72

Her lips part as she raises a hand to them, leaning against the peeling wall. We're silent until she takes a shaky breath and says, "There's a bathroom upstairs so you can clean up. And I'll find you some clothes. Looks like they ripped or stomped all yours."

I struggle off the cushion and limp after her. Through the second door and past a pokey kitchen, a hallway hosts a flight of bare wooden stairs. We climb to a landing, and a huddle of doors.

Pausing outside one, she pushes it open, revealing another sparse room with only a mattress, a small desk and chair, and another boarded-up window. "You can sleep in here tonight. It's not much, but it's safe for now. The bathroom's at the end."

"Thanks, Hallie." Tears warp my view of her face. I'm not sure if it's gratitude, homesickness, or just plain exhaustion.

The bathroom is grubby, and there's no hot water, but they've rigged up a kettle, so I make a decent attempt at a strip wash, drying myself with the least grimy corners of my cast-off clothes. After days on the streets, it feels like shedding a filthy skin. In the mirror, my face is scratched and raw, my eyes hollow and ringed with dark circles. When I turn and crane my neck, I can make out the beginnings of a purple bruise spreading between my shoulders.

Hallie has left underwear, a pair of jeans and a black t-shirt outside the door. Voices drift up the stairs, so I guess Gabe's back. I grab the clothes, dress, and scuttle across the landing to my room. It can't be that late in the evening, but my head is spinning as if I've been awake for days. I flop onto the mattress, retrieve the phone from the battered rucksack, and swipe the screen.

Still dead.

Heart pounding, I hold down the power button. "Please, please work. Please…"

The display lights. The battery icon says twenty-two percent. I flop back on the bed, light-headed with relief.

*Seth...*

A soft knock makes me jump. "Ess. Can I come in?" Hallie pushes the door open, a brown paper bag and a bottle in her hands. "I bought you a pastry and water. And—" she glances behind her, "someone wants to see you."

Even though he's the reason I'm here, my brain whirs as Gabe steps from behind Hallie. His dreadlocks swing as he nods at me. "Hello, Essie. Long time."

I can only glare at him.

"You ran into Jake Murray, I hear. You okay?"

"Everyone thought you were in London. Or dead, depending on who you believe."

His freckles stretch into a tight smile. "Who did you want to believe?"

I shrug and look away.

"Essie, I understand you're angry with me, but can we get past it somehow? We've all moved on a lot since back then."

My chest cramps. I spring at him, my fist slamming his cheekbone. He staggers back, his deadlocks trailing behind, and makes a noise that could be, 'Oh', but isn't quite.

I flex my punching hand. "Fuck you. *Moved on*? You got Maya killed that night at Langford's. For a stupid revenge trip."

In the doorway, Hallie makes a sniffing sound, probably thinking about her brother, Francis. Killed because he published an article questioning Langford's business practices. That's all it takes with Langford.

Gabe has regrouped. He takes a tense step towards me. "*I* got her killed? Seriously. The only reason we were *there* was because of your scientist mate. Why don't you slap him around?"

"That's a lie, and you know it. You wanted to get back at Langford for Francis. Jack had nothing to do with it."

"Oh, like you're the innocent. You didn't force Maya to come with you that night, then?"

My legs lose strength, and I flop onto the dusty mattress, hand to forehead.

Gabe scrapes a chair over from the corner and eases into it, rubbing his reddening cheek. "Look, I didn't turn you in,

74

did I?"

"My hero. You did hand over the pictures you took of Maya and me spray-painting Langford's house, though, didn't you? After you made us do it." The fury swells again. "And then ran away."

"I didn't hand them over. They raided my flat."

"Why did you take them in the first place if you weren't planning to use them against us?"

He huffs. "This isn't getting us anywhere."

"So it would seem." I'm too tired for this.

"You should rest. We can talk in the morning." He rises and replaces the chair in one smooth movement, then pauses next to Hallie at the door. "I am sorry about Maya. Really." He stares at the boarded-up window as if looking for an exit. "Too many people have died."

My eyes sting with momentary tears. "At least we agree on something."

The door closes behind them.

I sit for a long time on the makeshift bed, numb and exhausted, unable to shut my eyes. When sense returns, it's the loss of Maya that hits me first—hard, as if the pain is fresh. Like she just died today not six years ago, on the night I last saw Gabe. My ears ring with it. The tears roll and drip from my nose onto the already-damp mattress. There's no escape. Maya's face glows behind my eyelids whenever I close them.

Jack's voice, sharp with panic, echoes in my head. *'There's a storm coming.'*

What have I done?

*Got everyone killed? How do you think Seth and Willow are doing out there, Ess? On the run...or dead too?*

It can't wait any longer. I grab the burner phone and dial Seth's number.

# Chapter Ten

## Seth

**11th November 2041**

"Daddy, wake up." Willow's voice seeps into my brain. "The phone."

I sit up and grab the ringing phone from her hand. The number isn't one I know. Is it Essie's burner, or someone else?

"Daddy, answer it." She glances at the door. "Someone will hear."

She's right. Our latest shelter, a tiny summer house, is at the bottom of a longish, sloping garden, but it's not that late and the occupants of the house are still up. The light from their living room spills onto the patio at the top of the incline.

I press the button and with numb lips say, "Hello?"

"Seth." Essie's crying down the line.

"What's wrong? What's happening? You okay?" I turn my face away from Willow.

"I'm fine. Honest. It's just—" Sobs drown the words.

Panic forms a hard knot in my chest. "Essie, please, talk to me. Where are you? Are you hurt?"

She gives a wet sniff. "Sorry. I'm okay. I'm just glad you're alive."

"Same." My trapped breath escapes. "Where are you?"

Silence for a few beats. "I think it's best if I don't say. Where are you? Is Willow okay?"

"She's fine. Just past what's left of Scarborough."

"On foot? You made good time. Seth, you're not still in

Rich's car, are you? They'll have the plate number."

"I'm not that daft. We...happened upon an old car which got us part the way, before it clapped out."

"You stole a car?"

"Never mind. We'll be at Mum and Dad's by mid-morning tomorrow. Safe and sound."

She breathes into the phone, popping the mic.

"So now we only have to worry about you. Have you spoken to Jack? I heard about the hurricane. Tell him he's got to help you. This whole thing is down to him."

Another pause, then her voice cracks as she says, "Jack's dead. Have you seen the news? Cuba's under the sea. The prototype's gone."

*So this is all for nothing.*

I close my eyes. "Any chance he got out?"

"I haven't heard from him since that first night we ran."

Six days ago. It doesn't look good. "He could have lost his phone, or it ran out."

"Yeah." But her voice is tight. "Look, I have to go soon. Should I talk to Willow?"

I glance behind me, at Willow's wide, watchful eyes; her stiff, fragile composure. Then I think of Essie, barely holding it together with her secrets. "I'll tell her Mummy loves her more than anything in the world."

Essie makes a choking sound. "I love you both."

Then she's gone. I'm cold inside that I might not see her again, or even hear her voice. After all this time, everything we went through together, we're back where we started. Only worse, because half the world is under the sea and we're not together. My vision blurs as I stare at my bandaged hand. It throbs in response.

"Daddy?" Willow reaches around and puts a warm hand in mine. "Mummy will be okay. Whatever she needs to do, she'll find a way. She's clever."

Despite it all, I grin. "She certainly is. She married me, didn't she?"

Willow tips her head and gives me a grave stare. "Daddy, you're silly."

As much to hide my tears as anything, I scoop her into a tight hug.

\*\*\*

Early the next morning, it's my turn to shake Willow out of dreams. She mumbles and wipes dribble from the corner of her mouth.

"Wills, we need to leave while the house is still asleep."

"'K."

I pull the summer house door closed and we duck under a fence at the end of the garden. The field beyond the torch beam is dark, but not silent. Rustling and snuffles recede on all sides, making me imagine a sea of wild, hungry animals parting before us. When I sweep the torch, there's a glimpse of low, fleeing limbs and woolly tails. "Just sheep, Wills. Keep going."

After ten minutes of tense rambling, we reach a road that never used to be coastal. Now its edges crumble away, indistinguishable from the rocks that descend into the North Sea. The salt of it burns my lips as we pass more dark fields on the left.

"Daddy. I'm thirsty."

"Me too. We'll find water somewhere."

She frowns and glances at the sea but says nothing. I'm too tired to explain about salt and fresh water, so we trudge on in silence.

"How far is it to Nanny and Grandad's?"

"A little way." Like, seven miles. "Don't worry, we've got plenty of time." It's a strange thing to say to a four-year-old, but she nods, and her shoulders relax.

We settle into a slow, hypnotic rhythm. I listen for the sound of fresh water. Half a mile along, the tinkle of a stream joins us like a fellow traveller.

"Wills." I put my hand on her shoulder. "Water." Rummaging through the bag, I come out with the flask.

78

"Wait here and I'll get us some."

The verge is silky with clay that sticks to my boots as I stoop to capture the flow. Eventually, I descend to the slimy bed to reach it. Icy water spills into my boots. "Here." She picks her way to the edge and reaches for the flask. Her gulps come fast as I clamber back up the incline. She finishes the lot, so I have to brave the cold again for my share. When it goes down, the water is so sweet it makes up for the wet socks.

We walk again along the pitted tarmac, the restless breath of the sea keeping pace. Willow's head droops, flopping in time to her strides. The night is fading into a smudged, grey sky which makes the foam glimmer on the rocks below.

The sun burns off the sea haze while we walk. Soon, we've shed our coats and layers, but I'm still sweating. Willow slows. By the set of her jaw, I'd say she's tired and hungry.

"Wills, let's have a break. I've got goodies for breakfast." I scavenged them from our hosts' dustbin last night, but there's no reason to emphasise that fact. Willow nods with a tight smile and we sit, feet dangling over the new cliff edge.

"Let's see." I delve into the holdall. "We've got apples, lovely and ripe. And…a whole sponge cake. Think you can handle it?"

Her eyes grow wide and fix on the cake. "Yeah!"

"Apple first, though."

We eat watching the sun's slow arc rise above the sea.

"Daddy," says Willow, brushing crumbs from her lap onto the rocks. "Is Mummy in trouble?"

My throat tightens. "Why do you ask?"

"Every time you speak to her you cry." She peers closer. "Is she?"

God help me. "No, sweetheart. She's just got important stuff to sort out."

"About her friend?"

I nod.

"You don't like him, do you?" Her eyes won't leave my face.

A slate of cloud obscures the sun. Its shadow glides under the surface of the water like a basking shark. "It's not that. It's just…complicated."

Her features are blank, but I can't shake the feeling she doesn't believe me. Her gaze is too intense.

"Come on." I shove the remains of the cake in the bag and stand, holding out my hand. "We've only got a little further to go. We'll be at Nanny and Grandad's by ten o'clock." At the thought of seeing Mum and Dad, my heartbeat kicks up. I haven't been able to call and say we're coming in case someone's listening. It's over five years since I saw them last. With travel restrictions and the transport system failures, it's been impossible to come this far north. They've only met Essie once, and Willow never, though there have been a few stilted phone conversations. Mum's going to love her to pieces; will lose it over her curly hair that's so much like mine. I bet Dad will hang back, but his eyes will be wide and glazed when he looks at her, as though he beholds a heavenly being.

I take Willow's hand and quicken our pace.

Two hours later, the sky has clouded over. As we limp down the deserted lane towards Mum and Dad's, it occurs to me this could be risky. Kerry—and whoever she's working with these days—must know where my parents live. They could be here already. Why didn't I think of that? Too distracted with the business of getting here, I suppose. That, and worrying about Essie.

I ease Willow behind me as we reach the hedgerow concealing their front garden. They've let it go wild, invading the road, which is not like them.

The house is silent, its windows shut, stone walls glowing pink in a brief spear of sunlight. We ease around the shrubbery and creep along the inside edge to the back of the house and the tiny patio. Here, the long, narrow garden looks like I remember it. Neat but drab—normal for this time of year, except Dad's started a compost heap. At the bottom, a brown mound of soil and vegetation interrupts the otherwise smooth green of the lawn.

"You're Seth, aren't you?"

I whip around, nerves firing.

A man stands at the kitchen threshold. He's opened the top half of the stable-style door so he's visible to his waist. A scraggy, grey-blond beard stipples hollow cheeks stretched into a smile. Bloodshot, pale blue eyes peer at me. "I recognise you from the pictures." He grins. "You're all over the house. Almost feel like I know you."

*How does he know my name?*

They got here before me.

I back away, pulling Willow behind me again. The blood is pounding in my ears, but something feels off. This guy doesn't look like police or Unity. He just looks like a bloke who's been on the road.

*Or that's what he's supposed to look like.*

Willow moves beside me. My calves graze against the low wall bordering the lawn. "Who the hell are you?"

With another smile, he opens the lower door and steps outside. "Oh, sorry. I'm Rook."

I stare at his outstretched hand and, beyond it, his filthy bare feet. "What are you doing here? Where are my parents?"

The smile melts, turning moist and downcast. "Seth."

Something is wrong. It's coming off him in waves. I lunge and grab him by the shirt, my cut hand throbbing in protest. "What have you done to them?"

"Nothing." He wheezes. "Please."

Delivering him a vicious shake, I lean close enough to catch the smell of garlic on his breath. "If you've hurt them…"

"I didn't. Swear to God. I—I found them."

*Found them?*

Nausea closes my throat. "What does that mean?"

81

Rook sucks in his lips and stares at the floor. "I'm sorry, Seth." He looks up. "They're dead."

My legs lose whatever they had left. Hand to mouth, I stagger backward and collapse onto the wall. "What?" My voice has a hard edge I don't feel.

Rook shifts his blue eyes to Willow and then back to me. "Someone shot them. I'm sorry. I found them in the lounge. Looked like they'd been gone a couple of days."

Willow leans in close to me, her face slack. "Daddy."

I have no breath to reply, or strength to reach out to her. Every part of me is numb.

Rook remains still, watching us.

"Is this a trick?" Even my voice is flat. "Who do you work for?"

His brow furrows as he points behind me to the bottom of the garden. "I gave them a proper burial."

The compost heap.

My stomach convulses, and I vomit on the patio. Willow sniffs beside me as tears roll down my own cheeks. The thought of the dark soil graves tugs at my aching chest, but I can't turn around. Not yet.

"I'm sorry," Rook says again. From his accent, he's local. "I needed a place to shelter. We had awful storms. A hurricane hit the moors a fortnight ago. I lost everything. My old dog, Sally." He blinks and looks away over my head, maybe considering my losses. Or he's thinking of the next lie to tell. "Why don't I make us a cuppa?"

Like I'm a guest in my own parents' house, but I nod anyway.

*How did you know my name, Rook? From rifling through my parents' papers? Or from your Unity briefing file?*

Rook ducks into the kitchen. Spitting onto the patio, I rise and take Willow's hand.

"You okay, Daddy?"

"Yeah."

"Are Nanny and Grandad dead?"

Unreality threatens to choke me again. "I think so." Wondering if she knows what that means, I close the door behind us. Partly because it's started to spit with rain, but mostly so I don't have to think about the gravesites behind me.

Rook is busying about with the kettle, throwing tea bags into mugs and clattering teaspoons. I drop into a wooden chair at the table, and Willow climbs on my lap. The kitchen smells of hearty food. I sit motionless and dazed until Rook slops a mug before me. Opening the drawer underneath the table, I pull out a coaster with a picture of red and white flowers on it.

"There's no milk, I'm afraid, so I've been using the coffee creamer." He sits opposite me with his own tea, no coaster. "Might taste weird."

I open my mouth, but there's nothing to say, so I close it again.

"Oh, hey. There's orange cordial in the cupboard. You want some of that, little lady? Sorry, I don't know your name."

"Willow."

"What a pretty name. You want a cordial, Willow?"

She nods, watching in solemn silence as Rook springs up and bustles, making her a drink. The tap squeals when he twists it.

"I've been drinking the water, so I know it's safe." He hands her a glass and takes his seat. "Which makes a pleasant change. The places I've been. A wonder we haven't all died of cholera, I'll be honest."

He taps his mug in time with the rain battering the window. I stare at mine. It's the one I bought for Mother's Day years ago, painted with a beach scene, leaning palm trees supporting a woman in a hammock. *Take it easy, Mum* is scrawled around the bottom in freestyle script.

Now she's dead.

I glance at the door, clear my throat, and swallow. "How long have you been here, Rook?"

"Couple of days."

And he reckons they died two days before that. It could have been Kerry, then. But why? Was it revenge for the double-cross? If it was, wouldn't she want to goad us with it? It's the sort of shitty thing she'd do. Perhaps she tried, but we were out of reach, on the run. Or…

*Or Rook's lying.*

Maybe he killed them and took up residence in their house. He said he'd lost everything in the hurricane. I look at him across the table. He keeps twitching his shoulders up, as though he's got an itch or a stiff neck. He's tall, sure, and not old—I'd say around forty. He doesn't look very strong. Or the type to go about killing defenceless old people. And I don't think he's got a gun, or he'd have been carrying it when he came out to see who we were.

"What did they look like when you found them?" Dread swirls in my stomach, and I hate myself for asking in front of Willow, but I have to know.

Rook's eyes flit from Willow to me, dark despite their pallor. "Peaceful."

"You said they were shot."

"Okay, not peaceful. But I don't think they suffered."

"How can you know that?"

He shrugs, or it's his twitch. "They were head wounds. I doubt they felt anything. I've cleaned up as much as I can."

It's as if the conversation is happening in a bad dream, like my head is full of feathers tickling my brain, scratching the inside of my skull. Willow stares at me with wide, red eyes. Her mouth gapes, slack and wet.

Rook sniffs. "Are you hungry? There's stew on the stove. Your parents kept a well-stocked freezer. And an impressive veg patch, too."

I narrow my eyes at him. "You've been living well."

Rook flushes and looks down. "Sorry, mate. I don't mean to be insensitive. It's just… I haven't eaten properly for a long time."

"I'm hungry," says Willow in a small voice.

"Well," says Rook, springing over to the cooker. "Let's eat."

It smells good, and I try my best, but with my stomach tied in knots, it's impossible to eat. I'm thankful Willow hasn't the same problem as I watch her shovelling beef and onions into her mouth.

"I need the toilet." As I rise, I pat Willow's shoulder. "Won't be long."

She doesn't seem bothered about being left with Rook, but I don't intend to linger in the bathroom. Just long enough to experience the full blow of my face in the mirror: red eyes, wild hair and grubby skin. Mum would be horrified. The thought of Mum brings me to my knees on the bathroom floor. Shoving a fist in my mouth, I scream silently. Tears roll and I just make it to the loo before I throw up what little lunch I ate.

Shaky and weak, I pause outside the lounge and push the door open. The smell hits me right away; like copper and iron and burning. My eyes catch a red stain on the carpet by Dad's chair before I slam the door closed.

"I want to see their graves," I say as I enter the kitchen.

Rook gives me a sad smile. "Of course."

Willow sticks so close I almost trip over her as we walk down the garden. Probably unsure if he's wanted, Rook stays back, hovering on the patio. The afternoon air is hazy and warm and smells of smoke. He's made good work of the graves. They're straight and neat. Fresh, chocolate-coloured soil heaps in the middle, where Rook has set crosses made of wooden planks. It looks like he's nailed them together. I sway as the unreal feeling comes back. Willow takes my hand.

I try to remember all those mystical words of comfort that I spoke so easily when I was a cleric, but they've abandoned me. There's no sense in this. My free hand curls into a fist so tight my nails gouge my palm.

"Nanny and Grandad are in heaven now," Willow says. "With Mummy's family. Do you think they'll find each other?"

Not sure if what comes out of my mouth is a laugh or a

sob. What I wouldn't give to believe any of that stuff right now. "I think they will."

Back at the house, Rook has poured me a large glass of Mum's brandy. He offers me a cigarette. Feeling Willow's eyes on me, I take it and accept a light on the third cigarette I have ever smoked. It burns my throat and makes my stomach turn, but I inhale it like the sweetest perfume.

"I, er, took the liberty of plugging your mobile in to charge." Rook points to the phone on the kitchen counter. "It was out. I thought you might need it."

"Thanks." My voice sounds terse. I feel it. He must have been through my bag.

His cheeks flush, and he does his shoulder twitch. "Hope you don't mind."

"It's kind of you. Thank you."

He flaps his hand. "Hey, Willow, I found books in the front room. Do you want to have a look?"

"Is Rabbit Party there?"

Rook frowns. "Not sure."

"I don't think so, Wills. Those books were mine when I was young, and Rabbit Party wasn't written then."

"Come on. Let's see what's there, shall we?" Rook tips his head towards the door.

Willow glances at me, purses her lips, then trots off with Rook into the little room next door to where Mum and Dad died. Grateful I thought to close the lounge door, I follow. As I linger in the doorway, Willow's eyes grow wide at the sight of the stuffed shelves. Rabbit Party was more expendable than we thought.

Rook opens an enormous book with an array of colourful animals on the front and reads aloud. "It's morning in the jungle, and Stanley the snake stretches his scaly skin…"

Willow's gaze fixes on the page as she leans towards Rook. It's a strange thing, because as I watch him read, his shoulders stop their restless twitching and settle low and soft. Leaving the doors open so I can hear them, I wander back into the kitchen. I pour myself fresh brandy, light another of Rook's cigarettes, and sit down to think.

# Chapter Eleven

## Essie

### 12th November 2041

Murmuring, indistinct at first, resolves into words which still make no sense.

I open my eyes against a crust of dried tears. My fingers are still curled around my phone and I've a fierce, throbbing headache. Moving brings fresh pain in my back and legs, reminders of my meeting with Jake Murray and his baseball bat. Pulling the duvet over my eyes, I groan and try to forget the world is still here.

My doze fractures with a knock at the bedroom door.

"Ess. It's Hallie. Can I come in?"

"Er, yeah."

She elbows the door open with two mugs in her hands. Passing one to me, she sits on the end of my bed and cradles hers in her lap. The tea is strong and hot. After three eager sips, I put in on the bedside table.

"How're you feeling?"

"Like I've been ten rounds with Teddy Franks."

She chuckles at her own saying. "One round with Jake Murray will do that. Vicious bastard."

"Thanks for helping me. I don't know what they'd have done to me if you hadn't come along. It's lucky you did." I grab my tea again.

With a small smile, she says, "Not lucky. I was following you."

I pause with the mug at my lips.

"When you appeared at The Bank with Piper, we didn't know what the deal was." She looks away at the duvet covering my legs. "Sorry, Ess. We thought you might come for us. After…"

My face grows hot. "What? After Gabe sold us out? After he got Maya killed?"

At least she's bothered to look at me now. "We—"

"You thought I might bring the cops with me? No, Hallie. That's more Gabe's style."

"They did raid his flat, you know," she says. "All tooled up. I was there. We thought we were going to die."

It's hard to stay angry. The tremble in her voice kills it. I take another sip of tea, and it warms my sore throat. "Did you bomb Langford's factory? That's the official story. That you blew yourselves up with it."

She shifts on the bed and flicks her hair back. "We can talk about that later. The others are downstairs. I thought you could get dressed and come and meet them."

"Who?"

She smiles. "Our merry band of revolutionaries."

"Oh, God, Hallie."

"It's different this time. These people are professionals."

"Yeah? Professional what?"

Hallie nods towards the door. "Come and see."

"Okay, okay. Let me get ready, will you?"

Fifteen minutes later, I wander into the stuffy lounge, which still smells of orange. Gabe and Hallie are sitting on cushions together with three people I haven't seen before. They're clustered around an open laptop.

A broad woman with a dark curly bob who looks in her late twenties is gesturing at the screen, her eyes wide. "Gabe, the results are conclusive as it gets. Look at the model."

"Jasmine's right," says a woman with cropped, bleached hair and deep crow's feet. She's leaning forward, pale eyes shining in the screen's light. "It's doable."

"So now we have to figure out a *way* to get it done." This is a guy of about thirty with mousy, shoulder length hair. He looks at Gabe and taps a pencil on the table. There's another one behind his ear. "It's a hell of a distance from where we are now."

Gabe sighs and holds his hand up. "Benji, I know that. At this stage, it's about what's possible." His teeth glow blue in the laptop light as he grins. "And now we know it is."

"Within a margin of error," says Jasmine. "And within the bounds of my model."

Gabe rolls his eyes. "Uh huh."

"Which is to say nothing of the logistical barriers." The other guy is still tapping his pencil. "Or real global and domestic politics."

"You're a storm crow, Benji," says the blonde woman, who has caught Gabe's grin. "It's a start."

"A bloody good start." Gabe looks up and his smile widens. "Ess. You're awake." As if last night's fight didn't happen. "Let me introduce our friends. This is Benji the Grouch. And that's Jasmine and Luisa. Guys, this is Essie, and old friend and fellow warrior."

*Fellow warrior? Tosser.*

I respond to the hellos and smiles.

"Come and join us." Hallie points to the cushion pile. "We're still waiting for the delivery of breakfast, I'm afraid, but there's a full pot of tea in the kitchen. Help yourself."

"Never mind the tea, Ess. Come and get a load of this." Gabe nods at the laptop.

Yawning behind my hand, I move around to see the screen. "It's...a lot of numbers." Rows of them, but they mean nothing to me.

Benji snorts, drawing a frown from Jasmine.

Gabe holds up a finger. "A lot of numbers, Ms Glass, which add up to real change. These numbers prove we can do it."

"Do what?" I force my voice to stay flat. I refuse to get carried away with Gabe's dreams again. The price is always too high.

"A global renewable energy grid," says Luisa, her mouth

twitching. "Moving clean energy around, to every country on the planet."

Gabe jumps up from his cushion, grabs and drops another one, guiding me onto it. "Think about it, Ess. Every country producing and storing energy in their own way, using their most workable renewable resources. Except we all co-operate. We trade clean energy, but we regulate the market. We put in quotas and caps, so everyone keeps their lights on. What d'you think?"

I shuffle my cushion back a few inches. "Sounds ideal."

"And idealistic," says Benji, his eyes on Gabe. "My thoughts exactly. Geopolitics aren't that simple. Nor are energy markets."

Gabe tuts. "I'm not saying it's simple, Benji. But it's the start. Of an idea."

"One you won't get the world to sign up for in a million years."

But despite my fury at Gabe, my brain is awakening to possibilities. "What's the energy source?"

"Engineered hydrocarbons," says Luisa. "Or liquid carbon dioxide which can be converted to fuel at the destination."

My mind is whirring. Pathways wind from here to where we could be. "We'd have to take everyone with us. People are hurt, and scared. They need something to make them feel safe. If we can do that, anything's possible. If enough people believe, the rest will follow. No government can stand against that."

Gabe beams at me. "And we have people all over the globe working with us." He holds his hand up to silence Benji. "Not loads, I grant you, Benji. But enough to disrupt."

"Oh God, Gabe." The significance of this makes my heart swell. "Can we do this?"

Benji sighs and purses his lips. "You're talking about revolution here. That's the only way it would happen."

I gaze at the window, even though the only view is the wooden planks across it. If this could happen, Jack's death would have some meaning…and Maya's…and Piper's. "What have we got to lose?"

When I look back, Luisa and Jasmine are nodding.

A bang outside makes everyone jump.

"The delivery," says Hallie, springing up. "Ess, help me out."

She leads me down to the grimy corridor we entered by last night and trots over to the hatch in the floor. After some fumbling and clunking, she pops it open. A box thrusts up into her hands.

"Thanks, Dal. How many?"

A male voice echoes up from the hole. "Not so much today. Think we got there before a drop. Or they're on to us and using somewhere else."

"Let's hope not. Ess, could you take this up and come back for another?"

For the next twenty minutes, we shuttle box after box from the hatch to the flat. After we've piled around fifty, the flow ceases and we stand panting and sweating in the corridor. My legs burn and the bruises Murray gave me throb. The delivery man salutes us and disappears.

A second later, there's a shout from the hole.

Hallie's wide eyes stare at me and we both run to the hatch. Down in the dark, a head emerges, honey-blonde hair gleaming. "Hey, guys."

"Piper," Hallie and I say together.

Behind her, Dal has clearly decided we're safe, and he slinks off down the tunnel.

"Can you give me a hand?" Piper reaches up to us. "My shoulder's buggered."

I have no idea I'm crying until a tear drops from my chin. "I thought you were dead."

Piper gives a hoarse grunt. "As good as."

She's not wrong. As Hallie helps her up the last rungs of the ladder, it's obvious she's in a state. One arm is in a makeshift sling, thick bandaging on her shoulder. Her face and arms are a mesh of cuts and bruises.

"Christ, Piper. The police did this to you?" Stupid question, but nothing more helpful comes to mind.

Piper must think the same because she doesn't answer as

91

we help her up the stairs. When we return to the lounge, it's only Gabe. The others must have gone while we were heaving boxes.

Gabe's mouth draws down when he sees Piper. "Bastards," is all he says.

"I didn't tell them anything, Gabe." Piper eases onto a pile of cushions Hallie has arranged for her. "Well, to be honest they didn't ask many questions. It was just a quick beating, then call the doctor. She did a good enough job on the wound."

"So they did shoot you." I drop onto a cushion next to her, still stunned she's here.

"Just a graze. Bloody hurts, though."

"I'm so sorry, Piper."

She turns stiffly to look at me. "Why? You didn't shoot me."

Hallie crouches beside her. "Piper, how did you know about the tunnels?"

Her damaged shoulder lifting, Piper twists the other way to face Hallie. "I didn't. I was walking back up Corporation Street from the cop station and recognised Dal in his truck, so I sneaked on the back."

Hallie glances up at Gabe, who nods. She squeezes Piper's good shoulder. "Well. Looks like you're one of us now."

When Piper looks back at me, I've got nothing but a shrug.

"Anyone for brekkie?" says Gabe, ripping into a box in the stack. "We've got bread. Actual, real, sliced bread. So Marmite on toast is kind of mandatory."

Ten minutes later, we're gathered around a rainbow-striped teapot and a plate piled high with steaming toast. There's no denying my empty stomach—I gobble down slice after slice and gulp tea that warms my insides and makes me more alert. "Where does the food in the boxes come from?"

Mid-bite, Hallie pauses and glances at Gabe.

He puts down his mug. "You're better off not knowing that, specifically."

"But *un*-specifically, it's stolen, right?"

"From people who steal for a living, yes."

"The government?"

"Again—"

"Yeah, okay, I'm better not knowing. Kind of risky, though, isn't it?"

"Says the woman who tried to destroy the energy industry. We move premises every so often. Hence the two-star accommodation." He purses his lips, staring at his mug. "How is your ConservUnity friend these days, anyway?"

I'm not telling him about our dealings with Kerry, or the stuff in Cuba. "Dead."

"Oh. God. Sorry."

My hand flaps, a gesture to replace the things I can't articulate. "How did you meet those people who were here before? They seem very…together."

Gabe snorts. "Some I've known for years. Some came recommended." His face breaks into a grin. "Essie, there are loads of us this time. We've got scientists, doctors, lawyers, logistics, architects; big ideas. The global grid is just the start."

My heart kicks. "Gabe, have you seen it out there? The place has already fallen apart."

"Exactly the time to rebuild. We've come so far. Look at us." He points at the boxes. "We're redistributing the wealth right now."

Weary, I look at my tea. And yet I can't deny the appeal of thieving from Langford's mob to feed hungry people.

*Have you forgotten what Gabe did, Ess? You're just gonna forgive him like that?*

No.

"It's never going to bring Maya back, though, is it?" My voice comes out quiet, but it's shaking with entrenched rage. "Or make up for the fact she died because you betrayed us. And then ran away."

He sighs and looks at the door. "I am so sorry. I was a mess back then. Hell bent on revenge. On Langford… On the

93

cops. Everyone." When he shifts his eyes back to me, they're wide and earnest. He reaches out a hand, then seems to think better of it. "I would never have turned you in. You believe me, don't you?"

Hallie has been watching, but now she pipes up, "Ess, he wasn't well. They broke him when they arrested him. In that police cell..." She shakes her head and looks away.

The room grows hotter. All the possibilities of their plan swirl in my brain, colliding with my bitterness at Gabe's betrayal. I put a hand to my aching forehead. "I need some air. Can I go, please?"

My eyes open in time to catch Hallie and Gabe exchange a look, then Hallie says, "It'll have to be the tunnel. You can't leave through the front door."

The thought of fighting through that stink again makes my stomach clench, but I have no choice. I grab my bag and say goodbye to Piper, who is on her way to crash on the bed I slept in.

The tunnel's just as grim the second time around as Hallie leads me on the reverse route. Worse, because now I have a stomach full of toast which is determined to free itself. After an age, we're back under the manhole at New Street.

"How do I get out? There's no ladder."

"Aha," says Hallie, and produces a rope from her rucksack. She lobs it towards the manhole, and it catches on something like a handle sticking out of the brickwork. "Can't leave this here, it's too risky." As she feeds the rope, the end she threw reappears above us. She ties the two ends together and tugs. "There are enough nooks and crannies in the bricks to heave yourself up with this. You go first, just in case."

"In case what?"

With a nod at the rope, she hands me her bunch of keys.

I pocket them and climb, poking the toes of my boots in where I can. It's not pretty. My back and legs are still sore, and my hands burn on the rope, but eventually the hair on my crown brushes the manhole cover.

"The keyhole's to your right."

A few minutes later, we're standing in the rail tunnel.

Hallie crouches to release the rope. Bright sunlight bleeds in through the archway which will take us back to the station. A silhouette steps away from the wall and stops. I can't see their eyes, but from the stiff posture they're looking straight at me. With a movement of the shoulders, the figure lifts something to their face.

"Hallie." I blink, and when I open my eyes again, there's no one there.

"What?" She slams the hatch closed, turns the key, and starts shoving the rope in her bag.

"Erm, nothing. Just felt funny, that's all."

She pulls her mouth down. "Yeah, that shit smell will do that to you. Guess I'm just used to it. Let's go for a walk. Clear our heads."

"You're coming with me?"

She beams. "Course. You've been through it the last couple of days. And I've missed you. Be nice to spend some time together."

Being with Hallie makes me feel safer, so I'm glad. Still, I can't shake the suspicion she's here to keep me in check as much as keep me company.

# Chapter Twelve

## Kerry

**14th November 2041**

"I have good news, Kerry." Langford has a smile in his voice, but down the phone I can't tell if it's genuine or one of his fake ones. "I need you in London. A car's on the way to fetch you from the office."

My third day on the job and Langford's caved in. I guess he's decided I'm too valuable to waste in this backwater. Could be what I can do for him in Westminster is more important than the revenge trip he had planned. Or there's a better quality of retribution to be extracted in London.

I keep my voice cool, but my heart has gone crazy. "Sure, Alex. I'll be ready."

The drab journey to London takes over two hours. I'm sure it used to be less than half that time, but parts of the A24 are so degraded they're impassable. Langford's dour driver—I can't remember his name—has to take more than one detour. As we approach Westminster Bridge, he eases his window down and hangs out an arm. A huge gunmetal barricade spans the width of the road ahead, armed police pacing its length. There's a buzzing and a compact drone hovers inches from the car's open window. Langford's driver places his thumb on a plate built into the drone's shell. A green light flashes, and one of the police officers waves us on. As we move, a deep rumbling shakes my insides and the barricade lifts.

I gaze at the barrier as it glides up and away on its

mechanism. Its movement is smooth, almost balletic. "It's more secure round here than I remember."

"They installed it after the last attack," says the grim chauffeur. "Westminster is all sealed off now. Safe as it gets."

He's not wrong. There's another barrier at the far end of the bridge, which lifts on our approach without further admin.

There are no pedestrians and the few cars on the road are like the one I'm in—sleek, black and shiny limos, likely with the same leather seats. Ministers' cars.

"So no public access?"

"Nope. Officials only. All locked down."

"Good." So why is there a queasy feeling in the pit of my stomach? Westminster teemed with tourists and Londoners a few years ago. This emptiness amongst such grandeur is eerie. It's like a horror film I saw when I was a teenager about a virus that wiped everybody out and survivors had to hide in their houses. There were shots of a deserted Westminster Bridge and I remember wondering how they shut down London to film. Might have been easier than I thought.

After the bridge, we turn right on Whitehall, away from the Houses of Parliament, and past a Cenotaph draped in the George Cross and Unity flags. The wrought-iron gates that used to bar Downing Street have gone, replaced by a smaller version of the bridge barriers, which blocks the view.

"Wow. Alex *has* been busy."

The driver grunts as another drone approaches. This one operates on face recognition. The driver twists clumsily in his seat and gives it a full view of his features. When the barrier lifts, it reveals a line of men in camouflage, rifles in a low ready position. My stomach churns again. I try to recall the last time I was in Westminster. It's eighteen months, and Langford's had all this installed since then.

The barrier lifts and we roll past stone colonnades on to the foreboding inky brickwork of Number Ten. The driver pulls up outside the glossy black front door and waits. It's obvious he's not getting out to open the door for me, so I press the button on the armrest and climb out.

Someone opens the metal-plated door to Number Ten before I've made it up the steps. Inside, a young blond man in tight, blue livery makes room for me to move onto the red carpet, which is still flanked by those ridiculous, oversized chessboard tiles. From the smell and nap of it, the carpet is new, but it's the same shade I remember from before. Across the hall, an oil painting of St James' Park hangs in a gilt frame, representing a time when people could access the park. Two portraits face me on the opposite wall, one of Alex Langford alone, chin lifted in megalomaniac glory, and the other of the whole Langford clan—Alex with his long-suffering wife and son in tow.

The livery boy leads me through a doorway between the paintings into the airy corridor to the rear of the property. Two oak-panelled anterooms later, it seems we're going straight to the Cabinet Room. He knocks once.

"Come." Alex's voice pierces the wood.

My chaperone nods and retreats, leaving me to open the door.

I always thought this room looked a drab seat of power. Facing me, Langford sits alone at the long edge of the table, which is draped in its green cover that always looks like careless hands have tacked it down. Behind his head, an enormous iron wall sculpture depicting the Hands of Kinship is back lit in red. The carpet is beige with a pattern in a clashing shade of green. Beige drapes obscure the enormous windows, barring the bright sunlight from entering. It's airless in here, and it smells of warm fruit and pastries from the trolley in the corner.

"Kerry, great, you're here. Thanks for coming." As if I had any choice. "You can get acquainted with the place again."

"Is there a Cabinet meeting today?"

"In a while. It's just us for now." His eyebrows rise into his frown lines. "And an old friend of yours will be along."

Okay. "Foster-Pugh?"

"I thought you might enjoy a private reunion before everyone gets here." His damned eyebrows are still waggling.

"Great."

Right on cue, there's a knock at the door.

"Come on in, Oliver." Langford's voice switches to jocular mode as he springs from his seat and rounds the table to meet Foster-Pugh. Their hands shake and pump as I follow, then Oliver turns his sharp face on me. Standing side by side, they're comically mis-matched. Beaky and Beefy; hard to believe they're lifelong friends.

"Kerry, what a pleasure to see you." Foster-Pugh's eyes flick up and then lower along his hooked nose, and I know he's surveying my broadened figure, my cheap navy suit. "I heard you were working for Alex now. Needed a change? Good for you. Public Relations is a dirty business. Not like politics, eh?" He snuffles like a hedgehog, his mirthless version of a laugh.

*I haven't forgotten you fired me, you patronising asshat.*

I wrench my face into a smile and hold out my hand. "Oliver. It's nice to see you too."

Foster-Pugh sobers. Behind his wire glasses, his eyes glint. "Alex, have you updated Kerry on what we learned yesterday?"

"Not yet." Langford is back around the table, standing behind his chair. Like he's waiting for Foster-Pugh to sit first. "Kerry arrived a few minutes before you."

Foster-Pugh folds into a chair opposite Langford, who finally takes his own seat. Stranded in no-man's-land at the far end, I scamper around and sit next to Langford.

We peer at each other, then, at a nod from him, Foster-Pugh claps and rubs his hands together. "Well, Kerry. I have interesting information for you regarding an old associate of yours." He snatches up his briefcase.

"Really?" I frown at Langford, who grins until I itch to slap him.

The briefcase snaps open and Foster-Pugh pulls out a Manilla envelope. From it, he takes a pile of large photographs and slides them across to me. He taps the top one. "Recognise the one on the right?"

It's a dim snap taken in a railway tunnel. Two figures stand in the waning light. From the outlines, they are young females, but that's all I can tell. "Nope."

"Look at the next picture."

That one makes my nerve endings fire. Two young women again, walking around New Street station in Birmingham. One of them I vaguely recognise but can't place. The other...

*Essie.*

A hundred thoughts ricochet around my head. Obviously, Langford knows I know her, so Foster-Pugh does too. It doesn't mean they're aware of our business deal. Or Essie and Jack's betrayal. Forcing my voice to stay even, I say, "The Glass girl."

Langford snorts. "The scummy little bitch who bombed my factory." He turns in his seat and leans closer. His spiky, aggressive aftershave makes my nose itch. "The one you released that same night."

Slowly and evenly, I say, "I thought you bombed your own factory, Alex."

"The girl you double-crossed me with."

My breath stops.

He nods, his mouth twisted. "Yes, Kerry. I know about your scheme." He prods the photograph. "With that bitch and Jack Riley. Thought you'd make a killing on that prototype, didn't you? Thought it would be payback?"

I pull my eyes away and glance at Foster-Pugh.

He's staring at me, beads of sweat on his forehead and a nasty grimace of a smile on his lips. "That seems to have backfired somewhat, doesn't it?" That odious snuffling sprays me again.

I scowl at one, then the other. "I don't know what you're on about."

Langford thumps the table. "Oh, spare me the bullshit, Kerry. So you got fired. Tough shit. That's no justification for taking sides with those lowlifes." His face pushes into mine and the aftershave stings my eyes. "You're going to pay for that."

There's a knot in my chest. I swallow hard. "Alex—"

"Shut up." He breathes heavily, then his face relaxes as he turns back to Foster-Pugh. "Oliver, perhaps you'd be good enough to update Kerry on Glass's movements since she escaped justice."

Foster-Pugh curls a hand to his mouth and clears this throat. "Of course. Well, surprise, surprise, Glass has been consorting with criminals." He sifts through the photos. "This woman, the West Midlands police have been trying to trace for months. She's been running a theft ring, stealing from government warehouses, and distributing to the street vermin around Birmingham. Quite an operation. They've been moving premises every month, but one of our contacts got these shots yesterday." Foster-Pugh shuffles more photos from the pile. "He followed them for three hours and then bingo." He holds up a photo of the woman alone, standing at a red, metal door. "Their current distribution point. The street vermin are calling it The Bank. The rumours are these scum are connected with the riot on Monday." He shrugs. "Although, I doubt we'll be seeing a repeat of that for a while."

I peer at the photo. Is Essie hiding behind that door? "So what are you planning?"

Foster-Pugh looks at Langford, then turns back to me. "Raid them, of course. Who knows, we might catch the Glass tramp while we're at it."

"What if she's not there?"

Foster-Pugh's smile drips venom. "Oh, we've got a backup plan for her which can't fail."

Langford fiddles with a picture of Essie. "And if we pick her up, do you want a piece of her?"

*Oh, yes. Yes, I do.*

"Why would you do that for me?"

He drops the picture and cocks his head. "I like the idea

101

that you owe me."

The conference phone on the table buzzes and Langford reaches over to press a button. "We're ready. Send them in."

I rise, preparing to leave, but Langford snakes a hand around my wrist and, with firm downward pressure, forces me to sit.

The door opens and a procession of white faces appear. Among them are two women, both in their late fifties, both pert for their age with short but soft haircuts: Kamilla Slattery and Felicity Bland. I know most of the men's names too. My mind slides away from their forgettable faces as soon as they're through the door. This is it: the elite in the flesh. Clearly Langford and Foster-Pugh max out the Cabinet quota for charisma.

They file in and settle behind their wooden name plaques, some with glasses of juice and plates of tropical fruit from the hospitality trolley. Twenty briefcases click open and tablet devices appear. Twenty sets of eyes take curious peeks at me. Though many of them know damn well who I am, no doubt they are wondering what I'm doing here. They're not alone. The room grows warmer still.

"Good morning, everybody, good to see you're all so chipper." At the Great Leader's words, the room quietens. "Before we begin, I'd like to introduce our esteemed guest today. Kerry Tyler, some of you might remember, served as Homeland Environment Minister a while ago. Until we agreed to part on *very* amicable terms. I'm pleased to say Kerry has returned to work for us." He turns his sardonic gaze on me. "In an advisory capacity. This is her first week, so do be kind. Kerry will take the minutes today, won't you, Kerry?"

*You absolute wanker.*

While I fumble my tablet from my bag, I give him my brightest smile. "It will be my privilege, Prime Minister."

Years ago, the optics of the only black person in the room being there to take the notes would have bothered them. Not anymore. There are no photographers or film crews to worry about, no awkward questions from reporters.

There are a few confused frowns, but many more smirks—from asshats who no doubt think I had this coming. Jacob Peterson is actually laughing behind his hand. I press-ganged him into adding one percent to my budget when he was a junior in the treasury. Now he's Chancellor of the Exchequer. God, he's loving this.

"Excellent. Well, Kerry, I think you know most of the faces, and the rest you'll pick up. Let's crack on. Okay, Oliver, would you be kind enough to take us through Matters Arising?"

"Of course, thank you, PM. If you open enclosure document A, there's a summary of matters carried forward from the last Cabinet meeting."

There's a collective twitch as they swipe their screens. I'm left to squint over Langford's shoulder, but all I get is a reflected light from the chandelier above us.

"First item, the Precipitation Tenure Scheme. Well, that's mine and I'm happy to report the vexatious case against was dismissed by the Supreme Court yesterday, so we're clear to proceed with the preliminaries."

"Precipitation Tenure?" It's out of my mouth before I can stop it. "As in, buying and selling the rain?"

The room grows quiet as the heat of their stares presses on me.

Foster-Pugh glares at me. "As I was saying, we are moving on to implement the recommendations of the PTS feasibility study. I will bring a full progress report to the next meeting."

Foster-Pugh glances at Langford, who gives him an approving nod.

"Okay, next item is Cuba. JP, perhaps you should take this one as it's your baby."

Jacob Peterson flushes and gives a smug smile. "Thank you, Home Sec. More good news. I've been in touch with Brookers, and they confirm we will receive a transfer of one point six billion dollars into the Treasury coffers in due course. There's some tying up of loose ends as always—confirmation the island is permanently submerged, insurance implications of death toll et cetera—so it'll hit the coffers in Quarter Four. But...not to be sniffed at."

There's a smattering of applause while my brain wraps around the news. They bet on Cuba going under? I mean, of course they did. It's not the first time, but... *Cuba*. That means the prototype has gone and Jack Riley with it.

A fact not lost on Langford, because he turns a spiteful grin on me. "Fantastic, Jacob. Great work spotting that opportunity. Okay, Oliver, what's next?"

"Sherwood Forest fires, which is mine. The blaze is heading northwest. We've called in the army to airdrop retardants, so we're doing all we can on the ground. I'm more concerned about managing the message. There were rumblings of protests in Nottingham and Sheffield. To be fair, the air is rancid up there."

"Well, then we just hit them with the Dissent and Congregation Act." That was Kamilla Slattery, just promoted to Justice Secretary. "There's a reason we increased the sentence to twelve years."

Foster-Pugh nods. "But we need to nip this in the bud. Go in strong, like Birmingham."

He has my attention now.

"How many arrests were there on Monday?" asks Harry Carter, the Information Secretary.

Foster-Pugh swipes his tablet. "Sixty-two arrests; thirty-six shot by drones; twenty-one fatalities; eleven shot by officers. No fatalities amongst those, which is good. No *investigations* required."

My ears click in the brief silence as I swallow the bile.

"We have to go in strong," says Foster-Pugh, though his voice is less strident.

I haven't typed a single word of the minutes. Langford doesn't need them. He undoubtedly records all his meetings. It was just another power trip, another way to humiliate me.

Instead, I think about Carlo, try to imagine what my son is doing now. Is he in London? Has he joined a dissident organisation, as I suspected? Is he right now plotting action of the type Foster-Pugh wants to 'nip in the bud'? Could it get him hurt? Killed?

From Carlo, my mind wanders on to Essie. There was no sign of Seth and Willow in those pictures. Is she alone now? Where are her family? I hate the bitch for double-crossing me, but do I want her dead?

And if Langford keeps his word, if he delivers her to me, what will I do with her then?

# Chapter Thirteen

## Seth

### 15th November 2041

I'll give him this much: Rook's an excellent chef. I've watched him busying about the farmhouse kitchen. He loses his twitch when he's cooking, just like he does when he's reading to Willow. Last night, I asked him where he learned. He gave a weird laugh—well, his mouth opened, but no sound came out. Then he twitched and said, "It wasn't Le Cordon Bleu."

Tonight, he's making shepherd's pie. It was one of my dad's favourite dinners, though Rook's version is spicier.

"Double whammy of Worcestershire sauce and mustard is the secret," he says. "That and a generous glug of merlot." He takes a glug for himself.

"I'm guessing Mum and Dad's cellar is almost out," I say, watching him drain his glass.

"'Fraid so." Rook pulls in his wine-stained lips, in what I guess is an attempt at contrition. "But don't worry, I'm on it. I've started brewing homemade. There was a kit in the shed, unopened. We'll be chugging blackberry wine in a few weeks." His eyes go wide. "Hey, you're a cleric, aren't you?"

How does he know that? Pictures around the place, I guess. "Used to be."

He grins. "Maybe you could bless it for us. I could do with a bit of divine protection."

Couldn't we all? "Sorry, I've lost the knack. And the inclination."

Rook nods, as though that makes sense to him, and we slide into silence.

I've mourned Mum and Dad quietly, for Willow's sake. Doesn't feel real. Those mounds of earth are all that's left of them. What happened?

Rook says he found them in the living room, shot in the head. My insides go cold at the thought. Who shot them? My frazzled brain is trying to connect this to Essie and me, but I can't see how. If that were the case, why did they just leave, whoever they were? Surely, they'd wait around on the off chance we'd come bumbling up the A1 straight into them.

Nasty thoughts keep coming back. Rook's shown no sign of being dangerous or violent and he's so gentle with Willow. But...finding a house like this was a stroke of luck for him.

*When did you get here, Rook? Were they really dead when you found them?*

"When's dinner ready? I'm hungry." Willow is standing at the kitchen door, a carefully crayoned picture in her hands. Wax spirals of red hair spill out of a smiling face: Essie.

"Just dishing up now, Wills."

I haven't got used to hearing Rook call her that. Judging by the way her shoulders rise one after the other, neither has she.

"Shall we eat in the lounge?" Rook scoops steaming pie from a Pyrex dish and slops it onto three plates.

I dart to a cupboard. "I'll get the trays."

Rook and I settle in the living room, trays on laps. Willow kneels at Dad's footstool and balances her plate on top. Her movements are fluid. The cut on her leg is healing well and my hand has ceased its complaining too. I give silent thanks to Nathan for the elderflower salve.

Wasting no time, Willow tucks into the pie, though I can't believe it doesn't burn her mouth.

Rook swipes the remote to switch on the old-fashioned, wall-mounted television. "Ah, it's Clara James."

I glance from my pie. A young blonde woman standing by

large screen is reading the news.

Rook whistles. "She's a proper saucy bitch."

"Rook." I glance at Willow.

His beard twitches. "Sorry, mate."

Clara reads: *"Wildfires are being brought under control in Sherwood Forest, as a generous government aid package costing millions of pounds takes effect. The Homeland Environment Minister, Devon Devonport, said he hoped this would give the local authorities pause for thought and encouraged them to take better care of our precious woodland heritage."*

"Well, that's bollocks, for a start." Rook spits a fleck of potato as he speaks. "What are the local authorities s'posed to do about it when those arseholes are wrecking the planet?"

I give him a look to say, 'dial down the language', but his eyes are fevered and fixed on the screen. Plus, I can't argue with his point.

Clara swipes the screen behind her and a picture of a woman with a grey-blonde bob fades in. *"The Justice Secretary, Kamilla Slattery, has promised swift action to ensure safety and calm on our streets following the violent attacks faced by brave police officers in Birmingham yesterday."*

A jolt of electricity rocks my chest.

Clara continues, *"An out-of-control mob assembled in the city's Victoria Square, intent on causing damage to historic buildings and attacking all who stood in their way. Sixty-two arrests were made. Twenty-six members of the public were seriously injured by the mob, and twenty-one were sadly killed. Ms Slattery spoke to us earlier."* She swipes the screen again and a live version of Slattery appears in front of a bookcase adorned with yellow roses.

"We simply cannot allow heinous acts like this to go unpunished," says Slattery. "Mark my words, I will ensure by any means necessary that every perpetrator of this despicable violence—this heartless *slaughter*—is brought to justice before they injure any more of our heroes or cause more damage to the heritage of this great nation. Those murderers will pay a harsh price. That is what we stood for in our manifesto, and that is what we will do."

"You think it went down like that?" asks Rook.

"I doubt it." Glancing at Willow, happily engrossed in another book, I think of Essie. God, I hope she wasn't near that place. There's no reason to suppose she was. She'd have said on the phone.

Clara has moved on. *"Police have appealed for people to come forward who may know the whereabouts of a couple wanted on charges of planning terrorist activity."*

She swipes the screen. My heart stops.

Two photographs share the space: one of Essie; one of me.

*"Twenty-five-year-old Estella Glass, known as Essie, and twenty-seven-year-old Seth Fielding, a disgraced Unity cleric, have been plotting attacks on a series of government buildings."* Clara glares at me down the lens as my insides dissolve. *"Anyone with information should call the number on the screen urgently. Authorities are also increasingly concerned for the welfare of their four-year-old daughter, Willow. There is a generous reward for any information that leads to an arrest."*

At the sound of her name, Willow's head pops up. "Daddy, that's you and Mummy."

I lean over and grab the remote from Rook, whose eyes are wide and still glued to the screen. With a swipe of my hand, our pictures have gone, replaced by drone footage of Sherwood Forest, from before it went up in flames, accompanied by stirring orchestral music.

"That's enough news, I think." I smile at Willow, who blinks and frowns.

Rook watches the pine trees whizz by on the screen for a moment, then turns his weary face to me. "They really are lying bastards, aren't they?"

\*\*\*

Willow is shaking me awake. Except it's not Willow because the hand on my shoulder is strong and bigger than hers.

"Seth." It's Rook's voice in my ear. "Wake up. They're coming for you."

Willow stirs beside me in the bed, poking a toe into my thigh.

"What time is it?"

Rook moves away, tugging the covers. "I saw headlights coming towards us. No one drives past here anymore, since Crawton was abandoned."

I sit up and rub sleep from my eyes. "Abandoned?"

"Didn't you hear? Floods." Rook tuts. "Never mind. We have to move."

As Rook switches on the bedside lamp, I untangle myself from the duvet and run to the window. Half a mile away, dipped low, two sets of headlights glide along the lane approaching the house. "Rook, have you been keeping watch?"

He shrugs and looks down. "Thought after you appeared on the news, someone round here may have reported you."

Tears prick my eyes. "Thanks, mate."

Willow has wandered off to the toilet. I grab our few things and stuff them in the holdall as she returns. "Wills, we've got to go."

"I know," she says quietly. "Because of the news."

My chest aches.

*I'm so sorry, little one. You don't deserve this.*

The headlights spring into the room, sweeping the oversized poppies on Mum and Dad's wallpaper.

"Come on," says Rook. "We'll go out the back."

We sprint downstairs. As I pass the sideboard, I grab a photo of Mum and Dad at a restaurant on their twentieth wedding anniversary. They look so young. I shove it in the bag and hurry into the kitchen. Behind me, Willow is cramming her feet into her trainers her Minnie Mouse rucksack hanging from one arm. I snatch my phone and the charger from the kitchen counter and join her, fumbling on

110

my shoes, snatching up coats.

Rook is at the back door. He shrugs on my dad's old, green mac, then ducks behind the dining table. "Shit, they're in the garden. Come on. We can get out through the cellar."

There's a coal hatch that opens on the side of the house. From there, we could jump the fence to the next garden. Rook must have had a good look round to know that.

As glass smashes in the kitchen, Rook rips open the door to the cellar. He and Willow clatter down the stone steps. Diving after them, I grab the bunch of rusty keys from the hook inside the door and lock us in. At the far wall, I reach up and unlock the coal hatch. Above us, feet stamp on the hall and stairs. Rook scrambles through the hatch, then thrusts his arms back in and lifts Willow through the gap. I brace my hands against the frame and heave myself up. There's no way to lock the hatch from the outside, so I close it as quietly as I can. We're stuck to the spot, panting, listening to the bangs and rumblings of the raid.

There is some light in the sky despite the cloud cover, so it's near dawn. We're in the narrow alleyway between Mum and Dad's and the neighbours' houses. In the days since we arrived, we haven't seen them, so I assume they've left or gone away.

"Come on," whispers Rook. As he vaults over the low fence, a gust of wind rattles the coal hatch.

With a last glance toward the graves, I lift Willow over, then follow. As we duck around the building, the neighbours' dining conservatory comes into view. In the dim grey light, it's possible to make out the places set for dinner. Four empty glasses cluster in the centre of the table as though trying to toast themselves.

"They must have left in a hurry." My voice is hoarse with sleep and terror.

"Hey." A shout from Mum and Dad's garden. As the speaker moves, a glint of something at chest level is followed by a gunshot.

Willow screams. I grab her hand, and we sprint across the neighbours' garden, where Rook is scaling the next fence.

Deep rumbling accompanies our scramble.

Is that thunder or the raid?

Another gunshot rips the air, followed by grunts and thuds as our pursuers jump the first fence.

Stinging hail slams into us, bouncing on the parched field as we race across it.

# Chapter Fourteen

## Essie

### 16th November 2041

It's late afternoon in Gabe and Hallie's orange-smelling lounge. Hallie's downstairs, manning The Bank, handing out samosas. Piper is dozing upstairs on the tiny bed we use in shifts. Not that I get much chance. She sleeps half the time, healing from her wounds. Gabe's friends, Luisa and Jasmine, are back. We're settled around a half-empty plate of samosas and a pot of tea.

"Jez called me last night. London has been recruiting," says Luisa, her dark eyes sparkling. "They've got hundreds now, from everywhere. Kim's calling it their revolutionary village."

Gabe looks at me and grins. "Kim's the London commander. Ess, you should see it. It's a few months since I visited them, but even then, they had a real vibe going."

"Where are they all?" I'm wondering how that many people can hide in London without being targeted.

"The old underground system," says Gabe.

"Don't they patrol it?"

"The stations, yes. Not the entire network. Including the bits they shut down, it's vast. They've got a rabbit warren. Kim was a town planner, back when they used to plan towns instead of letting them go feral. She's a genius at living off-grid."

"Sounds interesting." I try to act cool, but my mind is racing at the idea of a community living literally under their noses. "I'd like to see that."

Gabe's smile widens. "We'll go there soon. I could do with a holiday."

"Might not be much of a holiday," says Luisa. "Kim's planning something big."

My heart thuds.

Gabe's eyes snap up. "Oh? What's that?"

Luisa shifts on her cushion. "Jez didn't say much, just Kim reckons it's time to do something useful with her recruits. I think she's thinking direct action. I mean, they've got the numbers."

Gabe sticks out his bottom lip and nods. "I'll call her later."

There's a gnawing feeling in my stomach. If Monday's events in Victoria Square are anything to go by, they'll get themselves killed. "Gabe, you saw the drones shooting people the same as I did. Do they know about those things?"

"Do who know about what?" Piper comes into the lounge, draped in Hallie's dressing gown, one arm in a fresh sling. She grabs a cushion and drops it next to mine.

"The killer drones," is all I say, then close my mouth.

Piper seems to deflate onto her cushion more than sit. I know she still has nightmares about what happened to her because she cries in her sleep. It reminds me of the flashbacks I have to Langford's attack. I stroke her hair as she gives me a sad little smile.

Gabe shakes his head. "I'll tell them, but Essie, you must see this is no time to back away. Their violence is a sign we're breaking through."

"It won't do us any good if we all get slaughtered, will it?" I refuse to let my gaze drop from Gabe's. "You taught me that yourself years ago. They crushed the twenties' uprisings by force. We can't beat them that way, because they'll always have more weapons. We have to be smarter."

"Smart how? You got any better ideas?"

I take a long breath in. "I *did*. It would have worked if I hadn't screwed it up."

Gabe frowns, and flaps his hands to say, 'go on'. It's time to come clean.

*So you're gonna trust this guy, now, Ess?*

No. I don't trust him. But right now, he's the best chance I've got of making it out of this nightmare. My mind runs away into the fantasy of calling Seth, asking him to bring Willow and join me. My heart hurts with the idea, because I know I can't. It's not safe yet.

Gabe is still staring at me, so I spill it all. In front of Piper, Jasmine and Luisa, who I'd never met a fortnight ago, I tell Gabe about my plot with Jack to build the prototype under Kerry's nose.

Gabe claps his hands. "Bloody hell, Ess. That's *brilliant*."

"It might have been." My face grows hot as I confess my stupid mistake with Lawrence.

"God. Lawrence," says Gabe. "I'd forgotten about him."

My lips pull into a sneer. "Well, he's probably dead, too."

*And you're as responsible for that as I am, Gabe.*

"The prototype and Jack are under the sea." I blink. Tears are no good to anyone. "My point is, if we're going to beat them, it's not just about smashing stuff up." Four pairs of eyes focus on me, and my face glows even hotter. I swallow. "If you've got all these geniuses, Gabe, then it ought to be possible to outthink them. I don't think Langford's that clever. He's just rich."

The room is quiet for so long, I wonder if I've broken some code and am about to get thrown out.

Then Gabe nods slowly. "You might be on to something there, Glass."

***

It's Piper's turn on the mattress, so here I am stretched awkwardly across a pile of cushions which keeps shifting under me. My bruised back throbs every time it scrapes on the floor. Piper is snoring. These hours in the middle of the night, I ache for Seth; for the knowledge of Willow sleeping in the next room. I miss them so much. Here, there's no chance of any sleep.

Sighing, I pull back the itchy blanket and ease to my feet. The bare wooden floors groan as I cross the room. Piper whimpers and I pause at the door. After a few mumbles, she settles. I slip out and down the stairs.

Everyone is in bed. It's cool, and silent until I draw myself a glass of water. The pipes behind the wall thump and clank as the water sputters. I chug the first glass, which tastes bitter, and fill it again. As I swig, the clanking continues, only it's not coming from the pipes, but from the hallway below.

My mouth goes dry as I creep across the living room then down the second flight.

THUMP.

It's the manhole cover. Someone's trying to get in. But everyone's here or gone home for the night.

Heart pounding, I sprint up, through the lounge, and up again. "Gabe! Hallie!" I burst into their room, fumbling on the light.

"What the—?" Gabe snaps up in bed, his freckled bare chest exposed.

"There's someone coming." My breath catches. I swallow. "Through the tunnel."

They're up in an instant, pulling on clothes, grabbing a bag each from under their bed. Piper emerges from her room as they race down the stairs.

"Piper, come on." I dive to the semi-dark stairwell.

She catches up to me as I reach Gabe and Hallie. We huddle at the open door to the flat. Gabe switches on a torch.

THUD.

We jolt almost as one, the torch beam convulsing. Piper emits a little scream.

"The Bank." Hallie takes the steps two at a time, leaps past the manhole cover and through a door beyond.

THUD.

That came from the direction Hallie fled. She bursts back into the hall, her eyes a glassy reflection of Gabe's flashlight. "They're at the front."

We're trapped.

"What are we gonna do?" My voice is shaking so much I'm not sure they understood me.

THUD.

"There's another tunnel," says Gabe. "For the canals. Come on." He joins Hallie in the hall, and they dip out of view behind the slope of the stairs, taking the light with them.

When Piper and I make it there, they've disappeared through a door I haven't noticed before. We crowd into a large, dark cupboard. Hallie drops to her knees at a square metal cover.

Fumbling in her bag, she pulls out the iron keys. "God, I hope they don't know about this one."

"Shit. My bag." I turn to Gabe. "I left my bag in the flat."

"Forget it."

"No. I need it. My phone... everything's in there."

*My only line to Seth.*

THUD-THUD.

Hallie thrusts the key in the lock.

"I'm going back for it." I grab Piper's arm. "Don't wait. You go."

"No."

"Piper, please. I'm thirty seconds behind you."

Hallie's jumps down. Gabe sits on the edge of the hole and looks up. "We have to go. Now."

The only way I can make Piper comply is to give her a shove before I race back up to the flat. I snap lights on as I go. It's not like they don't know we're here.

My phone is under a cushion where I was trying to sleep less than ten minutes ago. I grab it and my open rucksack and shove it inside. As I dash across the room, Boop the green rabbit drops on the floor and I almost trip.

"Boop, come on." I scoop him up, throw him in the rucksack and zip it closed. As I reach the foot of the stairs, a splintering crash comes from behind.

117

They're in.

I burst into the cupboard and close the door behind me. It's dark and silent. As fast as I dare, I stumble towards where the tunnel opening must be. I can only pray Hallie didn't lock it behind them and trap me in.

Voices echo in the corridor outside. I reach the manhole. The cover is on, but it lifts as I pull the handle. Sobbing with relief, I launch into the hole.

*Hallie, you absolute hero.*

I land hard, but the drop isn't as far as the New Street tunnel. My foot buckles as it lands on something.

The keys.

Hallie took a hell of a risk leaving them. Guessing what she meant, I reach a shaky hand up and fumble the shank into the lock. It takes two hands to force it home, then I shove the bunch in my pocket and run blindly to wherever the tunnel will take me.

Someone snatches my hair in the dark.

*Shit. They're here. It's over.*

I scream and jerk, trying to slap the hand away.

"Ess, it's me." Piper's hoarse whisper cuts through my panic.

"Oh shit, Piper." My breath explodes out of me. "I thought you were cops. Jesus."

She clutches my arm. "I didn't want you to get lost, so I waited."

I bend double, trying to suck in air before I pass out.

Piper's voice is harsh, edged with terror. "We've got to *run*."

Still gasping, I grab my phone for light and follow her. "D'you know the way out?"

"Er, sort of."

We run, our footsteps muted on the damp floor of the tunnel. I try to ignore the rats scuttling away from us.

Piper stops at an intersection, her head twisting left and right.

I listen behind us, but there's nothing except the sound of our breathing. "Which way?"

She purses her lips and points to the left. We set off at a brisk walk.

Trying to shake the feeling Piper's improvising, I glance at my phone. Sixty-four percent battery. They had chargers at The Bank, but I left without one, so that's all I've got.

We walk on through another intersection. The further we get, the more it seems we might have escaped the raid. Doesn't mean we won't starve to death if Piper doesn't know the way out.

"Is this the route Gabe and Hallie took?"

"I don't know." She stops. When she turns, the light of my phone picks out her worried frown. "I thought so, but…" She flaps her hands.

"Okay." I bite in my panic. "Let's just stay calm. We can't be far from an exit."

"Well, we've been walking for an hour and seen nothing." Piper's chest heaves with shuddering breaths. "Does it feel like we're deeper underground to you?"

"No, Piper. Let's not do this." I grab her shoulders. "We're not freaking out, okay? This is gonna be fine. Piper."

She looks at me.

"We're okay. Okay?"

Her breathing slows and she nods. "Okay."

"Right, let's think. We came out under Hurst Street and turned left about half an hour ago. What do you reckon, we could be somewhere near Edgbaston?"

She wipes sweat from her brow. "Possibly."

"Makes sense for a tunnel like this to lead to the reservoir." I shine my phone along the ceiling up ahead. "Let's keep going straight. It's got to come out somewhere, eventually."

We walk in silence. After fifteen minutes, my phone light catches on something square and dark overhead.

"Piper." I point the phone up.

She beams at me. "Thank Christ for that. Let's hope it's not locked."

It's not, and there's a slimy metal ladder to climb. Within minutes we're out, surrounded by a clutch of trees and shrubbery. I was right; we're at the reservoir. The sunrise glints pink on its glassy surface. Warm air is piney, musty with the smell of standing water.

Piper nearly knocks me over as she sweeps me in a tight hug. "You're a genius."

I laugh, untangling myself from her in front and a bramble behind. "Hardly."

Something snaps behind us. I whip around.

A grubby-faced Hallie approaches us through the trees, her tongue stud gleaming as she laughs. "You made it. Oh my God, I thought you were gonna get taken."

I giggle, a high-pitched, manic sound. Piper snorts.

"Shit, ladies." Gabe peeps from behind a conifer. He shuffles over and flops down on the crisp, leaf-littered ground. "I need a drink."

Still laughing, we collapse in a loose circle.

Hallie sobers first. "The Bank's gone."

Gabe puts an arm around her. "We'll start again. We've done it before. It's a sign."

Hallie pulls away to peer at him. "What of?"

"Time for a change." He takes a long, noisy breath.

"We should go to London," I say. "Join that community. What's her name? Kim?"

Hallie sifts the powdery soil through her hands. "I don't know, Ess."

She says something else I don't hear because my phone buzzes. The battery's only at thirty-four percent now, but there's something else. While we were underground, I had a missed call from a number I recognise.

There's a message. I spring up and turn away from the others, ignoring the confused look from Piper. With trembling fingers, I call the voicemail.

"Ess. It's Jack. Just wanted to let you know I'm okay. I got the last flight to America, but I can't say any more. I'll tell you everything when we speak. Hope you're okay."

*Bloody risky, Jack.*

What if they had taken me at The Bank? They'd have had my phone when he called. I can't stay angry, though. It's incredible he's alive. Ending the call to voicemail, I start to dial Jack's number. Before I've got three numbers in, the phone rings again.

I answer immediately. "Seth."

"Christ, Ess. I'm so happy to hear your voice." He sounds like he's crying.

I try to suppress my sob, make it into a giggle. "You're timing is so damn perfect."

Seth sniffs. "What's happening?"

"Oh, a bit of excitement. All over now. You?"

"Same." He murmurs something, I assume to Willow. "I, er, had to leave Mum and Dad's so we're on the road again."

"Why? Did they find you? Where are your parents? Did they hurt them?"

"They're dead." His voice splinters.

My legs collapse under me, dropping me to the ground. "Wh-hat? They killed them?"

"No. I don't know. They were dead when I got there."

"Oh, Seth. I'm so…"

*What Ess? You're sorry? More deaths on your account. When are you gonna stop?*

"No, don't. It's not your fault. I just…wanted to hear your voice. And tell you we're okay. I thought you could talk to Willow."

My chest aches. "I want to, so much, but I thought we said no…"

"Bugger that. Ess, we could all be dead by tomorrow."

"Yes." I close my eyes.

The phone rustles. "Hi, Mummy."

A sob rips from me. "Willow. Hi, baby girl."

121

"Mummy, have you finished the stuff you had to do yet?"

"Not yet. Almost."

"Good. I miss you. Nanny and Granddad are dead."

The tears roll down my cheeks, pattering on the dry leaves. "I know. I miss you too. I love you." It's only a whisper, so I'm not sure she hears.

Another rustle.

"Ess, it's me again. You okay?"

"Yep." I sniff. "I'm okay. I forgot to tell her I've got Boop with me."

"Really?" He gives a wet chuckle. "She thought she'd left him in Rich's car."

The silence in the wood behind me is so complete, I guess they're listening. "He's right here in my bag. He's a bit stinky, but he's in one piece."

"Ess, that's so great. I'll tell her." His sigh distorts. "We can't tell each other where we're going, can we?"

"No. Also, I don't know where I'm going."

"I love you so much."

"I love you too, Seth. Stay safe."

He's gone before I'm ready for the wave of loss. When I turn around, the pity in Piper's eyes makes me feel a hundred times worse.

I clench my fingers into tight fists, the dirty nails digging into my palms. "What are you all gawping at? Are we going to London or not?"

# Chapter Fifteen

## Kerry

One week in, and I've had enough. Seven days with these odious asshats is all it takes. How could I have forgotten how poisonous Langford is?

Either he's decided I'm trustworthy enough to stick around, or the ongoing opportunities to humiliate me were too tempting to resist. Either way, he told me Friday I was to be based in London and handed me the keys to one of his properties on Primrose Hill. Nice place, and I don't have to pay him a penny.

Rent free it may be, but I'm waiting to learn the price I'll pay in the end.

This morning, Langford has called a COBRA meeting, but he didn't tell me why, and I'm not invited into the windowless Cabinet Office briefing room where they're all huddled. I'm left guessing what it's about. There are rumblings of rebellion about the place; rumours of dissident groups organising around the country, so I imagine the meeting is to plan a new crackdown.

I'm stationed at a safe distance down the corridor in a lush, red-carpeted room in the Cabinet Office building. My task is to plough through a pile of reports and provide Langford with a briefing paper. He's given me free rein on the expanse of filing cabinets containing reports and previous briefing papers.

Big mistake, Alex.

The COBRA meeting will to continue until noon. I'd finished Langford's briefing by ten, so now I get to play among the papers.

Working my way through the 2041 files, I hit the briefing dated 7th October of this year. This has meat on its bones:

### Item 2A. Dissent and Mitigation
*Report ref HO41/10/463A [CLASSIFIED A1]*

*Report is an options appraisal for mitigation of dissent as the effects of climate change worsen (see items 1A and 1B).*

*Primary risks:*
1. *Disproportionate impact of climate change on already-dissenting communities such as the homeless, poor, anti-establishment, and ethnic minorities.*
2. *These communities, taken as a whole, comprise greater numbers than existing legislation and policing methods can suppress in the event of an uprising.*
3. *Current intelligence suggests the presence and expansion of cross-sectional dissident groups. No intelligence around specific threats, but expert advice recommends early intervention and mitigation.*

*Options for Mitigation:*
1. *Continue current methods of surveillance, including open and covert ops, and infiltration – ADOPTED.*
2. *Continue communications work around badging of dissident groups as terrorists: drip feed media stories of criminal damage and violence of 'fringe' groups – ADOPTED.*
3. *Internment measures included in report HO41/10/463A – RECOMMENDED.*
4. *Neutralisation measures included in report HO41/10/463A – COBRA TO DISCUSS (date tbc).*

Internment... *Neutralisation.*

They're talking about putting dissenters in camps; killing them if they don't comply? Why should that surprise me? Langford's been heading this way since he got into power.

Still, reading it in black and white like this, the nausea burns my chest.

Glancing around, I pull my phone out of my bag and take pictures of as many pages as I dare. Then I replace the paper in its drawer and thumb through the files behind it.

Ten minutes later, in a briefing dated 4th November, I find this:

*Item 4A. Unity Expansion*
*Report ref HO41/11/554*
*Report outlines proposals from the Home Secretary for the inception of two new arms of Unity\*.*

*\*For clarity, Unity refers to the organisation created in June 2029 to bring together all churches and education establishments under a single umbrella of enlightened institutions.*

*- Unity Devout will return the organisation to its roots in traditions of deep faith. This will include integration of Old Testament values with the rule of law. The report details principal values.*
*- Unity Power will support local law enforcement to manage the issues around dissent raised in report ref HO41/10/463A [CLASSIFIED A1]. Report HO41/11/554 names key individuals active in several major English cities, including London, Birmingham, Bristol, Manchester, and Liverpool. These individuals will form a bronze command team working locally to maintain order, gather intelligence, and keep dissident groups in check.*

Christ. They're organising militia. I pull out my phone again.

Glancing at the mahogany door, I move along the cabinets and fish out the report referenced in the briefing. There's summary of Unity Devout Values: reverence, penitence, respect for authority...

Further down, there's a heading:

*Bronze Command.*
*London South – Charlie Worth*
*London North – Archie Braiden*
*Birmingham – Jake Murray...*

A buzz of voices grows in the corridor. I check my watch: eleven thirty-five. They're out early. Shoving the report back in place, I elbow the cabinet door and spring away. The chair rocks as I flop into it back at the desk.

Too late, I realise the filing cabinet is still open.

The voices grow louder. Foster-Pugh is saying, "Well, PM, I'm delighted. We have a robust plan to proceed."

Langford replies in a low rumble I can't decipher.

Unable to breathe, I shuffle papers with an aimless, shaky hand.

The voices fade away down the corridor. My shoulders deflate as I finally force out a sigh.

***

Ed places an after-dinner coffee in before me and leans in to bite my neck.

"Hey, that hurts."

"You love it, though." His voice vibrates against my throat as he nuzzles in hard and bites again.

I shove him away. "Seriously, Ed. I'm working."

"Christ's sake, Kerry." He sounds like a sulky teenager. "Why have me drive you home, if you're just going to work?"

"Because this is different work." True. Researching Foster-Pugh's career in journalism is a job best done away from Westminster. And what a career it is. Editorials in all the major papers and political magazines. Rants about the 'cancer of red tape', mainly. This guy doesn't believe in any form of organised society. He wants a world populated by controlled masses, ruled by a 'superior class' who play the markets unfettered. It's no secret. He's been writing about it for years, if anybody had paid attention.

My laptop slams closed in my face.

"You know." Ed slips behind me, hands snaking around my throat. "I feel like you're taking me for granted." His fingers squeeze.

"Ed." My voice comes out high pitched and breathy.

"Hmm?" Keeping one hand wrapped around my throat, he yanks my shirt collar and bra strap down and bites my shoulder, stinging, breaking the skin.

"Get off me."

The biting stops, but he stays in place. His fingers tighten on my neck.

My personal phone rings. I peel Ed's slackening grip from me and grab the mobile from the kitchen table. "Kerry speaking."

"Mum."

"Carlo." I straighten my back in the chair, slapping Ed's probing hand away. "Are you okay? Where are you?"

"I'm fine. Everything's fine. Just wanted to say hi and let you know I'm in London."

My limbs flush with heat. He's been so close. "It's good to hear that. Why haven't you called before? You promised every week. I've been worried sick. What are you doing? Where are you staying?"

There's a pause. "Erm, I can't say. I've found these people, Mum, and they're gonna change things. We're going to make it better."

"Are you safe?"

He snuffles. "Safe as any of us are. Mum, these are good people. They've got my back. Kim's..."

In my kitchen, a million miles away, my work phone rings. Ed scoops it up and answers it, but his voice is muffled and echoey. It's as if I've jumped down the phone and am halfway to my son's side.

Carlo is speaking again. "I just want you to know I love you. In case something happens."

"What's going to happen?"

Silence.

"Carlo?"

127

"Never mind. Just know how grateful I am you let me do this."

*Well, I'm starting to regret it, kid.*

"Call me soon?"

He sighs. "I will if I can. Bye, Mum. I love you."

"I love you too," I say to an empty line. The phone slips from my ear on to the table.

*I found these people, Mum...*
*Kim...*

Who is this Kim? A girlfriend? All the questions I should have asked flood my mind. What are they planning? Why does Carlo think something might happen to him?

I force the lump down my throat.

"Alex called." Ed shoves my work phone at me. "And I'm leaving."

The door slams as I speed dial Langford.

He answers quickly. "Kerry."

"Alex."

"Sorry to call so late." Asshat doesn't sound sorry.

"What is it?" That came out sharper than I intended.

"I have good news." The smug smile comes out in his voice, making it higher than usual. "About our mutual interest. Thought you'd want to hear it straight away."

"You found Glass?"

There's a paper-shuffling sound. "The next best thing."

"Which is?"

"Well, as you know, we offered a reward for information regarding the whereabouts of Glass and her boyfriend, Seth Fielding."

"Someone called her in?"

"Not her. Him and the brat."

So they went separate ways. Clever girl. "Where?"

"Up north somewhere. Middle of nowhere. We're gonna pick them up. Got close two days ago, but we're back on their

128

trail. I thought you'd want to get back to London tomorrow and meet them when they arrive."

Do I ever? "I'll be there first thing."

# Chapter Sixteen

## Essie

### 19th November 2041

Two days' walking has taken its toll, and we're not even halfway to London. My bruised and aching back wakes me before dawn. I hoist myself onto blistered feet, wondering how the hell I'm going to get my boots back on.

We spent last night in an abandoned corrugated warehouse outside Daventry. Rusted engine parts lie forgotten along the walls, and the smell of oil stings my nose after a long, restless night inside. Hallie and Piper are sleeping, huddled in their coats. Piper shivers and mumbles.

I ease open the door and step outside into the warm, smoky air. The colour of the sky throws me. The red hue radiates from the southwest. In the east, a bank of dark cloud hides the sun. I assume it's rising, though nothing would surprise me.

"It's the Cotswolds on fire." Gabe's scratchy voice makes me jump. He strides around the corner of the building, a cigarette cupped in his palm, pointing with his other hand to the western glow. "It went up yesterday."

When he holds the ciggie out to me, I shake my head. "How do you know?"

"I was chatting to some locals." He barks out a chesty cough. "Catches the breath, doesn't it?"

I clear my throat, though it's the smell of engine oil that's bothering me most. "Gabe, are we gonna make it to London?"

"Course. I'm not planning to live out my days in *Daventry*."

"We're all exhausted. I'm not sure I can walk any further. And Piper's…not well. She's got a temperature, and I think her gunshot wound is going septic. She needs a doctor."

He grimaces. "I know. There's a doctor at Kim's place. And I've got good news on transport. We've got wheels waiting, just up the way."

My hope sparks. "You found a car?"

He screws up his lips and does a seesawing gesture with his palms. "Mmm…ish."

I glare at him. "What?"

"Milk float."

"A *milk float*?" I try to work out if he's serious from his expression. "We have to drive the remaining eighty miles to London in a bloody milk float?"

"No, you don't have to." He shrugs, his mouth pulled down, voice hardening. "You can walk."

"Will it even go that far?"

He huffs. "I don't know, Ess, if I'm honest. With a bit of luck, maybe we'll be in London by lunch. I thought it was better than wearing our legs down to stubs." Gabe's eyes narrow at me. "London was your idea, remember. I'm just trying to make it happen." Chucking his cigarette away, he marches off and disappears around the building.

He has a point. That was harsh, but I'm tired of Gabe overselling his own ideas. Thinking back now, it would be simple to let myself believe Gabe's the reason we're all in this mess; not accurate, perhaps, but easy.

As he drives it back around the corner, the whine of the milk float's circuits is higher pitched than the electric cars I've heard. It's like the world's loudest, angriest, slowest, green-and-white mosquito. Green plastic crates pile high in the back. Gabe puts the vehicle out of its misery as the rear draws level with me. Old cobwebs and dried leaves blanket the crates.

"Well…" I can't think of anything to say.

"What in all hell is that?" A pallid-looking Piper is at the

131

warehouse door, leaning on Hallie for support.

Gabe's pale eyebrows draw down. "Any of you are welcome to locate an alternative, if you think you can do better."

Hallie releases Piper's arm and steps forward with a smile. "It's great, my love." She plants a kiss on his cheek. "I'll drive.

I brush a hand over a crate, picking up the threads weaved by long-dead spiders. "We'd better chuck out some of this lot, then."

Fifteen minutes later, Piper and I huddle amongst our belongings in the flatbed as Hallie steers the float off the estate with Gabe beside her. With the roof of the float and the few remaining crates packed around us, we're safely out of sight of any drones. The rush of air is almost cool, and I lift my face. It's good to rest on the move for once. Hallie avoids the motorways, sticking to the scenic route where an ancient milk float might raise fewer eyebrows. Though its top speed is fifteen miles per hour, it feels like we're finally getting somewhere. After a while, the buzzing of the electrics becomes hypnotic, modulating along with the decaying road. Piper's head lolls against my shoulder and soon enough, mine follows.

***

The whine has taken on a lower pitch. That's what must have woken me up. Piper is sitting cross-legged, her back to me, facing the road as it trundles past. We were never flying, but I'm sure the float has slowed down. "Is the battery low?"

Piper's shoulder jerk up, and she whips her head round. "Jesus, Ess, you made me jump."

"Sorry." I peer at the road, but it offers no clues. Just a generic A-road with spacious, detached houses on one side and cracked, dry, brown fields on the other. Some homes have shiny-looking cars on the drive and neat but yellowed lawns. Others look abandoned and feral. "How far are we from London?"

"Dunno. I just woke up myself." Looks like the rest has done her some good. Her cheeks have colour, her eyes more spark. "You're right, though. Sounds like we're about to run out of juice."

As if Piper's given it permission, the float moans to a halt.

Gabe gets out of the passenger seat and peers back at us. "Ladies, looks like we're on foot again."

A glance at my still-throbbing feet encased in dirty boots elicits a self-pitying groan.

Piper sits, head bowed in silent defeat.

"It's only ten miles or so." He grins. The ride seems to have lifted his mood.

Hallie joins us, grabbing bags off the float. "Better crack on if we want to get there before dark."

A painful, sweaty walk follows, skirting fields and housing estates. We stay alert for drones, which pass frequently, their low buzz a malevolent echo of our lost transport. Each time, we scramble into a hedgerow or huddle against a fence.

As we approach London, the houses become smaller, some boarded up, the roads even more potholed. It's a good thing we left the float. There's no way it would make it over this terrain.

The air smells of burning rubber. There are a few grubby, hooded people scattered here and there, smoking and idling against walls or meandering in the road. Nowhere near as many as I expect for early evening. "Where is everyone?"

Gabe's head pops up at a pall of dark smoke rising from a pile of tyres. "Dunno. A curfew? We should get off the streets."

"We're almost there, anyway," says Hallie, pulling Gabe off course to avoid a chunk of burning wood. "Hey!"

The boy who threw it sneers at us and yanks a knife from his waistband. "Fuck off. These are *our* streets. Just fuck off."

Huddled together, we back away.

He follows, his hood falling to reveal a shaved head. His silver Hands of Kinship lapel badge shines in the twilight. "Yeah, that's it. Off you fuck." Glancing at each of us, he points his knife and ratty glare at Piper. "'Cept you."

Piper grabs my hand and squeezes hard. Behind us, rustling tells me we're being surrounded. My heart thuds with sickening force.

"Yeah." The boy leers at Piper. "You'll do. Haven't had a shag in ages. What do you think, lads? She look dirty enough for you?"

The gang behind us growls and clicks. Piper shudders, her breathing fast.

Ahead of me, Gabe fumbles in his bag. I glimpse the barrel of a gun in its folds. My mouth fills with metallic saliva.

The deafening bang is too quick. My body jerks and Piper's with it. The gun must have gone off in Gabe's bag. But the sound came from behind us.

"Put down the knife, Cabbage, you moron." The voice is fresh—gruff and commanding. "Leave these people alone."

From the rear strides an immense pile of a man pointing a gun at the skinhead boy.

Cabbage fumbles his knife away. "Archie, I was just…"

The big man, Archie, marches up to the boy and punches him between his eyes. With a throaty 'ahhhh', Cabbage folds onto the floor.

Peering behind us, Archie shouts, "The rest of you piss off home and look up the word *curfew*, would ya? Good lads."

With mumbles and scuffs, the gang scarper into the darkness.

Turning back to Cabbage, Archie jabs him with a foot, bends and rips off his Hands of Kinship badge. "You need to learn some discipline before you wear this again, lad. I'm ashamed."

Cabbage mutters something as he hauls himself up to sitting, clutching his nose.

"What was that?" Archie bends closer, hand raised as if to hit him again.

"Sorry, Dad."

Archie nods and turns his attention to us. A badge glints on his chest. "You had better get off the streets. I don't know

134

when curfew is where you crawled from, but round here it's six o'clock sharp or you'll be picking your teeth out of the gutter."

Gun safely hidden in his bag, Gabe holds his hands up. "Yes, sir. Sorry. We lost track of time."

"No more excuses. Get lost." Archie looms over Gabe, pushing him up the road.

With numb legs, I move to follow Gabe and Hallie. As Piper passes him, Archie reaches out and grabs her wrist. She squeals in fright or pain; I can't tell which.

"If I see you again, I'm gonna let my boy do what he wants with you? Understand?"

Piper gives a shaky nod.

"We don't want any trouble in our neighbourhood." He looks up and down the street, seemingly oblivious to the trouble all around him.

Piper freezes. After an age, he releases her with a shove that sends her stumbling into me. I take her arm, keeping her upright.

"Piss off," says Archie, as though to himself.

We stagger into the sanctuary of the dark. It's half a mile before we halt to let ourselves react.

Piper collapses, gasping onto a grassy embankment, and puts her head between her knees. As I drop beside her and put an arm around her shoulder, Gabe paces in front of us.

"Jesus." Hallie blows out a breath. "Who was that guy? Not police."

"Militia," I say. "Unity militia."

"God. Is that a thing?" Hallie flops down the other side of Piper.

"Guess it is now." I peer up at Gabe, who's ceased his prowling. "How far?"

He checks his phone. "A mile. Further if we take a quieter route, keep off the streets."

Glancing at Piper, who's still shaking, her hair over her face, I say, "We should take the quieter route."

Twenty minutes later, Gabe halts us in an empty lane on the outskirts of another housing estate. Without speaking, he glances around and dives into a hedge to the right. Hallie follows. Grabbing Piper's hand, I push into the gap Hallie left behind, but the brambles still scratch my face as we fight through them.

We're in a vacant car park behind the ruin of a factory. Most of the security lights are out, but there's enough from the remaining two to illuminate what lies at Gabe's feet: a metal disk embedded in the tarmac.

Piper sighs. "Is this another sewer?"

He smiles at her as he pulls a stumpy crowbar from his bag. "You're in luck, Pipes. It's just a service shaft for the underground."

As tunnels go, this one's sanitary. It smells of rust and the crumbling mortar. A rime comes away in my hand as I steady myself after the jump. Gabe hands Piper a torch and switches on his own. Hallie hands me a similar one.

As we walk, the brick walls open out beyond the torch beams. A gentle downward slope ends in a steel-latticed gate. Gabe reaches through a hole in the ruined brickwork. The gate opens with a squeal.

It leads into a much bigger passage. Gravel scrapes as I step forward and stumble over something hard. As I shine my torch at it, it gleams back. "Railway."

"Yup. We're on the underground lines now."

"Christ." Piper scrambles back against the wall.

Gabe grins. "Don't panic. There've been no trains here for a century." He shines his torch to our left. "Miles of abandoned track. No signal traceable from the surface. It's a perfect place to disappear. If you know where to hide from the odd patrol." He glances at me. "Wish we had this kind of network in Birmingham. Imagine it, Ess."

"I prefer fresh air." It reeks of mildew and hydrocarbons.

Gabe fiddles with his phone. "I can understand that. This section was one of the few that ever operated diesel tube trains in the nineteen thirties. Still stinks, doesn't it? Incredible. Come on."

A few minutes later, a light dazzles from up ahead.

"Bit late for a maintenance crew," a voice shouts from

behind the glare.

"Yeah." Gabe holds up two fingers in a peace sign. "Got stuck behind a travelling circus."

Hallie's face shows no sign of my confusion. Piper, at least, is frowning, so I haven't gone insane.

A whoop echoes up ahead. "Mate. Good to almost-see you." The light lowers as a figure steps forward, peering at Gabe. "Have you changed your hair?" The speaker emerges as a tall, broad young man with dark skin and dreadlocks.

"Well, Jez, I figured it looks so gorgeous on you..."

Jez claps Gabe on the back. "There are those who would accuse you of cultural appropriation. Not me, my friend. I know it's just because you're a lazy tosser who can't be arsed to comb it." He hugs Hallie and kisses her cheek.

Gabe chuckles. "You always understood me the best."

"We got raided," says Hallie as they pull apart.

"I heard." Jez glances at me. "Friends?"

Hallie looks at me. "This is Essie, and Piper. You can trust them. They were at The Bank."

He eyes us before switching back to Hallie. "Did they find anything?"

She sticks her bottom lip out. "Nothing to find. Some stolen food. Nothing that could lead them here. We were careful that way."

Jez nods and lets out a sigh, gesturing ahead. "Come on, then. It's a little further. Kim's moved the camp. In case you left a trail at The Bank. Not that it'd fool them for long."

I could live a passable life as a mole. After so long underground, I'm acclimatised to the dense air. My eyes can make out little details beyond the torch beam they wouldn't have before. Like the missing bricks overhead, the broken steel girders arching between them. And the rats scuttling away from our lights.

On we crunch while my feet throb and the toes of my socks dampen with what must be blood. Now we're nearing the end of the journey, I want to see what's waiting for us. Gabe and Hallie talked about an entire community living here. That's hard to imagine in these dark, airless tunnels.

Our route of bends and junctions leads to a dead end, but as we approach, the torch beams play on its ruined surface. There's a three-foot hole edged by enormous lumps of rubble.

"Nineteen-sixties construction." Jez kicks a rock out of the way. "Built like blancmange, God love 'em. Come on."

We clamber through in a chorus of grunts and hisses. Beyond the breach, our footsteps quieten on an earthy floor.

"Have we left the rail network now?" I ask, but nobody replies.

"We've had to move on a few times," says Jez over his shoulder. "We almost ran into another camp a few days ago. Bloody Redemption Charter bunker, by the looks of it. They weren't too fussy about hiding."

That sparks a memory. Kerry once told me Foster-Pugh and his fundamentalist mates were planning for 'Judgement Day'. Underground bunkers, hoarding supplies so they could wait out the collapse. I thought it was crap at the time; a fantasy to get me to do what she wanted.

Gabe snorts. "Lovely."

Jez's shoulders hitch. "Gotta love the poetry. Both sides burrowing underground while the shitstorm swirls above us." He reaches up and pulls down a rope ladder. Torch in his teeth, he climbs up and disappears into the roof ten feet above. His grinning face pokes out from a gap. "Come on, then. I'll get us in while you catch up."

One by one, we haul ourselves up. I make Piper go ahead of me so I can catch her if she stumbles. She's started looking pale again, and she's holding her shoulder at a weird angle. Rich-smelling soil breaks free of the edges of the gap and rains on us. We're in another earth passage running crossways to the last. The scent and the heat remind me of a trip to Cornwall when I was a kid. We went to this botanical place with tropical plants under a dome. Dad kept complaining about the prices and we lost Darya among the palm trees—until there was a tannoy announcement for the parents of three-year-old Darya Glass. Afterwards, Mum said it was the longest ten minutes of her life. That must have been our last holiday before things went bad in the twenties. We couldn't have known it then. Or that less than a decade later they'd all be dead.

Jez stops and reaches out to the side. As he shoves, a section of the wall gives way. When I blink again, a metal panel is jutting out across the passageway in front of Piper and me. Gabe, Hallie, and Jez have disappeared.

"What the—?"

"Ess." Gabe peeps from behind.

Feeling like I'm high on something, I grab Piper's hand and we edge around the obstacle. On the far side is a hole in the wall through which three sets of teeth glow.

"Revolving door." Jez emits a bass chuckle. "Impressed?"

Gabe whistles. "Sure am, mate."

"Heidi in the camp was a set designer. Before." He swings the panel back in place. "She rigged it. Glued all the soil in place. Even when you shine a light on it, you can't see the joint. But we've always got it guarded just in case anyone evades my outpost." He flaps a hand at a pale, thin boy with a shaved head lurking in the shadows. "This is Caleb."

He nods at us, and everyone mumbles a variation of hello. Caleb doesn't look very tough. I wonder what he would do if a gang of coppers burst in with guns. Trying not to think about it, I let my gaze drift along the orange lamps embedded in the walls at intervals where they intersect with the floor.

Caleb leads us as the passageway opens into a large chamber, a cave, supported by haphazard brickwork interspersed with more earth. It's the size of the theatres Maya and I used to half-listen to lectures in at college. The ceiling stretches twenty feet above us. We must be deeper underground that I thought. More orange floor lights stud the floor across its span, giving the room a warm glow. People cluster around several of them. A murmur of voices echoes in the space.

Jez pats Caleb's shoulder. "Thanks, mate."

"No worries," he replies in a deep voice. "I'd better get back." Then he trots away up the corridor.

"I'll take you to Kim." Jez flaps a hand across the

chamber. "Wait here."

He strides across the middle of the room and approaches one of the larger groups on the far side. It's just light enough to make him out as he bends and speaks to a broad-set woman, pointing in our direction. Her eyes seek us out as she says something in response and then nods.

Halfway back across the space, someone with bleached hair barrels into him and they kiss—Luisa, from The Bank. She must have fled Birmingham, too.

Jez waves us over and waits while we catch up. "Kim wants to say hi." He slips an arm around Luisa and looks at me and Piper. "Just relax and be honest. She's alright."

It hadn't occurred to me to be nervous until he said that. Kim's gaze tracks us as we approach. There's a warm enough smile on her thin lips, but I can't suppress the feeling of being assessed. Her broad shoulders are down, her dark-rooted blonde hair scraped back in a ponytail.

"Welcome, Piper, Essie." Kim angles her cheek up for Gabe to kiss and, on her other side, takes Hallie's hand. Dressed in a grubby white t-shirt and jeans, she can't be much over forty, but the others in her group sit hushed as though in the presence of an ancient oracle. "I'm so glad you've joined us."

The solemnity of her tone makes me think she means something more than 'nice to meet you'.

"Thank you for letting us in." My voice is quiet, and the words sound weak to my own ears, but Kim nods in acknowledgement.

"Gabe, Hallie, we were just discussing the plans, but that can wait. It's suppertime, and I'm hungry. How about you guys?"

There are murmurs around the gaggle. They rise as one and move to the corner, where a gap in the brickwork leads out of the room. Gabe takes Kim's elbow, glances at me, then mutters while they walk ahead.

As we file through, another space appears, humming with conversation. It's brighter, with more of those orange lights and a hotchpotch of patterned blankets. Spread across the centre, trays of bread, samosas, cheese and fruit send wafts that make my mouth water.

Kim tips her head toward me. "Essie, come and sit with me."

I peer at Piper, who shrugs and follows. We settle on a red-and-yellow checked blanket and Kim grabs the nearest plate of samosas, offering us first pick. Mine is spicy, and juicy with peas. I gobble it and reach for another while Piper picks at hers.

Kim takes my elbow. "Essie, it's so good to meet you. Gabe's spoken about you often."

*Has he, now?*

From a pitcher, she pours us a glass of water each. "He tells me you've been at the centre of our struggle up in the Midlands. Playing politicians at their own game. Almost beat them, too, with that carbon capture technology you were building."

So *that's* what he was whispering about.

*Way to be discreet, Gabe.*

"It wasn't me building it. It was my friend."

"But you risked your life to bring it into the world. Pretty heroic."

My cheeks grow hot. "Well, I failed. The original prototype was lost, and so was my copy. And my friend is dead."

"I'm sorry. And I heard about your family, too. Must have been rough."

"It still is." I clamp my mouth shut, not eager to discuss this with someone I just met.

She gives a solemn nod and looks at her plate. When she returns her gaze to me, her brown eyes glitter in the orange light. "You know, we could use some of your guts around here, if you'd like to stay."

I'm not sure what to say. Across the room, Gabe and

Hallie are talking to a lad who can't be more than eighteen. His dark skin is smooth, his eyes bright as his smile. He's beautiful.

"Essie?" Kim says. "No pressure. Take your time. Look around, see what you think."

"Thank you." I peer at Piper, who has grown paler than ever. "Gabe said you had a doctor."

Kim swallows the last of her samosa. "Yes, Halima's here. Are you sick?"

"Not me. They shot Piper. At the protest in Birmingham."

"I heard about that." Her eyes swell with tears. "So many deaths."

"Her shoulder's not healing right. Do you think Halima could help?"

"Ess, I'm sure it'll be fine. Don't fuss." Piper sighs, but even her voice is losing its strength.

Kim takes in a breath, peers at Piper, and frowns. "Of course. Halima's on a recce, but I'll get her to have a look as soon as she gets back."

"Hey, Ess." Gabe crouches next to me, making me jump. "Good scran, innit?"

"Yeah."

He grins and tilts his head behind him, where Hallie and the beautiful boy are hovering. "This is Carlo. Carlo Tyler." Gabe's grin breaks into a chuckle. "Guess who his mum is?"

# Chapter Seventeen

## Essie

### 19th November 2041

My heart hammers as I scramble to my feet.

*Tyler...*

"Kerry?" I gape at Carlo. "You're Kerry's son?"

Gabe laughs. "Relax. He's one of us."

How can Gabe know that? Suddenly, this camp feels like a net closing in. Breath jams in my throat. My toes grow numb as I take a shaky step back.

Carlo puts out an uncertain hand. "Look, I came here to join Kim's camp. Gabe explained your history with my mum. I'm sorry she screwed you over."

I turn an icy stare on Gabe. "Yeah, well. There's a lot of that about."

"It's nothing to do with me," says Carlo. "Until recently, I hadn't seen her for months. Years. I've been living with my dad."

"Why are you here?" My voice is louder and more accusatory than I intended. It grows quiet around us.

Carlo lifts his chin. "Same reason you are. To stop them before they kill us all."

"Essie," Kim says behind me. "I can vouch for him. We vetted him. He declared his connection and has never given us any cause to think he's not on the level. You can trust him."

Still unsure, I nod once, keeping my eyes on the boy. Carlo's slim chest deflates as he exhales. "Well, it's…nice to meet you."

*This isn't over, laughing boy. Don't you think I trust you one bit.*

I manage a tight smile. Around us, the silence dissipates as people bustle, clearing away the leftovers.

Kim claps her hands. "Well, now we're all acquainted and fed, time for business." She turns to one of her crowd, a blonde woman who has been gawping unabashed at the scene we've created. "Gemma, we're going into conference now. Halima should be back soon. When she arrives, can you come and let me know?"

"Sure." Gemma marches into the other room.

Kim turns to Carlo. "Please excuse us, sweetie. Work to do."

Wary eyes on me, Carlo steps aside. With her gaze and a tilt of her head, Kim gestures for Gabe, Hallie, Piper and me to follow her to the back. She unlocks a metal door and admits us to a corridor lined with the same red bricks, lit by the same orange floor lights. The passage slopes upwards, past several deep, darkened recesses, to another door. As she opens it, strip lights assault my eyes. It takes a moment before I can make out a conference room dominated by a low, wooden table in the centre.

Behind us, others troop in. Jez and Luisa are among them, along with other faces I recognise from the gaggle around Kim earlier. As they settle themselves around the table, I count ten of us.

Kim seats herself at the top. "Guys, this is Hallie, Gabe, Essie, and Piper from the Birmingham cell."

A broad-chested man with short-cropped hair clears his throat. "I usually do comms with Sal up there."

Kim leans forward, eyes wide and focused on the crew cut. "Well then, Fred, this will save you a job, won't it?" She settles back on her heels. "Okay. I don't have to remind you we don't have long to get this show on the road. The date is set for the 26th, which gives us one week. Shau, what news on supplies?"

A woman about my age with spiky black hair sits up straight. "As you know, we're expecting the recce crew back any minute. To be confirmed, but we think we've more consignments coming down from the Manchester cell."

"Guns?" asks an older man wearing a turban.

Shau grins. "Khesh, we've got guns, flash bombs, tear gas, and shed loads of battens." Her eyes flash at the ceiling. "I hope."

Applause eddies around the room, making my arms prickle.

*Guns? Battens?*

"*Police* weapons?" The words are out before I know they're in my brain.

Glares turn on me in a long moment of silence.

"Fight fire with fire." Kim kneels to high five Shau across the table. "Great work, Shau."

"We haven't secured them yet, but I'm optimistic."

"I have every faith." Kim beams at Shau, then sweeps her gaze around the room. "We need to toughen up, people. After what happened to the Yorkshire cell, and Birmingham, we can't take any chances. Okay, comms. Fred, how are the plans coming elsewhere?"

Fred scratches his crew cut. "Well, Manchester have tooled up, and they've been working closely with Liverpool. They're happy to go on the 26th. I've got a call with Erin at Cardiff and Sati in Bristol tonight, so I'll know more then. Birmingham, well, we've our guests here to update. Last I spoke to Sal, they were struggling to get supplies."

Gabe clears his throat. "All sorted. Birmingham is a green, too."

I stare at Gabe. Back at The Bank, when Jasmine mentioned Kim's big plans, he made as if he knew nothing. Has he tricked me? Was he in on it all along? Just like him to keep it to himself. They're talking armed insurrection here.

Giving myself no time to back out, I stand. "Listen." The heat pulses in my cheeks at their glares. "We have to think about this. Gabe, you saw what happened in Birmingham. You know about the armed drones. That was a *peaceful* protest. We go in armed, it'll be a massacre."

The silent stares continue.

Kim's hand closes around my wrist. "Essie."

"No." Fred's calm voice feels dangerous. "We go in armed, some of us will die. But some of them will die, too." He looks at Kim. "I thought you said she was onboard."

"She is. Aren't you, Essie?"

Looking around the table at the sharp, wary faces, I swallow and let Kim's grip pull me back down. "Yeah. Course."

"At least we know she can't be the infiltrator." I get the impression Fred wants me to hear his mutter. "If she was, she wouldn't make this scene. Unless she's an idiot."

*Infiltrator?*

"Or she's being clever," says the woman next to him in a Liverpool accent. Her pale eyes blaze out of a freckled face.

"Ami, Fred, that's enough." Kim's voice cuts across the table. "There's no evidence of an infiltrator. I'm surprised at you both, propagating a baseless rumour." Her head swivels from one to the other. "I would have thought you had enough to occupy yourselves right now."

Fred and Ami stay silent, heads bowed.

"Okay." Kim releases them from her glare. "Where were we?" Her pocket beeps, and she pulls out a small, black phone. "Kim. Hi, Gem…" Kim's brows knit together as she listens. "Okay, I'll be right there." She tucks away the phone, face stiff and unreadable. "The recce crew's back. Meeting adjourned for today."

She rushes out of the room, leaving the rest of us to exchange confused glances and file out.

***

146

An hour later, we're crammed into a dim little office off the conference room. Piper grips my hand and screws up her face as Halima eases the filthy bandage from her neck and shoulder.

"Yeah, it's infected." Halima flicks back a dark curl from her eye and tips her head to speak to Piper in her South African accent. Softer than Brian's, it still makes me miss him like hell. "I'll get you antibiotics, and this'll need a good clean. You've a fever, and four-hourly paracetamol for the pain wouldn't go amiss."

"Thanks, Lima." Kim peers at Halima. "Who's gonna treat you?"

"I'll be fine, it's just scrapes. Jules got the worst of it."

"They knew you were going to be there?" I hold the roll of clean bandage out for her.

Halima cuts a section of the cloth and sighs. "No doubt. They were ready for us."

"But who told them?" Kim flops her head back against the wall a few times. "Who would do that?"

Halima shrugs. "Someone who knew we were recceing the weapons store at that particular time."

I have a theory. "When did Carlo arrive at the camp?"

Kim squints at me, her mouth moving, then says, "Couple of weeks ago. It's not Carlo. He didn't know about the recce."

"That you know of."

She pivots against the wall to face me. "You're a little new to be throwing around accusations, Essie."

"I just know his family."

"You know his *mother*."

"And you don't know them at all."

Her eyes narrow as she murmurs, "I don't know you, either."

"Hey guys, everyone decent?" Gabe's voice drifts through the door. He bursts in before anyone can respond. Halted in the doorway, he switches his gaze between me and Kim. "What?"

Kim's eyes linger on me for a moment, then her jaw

flexes. "They ambushed the recce. Everyone got out. No one seriously hurt, thank God, but Jules broke her ankle jumping over the fence. Halima and the others are a bit bashed up." She glances back at me. "They knew we were gonna be there. Essie thinks Carlo's the infiltrator. I'm wondering if Essie has something to hide. That about cover it, ladies?"

No one replies in the icy silence.

Gabe's eyebrows rise in anguish. "Come on, Kim. Essie just got here. She's hardly infiltrated anything, has she?"

She shrugs and blows out her cheeks.

"How's the shoulder, Pipes?" Gabe's looking for a change of subject.

"Bloody sore. But Halima's got painkillers and antibiotics."

"That's great. Ready for the revolution, then?"

She gives a twitchy smile.

We leave Halima to tend her own wounds and drift back into the communal chamber. I trail the others, trying to gather my wits. The cliques have reformed, some settling themselves into sleeping bags, some still talking, but more sombre than before. Most of the discussion I overhear is about the ambush, and who might have betrayed the recce. Everyone has an opinion on how we should find the perpetrator and what we should do to them when we do. As I pass him, Fred gives me a hard stare. So he's decided I am the traitor, after all.

I swallow the bile. It's not just my confrontation with Kim or Fred's hostility. It's this whole situation. Three weeks ago, I was at home with my family. Now I've no choice but to go along with this violent revolution. How did I get here so fast? This feels like the endgame. I always knew it had to come, but when I pictured it, I imagined Seth and Willow by my side. Now we're at opposite ends of the country, and Seth doesn't even know what's coming. I have to warn him.

Losing the others, I huddle in an empty, dark corner and fish the phone from my bag.

No reception.

Gabe said you couldn't detect their phone signals from the

surface. I guess that means none penetrate down here either. They must have set up their own network for their devices. I can't even speak to Seth.

A wave of homesickness drowns me and my eyes sting. Will I ever even see them alive again?

# Chapter Eighteen

## Seth

**20th November 2041**

It's a tranquil patter of rain on the tarpaulin above that wakes me. Before I've opened my eyes, it expands into a luxurious roar.

Willow stirs against my shoulder. I plant a kiss on her greasy-smelling hair. Then again, I must stink, too, after four days hiding in this forest with only rain to wash away the fear and sweat.

In the dim light, I turn onto my side and watch Willow as she wakes. There's no sign of Rook. I suppose he's off foraging for breakfast. It turns out he's a resourceful fella, which doesn't surprise me. He made a home for himself in my parents' house. It was Rook who spotted the tarpaulin abandoned in a bramble bush on the first night. When we rigged it up between conveniently spaced trees, it made for a decent enough tent. Shame about the mud, but at least it's kept the storms at bay.

I reach into my holdall and pull out the phone. Five percent now. It'll be dead within hours. I redial Essie.

Out of service.

*Shit, Ess, where the hell are you?*

"Found mushrooms." Rook is clambering up the slope behind us. His clothes and beard drip, grime running down his face. He's carrying my dad's coat in a bundle. "Is that wood dry enough to burn?"

As Willow yawns and sits up, I reach out to check the collection of wood we tied to our makeshift roof last night. "Think so." I fumble the rope's knot undone and the wood clatters to the ground, releasing a piney, mossy cloud.

Rook ducks under the tarp and gathers the branches in a pile. "Not too damp." He grabs the curved slate of scrap metal we've been using as a saucepan-cum-cooking-tray and crouches beside the woodpile. From the unravelled raincoat, he palms an assortment of mushrooms and green stuff onto the pan.

I hand him the matches. "You sure none of those are poisonous?"

He gives a wheezy chuckle. God knows why. "They're fine. These'll cook up a treat."

A few minutes later, an appetising smell wafts up with the smoke from the sizzling plate. There's wild garlic among the leaves Rook foraged, and my mouth waters in anticipation.

We eat, helping ourselves to the cooling mushrooms with our fingers while the rain splashes off the edges of the tarp. The food tastes as good as it smells. Or I'm just hungry.

Rook smacks his lips and says, "Nice bit of bruschetta would go lovely, wouldn't it?"

"Hmm. Rook, who do you think those people were at Mum and Dad's?" I watch his reaction, though it's not the first time I've asked this question.

His shoulder twitches. "Dunno. Not coppers, though."

*Who else could it have been?*

"How can you be so sure?"

"Because if it was the police, they wouldn't be that stealthy." Rook glances at Willow, who pins her eyes on me. "And we'd be dead."

"Oh, come on."

But Rook nods as if agreeing with himself. "If they thought we were breaking in, they would've shot first, asked questions later."

"And if they suspected I was…me?" I am a wanted man. And there I was, curled up fast asleep in my childhood home.

"They would've killed me," says Rook.

"They tried."

"And then taken you. Nah, it was bounty hunters coming on the off-chance." His shoulder twitches again, or shrugs.

"Pretty professional bounty hunters." I wipe mushroom juice from Willow's face with my sleeve, though all I've done is smeared a patch of grime around her mouth.

"Most of them are," says Rook.

I shut my eyes, tired of the confusion. And the thing that flashes behind my closed lids is what I glimpsed in that last look back before we ran, standing by the neighbours' conservatory. That silvery glint at the gunman's chest… Adrenaline probably drove my brain to make weird connections, but I swear the shooter was wearing a Hands of Kinship badge.

Unity, my ex-employer, has guns now.

***

"What's the plan, then?"

"Huh?" I must have dozed off after we ate. The rain has stopped. The sun warms the canopies of tarp and greenery above us. Willow is darting among the trees nearby, picking up fallen branches, screwing up her face, and tossing them aside.

Rook holds his palms to the sky. "We've been kicking around this forest for days. I just wondered if you had an idea where you might go next."

*Where we might go…*

To dampen the panic, I scramble to my feet. "Look, mate. I'm grateful for your help. I am. But you've done more than enough for us. If there's somewhere else you should be, then please, go ahead with my thanks."

Rook stares at me, his face blank and slack. Then he

152

giggles. Which turns into a throaty laugh. "Good one, Seth. Somewhere else to be." He knuckles the corner of his eyes. "Nah mate, there's nowhere. Truth be told, I'm enjoying the company. It's been a lonely old time since I got out." His eyebrows shoot up, as if he's surprised himself.

*Since you got out of where, Rook?*

I think I can guess.

"What were you in for?" I keep my voice soft.

Rook twitches, his eyes glazed and fixed on me. "I'd never hurt you or Willow. You know that, don't you?"

"But did you hurt someone?" My ears tune in to Willow rustling in the leaves behind me.

Head down, wiping his eyes, Rook nods. "Only a scumbag who hurt someone I loved. He got what was coming."

"Daddy, there's no dry wood here." Willow peeps under the tarpaulin.

Rook shifts to the far end of the den and turns away, fussing at the dirty cooking tray with a pile of damp leaves.

Willow's frown switches between the two of us. "Have you two argued?"

"No, sweetheart. Everything's fine."

Rook turns back to me, his eyes still glistening. "I'll go," he says.

Willow gasps. "What? Why?"

"No." At an awkward crawl, I cross the forest floor to Rook and put a hand on his shoulder as it jerks. "I'm not saying you have to leave. I just...wish you'd told me."

"Told you what?" The edge of wariness in Willow's voice cramps my heart.

"And have you thinking I'd offed your parents, too?" He catches himself. "Sorry. That was..."

With a raised palm, I accept. "Please don't go, Rook." I glance at Willow. "Willow likes having you around. I do, too. Your past is your business. If you've paid, you've paid."

He gives a twitchy smile. "I have paid plenty. You're a forgiving man, Seth."

153

"Comes with being a cleric, I guess. Ex-cleric, I should say."

"Hey, mate. We all have our skeletons."

Willow giggles along with us. Though I've no way of knowing how much she caught of the conversation, and what she understood, she seems satisfied now the mood has lightened. Though no one has spoken the words, we bustle around, preparing to move.

"I've been thinking we go north." I untether the tarp and flatten it to a size that'll fit through the handles of the holdall. "See what's going on past the moors."

"You sure?" Rook puckers his lips.

"Sort of." I've been loath to leave the cover of the forest and expose us in the open country. We can't have moved more than ten miles in the four days since fleeing my mum and dad's. But the longer we hang around here, the more chance they'll find us. Risking the moors has become the safest option.

It would be great to navigate with my phone, but it's on four percent now, so we'd get two minutes out of it before it died. I need to keep it running as long as possible in case Essie calls. A thin hope, but one I'm not willing to give up. So we discern north by the watery sun and set off through the trees. Within the hour, we hit a single track cutting through the forest to the northwest. The pines dwindle, making way for the gorse and patchwork fields of the moors. The three of us pause at the threshold between mud and crumbling tarmac.

"This'll do." I heave the holdall-tarp hybrid higher on my back and grab Willow's hand. "Come on."

As we trudge, the land and sky widen. Without the burden of being fugitives, and the sun's unrelenting sear, the moors would be a tonic. Although there are no drones, I glance at the white-hot sky every minute. God knows where we'd hide if we had to. We see no one and nothing except empty landscape.

A long time after we run out of rainwater in our flasks, the broken road grows broader, dotted with stone cottages. They would have been quaint but that most have broken windows and several of the doors hang skewwhiff in their frames. Further on, a few burnt-out shops huddle together, facing a weed-addled green.

"Wonder what happened here?" I slow my pace, gazing about me at the decay.

Rook squints at the sky. "By my reckoning, we've just hit Narlton. I heard Unity raided it a couple of weeks ago. Some local yokel tipped them off about an underground resistance cell here."

"What?" Putting a hand out, I halt Willow with me.

Ahead now, Rook sniffs and nods at the pink sandstone church to our left, its blackened spire like a spent match against the sky. "Doesn't seem the type of place, does it? S'pose you never can tell."

Was it my imagination, or did something just move in the barber's shop window?

"We should get off the street." I try in vain to keep the fear out of my voice. If Rook heard right, three grubby strangers rocking up, one resembling a photo they've been force fed on TV all week, won't go unnoticed.

"Yeah, you might be right." Rook peers up the road and points into the heat haze. "There's a track up the side of the houses. Shall we see if we can find somewhere to hide out and rest?"

The lane squeezes between two modernish brick homes to a metal gate barring a field bordered by wild, crisp hedgerow. Rook and I vault over it while Willow climbs between the diagonal bars. Long grass carpets the field, yellow despite the earlier rain. It snaps as we walk, releasing a sweet hay aroma. We drop our things and flop down in the scant shade of the hedge.

Willow leans into my lap. "I'm thirsty."

"Me too, poppet." I turn to Rook. "I didn't see any streams or fountains, did you?"

He shakes his head. "The church? Might be a font or something." He blushes, perhaps remembering what I used to do for a living. "Bit sacrilegious snaffling the holy water?"

I chuckle. "I saw a pub too. Might be worth a try."

"Pub or church?"

"Either. Both."

He looks down at Willow, who has fallen into a dehydrated doze on my thighs. "I'll go. You're a wanted man. You rest."

"Thanks, Rook." As he scrambles up, I say, "Hey, be careful, okay? If it looks… unfriendly, then leave."

He throws a salute and lopes off.

Willow stirs, her hair tickling my arm. I stroke it flat and think of Essie. Where is she? Why won't she answer the phone? Or why *can't* she? I swallow the fear rising in my throat and close my eyes against the sun's glare.

***

"Daddy." Someone is shaking my arm. "Wake up. Where's Rook?"

I snap upright, lids fighting to open. The shade of the hedgerow has dissolved and the sun reaches out low across the hills beyond the field. "What time is it?"

She frowns at me. "I don't know."

"Course you don't." I stroke her cheek. "Sorry." Casting about me, I grab the holdall and fumble out the phone.

It's dead.

*No. No, no, no… Essie.*

Fighting the empty terror I'll never see her again, I force myself to concentrate on now. From the angle of the light, it's mid-afternoon, which means he's been gone for at least three hours. "Where's Rook?"

"I just woke up, and you were snoring, and he wasn't here."

*Shit.*

"Well. He went to get us water from the old pub. Bet he just got distracted by a pint of beer."

156

From her blank expression, even Willow's not convinced.

I grab the holdall, feeding my arms through it so it sits like a backpack, the tarp pressed against my shoulders. "Okay, we'd better see if we can find him."

The main road is deserted; no sign of Rook, no shoppers, no kids walking home from school. Even the heat shimmer has stilled. I pause and look left, to the pretty stone church, then right to the pub. Not keen to rush into a Unity building, I choose the pub. We keep to the shadows as we slink down the street. The place sits in silence, its peeling red door ajar. Stiff fingers clamped around Willow's, I reach out with the other hand and push it open.

At first, nothing is visible except a smog of dust motes lit by the sun. As my eyes adjust, upturned wooden legs of chairs on tables emerge. The mahogany bar is strewn with bottles, their dregs emitting a yeasty aroma. Other than that, the room is empty. I turn my head to the side, listening, but hear nothing. Willow lets out a breath she must have been holding.

Pulling her behind me, I creep across the sticky carpet. As we near the bar, I can make out the stools pressed against it. One has toppled on its side. Around it, beyond the carpet's gold edging strip, a dark puddle glints from the floorboards. Nausea rolling in my stomach, I crouch and touch the puddle. It's tacky and there's no mistaking its iron reek.

Blood.

"Rook?" Willow whispers.

There's a clatter beyond the rear wall. The stripped pine door to the back is ajar, but not enough to see behind it.

I'm torn. I don't want Willow to see anything awful, but I daren't leave her, either. "Stay behind me."

We duck under the flip-top section of the bar. There's a cry of pain from the back. My heart thuds. Fingers numb, I reach for the handle and push.

We're in a dark hallway that smells of yeast and spoiled milk. To our right, a set of carpetless stairs leads up.

Another cry. It sounds like Rook.

"Daddy, it came from down there." She points to a door

under the stairs that must lead to the cellar.

Giving myself no time to think, I grasp the brass door handle and pull.

It's locked.

Willow screams and struggles behind me.

Before I can turn, something cold presses into my temple. "Tell her to stop."

"Willow, stay still."

The scuffling halts, replaced by a single, sickening slap. Someone rips the holdall from my back. I'm turned around and slammed against the banister. A large shoulder in a grubby, bloodstained vest obscures Willow on the floor.

The man glaring at me is older than his strength suggests —late sixties. Thin veins snake across his nose and cheeks, and his eyebrows arch in rage. His bloodshot eyes flicker. "It *is* you."

Confused, I say nothing.

"Jase said it was you. Come on." He yanks me towards him, then spins me round to face the cellar exit. Reaching around me, he unlocks the door. As it opens inwards, stone steps, worn to a bow, appear in low light. With a shove in my back, he says, "Down you go."

I catch hold of the doorframe to stop myself falling. Heart pounding, I have no choice but to descend to the dim cellar.

*Wills, run.*

But she doesn't. He must have ushered her behind me because her shuffling footsteps follow.

At the bottom, I step onto an earthen floor. The yeast smell is unbearable. A brick wall faces us, extending two-thirds of the way across the space. Yellow light spills from its left edge.

"Seth?" It's Rook, his muffled voice echoing from behind the wall.

There's a thump and a yelp, and someone says, "Shut up."

The man behind me shoves me in the back as Willow draws level. We round the corner of the partition.

Rook is facing away, on his knees before two men. They're younger than the first but seem just as angry. Both are broad and blond; they must be brothers. They loom over Rook, who's bent so low his head is almost in his own lap. Blood is dribbling from a wound on his crown, soaking the collar of my dad's coat.

"You were right, Jase," says the older guy. "It's him. Looking for his criminal mates." He shoves me forward again. "Sorry, pal, you're too late. They're gone. Where they belong—jail."

One blond chuckles. "Or six feet under, I hope. And you —" He points at me with a knife I hadn't noticed. "I recognised you the second you slithered into town, you murdering terrorist bastard."

Willow presses close into my legs.

"I'm not what you think." But there's little point in arguing with them. Better to concentrate on a way out. It stings, though, knowing what the entire country thinks of me after the news broadcast. "Look, let us go, and we'll leave. No trouble."

Looks pass between them, then they laugh.

"You must be mental," says the older guy, flicking his gaze up at the ceiling. "Do you know what I could do with that reward money? Fix this place up proper."

"It's too late, anyway." Jase smirks. "They're on their way."

No need to ask who *they* are. Unity; police. It's the same in the end. Nausea rising, I glance down at Willow's terrified face. They'll take her away to God knows where. An awful foster home. Or worse...

I doubt they'd balk at interrogating a four-year-old.

I swallow the bile and glance around at each of them. "Look, guys. I can't compete with whatever reward they're offering you. You must know that. For the sake of the little girl...please. Let us go."

The old guy barks. "Yeah, right." He shoves me in the back with the gun. I stumble forward into Rook's huddled form, Willow tripping behind me. "She's better off without you, pal. Let someone who knows right from wrong bring her up proper."

Willow recaptures my thigh, and her grip tightens. I rest a hand on her arm, trying to disguise the shaking. "Please…"

The young guy that's not Jase steps close beside me and peels Willow away. She struggles, then yelps.

"Wills, don't fight them. It'll be alright."

Eyes welling with tears, she lets the guy push her back against the far wall and to her knees while Jase grabs my hands from behind and ties them with thick, prickly rope.

On the floor, Rook lifts and turns his face to me. The bruises forming round his eyes make the fear-filled whites standout even more. "I'm sorry, Seth." The last word hitches as the old guy grabs him under the arms, lifting him to his feet.

Jase pushes me towards Willow. "Sit."

I don't have any choice.

Snatching more binding from a pile on the floor, Jase advances on Rook. There's a second or two pause as they eye each other, then he whips out the rope, cracking it against Rook's cheek, forcing his head to snap back.

"Hey." But everyone ignores me.

When Rook recovers his position, a fresh wound has opened, blood coursing down his face.

"That's for before," says Jase.

*You hurt him back, then. Nice one, Rook.*

As the old guy steps away, pointing his gun at Rook's head, Jase grabs, spins, and rams him headfirst into the wall. He winds the rope around Rook's wrists and yanks.

When we're subdued in the corner, Jase says, "What now, Dad?"

The old man grunts. "They'll be here any minute. Todd, go upstairs and look out. We don't want to miss this boat."

The other blond trots up the cellar steps and disappears. In his wake, tense silence settles over the room. The three of us sit motionless. Jase and his father stand stiff-shouldered before us. The gun points at my head. My mind is whirring, but it's not kicking up any ideas. I think of Essie, and what she'll do when she finds out we're taken. Because that's the next thing that's going to happen, I know it. She'll come.

*Please, Ess. Just once, don't think about us. Think about everybody else. You need to carry on the fight. If you still can.*

"Jase." Todd's voice upstairs sounds agitated.

Jase looks at his dad, who nods, then canters up the stairs.

Just one of them now. If my hands weren't tied...

"Dad, it's them." Jase's voice comes from above. "They want to speak to you."

With a final glare at us, the old guy exits the same way as his sons, leaving us a moment's grace.

"Mate." Rook sniffs. "I'm so, so sorry."

"Not your fault." But my mind is darkening, hope extinguished while we wait. "We should've tried the church."

"Daddy," says Willow, tears in her voice. "What will they do to us?"

"Shhh. Wills, it's going to be alright."

A new pair of legs, clad in black jeans, descends the cellar steps. Across the male torso, stretches a black t-shirt decorated with a large, silver Hands of Kinship badge.

A woman in similar dress follows, broad arms swinging. She marches ahead of her companion and grabs Willow, hauling her up by the wrist. Willow struggles and tries to bite. When the woman delivers her a vicious shake, she coughs and goes limp. Beaten, she allows herself to be led away.

"Don't hurt her!" I try to get to my feet as they recede up the stairs. With no free arms to brace myself, I don't get far before the Unity guy reaches me.

With a heavy boot in my chest, he jabs me back down, then peers into my face. "Yep. That's our man, Geri." He smirks at me and rubs a hand through his crew cut. "Hello, Seth. Where's the missus?"

I glare at him. At least that means they don't have Essie. He drags me up towards his silver badge and pitches me at the exit. The old man appears at the top of the stairs, pistol in hand. Eyes fixed behind us, he descends slowly. From the back of the cellar, Rook gives a gurgling, strangled cry.

As the old guy passes, the Unity monkey grabs his elbow. "Do what we asked, and you'll get your reward." He eyeballs the old landlord. "You have a right to defend your property from intruders. With reasonable force. That man was armed and attacked you in your home." He reaches behind him and pulls another gun from his waistband, handing it to the old man.

"That's bullshit." I jerk against the Unity guy's shove. "Rook asked you for help. He just wanted water. Don't—"

A fist smacks into my temple, sending me sprawling over the steps. Unity guy leans on my back. "Shut up, pretty boy. You're in enough trouble." He hustles me up the stairs, and the sound of Rook's terror fades as we emerge into the hallway of the pub.

Willow sits rigid on a stool on the other side of the bar. The woman stands next to her, my holdall at her feet, her heavy hands placed on Willow's shoulders in a sickening parody of maternal concern. Perhaps she decided it was less revolting than tying up a four-year-old or holding a gun on her. The two sons are out of sight.

"Come on." The guy grabs my hair and shoves me through the gap in the bar where they've opened the flip-top.

We're at the door when a shot fires in the basement. Willow screams as my nerves fire. Then silence.

*Rook.*

There's no time to mourn him. In the lull, I take my chance. Clenching my bound hands, I jerk my head backwards, connecting with the Unity guy's nose. He yells and falls back. Willow kicks the woman, who shrieks and releases her.

"Wills, run."

God love her. She doesn't hesitate—bolts straight for the door and rips it open. She disappears through it, and I move to follow. I'm too slow. Unity guy has recovered and wraps an arm around my throat.

"You stupid tosser," he says in my ear, and squeezes.

My breath stops.

The door bangs and Willow pitches through it. A third Unity grunt follows. Willow's on the floor, but I can't see her face because black flowers are blooming in my vision.

"Cuff her," someone says, and the woman springs on top of Willow, who whips her hand out, scratching her attacker's cheek. The woman smacks Willow hard, wrestling her over onto her front. The pressure eases on my neck, and I reach up to touch it. A second later, a head blow knocks me sideways into the wall.

Then, darkness.

*** 

Darkness and movement. A whine of electric. My head throbs. There's a sniffle, which I pray is Willow. The rope still digs into my wrists.

"Daddy?"

"Wills." My confusion and pain lift a little with the relief. They haven't separated us. Yet. "You okay?"

"Think so. Did they kill Rook?"

I can't very well deny it. "They must have, sweetheart. I'm sorry."

My eyes are adjusting. I catch a movement, a sweep of hair against a thin, vertical slice of light behind her. "Are we in a van or something?"

"Yeah. There was one parked outside the pub after they knocked you out."

"Did they say where they're taking us?"

"No."

"How long have I... have we been in the van?"

"Don't know. A long time."

"Hours?"

163

"Think so. Daddy, I don't know." She shifts and says more quietly, "I need a wee."

*Oh, great.*

"You'll have to do it in the van. Here, out the back. Most of it will go out of the gap."

We shuffle around so she can position herself.

"Hang on. Move away a sec." Heart pumping, I turn my back to the doors, find the handle with my bound hands, and pull.

Locked, of course. I huff out my breath. For a moment…

"What's wrong?"

"Nothing, sweetheart. Just hope. Come and do that wee before you burst."

# Chapter Nineteen

## Essie

20<sup>th</sup> November 2041

I long for the floor cushions at The Bank. All we have are mats more useful for yoga than sleeping.

These are Kim's orders: until we find the source of the leak, and how they knew about Halima's recce, no one comes in or goes out without authorisation. More than a hundred of us stuck here, stretched out in the communal chamber, yawning and fidgeting through the night. Some are asleep, but most twitch in their allotted spaces. Beside me, Piper is snoring. I guess the painkillers have kicked in, so that's good for her.

At least, Kim has joined us to abide by her own edict. She's sitting nearby, propped against the brickwork. Her eyes are half-closed, but I know she's watching me. Despite what she said to Gabe, Kim doesn't trust me. I throw her a thin smile, which she barely returns, and switch my gaze to Carlo. He's lying on his back, arms behind his head, twenty yards past the Gabe-and-Hallie bundle. What we have here is a suspicion triangle—Kim watching me; me watching Carlo.

I can't imagine why he's here except to spy for his mother. Which raises the likelihood that Kerry knows where I am. Fighting back the dread, I blink my sore eyes and imagine her sending diggers to the abandoned station. Armed police crawling down the tunnels towards us, ready with the gas cannisters. I wonder what Kerry's orders would be regarding me. Shoot on sight? Or bring me in alive?

A rapid movement across the room catches my eye. It's Ami, the Scouser who sneered at me in the meeting. She hesitates where the chamber narrows into the passage to the outside. Must have caught the turn of my head because she looks my way. A flicker passes over her face, then she hurries along the wall towards the exit at the far end. With a glance back, she disappears through it.

Piper stirs, her hand flopping onto my knee. Surprised, I emit a squeak, which wakes her.

She scrabbles herself up to sitting with her good arm. "What's wrong?"

"Nothing."

"Your face says it's *something*."

I shrug, hesitate, then say, "That Ami looking shifty just now. Just makes me wonder."

"Bloody hell, you're suspicious," she slurs through a yawn. "Who else are you gonna accuse? Am I in on it, too?"

"No, I just…s'pose you're right. But I've reason to be paranoid."

"Hmm." Piper settles on her back, arm thrown over her eyes.

"I need the loo."

They've built toilets of sorts beyond the chamber where we ate. No more than holes in the ground. They stink. I don't want to think about their waste disposal set up now we're trapped down here.

The dining space is dark, but enough light spills from behind me to glint on the metal door at the far end. It's ajar, and the smell of stale urine and worse drifts across the space to sting my nostrils. I do need the loo. Wishing I'd brought a torch with me, and a peg for my nose, I pick my way across the room. The passage beyond is pitch dark, but I feel my way along the rough bricks, following my nose up the gentle slope to the first ammonia-fumed recess. They've dug the holes at the back of the chambers, so it's easy to find, but harder to avoid falling into it. I stay upright by bracing against the wall. Eyes watering, I pull my jeans down and squat.

"I told you, they suspect nothing." It's a Scouse whisper, echoing from further up the passage. "Too busy accusing newbies."

I freeze mid-wee.

How is she talking on a *phone* down here?

"Yeah, I know." Ami sounds annoyed. "Look, I did what you asked, didn't I? When are we gonna talk about Liam?"

Silence.

"You said that last time." She huffs. "Whaddya mean you gotta go? Hang on, we had a deal... *Fuckers.*"

There's a clatter, and I wonder if she's chucked the phone. Footsteps crunch towards me. I hold my breath while they pass. The door clangs closed, but there's no rattle of the lock.

*Christ. Is Ami the traitor?*

I'm frozen, crouching, my jeans around my ankles. Ami works in comms. She knows everything. And now, I guess, so does Langford. I can't believe we're not dead already.

It's several minutes before I dare finish my wee and make my way back.

I can't see Ami among the cliques, but she must be in here. Weaving in and out of the sleeping bodies, I head towards Piper.

"Wake up." I lean down and touch her shoulder.

"Hmmwha...?"

"I've got to tell you something." I shake her good arm. "Wake up. It's important."

With a sigh, she sits up. "Jesus, what?"

I lean close and whisper in her ear, "It *is* Ami."

"Who's what, now?"

"I heard her on the phone. She's the mole." I lean back, keeping my voice low while I recount the conversation I overheard.

Piper's mouth drops open and she covers it with a hand. "Shit."

"Yep."

"What are you going to do?"

167

"No idea. I mean, Kim thinks it's me, so if I go running to her…"

She chews her lip. "Let's tell Gabe."

"I dunno…"

"Ess, I know you've still got baggage with him—"

"It's not that."

"—but this is serious. If she's leaked the plans… I don't have to tell you." She lets that hang, peering at me.

I concede with a nod and follow her over to Gabe and Hallie. They're awake, propped up on elbows murmuring.

One of Gabe's dreadlocks coils on the floor as he lifts his face to us. "Can't sleep either, huh, ladies? Not exactly restful, is it? I'm missing the luxury of The Bank."

Though she was spark out ten minutes ago, Piper snorts. "Funny you should say that—"

"Gabe, listen." I glance past him at Carlo and crouch nearer. "I know who the mole is."

As I retell the story, Gabe's eyes grow wider.

Hallie swears under her breath. "You sure?"

"Hundred percent. '*I did what you asked*'? What else could she mean by that?" I take in a huge breath and let it out slowly. "Will you help me break it to Kim? She's not a massive fan of me."

I make myself wait while he thinks, his eyes on the floor. He twists around and squints over his shoulder to an alcove in the far wall. Now I'm closer, it's possible to make out a pair of legs poking out of it, and above, Ami's pale face.

Gabe looks back at me, his brows drawn down. "You know, it's a hell of a thing to accuse someone in the inner circle. Not sure Kim's gonna go for it."

After a silent beat, I say, "I know. That's why I asked for your help."

He bites the inside of his cheek, his face screwing sideways. "You're gonna need proof, Ess."

This is a waste of time. I glance at Piper and back at Gabe. "Proof? I'll get you proof."

Heart thrumming, I march to the alcove. Ami's smile dissolves as I squat in front of her. I guess she must see my expression.

"Ami, what's in your pocket?"

Her hand jerks to the bulge in her denim jacket. "Nothing. What are you on about?"

My arms shoot out, and Ami's to meet them. She's too slow. I shove a hand into Ami's pocket, and she squeals in protest. Eyes fixed on her face, I can feel the heads popping up behind me. My fist returns from the pocket clutching a phone.

*The* phone.

I can't believe she didn't hide it somewhere. Then again, she had no reason to think anyone had overheard her.

"So what's this?" I hold it up to her.

Her eyes flicker. She knows she's caught.

"What's going on?" Kim's voice cuts through a tense silence I wasn't aware of until she spoke.

I turn on my knees and show her the phone. "Ami is the leak."

A crowd grows behind her as Kim stares at me. "It's a phone. So what? Any non-community network phones don't work down here, so Ami couldn't have used it."

Beside me, Ami grunts and makes a grab for it, but I pull away and stand. Handing it to Kim, I say, "Why don't you check the last call details?"

Rolling her eyes, Kim takes the phone. As she presses a button, her jaw twitches. "How did you make this call through the signal blocker, Ami? No one's been above ground."

Ami springs to her feet. "Kim—"

"No. Who did you call?" She holds up the handset. "Who is this number?"

The crowd behind Kim pulls in closer, eyes peering at the phone and Ami's face.

"I can explain…"

"Please do." Kim's voice is flat, her eyes unwavering on Ami's face. "Essie, stay there."

I freeze.

Eyebrows arched high, Ami glances at me, then around at

the faces of the crowd.

"I'm waiting."

Ami breaks all at once, falling to her knees, head bowed. A sob drifts through the curtain of her hair.

Kim appears to notice the crowd gathered, glancing around her with a sigh. "Okay, let's take it to the conference room. Everybody, relax and go back to sleep."

Although they worship Kim, I doubt very much that's going to happen. The onlookers drift away, tense mutters ricocheting between them.

Kim's hand closes around my arm. "You come with me."

I return her fierce stare, wondering how *I'm* the guilty one. There's no choice, so I follow Kim and Ami. As we file past her, Piper shoots me a frown. I shrug and keep going.

In the conference room, Kim points Ami to the nearest chair and me to sit opposite. She settles herself at the head of the table between us and slaps Ami's phone down on the table. "So, Essie, perhaps you could explain how you knew this was in Ami's pocket."

Drawing in a long breath, I eye Ami. "I heard her talking on it. When I was in the loo."

Her eyes narrowing on me, Ami's nostrils flare.

Kim nods slowly. "How did you know it wasn't an authorised phone?" She peers at Ami. "Because it's not."

"Because of what she was saying. It was someone outside the camp. Someone who Ami was working for."

Ami sinks into the chair and shakes her head as I repeat what I heard as accurately as I can. Kim's face grows paler, her lips thinner, as I talk.

When I finish, Kim's silent for a long time. Then she switches her gaze to Ami. "'*We had a deal'*?"

Ami says nothing, her eyes on the table. Beads of sweat glisten on her upper lip.

"What deal, Ami? With whom?"

No answer.

Kim huffs. "You're caught. You might as well come clean."

Ami lifts her head and glares at me. "You…" Shoulders

high, she leans forward. My mouth goes dry. She's going to spring at me across the desk. Then she crumples like a piece of wastepaper in the rain. Her eyes fill with tears as she looks at Kim. "I had no choice. Liam…"

"Your brother Liam?" Kim's voice is still icy, but with cracks in it.

Ami nods. She picks at the old wood of the table.

"Ami?"

"I never told you. They arrested him a few weeks ago. Sedition, they said, though he's nothing to do with this." She rests her forehead in her palm and closes her eyes.

"Why, then?" When Ami looks at her blankly, Kim says, "Why did they target Liam?"

Ami shrugs and sinks lower in the chair.

An idea strikes me. "They were trying to get to you through him."

Kim's gaze skims me, then drifts over my shoulder. "Which means…" She's back with Ami now, eyes probing. "You must have done something stupid for them to notice you." A curtain of hair obscures Ami's face. Head dipped low, Kim reaches out and brushes it behind her ears, exposing her mottled skin. "What did you do?"

"I…" Ami gives a wet sniff and looks at the darkened ceiling. "Took someone back to my flat one night. He saw some comms stuff I forgot I'd left out."

"What stuff?"

"Weapons stocks, recruitment figures." Ami's voice is barely audible. "One of the cell locations."

Kim's head and shoulders jerk. "The Narlton cell."

Ami's eyes crease with a plea as she looks back at Kim. "I'd been working on the stuff all day. I went out for a drink or two. I just…forgot to pack it up. God, I'm sorry."

"You're *sorry*? Jesus, Ami. Seven people died in the that raid."

"I know."

My neck cricks when I move it. Seven people died? I swallow a bitter taste. "So this guy you took home was Unity, or something."

171

Ami jumps, as though she's forgotten I'm here. "Or just fancied earning himself a few quid as a snitch. Next thing I knew, they raided my mum's and took Liam. When they let us see him in Belmarsh, his jaw and leg were broken. His eyes... He looked like a prisoner of war. In two weeks, they did that to him."

My stomach churns with revulsion as I remember the state of Lawrence when I visited him; the state of Gabe when he got out after his four days in prison years ago.

"And then the calls started. *'We can make things easier on him, or harder. Your choice.'* If I did what they said, they'd protect Liam. If I did enough, they'd release him."

It's hard not to feel for her. I clear my throat. "What was 'enough'?"

No answer.

"Could it include the plans for the 26th of November?"

Ami glares at me. "No. I haven't told them about that. Kim, you've got to believe me."

It's hard to tell from Kim's face if she does or not. She holds out her palms. "But it did involve leaking the details of Halima's recce. And they gave you a burner phone. One that can penetrate the blocker. I wonder how they managed that."

My stomach swoops. "And if they can do that...could they be monitoring us right now?"

Kim drums her fingernails on the table, then stands. "Essie, stay here and guard her." She sweeps out of the door, her wake ruffling my hair.

We sit in silence; me staring at Ami, Ami staring at her hands as they knot around each other.

Ten minutes later, Kim returns with a flushed, stoney-faced Fred. As he looks at his former comrade, his lip curls. He grabs her arm. "Come on."

"Where?" asks Ami as she stumbles to her feet.

He shoves her through the door. Ami gasps in pain as their duelling footsteps recede.

"Where is he taking her?" I ask.

Kim regards me. "You did well, Essie. Thank you."

"What will you do to her?"

She huffs out a laugh. "Don't worry. She'll live. Right now, you and I have more pressing matters to resolve." I suppose my confusion shows because she says, "The mess Ami left."

"Liam?"

A little smile. "He's not our problem."

A broken jaw; a broken leg. God knows what else. "Jesus."

"Neither's he. I meant we need to check her flat. See what else she's left for them to find. Clean up."

"A bit late."

"I'm with you on that. But I have to see it for myself. Tonight."

"Do you think she might have leaked the 26th?" I have my doubts about Kim's plans, but the idea of getting ambushed is no comfort.

She stares past me. "I bloody hope not. Everything's in place. It's too late to pull out."

As we gather ourselves to leave, she grabs my wrist. "Not a word to anyone, got it? Not a single word."

"What about the scene in the hall? And Fred?" I bite my lip. "I told Piper about Ami's phone conversation. And Gabe and Hallie."

Pinching the top of her nose, she says, "Can't be helped. None of them know anything for certain. And I told Fred nothing more."

"They'll connect the dots, Kim."

"We'll have to risk it."

I raise my eyebrows.

"What else can we do? Confirm their worst fears? Last thing we need is a full-on panic." Kim pivots and grips my other shoulder, facing me head on. "This is just you and me."

She seems to need a response, so I nod. With a returning squeeze on my arm, she leads the way back to the hall.

"Essie." Piper darts towards me, reaching out, eyes wide with anguish.

I block her with a shaky hand. "Not now, Piper."

She frowns, her mouth turning down, but drops her arms

to let me pass.

Dwelling only to pack our bags, Kim and I regroup, pushing through the murmuring crowd, past a hundred pairs of expectant, confused and alarmed eyes, to the exit and onwards to the world above ground.

# Chapter Twenty

## Seth

**21st November 2041**

Willow picks at her egg and beans on toast, her pale face twisted, as though it's not her favourite meal.

"Wills, try to eat."

"She hasn't made it right. The toast's soggy."

*She* is our chaperone-cum-jailer, Emma, who skulks in the kitchen beyond the open arch, pretending not to listen. One of Kerry's minions, I imagine. Or Langford's. I can't be sure since no one has come to explain. Emma is slight but has a wiry grace that convinces me she could break my neck if I piss her off. And she doesn't miss a thing.

When the van stopped and the doors opened, we were in a windowless garage. The woman who hit Willow and the guy who knocked me out scowled at us, perhaps catching a whiff of Willow's urine. They yanked us out of the van, through a door, and up a flight of steps that smelled of damp.

The garage turned out to be the basement of this house, where we've been prisoners since. Thick, iron bars and heavy locks; the windows boarded up on the outside. With no view of the surroundings, and no electronics, I couldn't tell what time of day it was, but it felt like late night. I've been running with that timeframe ever since, so in my head it's morning now. As they hustled us up more stairs, heavy rain battered the boards. Sounds like it's still going.

Our new guards are less pushy-shovey. Emma and a lanky, sullen guy called Ed relieved the others. Ed has sloped off during the night—there's no sign of him this morning. More evidence, if it were needed, that Emma can handle herself alone.

At least, there was a mattress in the bare, plaster-walled bedroom. It was musty and damp, but softer than the floorboards. And, perhaps because of the state Willow made of their van, they'd placed a wee bucket next to it. Emma locked us in there and let us out about thirty minutes ago to clean up before breakfast. The water was icy, but it felt good to wash the dried blood from my face.

Trying to encourage Willow, I take a big bite of my poached egg and make an '*mmm*' sound. It tastes good after God knows how long since we last ate. And I want Willow to stay strong. I haven't a clue how we're going to get out yet, but when I do, she needs to be alert.

I've overplayed it: with a sigh, Willow slaps down her fork and folds her arms. "It's probably poisoned."

I suspect she's raised her voice for Emma to hear, though there's no sign from the kitchen beyond the archway she has.

Despite the knot of dread in my stomach, a dark chuckle escapes me. "If they were going to kill us, they'd have done it by now."

She gives me a grave look. Her eyes, usually sparky like Essie's, are puffy and ringed with red. "That's not funny."

I swallow, my thin smile fading. "I know."

Emma leans against the archway, drying her hands on a tea towel. "Anyone for more juice?"

Willow gives a sullen shake of her head. So much like her mum.

"I will, please," I say with false brightness. When Emma turns back into the kitchen, I whisper, "Wills, we will get out of here, I promise. Just let them think you're going to do everything they say. It'll make it easier."

"You're not getting out of here." Emma's right behind me. Christ, she's a ninja. "Not alive."

As she pours my juice, I glare up at her. "Give us a break, will you? She's four."

From her unrippled expression, that means nothing to

Emma. She perches on the table next to me and swoops her face close to mine. "Remember the deal, Seth? You get untied, you behave yourself."

From this angle, the handle of a pistol is visible, poking out of her waistband.

She smirks, as if she knows that. "I'd be just as happy to see you chained to that radiator." Eyes still fixed on me, she points over my shoulder. After an eternity of hard staring, she relents and stands. She has the decency, at least, to retreat behind the arch.

Willow eyes Emma's back as it disappears under the arch, a mutinous pout on her lips. "Think I prefer the one who hit me." Again, I suspect, meant to be heard.

I shush her and resume my meal when a phone rings in the kitchen.

"Kerry." A silence, then Emma replies. "Okay. They'll be right here, waiting. See you shortly."

Willow gazes at me, and I lower my fork. If I ever was, I'm not hungry anymore.

\*\*\*

"Jesus, it's bucketing out there." When Kerry appears in the back room, she looks dry in her ivory trouser suit. Likely she got Ed, who's lurking behind her in the hall, to hold a brolly over her. He's the type—repressed aggression, obsequious in the face of power.

Emma hasn't tied us to a radiator, but she made us sit on the dusty wooden floor next to one. Willow is squashed in beside me. Emma wouldn't let her sit on my lap. God knows why.

Kerry's mouth plays with a smile as she peers down at us. She just stands there, staring at me as if she can't believe her own luck. Then she turns on a stiletto, leaving a citrus perfume cloud as she disappears through the door and mutters something to Ed. Emma remains still beside the door, gazing over the top of my head as if she's bored. Maybe she can see the end of her shift approaching.

"Okayyyyy." Kerry's voice precedes her return to the room. With a dispassionate glance at Willow, she clacks over to stand before me. "Well, we have a situation here."

I say nothing.

"Your girlfriend is a bit of an irritant, isn't she?" Kerry taps a foot and sighs. "And by irritant I do, of course, mean a lying fucking bitch."

Willow's breath hitches. I take her hand.

"You've got to help me understand here, Seth. We had a deal. Building that prototype; we were gonna save the world. Then she and Jack fucking Riley decided that would never do." She paces back and forth in front of me. "They were more interested in screwing me over. Well, you know what? Good one, Essie. I'm officially screwed."

While she's been ranting, Ed has brought in a kitchen chair and scooted it behind her. She lowers herself onto it, laughs humourlessly, and shakes her head.

Outside, the rain hammers against the boards, but I hear no splashes of passing cars. Where the hell are we?

When I look back at Kerry, her mouth turns down, her eyes heavy-lidded. "Lawrence is dead. Hung himself in his cell." She gazes at the boarded window. "They should have seen it coming. No idea why he wasn't on suicide watch, poor lad."

*Oh, God. No... Lawrence.*

I open my mouth. Nothing comes out but a fractured groan.

"I'm sorry. I know he was a good friend."

My stomach churns as I glare at her. *"You killed him, you fucking liar."* My voice sounds bitter, alien.

She smiles, as though getting me to curse her was a victory in a secret battle. Reaching into her jacket, she comes out with my phone. Her thumb rests on a button and the display lights. They've charged it. So now they have the number of Essie's burner phone. My eyes follow the handset as she waves it around and, in my head, I beg it to explode.

"We couldn't reach Essie last night. No signal." Kerry sticks her bottom lip out and stands. "Hope nothing has happened to her."

"More lies."

"Why would I lie?"

"Any number of reasons. To screw with me; to get me to talk. I don't give a shit. I just know you're lying."

Two rapid, high-pitched coughs come out of her mouth. A second after, I realise she giggled. "We can talk about Essie later. I'm interested in what you said. About getting you to talk?" She pockets the phone and steps closer, pinching up her trousers so she can ease into a crouch. "As it happens, I need to clarify a few things."

Against my arm, Willow's chest hitches. I squeeze her hand, eyes fixed on Kerry's hungry face.

"Where's Jack, Seth?"

I wasn't expecting that. "Wha…? I assume he's dead. Cuba went under the sea."

"You assume he's dead." It sounds like she's speaking to herself at first. "Well, I made that mistake before. Riley has the luck of the devil. He escaped a burning building a few years back. Wouldn't surprise me to learn he'd survived a catastrophic hurricane, too."

"I can't help you."

"Can't or won't?"

"Why are you looking for him? He's no good to you now. The model he was building, the file… They both sank with Cuba. That's years of work lost. A decade or more. There's no time to start again, even *if* he's alive. Even *if* you could persuade him to do it."

"You're right, Seth." That giggle again. Something snags the back of my mind.

*There was another…*

The file Jack used in Cuba was the copy we made. There was an original: the one Lawrence took from Essie and said he'd keep somewhere safe. At the prison, he told Ess he'd

179

flushed it away. Was he lying—did he have it hidden after all? Has Kerry got hold of it? My guts roll as visions of what she might have done to Lawrence flash behind my eyes. Is Kerry still planning to build it and make her fortune? We're beyond that now. Jack's dead.

I shake my head. "You're clutching at straws."

With a sharp exhale, she fishes my phone from her pocket, glances at it, then returns it. "I'm not the only one, am I?"

It's only when two fat tears plop onto my hand from her chin I understand Willow has been crying silently for a time.

# Chapter Twenty-One

# Kerry

## 21st November 2041

I wonder if Fielding suspects I have the original prototype. The way his eyes bulged wider than his face this morning, I'd say so. Just as well he doesn't know the whole story, or he'd be bitching about another dead prole.

*Prole.* God, what a vile word. I've been hanging around with Alex Langford far too much lately. Jay sounded like a nice bloke. Like Lawrence, but I guess they're cousins.

*Were* cousins.

Both dead within weeks of each other. In the name of saving this godforsaken planet. Poor saps. Bless Lawrence's compulsion to make amends, and his intolerance to pain.

I assume Essie forgot she once told me Lawrence took the original prototype file from her. Then again, the day she said it, Alex had beaten her half to death. I can forgive her a few blind spots. And maybe she never knew Lawrence had sent the file to Jay in Scotland for safekeeping.

Those last few video calls with Jack in Havana… I knew something was wrong. He was evasive about his progress on the build, Essie sitting stiff-shouldered and quiet across the table. Call it an intuition. When I arranged for her to visit Lawrence, I hoped she'd spill it. It was so much easier than I'd imagined. She coughed it up, just to make him feel better.

I didn't enjoy ordering Ed to arrange either interrogation; either killing. But they were necessary. Lawrence led me to Scotland and Jay. Jay led me to the prototype. Easy as that.

The Scots have been used to softer authority for too long. When the crunch came, Jay couldn't hack it and crumbled within minutes. So Ed told me. I'll bet Jay never knew what he was sitting on, or how important it was. How rich he could be if only he'd known what to do with it.

It's back to square one, but at least that's better than square minus twenty. Seth's right. Jack's probably dead, but what if...?

With no more stray copies, and no Essie Glass to get in the way, that little file is my ticket. Getting rich is one thing. Being the person to save however many lives remain from the nine billion we started with...that's the real prize for me now. Langford's going to look utterly ineffectual next to my heroic actions. He and his greedy, corrupt mates will crawl back under their putrid rocks, and good riddance.

Not an entirely selfish aim. A win-win.

I mustn't get ahead of myself. There's work to do yet. Essie's still free, and Langford's still in power. And he's on his way right now, from the flat upstairs, to where I'm perched, waiting pertly on a chair in his private Downing Street office.

The door behind me sighs open. "Good afternoon, Kerry. Great to see you."

Time to focus.

I twist in my seat, a pliant smile on my lips. "Alex. Thank you for taking the time. I know you're busy."

Langford strolls past the desk in front of me to the window opening on a walled private garden. "This rain." He sighs. "I've got a report on my desk telling me it won't stop for days."

The side of his jaw twitches. If I knew him less, I'd say he was scared.

"They delivered Fielding and the brat last night?" Pulling at his cuffs, he turns and lowers his bulk into the chair. The leather gives an extravagant rasp.

"They did."

He grunts. "At least they got something right. And the lowlife who was helping them?"

"Dead."

"Anyone around to miss him?"

I shake my head. "So, what now?"

Taking in a deep, noisy breath, Langford leans back. The leather creaks again. He can't hide the smirk. "I'm happy to leave it to you to resolve the matter, if that's what you're asking."

*That easy?*

I blink at the ceiling rose, appearing to consider this for the first time.

"Frankly, Kerry, you'd be doing me a favour. I've got more important things on my plate than scum like Glass. You're welcome to her. She's a bad omen."

"She might be that. But she still destroyed your business." I return wide eyes to him. "You don't want closure?"

His guffaw distorts in my ears. "I'm over it. Fill your boots. Just don't leave any mess behind for me to step in."

\*\*\*

Ed's windscreen wipers are useless against the deluge, and we're not even in motion yet.

"Where to?" he asks as I put on my seatbelt. "Your place?"

"Back to the safehouse. I need to talk to Fielding."

He twists in his seat, gaze pressing into me. His hand snakes up my inner thigh, pinching at the top. "No. Your place."

I steady my breath on the short, tense drive to Primrose Hill.

An hour later, I'm curled on the sofa, hair half in and half out of its updo, face hot and damp and, I know, lined with creases from being buried in the pillow for too long. Ed ordered me to relax while he made coffee and toast. There's no denying I needed the stress relief, and it worked. My limbs were loose, not stiff and aching as they have been.

I can't afford to waste any more time. Grabbing my tablet,

I wake up the display screen. The OnTheWall icon is a black ink drawing of a fly. Dirty and underhanded, like its functionality. I click it open and select the last voice-activated recording.

"Ollie." Langford's voice is wheedling and dulled, considering the wooden panelling in his office. "You've still got a thing for her, haven't you? You can't hide anything from me."

Foster Pugh's snuffling response splutters out of my tablet. "I haven't a clue what you're talking about."

A door closes.

"Bet you could if you wanted." Langford's voice is clearer now. "She's desperate. No, I didn't mean it like that. She's clinging on to our coat tails. Trying to get a leg up. Which means you could get a leg *over,* no problem. And now she's no longer a minister in your department, it wouldn't look...improper."

There's clattering and something pours; probably single malt.

"I hardly think—"

"All I'm saying is you'd be doing us both a favour if you did. Chill her out. Get her to confide in you. Tyler's got an agenda; her sort always has. I just don't know what it is yet." A pause, a slurp, and the soft clop of glass on wood. "You could screw it out of her. She'd love it."

My stomach knots.

*I'll tell you my agenda, you disgusting wanker. Bugging your private office. Screw THAT out of me.*

Ed delivers my coffee, his movements stiff and jerky. Belatedly, I reach for my ear pods and pop them in.

A sigh from Foster-Pugh crackles in my ear. "I didn't come here to discuss Kerry Tyler."

"I know. So... Unity Devout?"

"Yes."

There's a smile in Langford's voice now. "What news from the Crusades?"

"Don't make fun of this, Alex. Some of us are quite sincere in our faith."

Langford chuckles. "Sorry, Ols. Old habits. Look, you know I'm fully supportive of the Devout scheme. We're going to need the crowd control going forward. Devout and Power are two important sides of the same coin. Good cop, bad cop; carrot and stick?"

"Well, yes. Exactly."

"So, what of the carrots?"

Foster-Pugh inhales. "I've got the Redemption Charter on board now. We're working through the stratifications; looking at areas of life, from transportation to grocery shopping. The more devout the prole, the more their privileges accumulate."

"What about evidence of devoutness?" Another glass clinks. "How to you measure faith?"

"Shibboleth."

"Huh?"

"Never mind. We're working on basic criteria like the Good Citizen assessment. I expect they will intersect neatly."

"Sounds good. That'll be easier for the proles to understand. More palatable."

There's a chuckle, then a brief silence.

"Ollie, there is another thing to discuss." Sounds like Langford is speaking into his drink.

"I know. And it's in hand."

"The reports are concerning. I don't have to tell you. A *network* of insurgents. Literally underground?"

"It's in hand, Alex, I assure you."

Langford grunts.

"We have access to good intelligence. We know there's been an escalation in operations. They're planning something soon. All we need are a few details on base locations; dates, times, places. Then we'll take them down."

"I need more."

There's a loud sigh. "We have the name of their London commander. Kim Vella. I have dossiers on her and a few of her lieutenants. It's a matter of time before we get to one of

185

the top table. Then it's over for them. And they won't like what comes next."

*Kim? The same Kim that Carlo mentioned?*

Has to be. How many underground movements could survive in London these days? My heart pounds so hard it throbs in my throat. Carlo's involved with these insurgents. I want to run out and scour the streets…under the streets until I find him and bring him home. But where would I start?

"You okay?" Ed mouths, gaze darting between my face and uneaten toast.

I rip the ear pods out. "You need to drive me to the safehouse."

"Now?"

"Yes, now."

I taste blood and swipe at my mouth. My teeth have cut into my bottom lip.

***

Drew's on duty at the safehouse, which is unhelpful. I assume it was Drew that bashed Fielding over the head in the arrest, and his being their guard now has done nothing to improve my prisoner's compliance. His dark eyes smoulder with suppressed rage, that almost erupts when he catches my eye.

"I'm trying to help you, Seth." I cross the floor to stand over him. He'd have risen and squared up to me, but Drew's got him cuffed to a chair. Fresh bruises bloom on his cheek and mouth, so I doubt they've become better friends since yesterday. "The PM has granted me latitude regarding you, but his tether is short."

"I love how you still call him PM. Like this shit is perfectly normal." He nods to the boarded-up window. Not sure if he means the safehouse or the world beyond it.

"What *should* I call him?"

He shrugs and sneers. "Führer?"

From the next room, there's a shout, a clattering of feet, and the girl squeals.

Fielding's eyes burn into the wall, then me. "Tell your attack dogs if they hurt my daughter, I will spend the rest of my life making them regret it."

"However long that may be." I don't mean to smirk, but given his circumstances, the threat is so ridiculous I can't help it.

"What do you want? I told you I don't know anything. Where Essie is, where Jack is—other than at the bottom of the Gulf of Mexico."

"Why?"

He stares at me, lips moving, shaking his head the tiniest bit. It makes him look stupid.

"Why did Essie screw me over?"

"You are fucking kidding me."

"It was a win-win. We get to save the planet; I get to secure my financial future. What was it about that plan she couldn't stomach?"

"I don't know, Kerry. Maybe she didn't trust you?"

"She'd rather watch it all go to hell than see me earn a penny." The truth of it makes so much sense I almost feel the click. I fix him with narrow eyes. "And haven't you wondered why she spent so much time plotting with another man? You can't have enjoyed that. Hardly adds up to the portrait of a hero she likes to paint of herself. Not that different from me, after all."

His arms strain against the cuffs for a moment, then relent. "I'm not a cleric anymore, Tyler. I don't take confessions. What do you want?"

I wasn't planning it for that moment, but before I realise what I'm doing, I've yanked Fielding's phone from my pocket. "Let's ask the woman herself, shall we? I feel like she owes both of us an explanation."

Before I can click the redial, my own phone rings. I fish it out of the other pocket. "Yep."

"It's Lenny. We got him."

It's all I can do to suppress an ecstatic laugh as I turn away from Fielding. "Where?"

"Florida. The bit that's left after the hurricane. We'll have to travel north to bring him back. The airports here are still closed."

"Great work, Len." He hates that name, but I keep forgetting. "Get here as soon as you can. Oh, Lenny..." *Hope, hope.* "The prototype?"

"Gone in the storm. Sorry."

"Okay." I force myself to sound deflated, though my heart is leaping. "Well. It was worth a try. Bring him back."

This never happens to me. I never get what I want. The years of work; tears and sweat, and I never seem to make it to the top. They never let me. Langford and his cronies are just the latest in a long line of wankers who've held me down.

Now I have the only prototype. I have Jack. Near-as-damn-it have Essie. The gang back together, except I'm the one in control. The bitch won't be able to double-cross me this time. If I have to keep her family locked up for years, I have the means. Hope it doesn't come to that. It's much better if we can work together.

I gain control of my expression and turn to face Fielding. Pocketing one phone, I retrieve the other. "Right. Where were we?"

"You were being a bitch."

Rude. Though I can hardly blame him. Wondering if he caught the drift of my conversation with Lenny, I click Essie's name on his phone. "Let's see if we can get through to her now."

There's no out-of-service whine. This time it rings. My eyes rest on Fielding's while I wait. His chest hitches, his eyes are moist and wide. Is he hoping she answers or praying she doesn't?

"Seth?" Essie sounds breathless, as if she's excited or just run to pick up.

"Hello, Essie."

There's a long silence, which I allow, then a flat, "Kerry."

# Chapter Twenty-Two

## Essie

### 21st November 2041

"You've been hard to reach of late." Kerry's silky smooth as always.

I fight the rising dread. "Where's Seth? Why have you got his phone?"

I can feel Kim's eyes on my back and turn to face her. She's standing in the door to Ami's kitchenette, hair still wet from the shower and pulled into a plait. Her eyes fix on me, dark with fear.

"I think it's past time for us to talk, don't you?" Kerry's voice drills into my ear.

"You haven't answered my questions."

Her sigh pops the line. "He's here. He's fine."

My stomach lurches. "Where's Willow? Put them on camera."

"Not yet."

As my hand shakes, the phone rustles against my ear, drowning out her next words. Legs numb, I collapse into Ami's armchair. "Let me see them, you bitch." But the strength has drained from my voice.

"You'll see them in the flesh soon enough."

In the background, Seth shouts, "Ess. We're okay. Don't come here. Screw them."

Another sigh, more rustling, and a door closes. "We both know you're coming."

I focus my effort on the struggle to breathe.

"They are unhurt. And will remain so if you co-operate. You have my assurance."

"Your assurance?" The words explode out of me with a bitter half-laugh. My eyes lift to Kim, who has moved to stand beside me, a frown frozen on her brow. "Fuck you, Kerry."

"You're in shock. I understand that. But you need to think well, and fast."

My legs come back to life, and I spring up, pacing around Ami's lounge. "You need to leave my family alone."

"I didn't start this. You're the one who lied. Pretending you and Riley were working on the prototype when all that time it was sitting in his goddamned *workshop*."

"You know where Carlo is, Kerry?" I ignore Kim's frantic gestures and turn away. "He's in a camp right under your feet, plotting to end you and your mates. How does it feel when your son hates what you stand for enough to want you dead?"

Silence at the other end, a click, then three short beeps. My own harsh breathing echoes back at me.

She's gone. That must have hit home.

I try to call her back, but she must have blocked me or something.

Heart hammering, I turn to face Kim's anger. She's not there. Racing to move the camp again.

Now I'm on my own.

Nausea overtakes me, and I retch, but there's nothing in my stomach. My nerve endings explode, every muscle burning. Before my brain catches up, I've hurled the phone against the wall. It smashes into pieces that clatter on Ami's floorboards. Dropping to my knees, I shriek with the fear and rage that's been building for weeks. The scream turns into a wail.

Hands are on my shoulders, rocking me, and Piper whispers, "Shhh."

*Piper?*

190

I give in, resting my head inside her arms and sobbing. I don't know how long we stay there. Long enough for my shoulders to cramp.

When I look up, Kim is sitting in the armchair, face pale, eyes fixed on me. "They have your family."

It's not a question, so I don't respond. Instead, I look at Piper. "What are you doing here? You should be resting that shoulder."

She flaps her hand. "I followed you from camp. But when you entered the flat last night, you locked the door and stranded me in the hall. I slept in the laundry room."

Last night, we searched the flat, retrieved Ami's gun, and burnt the documents in her grate. I persuaded Kim we should stay here instead of risking the journey back to camp. The constant torrential rain had emptied the streets even before curfew; we'd have been beacons out there. We didn't know Piper was in the hallway. If Kim hadn't agreed to stay, if we'd gone back underground, would I ever have received Kerry's call?

Pointless question.

"We'll do a trade." If Kim's angry at my indiscretion about the camp, she's squashing it for the moment. "Your family for her son. I can make a call, get Carlo locked up with Ami."

Mind whirring, I get to my feet and stare at the shards of plastic that used to be my phone. My only lifeline to them. I didn't even find out where they're being held.

Piper stoops over to peer at the remains. "Think the SIM card is still intact." She looks up and says, "You can have my handset."

I give her a grateful smile, so tired my head will hardly stay up. My voice shakes as I say, "Don't arrest Carlo. He hasn't done anything wrong. I don't want to be responsible for any more suffering. It's enough."

Kim is grim-faced. "What are you planning to do?"

"Whatever Kerry wants."

"Ess…" Piper grabs my elbow.

Shaking her off, I fix my stare on Kim, who holds her neck and shoulders stiff as she says, "No."

We're silent while I grasp the implications of the word.

"I can't let you do that, Essie." Kim lifts her chin. "You know everything."

After another beat, I pull Ami's gun from the waistband of my jeans. It hangs cold and heavy in my hands. It's loaded. "I'm not asking your permission."

Kim seems to weigh up the threat, squinting at the gun and my face in quick succession.

"I'll draw their attention as much as I can. Stop them." I glance out of Ami's small, grubby window at the floodwater swirling around the front gate. "This is our last chance, Kim. Burn it down."

She nods. "You're a massive pain in the arse, Glass. But I'll be sorry not to have you with us when we do."

Piper has been fiddling with her phone. She holds it out, clutching her own SIM card in the other hand. As I take it, her eyes swell with tears.

"I'll be fine, Pipes." I force my shoulders back.

*Who are you kidding, Ess? You're dead. Seth and Willow too.*

But…just maybe, if I surrender, she'll let them go. And while Kerry and Langford are concentrating on extracting whatever they can from me—information, revenge—they won't be looking for any other fights. These are slim chances, but they're all I have left. And if they give Seth and Willow better odds, I'll take them.

In the silence, Piper has been sifting through the wreckage of my phone. She hands me my SIM, compatible with her handset, thank Christ. Before I can fit it, she ambushes me with a hug so tight it makes me cough.

"Thank you." She sniffs in my ear. "I was a mess before you came along. You saved me. And I can't…"

"Piper. I'll be okay. They want me alive."

*Uh huh. Do they, Ess?*

When she pulls back, Piper's flushed face cramps with understandable doubt, but she moves away, wiping her nose on her arm.

Kim approaches me as though I'm a wild animal. "Things will get rough for you."

"I won't give you up, Kim. I don't care what they do to me."

"If it's a choice between us and your family?" Her eyes burn into mine. "It will come to that. You know that's the whole point."

"You only need a few days, don't you? If you move the camp, that should be enough."

"And the date of the uprising? If they ask?"

I twitch my mouth into a mirthless smile. "It's set for 30th of November. Start December with a clean slate. Makes a certain poetic sense. Can I help it if they should move the date forward in the meantime?"

She grows still. "I get it. I was a mother once." She shakes her head, as if to disarm a memory. "Good luck."

"You, too."

I force myself to hold on until the front door bangs shut. As I let the tears flow, my fist clenches so tight around Piper's phone, its edges cut into my palm.

# Chapter Twenty-Three

## Kerry

### 21st November 2041

The rain hammers me, making the end of my cigarette hiss. This dried-out old Camel that's been in my bag for a decade. It tastes like ruined blacktop. Fielding and the others are stewing inside the house. They can wait. I need to get my head straight.

Carlo's phone hums its taunt in my ear: no signal.

I slap the phone against the crumbling rear brickwork of the safehouse.

It freaked me out, Essie talking about my son and the rebels. It was like a train slamming into my chest hearing it from *her*. If he hadn't told me himself, if I hadn't had it unwittingly confirmed by Foster-Pugh, I'd have thought Essie was lying to screw with me.

Carlo's in that camp with Vella, and they're about to get stomped.

A range of options parade before me, none of them appealing. I could drop everything. Go looking for him before they hit. Essie said they were underground, but there's a shedload of underground in London. Where would I start? I'm powerless to help him. And if I go, what happens then? Will Langford hang on to Fielding and the girl for me? I doubt it. They'd be in a hole in the ground by the morning. Along with my chances.

I close my eyes, lifting my face so the rain batters against the lids. Carlo wanted to do this. It was his choice. He's a man now. Being a man means facing the consequences.

Taking in a wet breath, I throw the cigarette at the rising tide of rainwater drowning the lawn. I've never prayed, but my brain utters a silent plea for Carlo as Seth's phone rings from my pocket.

I need to get on with the job. The one I can handle. So I click *Answer*.

"I was angry. Sorry." Essie's voice is little more than a croak. It hurt her to say that.

"You weren't lying, though. Carlo's in that camp."

A sniff; a breath. "Yes."

"Foster-Pugh's coming for them."

"I'm sure." I'd swear to God she just chuckled. "Pity he won't know where to look."

We linger on the precipice. Maybe neither of us are certain of our first shot.

"Essie—"

"Release my family."

"I can't do that."

"Let them go. I'll do anything you want, but Seth and Willow go free. That's my only condition."

My turn to laugh. "It's not your place to set conditions."

"She's four years old, Kerry."

"She's a lever."

"You're a bitch."

"We don't seem to be doing any better this time round, do we?"

Silence.

I picture her clenched teeth biting in the rage and hatred. "Look, Essie. I don't want to argue with you anymore. Come see me. I think we can make a deal. And believe it or not I have good news."

"What news?" She sounds so tired, so defeated.

Good. This will go easier if she's beaten from the start. "Wait and see. Come."

"Where?"

"I'll send you a location in the morning." Let her tenderise overnight.

A rapid breath crackles in my ear. "You hurt them, I will kill you."

A click and she's gone. I calm the whirlwind of thoughts enough to return.

"You're soaked." Ed frowns at me from the kitchen doorway.

"Where's the kid?"

"Back room. Drew tied her up when she bit him."

"Christ's sake, Ed. She's four."

"Yeah. She's got teeth, though."

Shaking my head, I listen at the door to the front room. If they haven't knocked him out, Fielding is keeping quiet for now. In the back, Willow sits stiff and shaking on a wooden chair, her hands pulled behind her. Drew has slapped a length of gaffer tape over her mouth. He lurks behind her, sulking in the far corner.

I turn a glare on Drew. "Take that crap off her. We're not animals."

"*She* is." But he unties her hands and rips off the tape, ducking away from her, though she barely moves, just eyes me as I draw near.

I hold out my hand, but she just continues staring, so I take her upper arm in a firm grip and lift.

"*Daddy.*"

From the room next door: "*Willow?* Hey, what's going on? What are you doing? *Leave her.*"

The kid rockets her foot into my shin.

"Ouch."

While my grip is loose, she slips free and darts into the hall. I stumble after her, Drew behind me. Not quick enough to stop her from reaching her father. She wails, clutching at him as, still cuffed, he nuzzles her. Holding a palm out to halt Drew, I give them time, then move forward and take her arm. She clings harder to Fielding's chest, so in the end it's a tussle to remove her. As I hand her over to Drew, I shoot him a warning look: *easy*. He pushes her out of the room.

"No. Where are you going?" Seth starts a ferocious struggle with the cuffs. "You fuckers. *Bring her back.*"

I keep a safe distance. "This is the only way. I'm sorry."

He stops fighting and glares at me with such hatred my legs force me back a step. "You keep fucking with my family, Tyler. I promise you will regret it."

It's so desperate one could be forgiven a little pity. But I can't afford that. I offer him a small, consolatory smile for what will come next, and walk away.

Drew has passed the girl over to Ed and is hanging about in the hall. Through the open front door and rain, I can just make out her bowed head in the back seat of Ed's car. Drew has his instructions. I don't need to repeat them now.

"I'll call you when it's sorted," he says.

Back turned, I nod and leave.

She's calm and submissive as we enter my rent-free Primrose Hill house, but I keep my guard up just the same, and lock the door behind us. "Would you like an apple juice?"

She gives a solemn nod.

"Okay. Go through to the front room." I point to the door next to us and proceed to the kitchen. The chances are, while she's alone, she'll be searching for an escape route. Let her. She won't find any.

When I bring her the juice, she's staring out of the window. Checking out the opening mechanism too, I imagine, but she's out of luck. It's locked and painted closed.

She accepts the glass without looking at me. "Mummy says you're an evil bitch." She takes a swig. "I think she's right."

It's not just hearing that word from the mouth of the four-year-old that takes my breath away. Her tone is cold and dismissive, weary beyond her years. What I've done is part of that.

"Well. You're a forthright little thing, aren't you?"

She frowns at me. Maybe she doesn't know the word forthright.

"I bought you some books." I hold them out to her. A couple of gaudy princess stories and a colouring book with a packet of crayons taped to the front.

She takes them, but her eyes don't move from my face.

"Are you hungry?"

A little flick of her head, *no.* "Are you going to kill my daddy?

My ringtone saves me. It's Langford.

"Alex."

"Kerry. I'm outside your house. Let me in."

What the hell is he doing here? "Okay." Glancing at Willow, I dip into the hall and check the CCTV. It's him, his bald head glaring in monochrome. I open the door.

"Need a bloody doorbell here." He huffs and wipes rain from his face with a linen hanky.

I step aside to let him in. "You're the landlord."

He's on his way into the front room and stops in the doorway. As I squeeze past him, his gaze switches to me, a pursed "Wh...?" on his lips.

*Go on, ask.*

"What can I do for you, Alex?"

He rips his eyes from Essie's kid. "Perhaps we could speak in private?"

With a nod, I lead him through to the granite and steel kitchen.

As soon as the door is closed, he's at me. "What the hell are you up to?"

"What do you mean?"

"That's Glass's kid in there?"

"Yes. It is."

"What's she doing here? Where's Fielding?"

I cock my head at him. "You said this was my thing."

"Suppose I did."

"Then don't ask questions. It would be better for you to have deniability on whatever this is."

He screws his eyes up for a second, and I can almost hear him weighing up his compulsion to control with the logic of my words. Finally, with a tic of his head, he says, "I have new information."

198

"Oh?"

"There's an imminent attack. Insurrection."

"London?"

"Amongst others." His expression is stiff and grave; he's more ill at ease than I've ever seen him. "Our source in the London rebel camp is compromised, but the Birmingham cell is history. A hapless prole turned up at their headquarters. Ran straight into the secret service."

"When's the attack planned?"

"Some time in the next week. That's all he knew."

"He wasn't holding out?"

"I doubt it. A geeky sociologist drink of water called Benji. Think they snapped him in half."

I'm certain they did. "So, what now?" There's an irksome seed in my mind.

He glances at the door. "Well. That's where you come in."

*Uh huh.*

I blink a few times, cross my arms. "You said I would have free rein on this."

"That was then. Things have changed. I need information, and given who she's been associating with, Glass almost certainly has it."

"No." It comes out louder than I intended. It's my turn to glance at the door. "We had a deal. Essie's mine."

His face reddens as his shoulders pull back. At his full height, Langford is at least six inches taller than me, and he knows how to use it. "I don't know what pies you have your fingers in, Kerry, or what you're doing with them, but you should take care to remember who you work for."

I need to row this back. With a chastened smile, I say, "I know you're in control, Alex. I do. You're right: I have a score to settle with Essie Glass, and I was hoping this would be my opportunity. But of course, defeating the terrorists is a higher priority."

Langford smooths down his bald scalp. "Okay. We can come to an agreement."

I turn my gratitude on him as he peers down at me, searching for signs of deception. He won't find them. "Really?"

Alex the Magnanimous smiles. "If Glass co-operates. *If* I get what I want from her, then she's yours. And whatever revenge trip you're on, good luck. I won't pretend the idea of her suffering distresses me."

"I appreciate that."

He runs his finger along the glossy worktop. "I assume she's still at large."

"She is."

"And you have a plan to bring her in?"

"In progress."

He nods then smirks. "Like you said, plausible deniability."

"I'll call you when it's done."

He's silent, just raises his eyebrow.

"I will. You have my word."

"How about to avoid any confusion, I have someone assist you?"

*You wily, suspicious wanker.*

"Sure. That would be helpful. Thanks, Alex."

His grin broadens. "That's settled then. There's a guy I've used before for arms-length stuff. Ex-CIA. Name's Chet. Well, that's what he calls himself. I've always wondered if he made up that name. I'll have him make contact."

"Great."

*Yeah. Really great.*

He looks at his oversized, diamond-edged watch. "Good. Well, I've got a COBRA meeting to chair."

Oh? "What about?"

He snorts. "Take your pick. Surviving the Great Flood; quashing The Great Rebellion. Any number of other shitstorms I'm not aware of yet."

"Yeah. This governing lark can be tricky, I guess. Still, this rain... good for business, eh?"

His eyes rove my face, no doubt searching for signs I'm mocking him. I give him a sympathetic smile. On his way past the front room, he ducks in and peers at Willow, who sits staring at one of the book covers. It's a picture of a princess in a purple dress. Langford grunts and moves on.

He pauses at the front door and mutters, "I'll send Chet round as soon as. But you call me the minute you detain Glass. If I find out—"

"Alex, you have my word."

With a nod, he's gone.

Taking in a long breath, I rest my head on the door. There's no way of knowing if Langford will keep his word. In fact, it's entirely possible he will extract what he needs from Essie and have her killed. Likely, even. What choice did I have? Putting up a fight would have led to more awkward questions. I still have the prototype; and Jack. And I can still stick it to Langford, even with Essie dead. Shame, though. It pains me, but I respect the girl. She's got balls.

When I return, Willow is gazing at the purple princess again, tears sliding down both cheeks.

"Can I get you something to eat?"

She shakes her head, still staring at the book.

"Another drink?"

Her eyes lift to me. "That man tried to kill my mummy. Before I was born."

I can't think of a denial that would wash. "How do you know?"

She wipes her nose with the back of her hand and glares at me. "You're going to give my mummy to him so he can try again."

"What makes you think that?"

"Adults always think kids aren't listening when they talk about bad stuff."

"Well, that's true." I can't suppress a chuckle.

She gives a wretched sob. "I hate you."

# Chapter Twenty-Four

## Essie

### 22 November 2041

Kerry's fingers crush Willow's throat. They glare into one another's faces, Kerry's growing redder while Willow's turns blue.

I wake up, a tortured scream trapped and burning in my chest. Struggling to inhale, I sit up. When it comes, my breath is panicked and raw, scored by moans.

Ami's bedroom is airless. It doesn't help that the window is nailed shut, but the sweat soaking into the lumpy mattress stinks of my terror. Just an awful dream, yet the sobs come. As if it was a premonition. As if, by dreaming it, I might have made it happen.

*You're being irrational, Ess.*

No doubt.

Grabbing Ami's gun from under the pillow, I force myself out of bed and into the grubby kitchen. At least its tiny window is open, letting in a fragile airstream with the smell and hiss of the rain. It's dark outside; must still be early morning.

There's an upturned glass on the draining board. Tucking the gun in my waistband, I rinse and fill the tumbler with tap water. Lukewarm though it is, it soothes my aching throat. It strikes me how like my old flat back in Balmford this place is. Right down to the damp smell. I'm transported to a time before any of this happened. Before Jack's carbon capture tech… Kerry… Langford and his cold brutality.

*Before Seth and Willow.*

I had so little to lose. Even then, I understood that was why I was so dangerous. So hard for them to put down.

And now?

So much more to lose; so easy to trap.

I've been such a fool. Thinking I could live anything like a normal life. And to bring a child into the middle of this. Born to be weaponised. To pay the price of my desire for healing.

The glass slips from my hand and dinks on the floor. My fingers hook into my hair, tugging until strands rip free. Like I'm frozen in the dream again, my mouth gapes in a silent cry as I sink to my knees. Finally, a wheezing sob comes out, and that opens the floodgates. Reason is gone, and all I can hold in my mind are Seth and Willow, and what might happen to them because of me.

It's years since I've been driven to it, but my nails find my wrists. With horrifically accurate muscle memory, they resume their old gouging. The pain is immediate and soothing.

I stay that way for a time, until the blood trickling down my arms drips on the lino, swirling in the puddle of my spilled water. My stomach churns, my mouth is dry and sour.

I need air.

Pulling the gun out of my waistband, I crawl across the kitchen. I grab my bag from the chair, shove in the gun, and scramble to my feet. Outside, huge, warm drops slam into my face and wash the blood from my stinging wrists. I'm glad it's still raining.

Ami's ground-floor flat is up a dingy, inclined side street. When I reach the wider road below, something cold first laps at, then soaks my trainers. Further on, anxiety buzzes between hundreds of people who wade through dark water that reaches their knees. The air smells of the river. Though most of the streetlights are out, enough sickly orange light remains on the relentless motion of the crowd. They're all going in the same direction. A young couple pass near me, their legs wrapped in black bin bags. The man is dragging a plastic sled heaped with a few belongings and a toddler, asleep under a tarpaulin.

Disorientation washes over me. I don't know what part of London I'm in. When we arrived—how could it only be a day or so?—it was so late. Kim led me down a warren of tunnels, then through a maze of streets, until I lost my bearings.

Sloshing further into the road, I'm jostled by shoulders and hands, which push and pull me out of the way.

"Excuse me." I halt a bearded man by pressing a hand on his arm. "Where are we?"

He stares at me. "Hackney. Or hell, can't tell which." He sounds as if he's from the Midlands like me.

"What's happening? Where's everyone going?"

"The river's gonna bust with the rain. They're sayin' the Thames barrier might collapse."

"*Collapse?*"

But he's moving on, shaking me off like a mosquito. I gaze at the slabbed sky and concrete around me.

No drones. Or cops. No Unity thugs.

This many people on the streets, they should be here, tooled up and ready. Their absence could only mean things are going very wrong.

*Perfect time to start a revolution, Kim...*

But I've got other things on my mind. Sodden jeans clinging to my calves, I splash to the side of the road. Leaning against a dusty concrete of a tower block, I rummage in my bag for the phone and check my calls.

Nothing. Just the stark white display telling me it's six-fourteen am.

"Call me back, Kerry, you bitch."

There's cold river water, warm rain, and, in between, my trembling limbs.

I don't think, just dial Seth's number.

It rings.

Rings again.

Again.

I pace back and forth, the soles of my trainers slapping in the shallows.

*Pick up ... Please. Pick up.*

I'm about to give in when there's a click.

"Up early, Essie?" Kerry sounds wide awake.

"Where?"

"Well, good morning to you, too."

My free hand frets at the wrist below my phone and it throbs. "Don't fuck me about, Tyler. *Where*?"

She pauses, and I can almost hear her smirk. "Not yet."

*Bitch.*

"No, you don't." The words have to fight through my clenched teeth. "Tell me where you are. Now."

Another beat. "I'll send you a location."

She's gone.

I prowl the pavements, dodging evacuees who pay me no attention. Images of what I want to do to Kerry come at me in the dark. I picture my hands around her throat, like I dreamed hers around Willow's. My chest heaves with hatred and the want of Seth and Willow.

*Stop it, Ess. You're no good to them like this.*

I breathe deeply, trying to clear my mind, to focus on what I have to do next.

My phone buzzes. She's sent me a post code and, '*Come alone, obvs*'. I tap it into the navigator. It's five miles to the west, in Primrose Hill. Hitching my rucksack higher, I force my trembling legs to co-ordinate.

As I walk, the light grows warmer, bouncing off ruined

blocks of flats and shuttered betting shops. Further west, the river water recedes and the crowds thin, though the rain persists. By the time the flats morph into Victorian brick, nobody is on the streets. Perhaps they think the flooding will be localised, because Primrose Hill is not evacuating.

Neat Georgian terraces line Edis Street. I limp down the row, mouth dry as dust, realising she never gave me a house number.

"Don't go in there."

The voice behind me makes me cry out.

Piper's eyes bulge as she steps back.

"Would you stop bloody following me?"

She gives me a weak smile. "Kim's orders this time." She holds up a new phone which must have replaced the one she gave me. "I paired our SIMs so I could find you again. Sorry."

"Well, you can just *un*-find me. This doesn't concern you."

She opens her mouth to respond.

"Essie." From the other direction.

I whip around. Kerry's head pokes out of a door in a slate-grey painted house.

My feet plant on the tarmac. Her eyes darken as they rove me. Even in the morning shadows, I must look a state; filthy with dirt and blood; soaked with fear and rain.

Her gaze drifts to Piper a few paces behind. "You were supposed to come alone."

"I am." I turn to Piper. "Go. Now."

Piper doesn't move, except to shake her head.

Fury spikes my chest. "Are you trying to screw this up for me? This is my *family*, Piper. Go."

"No." Kerry glances behind her, then steps out, pulling the door to. With hands plunged in the pockets of her cardigan, she stalks towards us, looking at Piper. "If you've come this far, then you know too much."

Now she's close, the weight of the gun in her pocket is obvious. I think of Ami's pistol inside my rucksack. But it's on my back, and there's no way to retrieve it before Kerry intercepts.

206

Kerry clutches Piper's arm, tugging her towards the house, though Piper offers no resistance. There's no attempt to handle me. She must know I'll follow.

As we reach the flag-stoned porch, Kerry locks the front door, then pushes ahead and halts us with a hand. Nodding over my shoulder, she says, "Bag."

*Shit.*

I shrug off the rucksack. She takes it, grimacing at the filth caking the handles. As she deposits it on top of a small mahogany sideboard, a something scrapes behind a door ahead.

Kerry straightens. Her hand shoots out again, hitting my chest. "Stay—"

"Mummy?"

"Wills."

I shove through Kerry's arm to meet Willow as she bursts out of the back room, ricocheting against the side panel of the stairway opposite. And then she's right here. My daughter is in my arms. My limbs thrum with her. I drop to my knees and bury my face in her greasy, matted hair, tears flowing into her curls. She's crying too, an open-mouthed, abandoned sob.

When I can speak, I ask, "Where's Daddy?"

Her head shakes under my chin. "They took him away. Mummy, what happened to your wrists?"

I glare up at Kerry, who has slipped between us and the door Willow ran from. "Where is he?" I try to sound fierce, though tears still roll down my cheeks.

With a rueful downturn of her mouth, she says, "I'm sorry."

*Sorry? Oh God, he's dead.*

Willow wriggles. Aware I've been squeezing, I release her. Hot and cold flush me in waves as I stand. "What did you do to him?"

Willow's breath hitches. "He's done nothing *wrong*."

"That doesn't matter to these people." Piper steps closer from the porch behind. "Right, Kerry? Yeah, I know who you are."

Kerry looks at me, nostrils flaring. "You didn't leave me much choice. What did you think was going to happen when you fucked me over?"

"That doesn't mean—"

"I knew you were up to something those last few calls to Havana. Jack all vague and cagey. And *you*...sitting there twitching like a bloody bug on a pin. Do I look that stupid to you?" She whips out her gun, striding closer.

Pushing Willow behind me, I flinch back.

Not far enough. She grabs the front of my shirt and yanks me towards her, then pivots and shoves me into the wooden panelling on the stairs. Willow yelps, ducking out of the way. My shoulder blades flare with pain.

"You're going to pay for that." Right in my face, Kerry leans, then draws back. A moment later, her palm stings my cheek.

Inside my mind is a haze of grief for Seth; of panic for me. I keep my face smooth and calm. "Fine. Do what you want with me. You always have. But Seth w-was innocent."

She sneers. "He wasn't, though, was he? I learned that from your own sweet, deceitful bitch mouth. Remember your conversation with Lawrence at His Majesty's Pleasure? Seth copied that file. The *stolen* file." She pouts. "Poor Lawrence. Too soft for this world by half."

*Lawrence too?*

"You killed them both."

*No... No more.*

My left eye blurs, the vision doubles. Despite the pain in my shoulders, I'm glad of the panelling behind me. Without it, I'd collapse at her feet.

She flicks her head. "I'm afraid Lawrence took his own

208

life. It was the guilt, see?"

Though the gun remains in her hand, I risk a step away to the side. "*Guilt? For what?* He did nothing wrong, either. And don't say Maya. This is me you're talking to. We both know who murdered Maya, and it wasn't Lawrence."

"Ah, but he left a note. Confessing to everything. To Maya, yes. Also to harbouring stolen commercial property. Not just any commercial property, either. A planet-saving prototype. You know the one."

I can only stare at her. "*Harbouring?*"

He said he'd flushed the original down the loo. Did he keep it after all? If he did, that means Kerry...

With a widening grin, Kerry steps towards me. "Yes."

"He didn't leave a suicide note."

"But he did, though."

"You beat it out of him."

"I have a photo of the note, if you'd like to see it."

"And then you killed him. You have the prototype."

It's a full-on smile on her face now. "You don't have to worry about that anymore." She reaches down and takes Willow's arm. More gently than she grabbed me, but she keeps the gun in a firm hold with the other hand.

"What does *that* mean?" My limbs tense, ready to fight

As Kerry pulls her away from me towards the stairs, Willow takes in a sharp breath, but submits. Kerry pockets the gun, moves a little further, then turns Willow with her to face me. "Come on up."

Piper draws level and glances at me. How much of that did she understand? I have no ideas, and Kerry is pushing Willow onto the first step.

"Take your hands off my daughter." It's almost a growl from my twisted lips.

Hands in the air, Kerry leans back.

Willow looks up at her. "That man is hiding up here, isn't he?"

My neck stiffens. "Man?"

Kerry huffs, and shoves Willow again, harder this time. "Get up there."

My heart is thumping. "*Don't touch her.* What man?"

Kerry's feet are disappearing up the stairs and she doesn't answer.

I grab Piper's arm and whisper, "There must be a back door somewhere. Go. Get out of here."

Jaw fixed, Piper shakes her head.

"The back door's not an option, by the way." Kerry's voice drifts down from above. "Unless you've got a set of bolt cutters handy. Up you come."

All the breath and hope for Piper drain out of me. Any hope I had for myself went with Seth. I trudge after them to the first floor, and Piper follows. Kerry waits across the varnished landing in front of a gloss-white door. Grey light seeps in from the window beside her. She places one hand on Willow's shoulder. The other holds the gun again. I grit my teeth.

"Come on." Kerry speaks as though to a child, but she's looking at me.

The door slides open, revealing a sparse but stylish bedroom of white linen and exposed floorboards. Willow was right. A man is sitting on the bed. I recognise him from somewhere, but my brain is racing. I can't catch hold of who he is. When I glance behind me, Kerry shoves Willow inside the room. The man reaches out, pulling her to him and though it's gentle, it's enough.

I'm not going to run now. If I ever was.

"Well, hello there."

With his stupid accent, I finally place him. It's Bible Belt. The one who took me from Langford's house that awful night. Drove me to Langford's factory, where they almost killed Jack and me.

Kerry closes the door and leans against it, glaring at Piper so she moves further into the room.

"Langford?" I hate how scared I sound.

"He didn't leave me much choice." The rueful twist of Kerry's mouth could be genuine. "I might have my unresolved conversations with you, but Langford's are more important. For now."

My insides are hollow. The muscles in my legs melt. It's only by holding on to the wall I can stay upright. "He'll have me killed." I regret my weakness when Willow sobs.

"I hope not." Kerry seems to mean this, too. She glanccs at Piper, who is standing stiffly by the adjacent wall.

My eyes fill with hot tears. "Willow. She can't—"

"She stays with me."

"No," Willow and I say at once.

No matter how hot my hate for Kerry, she's my only lifeline. "Please, Kerry. Don't…"

Kerry shakes her head and hands Bible Belt a key. "You want to call him, or shall I?"

"You do it." He's pulling something out of his pocket. Cable ties. He moves towards Piper, who tries to back away, though she's huddled in the corner.

"You don't need to use those."

Bible Belt ignores me. He grabs Piper's arm and spins her to face the wall. The tie zips on her wrists and she groans, the shaking in her body coming out as a vibrato.

My brain scrambles to track everything as Kerry takes Willow's hand and pulls her out of the room.

"Nooooo." Willow's cries diminish as the door closes and Kerry takes her down the stairs.

I strain my ears, but moments later there's nothing to hear.

All reason gone, I lunge towards the door. "Kerry. *You bitch.* Bring her back!"

Bible Belt slaps a hand over my mouth and drags me backward. With everything I've got, I fight, kicking and punching whatever's within reach. My fist smacks into his jaw. He yells, falling backwards, but not far enough. Before I can move again, he's grabbed me round the throat. He throws me to the floor. My head bounces off the wood. In seconds, he's on me. Flips me over on to my front and locks the cable tie around my wrists. The sharp plastic pierces the wounds I made myself, and warm blood tickles my palms.

Leaving me on the floor, Bible Belt rises. Metal rattles on metal as he locks us in. Silence follows, except for Piper's hitching breaths and my panting. What's left of my strength gives way and my cheek slaps against the floorboards. I can't even raise my head to locate Bible Belt.

Knowing it's no use, I pull against the cable tie. So soon after I found her, I'm empty with the loss of Willow. The wound where Seth used to be is something I don't dare touch.

The burning in my wrists is a pain I can bear. That, and the instinctive, mindless dread of what comes next, fill me up so I don't have to think.

# Chapter Twenty-Five

## Essie

No one speaks. The bed groans as Bible Belt sits. Piper sniffles from the bedroom corner. A racing pulse drums in my ears. There's no noise from downstairs. Nothing but the rain sounds on the street. The whiff of floor polish irritates my nose.

After a while, I shift onto my side so I can look at the door's glossy paintwork. I try to make my mind white and smooth just like it, marking off the moments with blinks and breaths. When thoughts try to break in, I pull against the binding and reopen the wounds on my wrists. A hiss escapes my teeth, but the burning soothes.

The bed groans again. "You hurting yourself over there, baby?" He's crouched behind me now and pulls my arms away from my back, tutting. "You'll put me out of a job."

I relax my hands inside the tie and focus on the door. There's a bubble in the paintwork. I try to imagine how it would feel to dig a fingernail into it. I used to love doing that when I was a kid. Mum and Dad weren't great at decorating, so there were always plenty of flaws.

More bed sounds, so I guess Bible Belt has left me be for now. How long before Langford gets here? I doubt he'll be so restrained. My arms go cold with the memory of the beating; the scars he gave me.

Now he's coming to finish what he started.

*You're thinking, Ess. Stop it.*

Back to the paintwork. Imagine a smooth, straight road going to a peaceful place. That's what the therapist used to tell me in those early days after the bombing. When the loss of my family was so raw, it eclipsed everything else.

*Lost your second family now.*

Stop. Please.

A tear rolls over my nose and drips. I focus on the paint bubble. A knock on the door makes me jump. Bible Belt comes over and unlocks it, and my paint bubble moves out of sight.

Langford's presence compels me to sit. I won't grovel on the floor in front of him. This man I never wanted to see in the flesh again. He peers down at me, a sneer twitching at his lips. "Long time no see."

I narrow my eyes at him, but my heart is thumping, nausea churning. That night... I thought he was going to beat me to death. Is he thinking of the same thing? Does he want to finish me? I could bear that, but for Willow. I'm all she has now Seth's...

My hands pull against the tie.

Willow.

Though they've taken her away from me, if I can just survive this...

Bible Belt slips out of the room as Langford walks over to the bed and sits on its edge. He makes a louder creak than Bible Belt. He's a much bigger man. All I want to do is turn back to the door and stare at my paint bubble. My eyes are wrenched in his direction as I wriggle back against the wall. Still smirking at me, he plants his knees wide and clasps his hands between them. The stillness of him makes my skin prickle. The only other time I've met him, Langford was furious with me for stealing the prototype. His violence still dominates those dreams when I have them. This new, controlled version of Langford—it's no less terrifying.

He shoots a look at Piper, then back at me. "Still leading your friends to the slaughter, then?"

214

*Slaughter?*

He laughs. The contemptuous bark that's been impossible to forget. "You used to have so much to say for yourself."

It wasn't my plan, this silence. But since I've started, it's the best course of action for now.

"Kerry won't help you this time. She works for me." He leans his forearms on thick thighs. "You're going to jail for the rest of your shitty life, you know that?"

*Smooth, straight road going to a peaceful place...*

"How that goes is down to you. Well, to me. But you can influence my position on the matter." He raises his eyebrows, clearly expecting a question.

I say nothing, suppressing the urge to swallow.

"God, I've gotta hand it to you. I thought you'd be all hissy fits and cat fighting." He looks at the ceiling, raising his palms in a theatrical posture. "'*Why, whatever could you mean, Alex?*' Well, Essie, let me explain." He switches his cold eyes back to me and lets them burn for a moment. "Tell me everything you know about the rebellion. *Everything.* Dates, times, locations. Names. Where are they hiding? What weapons do they have? What are their objectives?"

"You're mental." Piper leans forward from her corner, her tone flat with mock wonder.

He pivots on the bed. "Shut up. I'll get to you in a minute." Then he's back. "Talk to me. This is your one way out of a bad situation. I'm usually a patient man." He ignores my scoff. "But I don't have time to soft-soap. It's not prototypes and factories anymore. This is about national security."

"You mean power."

*For Christ's sake, Piper, stop.*

Langford rises from the bed and strides over to Piper. They glare at each other. Then Langford pulls back a foot and

215

whips it into Piper's thigh. She utters a wheezy yelp and flops to the side.

My nerves fire, burning my limbs. "Leave her alone."

He twists. "Oh, it speaks." Turning back to Piper, he kicks her bandaged shoulder, then returns to the bed, breathing hard.

My eyes flit between Piper, curled up, whimpering on the floor, and his flushed face. "Like beating teenage girls, don't you?" I bite my mouth shut.

He barks. Probably because he enjoyed that. Also, I suspect, because I just played my hand and he clocked it.

"I'm giving you an opportunity to answer my questions now. If you co-operate, I can make sure you're both held in a reasonable place. I mean, it'll be a prison because you're criminals. But you'll be treated well enough. If you don't..." He lets it float in the air for a moment, and peers at me. "You'll spill everything in the end. It's just a question of how much you can take." A little twitch of his mouth. "Why not spare yourself?" He points behind him. "And her. You can save her suffering. Make something good out of this."

His argument is undeniable. I'm in no position to be a hero. Willow... And he's right, I have to protect Piper. Too many people I love have died in their custody for me to brush off Langford's threat.

*You're gonna kneel to this animal, Ess?*

My last conversation with Kim comes back to me. I could tell him the wrong date for the uprising. It might even help Kim; give them the element of surprise.

*So you're going to surrender. Then what was it all for? Why did Maya die? And Lawrence?*
*Seth...*

A sharp yank at the cable tie shuts down the thought. As the blood oozes out of my wrists, I lift my chin to him. "I have no idea what you're talking about. *Sir.*"

216

A purse of the lips, a brief nod, then he rubs his hands on his trousers. "Well, okay then." He stands and strides past me with barely a glance. At the door, he pauses and turns. "Remember this chance I gave you."

The moment he slams and locks the door, Piper explodes into sobs.

"Are you okay, Pipes?"

Stupid question, but she nods through her tears. Blood is seeping through her bandage.

"I'm so sorry you got dragged into this. My fault."

"No." She wipes her nose with her good shoulder. "My fault. I begged Kim to let me follow you. She wanted to come herself."

"God, then we would be screwed. Kim in custody, with everything she knows?"

In a small, trembling voice, she says, "We know enough."

"Pipes." Was she close enough to hear my conversation with Kim? "I'm not going to talk, no matter what. But if it gets too rough, you—we—tell them it's set for the thirtieth. Okay?"

She nods. "Ess…" Her eyes seek mine, but when she opens her mouth again, no words come out.

The lock rattles, and my mouth fills with metallic dread. It's not Langford, it's Bible Belt again, Kerry lurking on the landing behind him.

I cock my head to peep around him at Kerry. "Where's my daughter?"

"She's safe." Kerry sidesteps Bible Belt and enters the room. "I will make sure she's okay. You have my word."

"Your *word*?" I check myself. "Please. Keep her away from Langford."

She nods, and for some reason, I believe she'll at least try.

"There's a toy of hers, a green rabbit, in my bag. Boop." I have to stop and bite my lips in hard for a moment. Something else needles me. I lift my arms and twist to the side. "I don't want her to see me like this." My voice wavers, my eyes sting, because all I want is to see her.

"She won't."

217

"Come on, baby." Bible Belt catches hold of my arm and lifts me to my feet.

Piper is sliding herself up the wall. He moves to help her, lining us up for departure. My eyes find Kerry once more. She's frowning, hands clasped together. All the same, she moves aside, letting Bible Belt hustle us onward and down the stairs.

There's a black van waiting in front of the house. Heavy drops of rain bounce off its bonnet. I wonder at their doing this in daylight, grey as it is, but a second later I almost laugh at myself. Langford is untouchable. Nobody is around, and if they were, they wouldn't care. For all I know, he owns this street. Bible Belt opens the van doors and watches while we struggle into its windowless back. The doors slam, throwing us into darkness. I close my eyes and rest my head on the bare metal interior, exhausted now the fight is over. With a judder and a whine, we're in motion. Piper shuffles closer and leans against me, her breathing unsteady.

"I'm sorry," I say. "So sorry."

I'm not sure if I'm addressing Piper or Willow. Every turn takes me further away from my daughter, and closer to the place I'm going to die.

It's only fifteen minutes' drive, but it's long enough for Piper to doze off, her head lolling against my shoulder, breath deep and hoarse. Sleep won't come for me, which is just as well. The horrific dreams would surely follow.

The van slows, then idles. The whine of a drone approaches, drowning out the electrics. When it recedes, we roll on. The deep rattling up ahead wakes Piper. She smacks her lips and mumbles something unintelligible.

"I think we've arrived, Pipes."

We sit in tense silence as the van halts. The door on the driver's side opens and bangs shut, rocking us. Footsteps crunch and then light floods the van. Though it's still raining outside, the glare stabs my exhausted eyes.

Bible Belt steps aside to make room. "Out."

With arms tied behind us, the only way to get out is to sit and shuffle off the edge. Bible Belt stays back and watches our performance. Rain pelts us, thrumming on the sticky red ground.

We're in a penned yard bordered by high mesh fencing, topped with razor wire. Huge yellow signs nailcd to its posts warn us the fence is electrified with lethal charge. Beyond the boundary lies an indistinct grey landscape of rubble dominated by a hulking low-rise concrete building. Bible Belt bends, removes a knife from his sock, and cuts our ties, first Piper's, then mine. Pressure released, my wrists bleed in earnest, but the pain diminishes.

A guard approaches us from the towering concrete building ahead. He's dressed in a black jumpsuit and flak jacket, the Hands of Kinship sewn on his lapel in white.

He glances down at my wrists as he mutters, "Welcome to Broadwater." Only he doesn't sound very welcoming.

Bible Belt clears his throat. "Personal orders of Prime Minister Langford. The details have been sent ahead."

The guard nods at Bible Belt, who ducks against the rain and scuttles back to his van.

"Let's get you booked in." The guard takes my arm. His manner isn't threatening, but the strength of his grip rachets up my dread another few notches.

We're led inside through the reinforced metal entrance and down a grey corridor to a row of doors. The guard halts at the end, wrestles the last one open, and gestures us inside. Without speaking, he slams it closed. The lock rattles and he's gone.

Eyes screwed shut, Piper slides down the wall, her boots scraping the tiled floor. "Shit. Oh shit, Ess. What now?"

"Shhh. It's okay." Am I trying to comfort her or shut her up? Both. There's a camera high on the wall, which is no doubt recording us. I move over to sit beside her, catching her attention with a wave and pointing up to the lens. She pulls in a breath and clamps her mouth shut.

We sit in silence, in this room that smells of metal and sweat, for I don't know how long. The door rattles again. A tall guard with a scurfy beard marches in and tilts his head at me to move. Glancing at Piper as her brow furrows, I rise to meet him. He takes my arm and leads me through a maze of corridors. All have grey walls that seem to bend in towards me and are lined with metal doors. We arrive at one that opens on a white-tiled room. The brightness, after so much time in the dark today, makes my eyes water. A metal table and two opposing chairs sit in the middle of the small space. There's a disinfectant smell in the air. A steel medical trolley nestles against the far wall with a small metal cabinet. Every part of this place is metal or grey or both. On top of the cabinet sits a folded red garment.

A woman wearing the black Unity uniform with her hair in a tight bun and a brisk manner enters the room. She pastes a tight smile on her bronzed face and bangs the door closed. "Estella Glass?"

I suppress my usual response. I hate my full name, but I doubt this woman would care. "Yes."

She drops the clipboard she's been clutching on the table. "I'm Prison Officer Thornberry. I'll be processing you."

"Processing?" My tired brain pictures my legs being fed through a sausage machine.

She huffs, as though this is a waste of her time. "Paperwork, security checks, hygiene and medical." Her eyes flick over my bloody wrists.

"Oh."

"Sit." She gestures to the nearest chair while moving around to the far one. "You need to sign these forms." Several papers are attached to the clipboard.

"What are they?"

She arches an eyebrow at me. I guess prisoners rarely dare to ask. "Just formalities." Another sigh. "Look, you're in Broadwater. This is the end of the road for you. Either way you belong to the state now. What does it matter what forms they are?"

I grab the pen tethered to the clipboard and sign the forms with a shaky hand. The last sheet is titled 'Mental Health Screening Form'. I'm instructed to answer a series of questions aimed at finding out if I'm going to top myself. I make my answers as jolly as possible. The last thing I need is more attention.

When I'm done, Officer Thornberry nods and points behind me. "Okay, take your clothes off and lie face down on that trolley.

"What?"

Her face and neck grow blotchy red. "Cavity search. It's no more pleasant for me than you, love. Get over yourself."

A lump growing in my throat, I obey. There's no curtain, so I have to fumble my jeans and knickers off with her watching. I struggle onto the trolley, its cold steel biting at my skin, giving me goosebumps.

While her hands glide and probe, I try to imagine that smooth, straight road to a peaceful place, but the thought just makes my eyes sting with wretched tears. I wipe them away.

"You're not the first to break down on this trolley, love. Don't worry about it." She mumbles this, but her tone is softer. "Okay, done. You can put that on." She points to the red fabric, which turns out to be a thin cotton robe.

Officer Thornberry busies herself disposing of her equipment and tidying the paperwork while I dress. The robe smells musty, like badly washed hotel sheets. Then again, I don't suppose I'm too sweet underneath it either. I haven't had a proper wash in ages, and there's been a fair bit of muck, sweat and blood since then.

As if she heard my thoughts, Officer Thornberry says, "Right. Shower next. Your first day you get to shower alone. After that it's communals, so make the most of it."

She leads me along more corridors to the shower block. It looks so like my old school showers, as if I've slipped back in time. Grey floors, white tiles and grubby, limescale-encrusted shower heads. Thornberry gives me a bottle of liquid soap to use and steps back to watch as the showers spray. The soap stings my skin and sets my wrists on fire. Disinfectant, I guess. They've tried to make it smell nice, but the strong piney stink just reminds me of the stuff Mum used to clear up Darya's sick when she was a baby.

"Wash your hair," says Thornberry.

221

*With this? It'll fall out.*

I obey. Feels like it's stripping half of my hair away, but then it was half made up of grease and sweat. She hands me a towel and a different pile of red material with underwear and a pair of black plimsoles on top. The fabric is a stiff denim jumpsuit. A series of numbers are dyed on the back and lapel.

41-77986.

My prisoner number. The tears well again.

After where her hands have been, I guess she thinks I've got nothing left to hide, but my cheeks still burn as I dress.

*Better get used to it.*

It's a miserable voice speaking to me from the pit of my belly. I block it out, think of nothing as she leads me to yet another room and takes my photograph.

"Right then, let me show you to your suite."

I'm sure she means that to be humorous. She's set off ahead of me, so can't see my scowl. More corridors punctuated with hefty, barred gates. Then we're in the prison wing. A great expanse of metal walkways and stairs opens. At least it's lighter in here. Cream metal and skylights high above us have replaced the grey metal and let in some light. The air is burning hot and the smell of stale sweat catches the back of my throat.

Officer Thornberry leads me to a door halfway along. "You're lucky you're in the ones. They try to allocate new fish to ground floor cells. In case anyone tries to…" She mimes a push.

I swallow the lump. I get the idea. "Where's Piper?"

Thornberry unlocks the door. "She'll be on another wing. They separate associates." She tips her head. "Come on."

I step past her into my cell. It's just big enough to house a single bed, a toilet, and a small sink. A pamphlet entitled *Life in Broadwater* sits on the bed. The front cover shows a picture of two women in natural-look makeup and red jumpsuits smiling as they walk together in what I assume is the exercise yard. There's no window and sweat soaks my clothes in moments. No wonder this place stinks so much.

From the door, Officer Thornberry gives me a rueful smile. "Get some sleep if you can. It's a few hours until dinner."

The bang of the door as she leaves distorts in my ears. I collapse onto the hard, lumpy mattress, desolate tears rolling down my cheeks. Even after everything that's happened, I can't remember feeling so adrift.

# Chapter Twenty-Six

## Essie

### 23rd November 2041

*Essie.*

Seth's screaming for me across a marshy wasteland that smells of rot and petrol. Storm clouds flit across the sky—left to right, then back again. As though they're in a sandbox, and a giant toddler is shaking it. I can barely see my own feet in the gloom. Twisted reeds tangle and trip me.

More cries, from further away. I try to follow the sound, but my feet wedge in the bracken and gunge. My throat closes in on itself as I fall, but not enough to bar the putrid marsh water. It burns and chokes...

The sound of my stomach convulsing wakes me. I roll and vomit over the side of the bed, wiping my watery eyes with my forearm. The sulphur still clings to the inside of my mouth and nose.

Just a dream.

*Yes. A dream. Seth's gone.*

I vomit again, and the tears are more than a reflex. I bury my head in the stale pillow and emit a silent sob. Less than twenty-four hours in jail, and I've learned to keep my weak spots hidden.

Thornberry was right, they took Piper somewhere else. I haven't seen her since my processing yesterday, not even when they released me from my cell for dinner last night.

Dinner. A slop of salty, lumpy mash and a hunk of

unnamed, unidentifiable protein which took some chewing. Jaw aching, I sat in the sweltering grey-painted hall and ate every mouthful and then crunched on the slice of dry sponge cake served for pudding. I hadn't realised how hungry I'd been until my belly was full. Sitting alone, I spoke to no one, though the hall was two-thirds full. Sixty other women prisoners scattered in groups at the nailed-down grey steel tables. Not the hard-eyed, wide-shouldered mob I'd been expecting. Some of them looked like people I could be friends with. Others seemed weary and beaten down. One girl, a couple of years older than me, smiled through a heavy gloss-black fringe as I passed her table. She reminded me of Maya. I decided I would say hello to her later.

It wasn't hard to pick out the Queen Bitch, even before she spotted me.

That's what they call her, though not to her face. In her presence, they use her self-appointed title of Bee—presumably also as in Queen. Bee is not wide-shouldered, but she is hard-eyed. She's a redhead like me, and wire thin with a wrong-footing, coiled air. She's ready, whatever.

At the end of dinner, the guards lined us up along the breeze block wall to take us back to our cells. Someone closed in behind me and a sharp pain flashed in my kidney. With a muffled yelp, I whipped around and there was Queen Bee, her eyes narrowed.

"Another fucking Polly scumming up the place." To the ripple of laughter behind her, she stepped closer and pressed her face into mine. The fist that grabbed my jumpsuit had the Hands of Kinship tattooed across its freckled back. "We don't want any of you people here causing trouble, okay? You better keep your head down if you don't want it stamped on." She leaned back, leaving a trail of eggy breath behind her.

"Calm it, Bee." A male guard took her by the arm, though not roughly, and led her ahead of the line, muttering platitudes as he pushed through the doors.

I swallowed the nausea, willing my heart to slow its hammering.

"Psycho bitch," said a soft Yorkshire accent. The girl who

had smiled at me earlier was scowling at the door where Bee had disappeared. "Bet she's letting that guard feel her up now, so he doesn't file a report."

Something red flashed behind her. A hand thrust into her hair and yanked it back until her face was pointing at the ceiling. A stocky woman spat in her face. "Fucking shut it, Pol."

"Okay, break it up, ladies." Officer Thornberry was cantering towards us from the back of the line. "Melody, cool it."

Melody released the clutch of hair and stepped back into line, an obsequious smile on her face, through which she said, "I'd watch your fucking step if I were you, Paki bitch."

"My family were from India, not Pakistan. Like, a hundred years ago." The younger woman rubbed her scalp and glared at Melody. I put a hand on her arm and shook my head. Her jaw remained clenched, but she kept her silence after that.

Clearly deciding the fight was over, Officer Thornberry drifted away. With a last hate-filled glare, Melody turned her back on us.

"I'm Idika." The girl who reminded me of Maya thrust out her hand.

It was such a courteous gesture, I took it. "Essie."

"You're a Polly, too, I guess."

"Polly?"

"Political prisoner. The con bitches in here hate us." She grinned. "Guess you've worked that out for yourself." As the line moved, Idika shuffled with it. "Don't know why they throw us in together. Except to make us Pollys suffer more." She rubbed at her fringe, revealing a bruised swelling on her forehead.

"Why do they hate us?" I arched my back as shooting pains burned from Melody's punch.

"Think we'll cause trouble, I suppose. Or they're Nazis. Dunno. Fuck 'em."

A gap had opened in front of her, so I nodded ahead. She trotted on, then turned back to me and said, "Were you at Kim's camp?"

226

It was so out of nowhere, I couldn't respond for a few beats. "Briefly."

"Kim's great. Got so many plans."

"Yeah." I glanced around, catching the eye of a squat, bald guard standing by the wall a few yards away. Trying to keep the edge out of my voice, I said, "Keep moving."

"Sure. See you at breakfast, then?"

In the corridor outside the hall, Idika followed a group down the corridor to the right. Officer Thornberry reappeared to herd the other half of us in the opposite direction, back to our cells. For a night that I passed caught in a mesh of terror and grief for Seth that won't let me go even now I'm awake.

I rise from the bed and shuffle over to the sink. Using the frayed flannel slung over its edge, I do my best to clean up the sick. I don't want to draw any attention. And besides, it's stinking out this tiny cell. My back protests with every movement, nerves shooting fire up my spine. Whether it's down to Melody's assault or the needling bedsprings, I'm not sure.

The worst of it comes up, but the stench hangs around no matter what I do. It's unlikely I'm the only inmate to throw up on her first night, so maybe there'll be no repercussions.

I've no idea of the time, but it feels like early morning. Perhaps I can settle back to doze for a short while before breakfast. My limbs and chest are leaden with exhaustion; my eyes, now they're dry of tears, are sore and crusted.

A clatter makes me yelp. The hatch is open, a pair of narrow, blue eyes peeping through it.

"Stand against the far wall," says a strident female voice through the gap.

Heart still thrumming, I drop the flannel and obey.

The eyes disappear as the hatch bangs closed, then the lock rattles and the door swings open. A female guard steps in. She's broad and tall but silhouetted against the strip light outside so I can't see her face. "Turn around."

"What's happening?"

She puts a hand to her side, where the outline of a batten protrudes from the curve of her hip. "Do it."

227

I turn.

"Hands behind your back."

Cold metal clamps over my wrists. They had healed a little, but they start up their familiar prickle as the guard grabs my arm and spins me to face her. My dread mounts while she marches me out of the cell, along the walkway and back through the door I came in yesterday.

*Only yesterday?*

No time to philosophise. Down the warren of dark corridors, the room she pushes me into is empty except for a chair in the centre. A single spotlight shines on it. Like something out of an old quiz show from when I was a kid. It's so corny I almost laugh, but it's not funny. The guard pulls me around and down into the chair, my cuffs clinking against its metal. She leaves without looking back, locking the door behind her.

Silence stretches.

"H-hello?" My voice quivers in time to my heart.

No answer comes. I shift, trembling in the chair, and swallow bile—all that's left after my vomit wake-up call. Sweat turns cold on my forehead, though the room is sweltering.

The door bangs open behind me. Shock expels air from my lungs. My head whips around. All I can see is movement and shadow. Footsteps grind on the concrete floor. To the left, then right, just out of the spotlight's reach. It's a tall man.

He stops in front of me and steps into the light. His black guard's uniform sags at the throat and is too short in the arms. Slicked-back white-blond hair drags on his collar. Almost-black eyes focus on me from a veined face. His aura calls to mind Queen Bee. That coiled manner, the lifted chin that forces the gaze to angle down the nose.

Shoulders cramping with terror, I return his glare. We freeze for a few moments, then he sidles behind me again. When I try to track him, my back spasms, so I return to the front.

Through the gap in the chair back, his fingers peck my arms. With a rattle and click, the handcuffs are gone. I pull my throbbing arms around, rubbing at my wrists. Blood slickens my grip.

He's back in front of me again.

*For Christ's sake, speak.*

Anything, the vilest threat, would be better than this silence.

"What do you want?" I *hate* myself for breaking first.

He crouches, peering into my face. This close, it's obvious he dyes his hair. Dark roots infest his temples. He reaches out long fingers and clutches my wrist. Clamping his hands like a bracelet, he twists them in opposite directions, quick and hard.

The burning is white hot.

I scream and jolt in the chair. He squeezes my wrist for a moment longer, then rises and steps back, yanking at the front of his ill-fitting jumpsuit, smoothing his hair, yanking again.

I cower into the chair, breathing hard and cradling my bleeding wrist.

The man steps behind me, but I don't have the strength to track him this time. A moment later, something thin and cold wraps around my neck. It tightens. That choking sound must be me, but it's fading as the pounding in my ears grows louder. My vision blurs, doubles. My lungs burn for air, but none will come. Limbs heavy, I watch my vision shut down in a haze of static.

The pressure eases. Breath rips into me, my chest convulsing. I fall from the chair, retching up the bile I swallowed. My hands fly to my throat and find blood.

The man's boots scuff in front of my face. My eyes climb two black-clad legs, a crotch, torso, unconcerned face.

His breathing is even, the only sign of exertion a slight flopping curl on his forehead which he smooths away. "Information."

I take a moment to twig he's answering my question.

"Get up."

When I don't move, he grabs my hair and lifts me back onto the chair. The handcuffs are out again. It happens before I can fight, my brain still sluggish. Just as well. Within seconds, he's cuffed my wrists to the post at the back of the chair.

Low light shines ahead of me. The far wall is one huge dark-tinted window. There's movement in the dimness beyond. A face looms the other side of the glass, underscored by a white collar and dark tie, topped by a gleaming bald head. I know that face and it turns every part of me cold.

Langford.

*No. No, please.*

Here for information, revenge. His greedy, craven eyes bore into mine as his sneer widens. He knows I can see him. And I'll bet he *likes* it.

This was inevitable. From the second I walked into Kerry's house on Primrose Hill. Before, even. This is where I've been heading.

Kim knew it. *Things will get rough for you.*

Time to deliver on my promise. There's nothing to lose and only one job left to do.

*But... Willow.*

I can't help her now. All I have is hope that Kerry keeps her word and keeps her safe.

*I'm sorry, little one. So, so sorry.*

I have to let her go so I can do this. I fix my eyes on Langford's face, let all the hate drown thoughts of my child. Everything he's done stokes the fire. Everyone he's killed. Maya... Seth. Millions more, in the end, with his callous greed for power.

Give Kim and the others a fighting chance to finish him. It's *for* Willow. The thought of not being there as she grows, of making an orphan of her when she has so much to face. The tears drip off my chin before I even know they're there.

Something slams into my temple, tipping me sideways on the chair.

"Pay attention." He's holding up a black rubber batten. "What do you know about the planned insurgency?"

"What?" My vision swims, the eye Langford damaged last time we met only seeing blurred shapes.

The batten smashes into my other temple, shoving my head to the opposite side.

"I want dates and locations. Now."

"I—I…" I don't have to fake it. My brain is scrambled, my head throbbing. Blood courses down the side of my face, trickling over the scar on my left eye.

"What do you know about Kim Vella?" The batten sways and jerks in the air as he paces. "Her whereabouts, plans, objectives." He stops and raises the batten level with my face. "Where is the London camp?"

My eyes slide past the weapon and find Langford's gaze again. He smiles coldly.

"Tell me the date." The blond man leans closer. "Now."

Langford's eyes probe me. He turns to the side and speaks to someone lurking in the deeper shadow.

I look Blondie Man hard in the eye. "I don't know what you're talking about."

The batten whips down.

*\*\*\**

The place I wake in is different. Not the hell room I was before. A smaller cell than mine, not quite dark. A little light bleeds from a crack under the door. I can see my hand, fingers clenched, silhouetted by my face. The metallic odour of blood spikes in my nose. Probably mine. Another light, tiny and red, twinkles in a high corner.

Camera.

It's cold—how do they manage that when the rest of the place is like a pipe stove? Asking even that silent question makes my head pulse. I stir, and my hip and throat throb in unison. A groan escapes me as I close my eyes.

Behind the lids, the batten comes down. I gasp and sit up, heedless of the pain all over. Hunched against the cold brick wall, I let the huge, whooping sobs escape.

I'm going to die in here. Nobody will know.

*And there's no one left to care but your helpless child.*

I scratch at my swollen wrists. My little rebellion: a punishment I can deal myself. But it doesn't help, only makes me cry harder. They've even taken that from me.

I barely react as the door bangs open. Or as I'm yanked up and shoved down corridors. I have no interest in them, or in the person who is pushing me. Or the pain they're inflicting. What does it matter? All that counts now is they get nothing from me.

My legs move on automatic, checking and switching with my guard's whim. I let my head and shoulders droop, watch the tiles track under my feet.

I'm back in that room, back in the chair under the spotlight. Waiting for Blondie Man to return. Let him come. I'll move my head to meet his batten this time. Hope to make up the critical velocity that will split my skull open.

Then it'll be over quicker. And they still get nothing.

I'm left alone. No handcuffs this time. No doubt they think I'm beaten. I stare at the rivulets on the concrete floor, rubbing the dried blood from my swollen cheeks.

How long was I out? Hours? Days?

Panic twists my guts when it occurs to me the uprising might have already erupted and failed.

*If that's true, why aren't you dead, Ess? Why this room again?*

The door opens. This is it.

Keeping my eyes down, I listen to his heavy, slow footsteps draw near. A different rhythm, so it's a different torturer. It hardly matters, but I look up, curious in a distant way. Who's going to deal the fatal blow?

Langford.

Poetic.

"Come to finish the job?" My voice cracks.

He blinks down at me, then reaches into the inside pocket of his jacket. My limbs tense, but he only pulls out a small, clear bottle, holding it out to me.

Frowning, I shake my head.

He rolls his eyes. "Jesus Christ, Glass, it's just water." He unscrews the top. "Drink."

Well, if he's attempting to poison me, he's doing me a favour. Trying to avoid touching his fat fingers, I take the bottle, then a large swig. I pour some into my palm, splashing it on my sore and throbbing face. It soothes the pain and makes me more alert. On impulse, I take another swig, but instead of swallowing it, launch it at Langford. It hits him in the chest, darkening his white linen shirt.

Face creased with affront, he darts back. "Nice." He lunges and slaps me on the ear. "Fucking animal."

"You've got a lot of time on your hands for a despot." I flip my hair out of my eyes and shoot him a glare. "Shouldn't you be dealing with the floods?"

His cheek twitches. "Right now, I'm dealing with you. Low life that you are, you're still a significant threat to national security."

"I could say the same about you."

His face jerks into something between a grin and a sneer. "There's the hell cat we've come to loathe. You're more fun when you're bitching."

I bare my teeth at him, but I'm oddly grateful for his appearance. Minutes ago, I'd all but given up. Langford's vile presence, and this rekindled hatred, give me something to fight.

A bright light flickers high behind the glass wall, which is no longer tinted dark. The door in the room beyond opens and Piper stumbles through it. Her blonde hair is dull and limp around her shoulders. There's a cut on her forehead, but she seems otherwise unharmed. Relief at seeing her alive disintegrates as my brain catches up. When Blondie Man follows her through the door, my whole body pulses in cold horror.

"No." I sound so weak, so already beaten.

Langford leans down to my level. "Okay, hell cat. Let's see what you're made of." He holds a hand up to Blondie Man, who throws Piper in the chair. "It gives me no pleasure that we've come to this."

"Really." I swallow bitter saliva from my stale mouth. Piper looks up and smiles, but even through the glass, it's obvious she's shaking. I wipe away the tears, only for more to replace them. My chest hitches.

"Nevertheless, time is a factor." Langford steps in front of me, obscuring my view of Piper. "So, one last chance to tell me what you know. The planned insurrection—give me the date, the locations. Where is Kim Vella's camp? Who else is involved in the conspiracy? I want names."

I try to calm the hurricane inside me, to slow the panic, but it's impossible. What day is it? How long do I need to hold out? And Piper...

It's useless, but I make the only choice I can. I turn my eyes up to his. "Wow, you are paranoid."

Perhaps I surprised him because he straightens, eyebrows raised, and laughs. With a finger in the air, he turns to the window. Blondie Man nods and holds up his hateful batten.

I clamp my eyes shut.

A muffled thud. Piper screams. Another. More.

Head bowed, I let out a sob.

Langford grabs my hair and tries to lift my gaze. "Open your eyes."

When I defy him, he jerks the fist entangled in my roots. Eyes still screwed shut, I'm raised from the chair and shoved forward, my scalp burning.

"*Open your fucking eyes.*" Langford pushes me again and I collide with something cold and hard.

My lids lift reflexively. He has me pressed against the glass. On the other side, Piper is curled up, legs still entangled with the overturned chair, hands over her head as Blondie Man looms. Her posture is stiff, and she's making a damped gurgling noise. Or the glass is distorting the sound. My breath freezes as Blondie Man grabs a knife from his belt. He bends down to Piper and presses it into her throat. She twitches her head.

Langford spins me around and presses against me, his hand still loosely grasping my hair. "Don't think she'll survive too much more, do you?"

*Say it, Ess.*

My knees buckle and Langford releases his hold, stepping back to let me slide down the glass.

My mouth and throat move, but even I don't hear my words.

Langford squats and grabs my chin. "What was that?"

"Stop. Please."

He holds up a palm to the room behind, then switches his gaze back to me. "Talk."

Pulling away from his grasp, I let my head loll. "The thirtieth. That's all I know."

"November?"

I nod.

"The camp?"

"They blindfolded us. Underground somewhere. They didn't let us share names, so I can't give you any."

Even in my anguish, I'm impressed with the security measures I've imagined. Maybe I've convinced Langford, too. He sits back on his heels, eyes narrow and focussed over my shoulder. A second later, they bulge. "What the fuck?"

I whip around in time to see blood bubbling out of a wide slice on Piper's neck. Her eyes are wet and fixed somewhere near me on the glass. Blondie Man stands over her as she bleeds.

My heart lurches and burns as I spring to my feet. "He cut

her." I turn to Langford, fists clenched. "I told you everything I know. *He cut her.*"

Langford pales as he shakes his head. "She grabbed the knife…"

So much blood.

Blondie Man spins, slipping in a pool of it, and lunges for the door. Moments later, he's in the room with us. "She just…" He mimes a throat cut, his movements slow and unsteady, like he's in shock.

"I saw." Langford's voice is far away.

"She's a goner."

"Suicide in this place. There won't be too many questions asked."

I let their words float over me as I watch the life drain out of Piper. Her eyes find mine. She screws hers up, as though trying to focus. A smile dies on her lips as her face goes slack. Her body convulses, splashing up the blood around her, silent behind the glass.

*No.*

This room is silent too. The two men behind me stand rigid, reflected in the glass, the still form of Piper between them.

*No.*

Reflected Langford puts a hand on Blondie Man's shoulder. "Better tell the guards. They'll clean up. I got what I needed."

*No. No, no, no.*

It's only when Langford clamps a hand over my mouth that I realise I'm screaming the words. I only know I'm fighting him when he punches me, splitting my lip. I lunge towards the door, but his grip is too strong.

"Jesus. Somebody give her a shot of something."

People rush in and pin me down. They shove up the sleeve of my jumpsuit. My upper arm stings as something punctures the skin.

Whether the scream continues from my mouth or just in my head, it persists even as my vision fades to black.

# Chapter Twenty-Seven

## Kerry

### 25th November 2041

She's a brave kid, I'll give her that. Stoical, though she must be a mess inside, losing both parents within days.

Wary and sullen when I try to draw her out, yet she doesn't appear broken. She pauses while tucking her green rabbit into bed and gives me a sideways look. The only tears she's shed were when I pulled her favourite toy out of Essie's rucksack. I forgot how raw young kids' tears could be.

The phone rings—Langford's number. Oh, Christ, what now?

"Alex."

"I'm outside. Let me in."

Why can't this asshat knock on a door? "'Kay." To Willow, I say, "Stay here. Do not leave this room."

She looks like she's going to do as I say.

Langford pushes his way in before I've got the door fully open, wide shoulders banging against the wood.

"Jesus Christ, Alex. It's only rain."

He ignores the wisecrack. "I need the kid."

"What? No. The family is mine. We agreed."

He's sweated through his jacket. Intense patches of it collect under his arms. He marches past me to the back room. "She in here? The Glass bitch won't talk. And now she's out cold." He disappears inside for a moment and comes out scowling.

"What have you done?"

He glares, then ducks into the front room. "I did nothing. Where is she?"

"Right. Calm down." Glancing up the stairs, I follow him and gesture to the sofa. "Tell me what happened."

He hitches his trousers up and sits, passing his palms along his shiny head as if he still has hair to ruffle. "She wouldn't talk. So, I tried a little leverage with her friend." His hands are rubbing his knees now. "The stupid bitch slit her own throat."

"Essie?" My skin goes cold.

He flaps a hand. "The friend. Grabbed the knife, turned the tables. Stupid bitch. We were just getting somewhere. Had to sedate Glass, but they were heavy-handed on the juice so now she's passed out."

"Jesus, Alex." But am I surprised?

He shoots me a grimace. "Spare me the indignation. This is a fucking insurgency. So now I need the kid. Or her father. What did you do with him, anyway?"

"You don't need to know."

He pauses a couple of beats, probably deciding whether to press the issue. "When she wakes up, Glass is going to talk. I don't care how tough she thinks she is."

"Have you tried asking her nicely?"

His face turns a satisfying purple. "Are you taking the piss?"

*Careful, Kerry.*

I shrug, trying to look sympathetic.

His head tics, like a fly's landed on it. "Doesn't matter. She's given me a date. I need to be sure she's telling the truth. And she's got more than she's letting on, I know it."

I'm thinking fast. "Well, you can't use the kid."

The purple darkens. "Kerry—"

"It'll raise too many questions. And it might just tip her over the edge. If she's not there already. You'll get no sense out of her if she loses her mind or ends up getting killed."

To my ears, it's a weak argument, but Langford appears to

consider it. "The father, then. Where's he?"

I straighten my back. "Unavailable."

His eyes glint. "D'you kill him?"

"Leave it."

"Yeah, yeah. Plausible denial." His shoulders slump as he lets out a slow breath through his nose. "What the fuck am I going to do?"

"She gave you a date?"

He nods. "Thirtieth of this month, she claimed. But she's a lying bitch."

"You were torturing her friend, Alex. She's not *that* tough."

"What would you know about it?" He's back to rubbing his knees again. "There's a circuit missing in that bitch's head. She'd have watched me kill her friend if it suited her purpose."

Circuit missing in *her* head. Jesus. "She didn't need to, did she?"

By the time he leaves five minutes later, Langford has worked himself up into a near-frenzy. He stalks out of the house, back into the interminable rain which he barely seems to notice, and down the road to his waiting car. As it speeds away, I try not to dwell on what it means for national security that when we're set to grapple with the most dangerous floods in the country's history, our leader is tripping on his loathing for one young woman.

As I step on the first riser back to Willow, my phone rings.

"Lenny. Where are you?"

"At the safehouse."

"Jack?"

Lenny scoffs. "Yeah, he's here. Bit grouchy, though."

"I'll be there in twenty. Got childcare to sort. Oh, Lenny? Try to cheer him up, will you? I need him on side."

If Lenny wonders what all that means, he has the good sense not to ask. I clear down and call Ed. While I wait for him to arrive, I go back up to Willow. She's asleep, curled up with Boop under her chin collecting spittle, though it's not even ten in the morning. This whole situation is taking it out of all of us. Perhaps a huge tidal wave breaking over London wouldn't be a terrible thing. A clean sweep.

Christ, I'm getting fatalistic.

Ed's sulky about being left to babysit at Primrose Hill while I drive off in his Range Rover, but he'll have to deal with it. There's serious business to take care of. I don't know what will happen to Essie. Odds are, Langford's going to end up killing her, accidentally or otherwise. I still have Jack, though. He's my ticket now. But how to approach this? He hated my guts even before I had him kidnapped and dragged halfway across the world, so charming him will be tricky.

Got to try. And if it fails, I have other options.

They've attempted to make the safehouse blend in with the shabby nineteen thirties frontages on the street, but the barred and boarded windows scream covert ops. Not-so covert ops, I guess. Lenny answers the door before I reach it and ushers me inside.

"Nice weather in Florida?" I ask, eyeing his bulky, bronzed arm.

He grunts and leads me up the stairs. "Wet."

Jack's in the far corner of the bedroom floor, fingering a bruise on his cheek. He looks thin and leathery, his red-brown hair lank and matted, the scar on his face a deep, jagged pink. Lenny has chained him to the rusty radiator. He has a little slack, but not enough to reach the mattress a few feet away. Excessive, but I suppose I haven't been with them for the last four days, so it's difficult to judge. Jack turns his dull eyes on me and tracks my approach. Maybe he's jet lagged.

"Hello again, Jack." I flash him a smile and step closer to the lumpy mattress. "Good to see you made it out of Cuba."

He stays silent and still, jaw fixed.

Undeterred, I move around the mattress to within a couple of feet of him. "I'm serious. We've had our differences, you and I, but I'd never want to see your talent go to waste."

"You want to make up. Right now? Really, Kerry?" He rattles his chains.

It's a valid point. I turn to Lenny, who's loitering by the

door. "Can we…?"

Lenny stomps across the room to release Jack, though not without a little shoving. What a testy four days it must have been. Jack rubs his wrists but stays put.

I perch on the corner of the mattress. "Can I get you anything? Cup of tea, painkillers… Are you hungry?"

He scoffs and shakes his head, looking away to the bedroom window, though it's boarded up like the rest. "You must be planning some revenge trip." His voice is distant, too. "Have you got Essie locked up somewhere? Or am I the bait?"

"She's fine. For now." God forgive me.

His eyes flash at me. "Where?"

"We'll get to that. My business right now is with you." I lean forward, inches away, and give him another smile. "There is good news, though." I pause a second for him to ask, which he doesn't. "I have your original prototype file."

Jack doesn't react to this, either. His head lowers, hiding his face.

"Did you hear what I said? We can—"

"I heard." His gaze remains in his lap "So now I'm to be coerced into making the carbon capture for you. Or you'll hurt Essie. Right?"

"No. *No.* Wrong."

"We're back at the start line." He lifts his face now, eyes dark with, what… Resignation?

"I want to work *with* you."

"Except it's six years closer to midnight. With even more carbon in the air, poisoning us faster than we could ever extract it."

"Come on, Jack. We still have time."

A sound somewhere between a tut and a bitter laugh bursts out of him. "Tell that to the Cubans." His gaze returns to the window. "If you can find any alive."

Of course. *That's* why he's so vague. "Must have been awful over there."

"Yeah. But being abducted, beaten, dragged to London when it's about to go under water, and chained to a radiator has taken my mind off it."

I shoot a frown at Lenny, who has the humility to look away at least, then switch back to Jack. "I'm sorry."

He squints at me. "Why are you being so nice when we lied to you? I thought you'd be raging."

"I was. But I understand you had your reasons." I shrug and look down at the mattress, stroking my hand along its frayed edge. "This is bigger than any of us. I don't need to tell you that."

"I'm not doing it just so you can make a shitload of money."

"I don't want money."

"Oh, come on, Kerry. You expect me to believe that?"

"Believe it or don't. Either way, you don't have much choice."

He lets his head flop back on the wall. "Where's Essie?"

I hesitate, work my jaw. "In prison. Langford has her now. I tried to stop it, but…"

"No." With a groan, he half-rises, clocks Lenny's stiffened posture and drops back. "Christ. He'll kill her. Get her out of there." He closes his eyes, pinching the bridge of his nose. "Get her out, and I'll build your prototype."

*Bingo.*

"I'll do everything I can to help her. You have my word." Fixing him with a solemn gaze, I say, "You're doing the right thing, Jack."

"You'd better hurry and get me a lab to work in." He nods at the window. "By the sounds out there, look for something outside London."

As I open my mouth to respond, my phone rings. A number I don't recognise flashes on the screen. I step outside and answer it. "Kerry Tyler."

"Mum." He sounds tired; faint, as if he's calling from far away.

"Carlo?" I head to the stairs, dropping my voice below echo level. "Where are you? Are you okay?"

"I'm fine. Look, I haven't got long. This is a borrowed phone."

"What happened to yours?" Has he been mugged?

"Doesn't matter. I just wanted to say I love you. Where I am, it's… the water's started coming in—"

*The water?*

"Where are you?" I grip the bannister as my shaky legs stumble on a riser. "Tell me."

"Doesn't matter. I won't be here for long." His voice cracks. "We're… It's starting."

I'm pacing the hallway now. "What? What's starting? Carlo, are you in that camp?"

"I—I can't say. Just—"

"You can't say? What does *that* mean? I'm your mother."

"I love you."

A click and a whine.

"Carlo… Carlo? CARLO."

He's gone.

The phone drops to the floor as I collapse on the bottom stair. Tears I've held back for so long won't be denied, so I cry them, my fist thrust in my mouth to stop the scream.

# Chapter Twenty-Eight

## Seth

**25th November 2041**

I gave up yelling a few days ago, just after I abandoned trying to force the door. At least, I think it's days. It's hard to be sure in here. I don't know where I am, or how long I've been here; what they've done with Willow. If Essie is still alive.

I do know this cell is six paces by five, smells of rotting bin juice, and has no windows. And that I've lost everything. My family; my phone; the picture that was all I had left of my parents.

The light comes on in the morning, and I imagine when it goes off it's the evening. I have a toilet, at least, in the corner. There's a damp bed roll and a cold tap that discharges straight onto the concrete floor. They shove food through a hatch in the bottom of the door, but all I see is a set of dirty fingernails and a plate of bread and cheese.

The only voice I've heard was after the first meal. A throaty, low growl demanding the return of the plate. If it's a prison, it's a bloody primitive one.

I shift on the bedroll and open my eyes. For all the good that does. It must be early because the light is still off. Perhaps I slept a little because my thoughts are sluggish and fractured. The night before last, terror dreams gripped me, so vivid they seemed to project on the walls after I awoke. Nightmares invaded by Alex Langford pressing a knife to Essie's throat, of Kerry Tyler shooting my dad in the head while Rook strangled my mum. I opened my mouth in the dream to shout at them to stop, then my voice turned into Willow's as she screamed and screamed…

My head throbs as I sit. The cut Drew opened when he knocked me out is raw and itchy.

But I'm alive. Which is more than I expected when Tyler walked away with my daughter. Being smacked around and dragged into a hole I can handle, if I'm still breathing, with the remotest possibility of finding my way back to Essie and Willow.

"Morning." I've taken to talking to myself with my developing croak. Not all the time. When I wake, last thing at night. A *bon appétit* when the bread and cheese arrive. Not always just to myself, either. Ghosts surround me now, of the living and the dead. And sometimes I talk to whichever one of them is foremost in the crowd. Last night at lights out, Lawrence sat on the end of my bedroll and sang to me. Without opening his mouth, he just sang into my brain. Though when real Lawrence sang, he sounded like a rusty hinge, this was sweet as an angel. Right now, Mum's close, her wiry salted-brown hair piled high in what she likes to call a pineapple head.

"Always suited you, that style."

She smiles, but it's uncertain and lopsided. She never could take a compliment.

None of the ghosts have replied yet, so I'm not completely gone. The minute my cell version of Essie gives me stick like the real Essie, I'll know there's no hope for me. Hard to rule it out. I'm on the road there, and this place can play nasty tricks. Need to put on the brakes.

With a little buzz, the light flickers on. I duck my head away from the glare as the hatch clangs open. A small plate of bread and cheese appears. Though I'm famished, the thing that catches my attention is the sound of rain that leaks in through the gap. It's torrential; great pattering streams.

"Hey, Mum. Stay for breakfast?"

"Lunch," says the gruff voice. "Bloody road's flooded out there."

It makes no sense, so I let it go.

Mum doesn't offer to take any food, so I tuck in as I continue my musing.

As for the prototype, Essie's drive to save the world, to serve Langford and Tyler a glass of neat justice? I'm letting that go, too. Of all the ghosts with me, only two have a possibility of being alive. However remote that chance is, I exist now for one purpose alone. If Essie and Willow aren't dead, I'll aim my entire being at getting back to them. So we can be together for whatever time we have left.

# Chapter Twenty-Nine

## Essie

### 25th November 2041

My temples throb like twin abscesses. I daren't open my eyes, though I can't remember why. It smells of disinfectant. Wherever I am, it's quiet, apart from a soft rustling on my left. Something stings the back of my hand, and I suck in a breath.

"Hey." It's a deep, accented voice I don't recognise.

I keep my eyes closed as somebody moves my arm. A cold sensation spreads under my skin. It must have awakened nerves around there because my wrist burns. The other one follows and, moments later, a memory.

*Piper.*

My eyes are open before I can stop them, though I can't see beyond light and dark shapes. The world spins. I try to say 'No', but my raw throat won't respond with anything but a groan that makes my stomach clench. I let my lids drop again into dark relief.

The movement around my hand stops, replaced by a soft, warm grasp.

"Hey, there." That deep, warm tone again, inviting me back.

I accept, lifting my eyelids with effort that makes my head pulse. My vision clears a little when I blink and stare down at a stiff, white sheet covering my torso and legs. Bandages encase my wrists, and I'm hooked up to a drip, which must be responsible for the cold sensation. I lift my gaze further, wanting to see the body attached to the smooth, black hand holding mine.

He's broad, and light blurs behind him, surrounding his head like a halo. I blink again and it turns into a plain old strip light.

*What's wrong with you, Ess? You high or something?*

I might be.

The angel smiles. "Well, hello. Essie, isn't it?"

"Wh…?"

"This is the hospital wing of HMP Broadwater. You came in unconscious after an overdose of sedative about…" he glances at the wall clock, "…thirty hours ago. We treated you with charcoal through a tube, so your throat and tummy might hurt. I'm Jonah, your nurse. That probably covers the top four or five questions you have."

The undulations of his speech lull me, and my eyes drift closed again.

*Charcoal. How about that?*

In the days I used to sketch, it was my favourite material to work with. Wonderful stuff, charcoal.

"Hey, lady. Stay with me." He gives my hand a squeeze.

"Wh… happ...?" With effort, I focus on his face.

"They told me you were hurting yourself, so they tried to sedate you. Someone got the dose wrong." There's something spiky behind his tone, though it seems he's trying to keep it even and soft. "That true?"

I can only shake my head. The things I've been trying to block out are breaking through. I don't have the strength to fight them.

*Piper.*

249

Tears squeeze out of the corners of my eyes and run down into my ears.

"Hey, now," he says softly.

"My friend. She…"

His brow creases, pulling down his close-cropped hairline. "I'm very sorry."

The last walls crumble and I remember everything. Langford; the torture; Piper with the knife. Such a tormented sob comes out of me, it must scare Jonah. He sits forward in his chair, eyes wide. Then, seeing I'm not in any physical trouble, he settles back and takes my hand again, letting me cry it out.

"What did she look like? When she was gone?"

*Weird question, Ess.*

I want to hear the word peaceful. When my sister Darya died, days after the bombing, that's what the nurses told me. It helped, though it can't have been true. I knew that even then, because I never went to see her afterward.

"I'm sorry, I didn't see her." Jonah's mouth twitches in consolation. "The guards don't bring people to the hospital wing if…"

*If they kill them?*

My stomach clenches, and I swallow hard. "It's a hell of a job you've got here, Jonah."

"Been thinking the same thing." His mouth twists, like he's fighting off tears. Or the spiky thing he's been trying to hide.

Perhaps to distract himself, he reaches past the top of my bed and retrieves a plastic cup, which he brings to my lips, lifting my head from behind. I drink the tepid water, feeling both foolish and moved by his kindness. When I pull back, he returns the cup. The water has eased my throat and the banging in my head.

"Why were you sitting with me just now?"

"I was flushing your IV line." He flaps his hand at the empty ward. "Also, you're my only patient right now."

I let my head loll on the pillow, mulling over an idea.

*What's to lose, Ess? How could it make things worse?*

"Jonah, what day is it?"

"It's Monday."

"I mean date."

"Oh. November 25th." He tilts his head, the shift causing the light to catch the whites of his eyes. "Why?"

I hesitate on the brink. If he's not what he seems...

Fuck it. "Tomorrow." I screw eyes closed against the renewed throb in my temples. "You might have a chance to do something about your shitty job." Even though it hurts my eyes, I fix them on Jonah's sad, kind face.

He holds my gaze for a long while.

No going back now. "Is there a way out of here through —?"

"It's true, then. Rebellion?"

I nod once.

His chest swells. He whistles. "Where?"

A needle of caution prods my brain. "When it happens, I don't think you'll need to look very far. Jonah?"

"Yes?" His mouth switches between a grin and a solemn, flat line.

"Can you get me out?" Something occurs to me. "And a friend. Idika; not sure of her last name."

"Dayal. I know Idika. Treated her in here more than once." That spiky undertone is there again. He breathes in then lets it go, frowning as he looks down the hospital wing. Seven empty beds besides mine; a jumble of trolleys and equipment; at one end, a tiny, partitioned office and an adjacent exit with a series of locks and bars on its window. At the other, a red metal door behind a set of thick, horizontal bars.

"Jonah?"

He snaps his head back to me. "I don't know if I can help

251

Idika, too. But I'd be honoured."

I open my mouth to thank him, but the phone rings in his little office.

"One moment." Jonah springs up and trots down the ward.

I watch him go, then my eyes slide back to the red door. For the first time since I arrived in this hellhole, hope sparks. I only need to stay alive another day, then…

*Too late for Piper.*

The thought stabs me in the chest. It dulls the hope kindling there and brings stinging tears to my eyes again. How many more deaths before this ends?

Jonah appears at the door, eyes wide, shoulders raised and stiff. He strides back to my bed. "Jesus. The Pr… the Prime Minister is coming here. To see you."

He looks like he expects that to be an enormous shock to me, but I can only raise a sigh. "When?"

"Right now." He holds his hands up in a *can you believe it?* gesture. "He's at the gates."

Despite my exhaustion, my heart kicks up a gear. "Do they know I'm awake?"

He moves slowly, as if he thinks he might be dreaming. "I didn't tell anyone."

"Then I'm not." I beg Jonah with my eyes as my limbs tremble. "He wants to kill me. Would have done already, but I know too much."

Jonah's jaw thrusts forward as he looks at my wrist bandages. "He's the one who did this."

He doesn't need an answer.

With a grimace, he says, "Close your eyes and don't move. I've got this."

Wiping my free arm over my eyes, I settle lower in the bed. "Thank you. I mean it."

Though his breathing is shallow, his brow greased with sweat, he pulls his shoulders back and winks at me. "You bet, lady."

Fixing on his smile last, I close my eyes and try to make

252

myself floppy, to calm my breathing. How do unconscious people breathe? Shallow and slow, I guess. I've got the shallow bit down, but... My legs itch with tension. The sheet scrapes my arms. I shift my neck, and the strangle wound flares.

"You'll have to do better than that," says Jonah. "Chill, lady."

"Easier said than—"

"Shh."

The door buzzes, and then it's too late. Langford's heavy footsteps scratch in my ears as they approach. My body tilts as he sits on the bed. His aftershave tickles my nose. The weight of him makes me want to turn away. I remain frozen and try to release my muscles down into the mattress, to think of nothing. Try not to remember Piper's eyes on me as she lay, the life bleeding out of her. Or his hand over my mouth.

"Any sign of waking?" His voice is flat and off-hand, as though he's discussing a stunned heifer.

"I'm afraid not."

"Shit." Langford enunciates the *t* as a sharp stop. "Is there anything you can give her to bring her out of it?"

*Christ, I hope not.*

"Nothing that doesn't stand a chance of killing her first."

Langford grunts. I bet he's willing to risk it.

Perhaps Jonah senses that too, because he says, "No doctor would sign off on further medication now she's out of danger. Her body needs time to metabolise the drug. Nothing more."

*Love you, Jonah.*

Langford tuts and shifts on the bed. "Too bad."

I ease my held breath out and try not to move. A ringtone sings, very close, and my muscles tense.

*Stop it, Ess. He's going to notice.*

"Yep," says Langford.
A scratchy female voice chirps at the other end.
"Kerry."

*Relax. Relax. Relax.*

More chirping. "Fielding? I thought he was dead."

*Seth?*

My fingers twitch before I can prevent them. My heart thumps so hard Langford must see it through the sheet. Seth's alive? I want to cry and scream and laugh. I close my throat around them all, though it's fit to burst with the pressure.

"Well, what the hell possessed you to lock him up on a bloody *flood plain*? Don't you watch the news?"

Oh my God. He *is* alive. Imprisoned, but alive.

The chirping grows tense.

Langford huffs and rises from the bed. My limbs loosen, but my mind is racing.

"Calm down, Kerry." Langford's voice is muffled, like he's turned away. "You're in luck. I have a place you can use. But I'll need him out within a day or so. And you will owe me a favour. Another one."

After a beat, Kerry speaks two short syllables.

"The Charter has somewhere." There's a smug smile in his voice.

Kerry again.

Langford chuckles. "Yes, the Redemption Charter. They've got a…facility underground, Swiss Cottage way."

Underground? Could that be the bunker Kim's crew nearly ran into? Got to be.

Langford's heavy feet clop while he listens. "Well, if it's not good enough for you…"

Kerry's voice rises, then falls again.

"Good, then. I'll talk to Ollie, get him to call you and

make arrangements. You, er, might want to be nice to him, you know? Grease the wheels. Poor sap still has a crush on you."

I wish I could hear her response to that.

"Oh, and Kerry? I'm calling in the first favour right now." Langford's voice is louder. "You want to hold him in the bunker, you bring his kid with you, okay?"

My fingers twitch again. He means Willow. And I have a horrible feeling I know why he suggested their bunker to hold my family.

Leverage on me.

"Yeah, I know what we agreed, Kerry. I've changed my mind. Now I want the kid. You can have Fielding."

Dread floods over me as I fight to stay limp.

The phone call over, Langford rocks the bed again as he sits down. "Hey, nurse?"

"Yes, sir." The spike in Jonah's tone is close to piercing his cool shell.

"She moved. When I was on the call, her hands moved. She's waking up."

*Shit, shit, shit.*

My legs and chest are aching with the stillness. The light beyond my straining eyelids shifts as someone draws near and presses on my bandaged wrist. It's gentle, but I have to suppress a grimace of pain.

From just above my head, Jonah says, "It's just her nerves firing on automatic. Happens a lot. Her obs are showing no signs of waking. It'll be a couple of days at least."

I'm left bouncing when Langford rises from the bed. "You call me the second she shows signs. The *second*, you get it?"

"Yes, sir."

Langford's steps clack on the tiles, then pause. I hold myself mid-breath. After an eternity, the footsteps resume, receding. There's the sound of a door closing, but I'm frozen. If I blow it now, it's over. Still, my muscles burn to move.

A soft hand takes mine again. "He's gone."

I open my eyes to Jonah's smile and return it weakly. "Thank you."

"Sure thing, lady." Like he's just held a door open for me.

"Jonah. When you're finished here, get out of London. It's going to get messy."

He surprises me by releasing my hand to cup my cheek in his palm. "Lady, it already got messy. I want to be around to clean it up."

My weary head rests on his hand and I close my eyes.

He takes in a breath and blows it out so hard it tickles my cheek. "Lady, rest now. If you're right about tomorrow, we've got to get you strong again."

There's no arguing with that. I need to sleep more than anything. But through the fog of my exhaustion shines the knowledge that Seth's alive. And my heart is so full of him, it makes me dizzy.

# Chapter Thirty

## Seth

**25th November 2041**

There's water coming in. For hours I've been cooling my heels in here while a puddle turned into a lake, now a sea of cold, silty water a foot deep in my cell. My toes ache with it.

For a while, I called out for help. By the time my empty lunch plate sank, I'd given up and rested here half-squatting, trying not to panic.

It's coming from under the door and not through the roof. Which, to my tired logic, means at least I'm not underground. There's a thin hope they will find me before I drown. Maybe.

"Oh, Ess. What a state I'm in."

She nods, mouth pulled down in a sardonic pout. "Yeah. You're proper screwed."

I try not to think of what it means that Cell Essie is talking to me.

The door rattles, making me cry out. When it opens, more water surges in with the torchlight that stabs my eyes. Drew is standing knee deep in it, scowling. He's wearing the same black gear, the same ridiculous silver Hands of Kinship badge. "All right. Against the wall."

Is he kidding? Squinting, I hold out my hands, showing I'm here.

He's not amused. "Turn to *face* the wall, smart arse."

I turn, the water riding further up my jeans with the motion. There's a wading noise, then Drew grabs my wrists.

"What's going on?"

"Upgrading accommodation." His voice modulates in the middle with the effort of tightening the handcuffs.

"Where to?" I rotate my wrists against the metal, but it burns, so I stop.

He spins me around to face him and grabs the torch from between his knees. "Just be grateful we didn't leave you here to drown."

"Are there floods?"

He drags me through the door. "You'll see."

They've held me in a broken-down warehouse. My cell opens into a vast brick-walled and pillared space. High, broken windows let in miserable, grey light. Heavy rain clatters on the corrugated roof forty feet above.

"Come on." He yanks me, sloshing us to a metal side door.

Outside, wheel-deep in floodwater, is a hulking green four-by-four. The air smells of river and rotting garbage. The expanse of industrial estate resembles an urban paddling pool. Rain bounces off its surface. Dismal though the rebounding light is, my eyes sting.

Drew opens the rear passenger side door and jerks his head. I struggle to climb in, landing face first, the aroma of wet dog replacing the decay. The back seats are covered in thick plastic sheeting and my heart thumps in renewed panic.

"Where did you say you're taking me?" I eye the plastic, trying to ignore the tremor in my voice.

Drew watches me in the rearview and laughs. "Don't freak out, pretty boy. The plastic's not for you, yet."

"Comforting. Thanks."

He narrows his mirrored eyes at me, then starts up the car with a click and a rumble. The Jeep moves, pushing a wave in front of us.

"Can this thing drive through floods?"

He squints in the mirror. "You'd better hope so. If we get stranded…" He reaches into the glove compartment and comes out with a gun, which he aims at me.

Point taken, I lean back on the plastic and close my eyes. My head spins, so I open them again, and pain lances. I shift in the seat—my cuffed and sweaty hands squeaking on the

258

plastic behind me—and look out of the window. We're on a main street, lined with a mixture of shop fronts and squat blocks of flats. My heart lurches.

There are people, hundreds of them, though judging by the light, it's too early for the evening rush hour. Waist-deep in filthy water, many are pulling sleds and dinghies loaded with possessions and wide-eyed, sobbing children. Others are alone, wading with heads down against the downpour. The hum of anxiety is audible even through the thick Jeep windows. Shop fronts are piled to the lintel with hopeful sandbags. A few of their owners lean out of upper-floor windows, gaping at the chaos below. Drones buzz overhead, but there's no other sign of security forces. These people are on their own. The few cars around are empty, most floating. Just ahead of us, a red Mini glides into a young couple, capsizing the dinghy that moments before had carried a child. The woman shrieks as her partner dives under the water.

"Careful," I say. "The kid's gone under."

Drew doesn't seem to hear me. We pass the couple and the Mini, leaving a wake to thwart their desperate thrashing. At least there's no bump of collision with any bodies.

"Jesus." The breath rushes out of me. "The river must have breached."

He eyes me in the mirror. "You think?"

It's almost dark now, but no lights illuminate the streets or buildings. There's only sweeping torch beams and our headlights bobbing in and out of the flood.

I lean forward in my seat. "How bad is it going to get?"

"Pretty bad, I hear."

"What are they doing about it? What about the flood barrier?"

He scoffs. "The barrier's been falling for years, barely keeping up with the estuary tides. They just didn't tell anyone. Besides, the water's coming from up there." He points to the roof. "We got no barriers in the sky."

"Jesus." I've no idea what part of London this is. From the direction of the dying light in the sky, and the flow of people, we're south of the river and heading towards it. "We're planning to get out of the city, though, right?"

Keeping his eyes on the road, Drew points the gun over his shoulder. "Time to shut up, okay?"

I clamp my mouth closed and sit back. No sense antagonising a Unity fascist while handcuffed in his car. Wiser to wait for a better opportunity. And pray it comes in time.

We reach a wide, staggered intersection boiling with a confluence of water. An abandoned double-decker bus straddles the carriageway, so the few vehicles negotiating their way south have to work round it. On the opposite corner, an underground station sign protrudes from the corner of a low-slung brick building. It's too dark to see the name on the sign, but even from this distance, I can smell the foaming effluent coursing down its steps.

"Bollocks." Drew peers through the windscreen in that direction. "My brother works security at Stockwell tube. He's on duty today."

Stockwell. That's a couple of miles south of the river. We're heading straight into the shitstorm.

"Listen, Drew—"

"Shut up." He kills the power on the car, then grasps the door handle, hesitates, opens it. "Bloody hell, Alfie." Glancing back at me, he slams the door again. After a moment's silence, Drew slaps the steering wheel, then drags his fingers down his face.

He's as distracted as he's ever going to get.

Slowly, I twist my back so that it's facing the door nearest me. The cuffs cut my wrists as I stretch numb fingers, searching for the door handle. They fumble against something. Screwing my eyes closed against the pain, I grasp and pull.

Nothing.

A scrambling, then something hits my head and whips it back against the glass. When I open my eyes again, Drew's flushed, twisted features fill the space between the front seats. "Any more pissing about, and I'll kill you myself."

*Kill you myself.*

As opposed to who's going to kill me?

If I'm going to die, I've nothing to lose. "Where is my daughter?"

"The rabid animal that bit me? I hope they put it down."

"She's four years old, you psycho."

He scowls at me, then turns around and delves back into the glove compartment. Hands full of something, he opens the door and splashes down in the water, reappearing seconds later to open my door. I jerk away from him, but he grabs me by the hair and yanks me back, shoving a wad of dirty cloth in my mouth. A bit of it hits the back of my throat, making me gag, but I can't spit it out. I contract my windpipe to move it forward a little.

He produces a roll of duct tape, ripping off a section and slapping it onto my lips. "Problem solved."

Breathing hard through my nose, I watch him return to his seat and start up the car.

There are no more distractions. He navigates the turbulence at the intersection and in minutes we're heading north again. As we reach Vauxhall Bridge, the river swirls around the red steel railings on the left, flanking an enormous steel barrier across the road. A drone swoops down as Drew opens his window, letting in the rain, and turns. It hovers, lens zooming on his face, then glides away. With a rumble that vibrates the chassis, the barrier sinks into the road surface. Jesus, when did they put these things up?

When the barrier's gone, it reveals a clear way ahead onto the bridge as water rushes over it. Even after it's down, a hydraulic hiss surrounds us. The water churns, moving towards, then past us through the open barrier. The steel blockade thunders closed.

Realisation hits me. They've pumped the flood water out. Back south to Stockwell to flood the tube. Or upstream to flood the bloody power station.

The river on the left is high and frantic, whirling around the railings. On the right, it's ten feet below. What is this, a dam?

There's another barrier at the far end, accompanied by a bunch of four stiff-armed guards in flak jackets with the Unity sign emblazoned on the lapel and across the back. As we draw near, they flag us down. One of them holds up a device to Drew's face and there's a pause while he's scanned. The barrier grumbles down and on we go.

Drew turns left off the bridge, away from a roadblock. We trace a northern route, this time slowly, with the flow of people wading thigh deep. At intervals on our right, barricades and checkpoints line the circumference of Westminster. More guards squint through the rain. We pass several confrontations between the guards and people fleeing. As our Jeep crawls by, a young lad pulls a knife on a guard. The guard's colleague aims his rifle. When he fires, the lad's scream cuts off and he hits the water.

There are scuffles between the people, too. Panic, I guess.

Inside the car is a different world; silent. As we crawl away from the river, the flood level drops to below the knee. The Jeep moves more easily. God knows how it got through what's behind us, but its electrics are unaffected. We come to a boarded-up estate agent with a red sign. Beside the frontage is an iron gate, sitting higher than the flood, up a concrete ramp.

As Drew corners the Jeep onto the slope, a drone sweeps down and he lowers the window, repeating his mugshot posture. The gate swings open. I gaze out of the window, nausea rising. This isn't a place you hold a prisoner. It's where you take someone to execute them.

Drew pulls up in a tiny, high-walled car park at the back. The concrete surface is crumbling, but only pockmarked by puddles. We must be on higher ground now. Drew swings round and rips the tape off my mouth. It burns, and a little yelp escapes me as I spit out the rag, which makes him laugh.

I drive my nails into my palms. "Where are we?"

He opens his door and jumps down, coming around to mine to open it. He's holding his gun again. "Come on, sunshine."

Unable to brace with arms, I land heavily and my knee

jars. Not waiting for me to steady myself, Drew marches me to the rear of the brick building. We're met at the door by a guard in similar garb as those at the blockades, same rifle slung across his chest, but he also has on a bright yellow safety helmet. He nods and steps aside for Drew to shove me through the door.

Inside is a shell, with bare brick walls and sporadic floorboards interspersed with nothing. I hit two boards, then miss, ankle scraping against a joist as my foot plunges into a hole. I yell and go down with a thump.

"Fuck's sake." Drew huffs and yanks me up, paying no heed to the further damage he's doing to my leg. "Take this tosser down, will you?"

"Take me down?"

"Your new digs." He chuckles over my shoulder as he releases my hands from the cuffs. "Subterranean, mate."

"Is that wise? Going underground in a flood?"

He comes around to face me and smirks. "You're a nervous little thing, aren't you? Relax, sunshine. It's flood-proof down there."

"Didn't they used to say that about up here?"

But Drew's heading out the door.

# Chapter Thirty-One

## Essie

### 26th November 6.00am

"Don't you ever go home?"

Jonah lays the tray on my lap. His laugh is rich. "Not when there's a revolution, lady."

He's made me bacon and egg sandwiches, though the clock tells me it's early for breakfast. God knows how he got hold of the meat in this place. He must have bought it himself, because I doubt prisoner rations stretch to such luxury. I take an enormous bite, unconcerned by the yolk and ketchup running down my chin.

He grins at me. "You look miles better this morning."

"I feel it," I say through a half-chewed mouthful.

I slept for twelve hours and when I awoke half an hour ago, free of needles in my arm, my head was clearer than it's been in ages. It's like all that poison they put in me blew away in a long, dreamless night.

"That's just as well." He places a green mug of steaming tea on my tray and eyes me. "And just in time."

"Yes, it is." Electricity is radiating from my heart, coursing down my limbs. I haven't got out of bed yet, but I feel strong. The awful weight of Piper's loss, the horror of the last four days in here, still crush my chest. They're more reasons for me to get up off the mat and fight. If I needed more.

Jonah squeezes my hand. "Eat, lady. Got stuff to do. I'll be back soon."

I don't need telling twice. As he strides away, I rip another bite out of the sandwich and oh, my God, it's the loveliest thing I've ever tasted. Apart from this cup of tea. Jonah has put sugar in it, which I don't take, but it's like hot nectar going down.

*You're alive, Ess. Seth and Willow are alive. You're still here despite everything they've tried to do to you.*

It's payback time. For all of us.

I gobble the rest of my sandwich and swig the tea. Opposite my bed is a door with a picture of a sprinkling showerhead. Jonah or someone must have given me a bed bath while I was unconscious, but dried blood still flakes in my hair and on the bandages around my wrists. I move the tray aside, pull back the blanket, and plant my feet on the cold floor. When I stand, my chest constricts, the room spins and I gasp, flopping back down on the bed.

*Not as strong as you thought, Ess?*

Yes, I am. Taking in a breath, I push the panic down and stand again. This time the room only wavers a little, and it passes quickly. I hobble to the door. Inside is a white-tiled wet room with a shower and toilet. A threadbare towel wraps around a rail on the back of the door. I strip off my hospital gown and knickers and turn on the shower. It's not powerful and the only soap is a harsh antiseptic-smelling liquid from the handwash dispenser on the wall. Still, the water is warm, and that's better than what I've had lately. My wrists sting as it soaks through the bandages. The cuts and bruises on my face wake up shouting when the soap hits them. There's a mirror by the loo, and once I've washed the blood from my skin and hair, I peek.

The face that confronts me is swollen, marbled with purple bruises. Pale skin and hollow eyes above a neck scored by an angry, scabbed wound. I turn away.

The towel scratches at my raw skin as I dry. My face is tight and sore from the soap. There's nothing else to wear, so I redon the gown and hobble back to bed, panting. My eyes slide closed.

***

Someone's tapping my hand. "Hey, lady. Wake up."

My eyes spring open to Jonah's kind face.

"Enough sleeping." He grins. "I have someone to see you."

I sit up, panicking, my head pounding. "Who?" Please, not Langford.

Jonah steps aside to reveal Idika behind him. She smiles, but it turns wonky as her eyes rove my face.

"I know. I don't look my best." Peering at Jonah, I say, "How did you get her here?"

He shrugs. "You don't need to know. I filled her in on the plan."

Idika leans a knee on the bed, as if trying to keep herself upright. "Look what they did to you."

"I'm okay." I fight the tears. "Piper…"

Idika's eyes are wet, too. Her fringe twitches as she blinks it away. "Jonah told me. I'm so sorry. These fuckers." She thumps the bed.

Jonah steps up next to Idika, glancing at the clock. "Listen, lady. If you want out of here, you'd better get a move on."

"What's the time?"

"Eleven thirty."

"Bugger." I've slept for hours. My heart thumps as I scramble at the bedclothes about me, God knows what for. I have no belongings left. "Clothes." I glance at Idika, who's still in her red prison jumpsuit.

"Chill, lady." Jonah reaches behind him to a chair and scoops up a pile of jeans and checked shirts. "From the spare clothes store. For the lucky ones who get released. The sizes might be wrong. I think the shirts are for men, but…"

The top one is red and green and the same as one of Seth's. The exact one he was wearing the last time we were together.

My eyes burn again, and this time the tears spill. I'm so lost, so far away from him.

Idika puts a hand on my shoulder and her mouth moves, but nothing comes out. I'm grateful for the lack of platitudes. There are no words she could say.

Jonah clears his throat and glances at the door. "Ladies, I won't lie. This is a hell of a risk. When I went down to arrange Idika's visit, there was a buzz."

"What kind of buzz?" Though I fear I can guess.

"Word is, something's brewing."

Idika nods. "It's true. I've heard a few of the girls whispering about a riot in here. They must smell the trouble coming."

"We don't have long before they lock us all down. Including you." Jonah looks at me. "You'll be back in your cell, overdose or no overdose. Then it's game over."

We don't need convincing. Idika chucks me the top set of clothing and starts fumbling off her jumpsuit while Jonah turns away, fiddling with the curtain. He pulls it around us and leaves us to it as I ease out of bed and pull off the gown. The jeans are long, but not a bad fit. The shirt is Seth's size, and it feels like his on my body, though it smells musty and not at all like him. I pull on my prison-issue plimsoles.

When we're changed, Jonah is waiting at the far end of the wing by the thick metal door fronted by iron bars. "It's this way."

I hesitate, glancing back down the ward. "Isn't that alarmed?"

"Yeah, but it's disarmed for medical supply deliveries. There's one due this morning." He looks at the clock behind us. "In fifteen minutes."

I could kiss him, but... "You'll be in trouble here."

"Meh." He waggles his head. "Maybe I'll just quit."

Worry cramps my chest, but there's no choice. I need his help. Jonah strides up the ward and into his office. His head bobs up and down as sounds of rustling papers and banging drawers seep out.

Idika squeezes my shoulder. "Thank you. For getting me

out."

I shoot her a tight smile. "We're not out yet."

For the next ten minutes, we take turns glancing at the door and pacing up and down the hospital wing. Jonah stays in his office, head down at the desk like he's working on something.

After an eternity, a phone rings in the office and Jonah says, "Okay, man. I'll be right down." He strides out of the office, a rucksack slung over one arm. From the angle of his shoulders, it's heavy. A pang pulls at my chest when I remember my backpack and my phone, left behind at Kerry's house. Or, more likely by now, in an office belonging to Langford.

"Show time, ladies." Jonah unhooks a bunch of keys from his belt loop and unlocks the bars, wrestling them open. There's a panel beside the door, which he holds a palm up to, before using a conventional key card. Stepping out, he twitches his head for us to follow.

My heart is thumping so hard it squashes my breath into gasps. We're in a dark corridor. At the end, through a small window set in another heavy door, shines a dull, grey light that can only be the outside. My head is so woolly it's like a dream as we near freedom, our footsteps muted in the closed space. Jonah pauses at the door, his hand hovering over the ID panel, and mutters something inaudible. For an agonising second, I'm sure he's going to change his mind and turn us in. Then he blows out his held breath and slaps his hand against the scanner.

The door opens, blasting us with warm, wet air as Jonah ducks back inside. It's still raining heavy drops that bounce off the walls of the prison and into our faces. The tears roll down my cheeks.

I'm free; and alive.

There's no time to get religious about it. We're one floor up on a rusty iron fire escape overlooking a weed-throttled parking area that looks like the industrial guts of the prison. Beyond, that huge, low-slung building I saw on my arrival. A line of prisoners snakes to its entrance from the prison yard on our left, walking parallel to a similar line in the opposite direction.

Idika hisses and pulls me back against the wall. "Twelve o'clock slave change."

"Huh?"

She squints at the line then back at me. "We're a free, twenty-four seven production line. You ever wondered how they keep food on the shelves with all the supply chains broken? Unity innovation at its best."

When the prisoners have gone, Idika releases me as Jonah re-joins us on the fire escape. For a moment we're frozen, gazing down at the car park.

Wooden pallets stack along a brick wall that reaches the level of our feet on the stairs. Idling beside them is a white truck with *MedUnity* scrawled along its side. Underneath, the foul drowning Hands of Kinship.

My limbs flash hot and cold and I grip the slimy railing. How the hell do we get out? That wall must be twelve feet high. There's no way a Unity delivery guy is going to help us. When I turn to Jonah to ask, his jaw is tight, and he's holding his hand inside his bag.

"Stay back." His voice is as tense as his face. It's weird, seeing his soft features arrange themselves in such a cold way.

He leads us down the slick steps, hand still inside his bag, so I develop a suspicion. The driver of the van swings his long legs and jumps down from his cab, thin face arranged into greeting as he strides to his rear doors. "Hey, Jonah. Short day today. You're my last drop." He doesn't appear to notice Idika and me skulking behind Jonah.

When the deliveryman jumps into the truck bed, Jonah moves swiftly. Whipping his hand out, he lets his bag drop to the floor. He's holding a gun.

"Stay here." Jonah runs and vaults into the van behind delivery guy.

There's a cry, then Jonah says in a low voice, "I don't want to hurt you. Just do as I say."

The van wobbles, there's a thud and Jonah screams.

269

"Shit. Jonah." I race to the rear of the truck and throw myself in.

He's lying face down, trying to lift his head. The Unity guy straddles his back, pinning Jonah's arms, the gun hanging from his fingers. With his other palm, he mashes Jonah's face into the floor. I run at him, kicking the gun. It spins behind and thuds into a box. As I move to retrieve it, the guy grabs my ankle and yanks. My chin scrapes on the wooden floor when I fall. He squeezes my ankle. Jonah struggles, trying to kick the man off.

Idika flashes past and scoops up the gun. "Okay—" She pants. "That's it. "

While the Unity grunt is distracted, I kick away from him and scramble up to stand by Idika. "Get off him."

He obeys, hands at chest height. Trying to push up off the floor, he gets to one knee.

"Stay down." I grab the gun from Idika and stand over him. "I've got a job for you."

Sweat shines on his bald head as his gaze tracks the gun.

Jonah coughs, his shoes scraping as he rises. He tries to take the gun from me, but I pull away. I've got this guy where I want him and there's no time. Someone could have heard us. Guards could discover us any minute. My vision swims, and I lean on the box behind me as I give my instructions.

Minutes later, I'm jammed into the passenger footwell, folded double under a sheet of black tarpaulin. Inside my den, I grip the gun, aiming at the Unity guy as he drives the truck. I can hardly breathe, the fear and canvas pressing in. A brief image flashes in my mind of Maya. That's how my best friend died. Suffocating in a tarp in Langford's basement.

I shake the thought away.

The truck stops and my heart jumps. A drone buzzes near and fresh air pokes at the cover as the Unity guy lowers his window. I hold my breath until my chest aches and dark flowers bloom in my vision. The drone whine fades. The truck crawls on.

"Hold it." A deep voice booms ahead of us.

270

The drone must have seen me. My nerves spark white hot, breath squeezing out of me. I'm desperate to look, but that would be fatal. My panicking brain pictures Idika and Jonah hunched in the truck bed, sitting ducks if they check back there. Even if I wasn't spotted, Unity Guy could decide to give us up any moment. I might get a shot at him, but they'd kill us. And if he's discovered harbouring prisoners, under duress or not, he'll be in a red jumpsuit with a number on his back.

Unity Guy lowers his window to the rain again.

"The drone screwed up," says the deep voice. "Need to log you manually."

I force myself to hold in the relief.

"Cheers, mate. You're set."

Moments later, we're on the move.

It's all I can do not to cry again as the top of the huge, electrified fence rolls past Unity Guy's window. "Well done."

He glares down at me with bloodshot eyes, then back at the road. "I've got a family, you lowlife bitch."

"Do everything right, and you'll be sitting down to dinner with them later."

"Fuck you."

This is not good. The guy is pissed off enough to turn us in if we free him. I need to speak to the others, but we're still too near the prison to pull over. Sitting up in the footwell, I untangle myself and point the gun at him. "Where's the quietest place around here?"

He scoffs. "There's a park not far ahead. You're gonna wish you'd bought your scuba gear, though."

"What?"

He nods at his windscreen.

Keeping the gun low and pointed at him, I scramble onto the passenger seat. We're crawling along a road lined with shops on the right—boarded-up hairdressers and greengrocers with sandbags piled in their doorways. A foot of water swirls past us as we move. People are bustling around, crossing the road, scurrying down side streets between the shops.

"It's flooding."

He gives me the side eye. "No shit."

"Can you drive into this park?"

"Usually. But…" He nods at the scene outside.

"Then take us there. As far in as you can get."

"You'll get caught, you know. And fuck knows what they'll do to you then."

"That's not your concern. Your job is to do what I say. Keep going."

We drive in silence. It's just the swish of the water and the hum of the people on the streets. A few minutes later, he turns up an empty side street, low-rise blocks of flats on one side. On the other, a featureless field turning into a lake under the barrage of rain. I scan the road but see no people. Either the residents have left or they're hiding.

"Okay, pull over by the field."

He does. We sit for a few moments. He looks at his hands, then glances at the dashboard. A comms handset rests in a moulded holder by the steering wheel.

I grab the device and yank it, ripping the wire out of its base. "Don't move."

Snatching the key, I open the door and splash down to the ground. The air reeks of river mud. Cold water soaks through my jeans and trainers as I wade around the to the rear, opening the doors. Jonah and Idika spring out as I scurry to the passenger door before Unity Guy can escape.

"Christ, look at this place," says Idika behind me.

Jonah wades through the mud and silt, holding up a bunch of cable ties. "Let me handle this guy."

"Gladly." I step back, holding the gun up.

Jonah reaches in and grabs Unity Man by the collar, forcing him out.

With a glance down the street, I huddle against the driving rain. No one's around, and though it's lunchtime, the light is dreary as dusk.

The truck wobbles as Jonah slams the driver against it, wrestles his arms back, and zips a cable around them.

Unity Guy grunts. "When I call this in, you are fucked,

mate."

Jonah spins him around, leaning down in his face. "Then we'll have to make sure you don't. Come on."

They scuffle to the back of the truck, kicking up wads of dirty water. Jonah throws him inside and jumps in after. The truck shakes and emits yells and groans as they struggle. Idika steps beside me, taking my hand. There's a bang, a thump and something tears. Unity Guy shouts, then his voice dies.

Jonah jumps down, slamming the doors, and rubs his jaw. "Arsehole headbutted me."

The truck rocks again, brushing against my back. In one of the dark windows of the building opposite, something moves.

My limbs jolt with icy fire. "Someone's there."

The others follow my gaze in silence. I can't breathe.

"You sure?" Idika grips my hand even tighter.

The window is empty now, but they were there. I swear there was a face, a hand with a phone.

As if summoned, a drone whines nearby. We crouch low against the truck as Unity Guy gives its side a jolt. Are they looking for us already? I peer at the sky, but I can't see anything. The buzz is coming from behind the houses. Which means it'll be in view any second. And when we can see the drone...

"We'll have to get under the truck," I say.

Jonah stares at me. "You're kidding. We'll drown."

Tucking the gun in the back of my jeans, I lean down, my hair dragging in the water. "There's a gap. Come on."

Not waiting to see if they'll follow, I suck in a breath and duck under the filthy water and the truck bed. I come up for air with the stinking underbelly of the truck inches away from my nose. My limbs rest on submerged tarmac, cold water covering me, making my wrists and neck sting. The gun digs in my back. Gasping, I tilt my chin up to stay above the waterline as Jonah and Idika breach the surface behind me.

"Ugh. Ess." Idika wipes mud from her eyes.

"Shhh."

We lie silent, shoulder to shoulder. The buzz of the drone grows louder, hovering above us. Unity Guy must have heard it too because he starts his muffled yell again.

"Glad I gagged him," whispers Jonah.

For excruciating minutes, nothing happens. My heart is pounding, the breath trapped in my chest. After an eternity, the drone fades away.

My shivering breath bounces back at me from the undercarriage. We wait.

Eventually, the risk of it coming back weighs too heavy. I shift and peek out. "I can't see it. Let's go."

I'm soaked through and trembling as we scramble out, careful to remain hidden from the houses. My head swims and I blink to clear my vision.

Idika wraps her arms around herself. "What now?"

Now I'm free and the immediate danger has passed, my body thrums with the desperation to find Seth and Willow. I grab Jonah by the shoulders. "Where's Swiss Cottage from here?"

He frowns. "You'd have to go through Hampstead Heath. It's miles away. Five or more. Why?"

"You and Idika need to leave the city. If they find you, you're dead on sight."

"Essie—"

"No. You need to go now. That drone was looking for us and it found the truck. Just tell me which way and then get out."

Idika steps behind us, putting an arm on each of our shoulders. "No bloody way am I leaving town. You said it was starting? I'm gonna find where the action is. You up for it, Jonah?"

Jonah's eyes stay on me as he hesitates.

"Jonah, I owe you everything. You saved me. The rest is my fight, not yours."

He shakes his head.

"Please." I squeeze his arm. "I'll be fine."

With swift movements, he sweeps me into a bear hug. Then he pulls back and fixes his gaze on me. "You be careful, lady."

I blink back the tears. "Always am. Thank you."

Idika wraps her arms around my neck and plants a kiss on my cheek. "Thank you, Ess. I'd still be rotting in that hellhole if not for you. I owe you big time."

I wave it away, and now there's nothing else to say. Jonah points me in the right direction for Swiss Cottage. Then, with final hugs and *'good lucks'*, they turn and head in the other direction, towards the river. Idika is chattering to Jonah as I watch them go, almost hopping with excitement. At their every step, I'm tempted to call out, ask them to stay with me. But that wouldn't be fair. Where I'm going, my odds of survival are slim. Theirs may not be much better, but they deserve the chance.

I watch them until they turn the corner. With a huge breath in to slow my heart, I set off through the flooded park toward Hampstead Heath and beyond it, my lost family.

# Chapter Thirty-Two

## Seth

### 26th November 2041 12 noon

No one has come down here since I arrived in this latest cell. The only thing to look at through the bars is the ridiculous steel Hands of Kinship sign on the wall. It gleams, as if it's mocking my weakness.

It's one hundred percent right. I've failed them.

From my exhaustion, I guess I've spent a night here, but I've no way of knowing, since the dim lights have stayed on. I catnapped for an hour or two then woke up needing a pee, which I deposited in the stained, stinking loo in the corner. Since then, I've been sitting here alone, torturing myself with visions of Willow. None of my cell ghosts followed me down here. Can't say I blame them, but it leaves me with no one to distract me from the weight of grief on my chest.

I'm underground is all I know for sure. The last road sign I remember seeing was for Swiss Cottage and Hampstead before we turned off into the scruffy minor road with the boarded-up estate agents. Then again, what does it matter what's above me? The silent guard led me down a tunnel, then through a maze of concrete corridors, one enormous well-stocked warehouse labelled *Med Store B* on a Unity-branded plaque, and into this cell.

A distant clang makes me straighten, my back pressing into the cold concrete of the wall. The metal door at the end of the room opens.

"Daddy." Willow bursts in, sprinting up to my cell and

reaching out to me through the bars.

I throw myself against them despite the bite of the iron and clutch her through the gap. "Wills," I say into the back of her hand. My palms run over her face, her shoulders, as though looking for damage. She seems unhurt, on the outside.

Cream-trousered legs approach behind Willow. My eyes creep up a blue silk blouse and a smooth, dark face with gleaming eyes.

"Hey, Seth." Kerry's smile is casual. As if the last time I saw her we just met for coffee, and she didn't rip my daughter away.

"Let him out of there." Willow's voice is fierce.

Kerry smiles without parting her lips. "As it happens, I was about to." She stretches up, touching the scanner with her palm. The bars rumble open between us as we glare at each other. Willow thuds against my legs, sobbing into my filthy jeans. With a firm grip on her arms, I move her aside. My heart sears my chest as I spring at Kerry, driving her back into the Hands of Kinship sign. Her head rebounds off a knuckle of the lower hand that Essie always says looks like someone drowning.

Kerry is trying to slip downwards, out of my grasp. My fingers squeeze around her throat, and she makes a low gurgling noise, which a savage part of me revels in.

Again she tries to talk, so I slam her against the metal. "I told you if you kept fucking with my family, you'd regret it."

"Daddy." Willow's voice is low and flat.

"Not now, Wills." I shove Kerry again.

Willow waggles my shirt and points towards the exit. "They've got guns."

Of course they have. Kerry's not going to come unprotected. There are three of them in a V formation, rifles pointed at me.

"Step back and face me," says the middle one with a wheezy bark, then, when I obey, "On your knees."

As I drop, Kerry steps in front of me, hand exploring her neck. The other hand reaches for a sobbing Willow and yanks

277

her towards the door. A guard slips behind me and lifts me to my feet, pushing me out after Kerry. We move through dark corridors, past metal doors and Hands of Kinship signs. The ceiling rises to twenty feet; the passages grow wider. Kerry stays several steps ahead, out of reach, Willow jogging along with her. A variety of smells accumulate and dissipate; engine oil, bleach, and frying food. If this a bunker, it's an immense one.

The guard at the front stops and scans us into a room. Inside is the same concrete floor, but rich, red-glazed tiles line the walls like in a Victorian pub. Two further doors are set in the opposite wall, but these are oak-panelled and dark-stained. The leading guard steps forward and knocks the one on the left.

"Come." It's a male voice, familiar but hard to place.

When the door opens, it's the shock of recognition that hits me first. His bald head and superior sneer gleam in the light from the banker's lamp on his oversized mahogany desk. Stretching twenty feet to the left, the room is all oak panelling, leather chairs and dark-patterned carpet. The smells of polish and sweat swirl in the hot air, propelled by a steel electric fan on a side table.

What the hell? One minute I'm in a concrete bunker, the next a presidential office staring at the damned Prime Minister sweating through his shirt. A rifle slams my back, and I fall to my knees.

Langford rises from his chair and plants his knuckles on the desk, peering down at me. "Mr Fielding. Good to see you in one piece." He glances at Kerry as she moves to the left with Willow and a guard. The other two loom behind while Langford comes round the desk to stand over me. Everything spins and shifts to the side, and I rock back on my knees to steady myself.

"Okay, Alex." Kerry steps forward, pushing Willow with her. "I brought the kid." She nods at me. "He's mine. We agreed, remember?"

Langford ignores her and continues to stare at me. "Your bitch girlfriend has screwed with me once too often."

278

A tide of nausea and hate swells, obliterating the exhaustion. "Where is she, you sociopathic prick?"

"Alex—" Kerry takes another step, glancing behind her.

"Quiet." Langford holds a forefinger up to her, never taking his eyes off me. "She *was* in custody. But the sly cunt hijacked her way out."

My heart hammers in my ears as my mouth twitches with irrational triumph. She's still alive.

Langford lifts a foot and slams it into my chest, crushing the breath out of me. Yelping, I collapse back into the guards' legs.

Willow screams.

Langford's face is in mine, the sneer twitching between greasy, purple cheeks, stale sweat wafting at me. "You may think it is, but I promise that's not good news for you."

The thumping in my ears continues in double time.

A beat later, it goes out of sync. Something else is knocking beyond the walls.

Langford must hear it too, because his eyes flick to the side before snapping back to me. "Because I'm getting the bitch back here, and I'm going to use you to do it. Her phone may be in my safe, but eventually she's going to catch the news…"

"Alex." Kerry's voice is tighter than ever.

"*What?*"

"What's that noise?" She stares at the wall, gripping Willow's shoulder, making her squirm.

Langford huffs. "They're still building. It's a massive project, Kerry. What do you want, the Savoy?"

"Not building. *Breaking*. And dripping."

The hammering has turned chaotic, punctuated with crumbling and rapid thuds. And under it, a *plat, plat, plat,* like a leaky tap.

My stomach swoops. "I thought this place was watertight."

Langford ignores me. His narrowed eyes fix on the wall behind Kerry. "Wait here." With a sharp inhale, he strides out of the door, slamming it behind him.

The three guards stand stiff, hands on rifles. One of the two behind me coughs. Kerry's hand picks at her mouth as she stares at the wall, then the door Langford disappeared through. While she's distracted, Willow frees herself from Kerry's loose grasp and edges away. As she gets within reach, her legs fold under her and she collapses into me.

I breathe her in, her lank, greasy curls, her stale clothes, and hug her tightly. "It's okay, Wills," I whisper. "We're okay."

*And Essie's alive.*

The banging grows louder still, behind the wall to the left, then stops. A splintering crack follows. Kerry gasps. Willow jolts in my arms, but her face stays nestled in my chest. Hushed voices are followed by a yell. A gun fires; a scream.

"Down on the floor. NOW."

Our three guards exchange wide-eyed looks and dive for the door. Pushing Willow behind me, I follow them out through the anteroom.

The corridor is a mess of shattered brick, concrete, and muddy, flailing limbs. Ten feet away, before a left-hand bend, filthy water foams around a hole in the wall. It swells to ankle level in the corridor. Spewing out with the flood, more thrashing bodies.

Someone shouts, "There's another breach."

Guards appear from the other side. Bullets rip the air and ricochet, sending sparks and a burning stink. My ears ring.

"They broke in." Kerry grips my shoulder.

"Who?"

She pulls me backwards. "Come on."

Grabbing Willow's hand, I wade away, following Kerry as she bounces off the wall and turns left. We take a flight up from the water. We're out, but the gushing and yelling continues downstairs. More shots fire. Willow is sobbing as I gasp for air. Ahead of us, Kerry plants her hands on her knees and coughs. It flashes through my mind that we could run. Christ knows what's happening down there, but Kerry's as confused as I am. What if we just took off?

It's too late. She recovers herself, drawing a gun from a strap on her calf. Holding it up, she grasps Willow's wrist and pulls her close. "Don't think about it, Seth. You wouldn't get very far in this place."

I glance behind me, into the dark stairwell. "What the hell is going on down there?"

She flicks a strand of loose hair out of her eyes. "I'm guessing it's the London rebels." She giggles, a manic gleam in her eyes. "Langford's been going insane trying to locate them, and now here they are, crashing into us." She circles to her right, forcing me to pivot away from the stairs. Her eyes darken, flickering down the steps, then fixing on me. "Forget about them. You're with me now."

"I don't fucking think so." Langford's voice slithers up the stairs, followed by his gleaming bald head. He draws level, shoving me back into the wall with a hand on my chest, then turns away. "Kerry, what the fuck?"

Her eyes track his face. "I was trying to—"

"Steal my hostages?" He plucks the gun from her hand, grabs her shirt, spins, and shoves her next to me. When Willow stumbles, he snakes a thick arm around her neck and pulls her backwards out of reach, resting against the opposite wall. "When will I learn? You are a snake in the grass, Tyler. Can't believe I let you back in."

The gun flicks between Kerry and me. Willow whimpers and my heart lurches. Down below, the shouting has quietened to the occasional barked instruction and yelp of pain. They must have subdued the rebels. From the sound of it the water is still rushing.

Langford looks down at Willow then glares at me across the landing, his face a rigid landscape of rage. "You know what? Why do I need two of you? Your bitch whore girlfriend will be just as compliant with only one of you to save. Maybe more so. In fact, I don't even need her for information anymore."

Kerry's shoulder shifts against mine as she glances at the steps. It's gone terribly silent down there.

281

Langford's eyes grow misty with hate. "I'm thinking a primetime TV appearance. Glass denouncing the rebels; declaring her support for my government. A plea for the end to this senseless violence. That'd be apt."

Fury scorches my insides, forcing the breath out of me. "Mate, you have picked the wrong girl for that shit. She'd die first."

A gun fires below, followed by screams quelled to sobs.

Langford inclines his head. "If her daughter's life was in the balance..." he tightens his grip on Willow's neck, "she might."

Another shot explodes downstairs, more sobs. Are they being executed? I swallow bile as Kerry glances into the darkness again.

"Daddy." Willow's voice shatters with terror. Her wet eyes plead as she blinks back the tears.

Langford's gun hand tenses. The barrel seems to swell as it points at me. "Sorry, *mate*."

A figure bursts from the stairs, leaping in front of Langford. There's a flash of red hair; an animal roar. My crazed brain thinks *lion* and then a shot slashes the air. Blood sprays, the yell warps to a scream of pain. The figure thumps to the floor, limbs stuck out at awkward angles. Langford stares at the thing he shot, eyes unfocussed. The gun drops from his limp fingers, clattering on the concrete. When I follow his gaze, it's like an electric shock bolting through me.

Gabe lies groaning, hand clutched to his stomach, blood bubbling out of him and spreading. The air turns to hot metal and fire. This is Gabe. The guy who betrayed Essie, who we thought was dead but isn't. But now he might be.

He just saved my life. Why did he do that?

Another shot fires further away downstairs.

I squat down to see if he's breathing. "Gabe?"

"Seth..." Gabe's eyes are closed, and his breath is wet. Blood foams around his lips. He coughs, then turns aside and vomits onto my shoes. "Sor..."

"Gabe. What the—?"

He grabs my hand, his fingers cold. "Shh. Parl..."

"What?"

"Palm… parmunt. Hallie. Go." Another gurgling cough.

"Parliament?" I can't make sense of this.

He nods, eyes red and feverish. "Yesss. The others. Go."

Fast movements rouse me. Too late, I realise it's just me and Gabe. Langford's feet disappear up the stairs, his gun gone from the floor. Willow's tiny pink trainers scuffle along with them.

"Hey." With a glance back at Gabe, I sprint after Langford.

As I climb flight after flight, it grows dimmer and hotter. It's just sobs and slapping, stumbling feet. I follow the sounds, gasping. "Langford. *Bring her back*."

The footsteps stop above. A door slams. Then silence.

"LANGFORD." Scrambling up the last steps, I run full pelt into metal. "SHIT." I slam a fist into the door, a bolt of agony ripping up my arm into my shoulder. A yell of frustration and despair rips out of me as I grab my wounded fist and kick the metal.

"You'll break your foot doing that." Kerry descends from the floor above, panting. She's holding her gun pointed down. Behind her, a figure lurks in the dark. Other than our breathing, it's silent up here. "They're gone, Seth. You can't get to them."

"So I just let him take my daughter?" Icy panic presses on my chest, despite the sweat running down it. I've lost her again.

"I'm not saying that. But we need to get out of here in one piece."

"How?"

She nods up the stairs. "I think there's a way out up here."

I want to believe her, but… "You expect me to trust you now?"

The figure steps to the side of Kerry, out of the shadows. "Trust *me*." Her tongue stud glints in the dim light.

"Hallie." I glance down the stairwell. "Gabe's…"

She swipes her eyes with a shaky forearm. "I know. But he made me promise if anything went wrong, if I needed to, I would leave him. 'Just keep going,' he said. 'No regrets.'

I…" She breaks in a sob. "They're killing people down there, Seth. What choice do we have?"

"He said parliament. That place is so heavily guarded, without an army you wouldn't stand a chance."

Hallie sniffs. "When our camp started letting in water, we split into two groups. We were to find the way to the Unity bunker and try to take it. The others went to Westminster to hit them there." Her voice is hoarse and rapid. "Only, we thought we had more time, then the water started pouring in, so we had to run. No time to get the weapons. Seth, we'd built an arsenal. Then we're fumbling around lost in dark tunnels. It was your worst nightmare. I thought we were going to die out there." She sobs. "Instead, we just died in here."

Kerry's gaping at Hallie. She grabs her shoulders. "Was a boy called Carlo there? He's seventeen."

Hallie nods, her lip curling. "Your son. He was in the group that went to parliament. Said he wanted to see your expression when everything crumbled around your ears."

Kerry puts a hand to her mouth, then glances around her. "We have to go. This way."

Hallie's eyes linger on mine, and she moves her lower jaw as though chewing on her tongue stud. Then she turns and trails Kerry up the stairs.

Insides cold with fear for Willow, I follow.

# Chapter Thirty-Three

## Essie

### 26th November 2041 12.15pm

"This way," whispers Caleb from the mouth of the tunnel. He takes one last glance above ground before descending the ladder, diver's torch in hand.

I could have kissed him when he appeared as I waded through the gates out of Hampstead Heath. He must be a good lookout, because he pulled sentry duty again, guarding the surrounding areas while the others attack the Unity bunker and parliament. When I asked him how they planned to get past Westminster security, he gave a wry smile, which made the bile rise in my throat. If he was pissed off to be left out of the action, he's over it. It took some initial persuading to make him abandon his post and show me the way.

It's a relief to be out of the rain, though the tunnel's diesel smell is suffocating.

"It's not far," says Caleb as I follow him. "But it'll take longer because we have to use secondary tunnels. The main ones flooded."

"Any chance the secondary ones will too?"

He shrugs "Maybe. It's guesswork now. I haven't been able to contact the others for the last hour or so." His brow furrows. "They had to leave most of the armoury behind in the flood. I just hope…" He shakes his head and moves on.

Ten minutes later, my socks are soaked inside my trainers as we wade through stinking, ankle-deep stuff which isn't exactly water. We halt at the top of a ramp descending into a filthy lake.

Caleb points down it. "This is the only entrance."

"To the bunker?"

He nods, then takes a phone out of his pocket and slots it into a gap between bricks high in the wall. "We'll have to swim."

"Oh, Jesus."

There's no time to freak out about the stench. We wade in until it becomes quicker to swim. The curved ceiling of the tunnel, its warped copper pipes, are less than a foot above my head. All the world's heat is concentrated in the tiny space. My cheeks burn. Though I bite my lips closed, the fumes of shit and rot invade my mouth and the cuts on my wrists and neck. My eyes sting.

There's another ten minutes of hell before Caleb turns in the water. "This is the last bend before the breach. It's a hundred yards, on the right."

I put my foot down, but the floor of the tunnel is too deep, and I'm forced to tread water. "Thanks, Caleb. I'll be fine from here."

He shakes his head. "You'll need my help. There'll be guards and they'll have blocked the tunnel."

"No. You need to get back to your position. They're relying on you." I try to hold my mouth above the water as I speak, but the disgusting filth gets in, making me gag. "What if someone finds the phone you hid in the tunnel? What if Kim finds a way to call you and you don't have it on you? Go back."

His smooth head twists the way we came, then back. From his furrowed brow, he knows I'm right. He turns off the torch and hands it to me. "I don't need this. I know the way. Hope you find your family." The water eddies around me as he backs away.

"Good luck." I listen to the lapping, feet kicking the dirty water up around my head, heart thrashing just as hard. His splashes and grunts recede.

It's just me now. I swim on towards the bend in the tunnel. Flat against the brick, I peek around the corner.

Darkness stretches with silence. Taking in a shaky breath of putrid air, I ease out into the open, keeping my limbs below the waterline. I daren't switch on the torch. If someone comes now, there's nowhere to hide. Caleb said the breach was to the right, so I swim that way until my fingers brush the curved wall of the tunnel, and I pull myself along. The hot air presses around me. I swallow the panic squeezing my chest. After a few minutes, my fingers brush a jagged edge of brick. My foot kicks something hard and it shifts away. If there were guards here, they've gone now. The place is near enough submerged. Heart hammering, I risk the torch and shine it at the wall. There's a three-inch gap above the waterline, no more. And God knows what's beyond it. With a huge inhale, I duck below and propel myself through the breach.

Rising to the surface again, I spit rancid water and gasp. I'm in a flooded concrete corridor. My foot brushes against something yielding. Instinct throws a nasty thought into my mind and a groan escapes me.

*Please, no...*

I have to know. Eyes wide, I point the torch down. Through the filthy fog, something is floating, like seaweed fronds. I duck below the water again. It stings my eyes, but I keep them open and push myself down. Floating inches away from me, a blank, staring face. Pale, distorted, but I know it.

*Kim.*

I thrash up, breaking the surface. My hand clamps over my mouth, stifling a scream. Breath spits between my fingers, my eyes streaming with fumes and shock. Kim's dead. There were others down there, too, hands and wisps of hair behind Kim. They killed them. Or they drowned.

A strangled sob bursts out before I can stop it. Dark shapes spread in my vision. I rest my head on what's left of the concrete wall and breathe in gasps until my eyes clear.

*Get it together, Ess. Seth and Willow, remember?*

I shine the torch up and down the corridor. It's empty. Silent except for the hammering of my heartbeat in my ears and the quiet, eerie lapping. To the right, the corridor stretches away into black. Twenty yards ahead, on my left, a concrete staircase rises out of the water. If there is an escape, this is my best bet. Limbs quivering with exhaustion, I pull myself along that way. My feet stumble on the bottom step. Several risers guide me up and out of the godforsaken muck I've been wallowing in. At the half-landing, I follow the right-angled turn and freeze.

A forearm flops through the railings of the floor above. A groan echoes.

Trying to prevent my trainers from squelching, I creep up the last steps. As I gain the landing, my foot slips in something dark and I fall to one knee. The tang is unmistakable.

Blood. Still wet.

Another groan makes me look up. Red-blonde dreadlocks glimmer in my torch beam.

No. Oh, no. "Gabe?"

"'ssie?" He shifts his head one way then the other. I'm out of his eyeline.

"Oh, shit. Gabe. They shot you." I move around to his front and drop to my knees again. Blood is oozing out of a wound in his stomach, running over his fingers, pooling on the floor. His mouth is caked in blood and vomit.

"Seth…"

"You saw Seth? He's alive?"

Gabe closes his eyes and nods. The movement racks him with a cough. He twists his head to the side and spits blood. "Hallie. Parlment."

"Parliament? That's where they've gone?"

He grunts, his head moving the tiniest bit.

I have so many questions, it's hard to choose the right ones. "When? Does Langford have him? Kerry? Where's Willow?"

"Ysss. Ke…. Five m-mi. Up." His eyes squint up the stairs.

I'm five minutes behind them, that's all. "I'll get help."

"Nnnn." His eyes close again. He's shivering.

"Gabe." I shake his shoulders, heedless of his wound. "Gabe, don't. Open your eyes. Open them."

His eyelids twitch but stay closed. He gives a deep shudder, then lies still.

"Gabe, please." I sob and shake him again. "Please."

I must leave. Wiping my eyes, I rise and back away from Gabe. A few steps later, I turn and sprint up the stairs. Gabe meant they went up. It's the only way they wouldn't have drowned. I gasp for breath and race up flight after flight, flashlight bouncing. I've no clue what's up here, what's next, but it's all I have. Forward is the only choice.

I run out of stairs. At the top, I slam into a metal door. With no real hope, I push, and it gives way. I stumble into the open. Rain hammers my head and already-soaking clothes. Shitty water runs off me in rivers.

I'm in a dim alley between the windowless walls of two tall brick buildings. Sodden cardboard boxes lie scattered on the crumbling tarmac next to a row of dumpsters. The air reeks of river and rotting waste.

"How the fuck are you still alive?"

I squint down the passageway towards the voice. Langford is holding Willow by the throat.

"Mummy." Her whole body is shaking.

My heart cramps with joy and rage. "Let her go, Langford." The weight in my back imprints on my brain. It's been there all along, in the waistband of my jeans, but in my grief and panic I forgot.

I yank out the gun as he points his at Willow's head.

"Don't be an idiot, Glass."

My hand tightens on the handle, its lattice pattern burning. He's using her as a shield, but Willow's half his height. Could I shoot him over her head?

*This isn't a Western, Ess. And you've fired a gun only once in your whole life.*

"Yeah, you could try it." As if he can read my thoughts, he hunkers lower behind Willow, keeping the gun at her temple. "Don't like your chances, though." He lifts her up as he backs away.

I make a sound between a sob and a yell. "*Let her go*."

"You could shoot me right now." He grins. "Right through *her*. Go on, Glass. How much do you want me dead?"

Willow struggles in his arms, dips her head, and bites his gun hand. He roars and throws her to the floor. There's a horrible thud and Willow screams.

"Don't." I pull back the slide. My fingers tighten on the trigger.

Langford laughs, then looms over Willow as she tries to sit up. He lifts a foot and thrusts it into her chest. She quietens as Langford raises the gun. "You won't risk shooting at me. What if you miss? I'll blow your little girl's head off. Drop it." When I don't move, he lowers his aim at Willow, who's still on the ground, her wet hair splayed around her. "Maya... Lawrence... Piper. Now Gabe. How many more people you love are going to die before you learn your lesson, Glass?"

"Lesson." It's all I can get out as Jonah's gun clatters on wet concrete.

"Back off." He advances as I retreat and picks up the gun with a sigh. "Better. You are nothing. About time you acted like it." Behind him, a massive Jeep pulls up, blocking the alley's exit. "Get over here, you stupid bitch."

There's no choice; nowhere else to go. With every step closer, my legs grow weaker, my hope dimmer. Willow scrambles up, throwing herself against me with a sob.

The Jeep door screeches as Langford yanks it open. "In."

The seats are lined with plastic.

Langford climbs in after us, his nose twitching. "You stink, Glass." Then, to the man in front: "Take us to the HP. The secure way."

The driver nods and pulls away, sending a muddy spray past my window. Willow clutches my arms and hides her face in my lap as she weeps.

"Shhh. It's okay, Wills. We're okay."

But even a four-year-old can see how far from okay we are.

# Chapter Thirty-Four

## Seth

### 26th November 2041 1.00 pm

Hallie kneels on the roof of the truck and reaches down to help me out of the torrent. A Fiat 500 glides past the space where I've just been thrashing about, sliding sideways into a BMW with a muted thump.

"Need help here." Kerry's voice cracks, coming from the rear of the vehicle.

We scamper that way and peek over the edge. She's clinging to the rear door, which is swinging open, pulled back and forth by the current. Her head keeps going under the waterline several feet below us.

Hallie glares down. "Leave her."

"We can't leave her."

"After everything she's done? Bitch deserves to drown."

Kerry coughs, her blue shirt ballooning around her head as she peers up at me. "Please, Seth."

"Oh, fucking hell." I lean down and grab her hand. "Push yourself up."

She fumbles in the water, finding a foothold.

"One, two, three, go."

Kerry launches out of the water, gripping me, her nails digging into my wrists as I haul her onto the roof. My shoulder screams. She lands with a wet plop and curls into another coughing fit as Hallie stands over her, nostrils flaring. She looks like she wants to kick Kerry back into the water.

I stand and rest a warning hand on her arm. "Hallie."

She shakes me off. "You should've left her."

"Thank you, Seth." Kerry sits up, gasping, and gazes about us. "Jesus."

Westminster Bridge is submerged, indistinguishable from the river. Anything smaller than the delivery truck we're standing on is floating or sunk. Water gushes around us, roiling with foam, stinking of raw sewage and oil. Rain clatters on the truck's roof. The atmosphere is thick with shouts of fear and anger. Way off somewhere, a loudhailer harangues the air. Shots fire; drones whine. People thrash in the water, clinging to whatever they can find. More than one body has floated past us.

"The security barriers've collapsed." Kerry nods ahead to the end of the bridge, where water cascades towards the Houses of Parliament. "Last week, this place was like Fort Knox. Armed guards, drones, the lot." Her voice is flat and distant, as though she's concussed.

"Their pumps have failed, too." I glare at Kerry. "That's what they were doing, isn't it? Pumping the flood away from themselves, back to the poor neighbourhoods."

She ignores the question and turns to Hallie. "You said Carlo came here?"

Eyes narrowed, Hallie nods. "He'll be up there somewhere." She flaps a hand towards parliament. "If he's still alive."

Kerry must feel the heat of my stare because she looks back and gives me an unstable smile.

"Where is Langford, Kerry? Where's he taken my daughter?"

"I've no idea where he'd go."

"Bollocks. You've been his lackey on and off for years."

She sighs and looks down, rubbing a nail along a gouge in the paintwork. "Knowing him, he's gone where the action is." She nods up at the parliament building. "But don't quote me. Langford's a law unto himself."

"You got that right." Hallie stares into the looming face of the Clock Tower. "He killed my brother. Gabe thought so from the start. I didn't believe it at first. Now I'm sure of it."

I follow her gaze. The clock reads eleven-thirty, though it's surely past one in the afternoon. Maybe the rebels have captured the building and stopped it. Or the storm has buggered the works.

"Bloody hell." Eyes wide, Kerry grabs my shoulder and points.

The black bow of a boat is gliding right for us. "Oh, shit. Hallie, hold on."

The craft strikes with a deep thud, rocking the truck sideways, launching us towards the opposite edge. Hallie screams and grabs on to my arm. Her legs pedal furiously over the precipice. I roar and grip tighter. The roof lurches back, thumping us down again. Hallie scrambles up and huddles next to me.

"Oh Jesus." Kerry is clinging onto the other edge, eyes bulging.

We're flat to the roof, gasping for breath. I crawl closer to the edge and peer at the boat. It's nestled in a huge dent in our truck, anchored there. The windscreen, if that's what it's called, is the right height to overlook us. The sign at the top glowers in blue and white.

*POLICE.*

Hinged to the bow, pointing at us: a gun.

I blow out a wet breath. "It's a patrol boat."

"Thank Christ it's empty," says Hallie.

"This is great." Kerry grins. "There'll be life jackets. Might be a dinghy."

She scampers to the edge, swings her legs around, and drops with a grunt. When I look over the edge, she's standing on the bow, shading her eyes with her hand as she squints up.

"Come on." She ducks around the side of the cabin, gripping the rails.

With a glance back at Hallie, I lower myself over the side. My knees jar as I land on the boards. The boat sways, squealing against the damaged flank of the truck. I follow Kerry into the cabin. It's a waterlogged mess, with random

293

equipment floating in the small space and broken instruments on the dashboard.

Kerry is knee deep in filth, delving underneath the waterline. "Gotta be something down here... Ah." She pulls up a yellow life jacket, flicking off the mud, and holds it up. "It's gotta be worth a try with one of these." The boat rocks back and forth and Kerry falls against the wall. "Might be able to float up to the tower. The water's only risen a floor or so there."

"Are there more jackets?" If there's only one, no doubt she's earmarked it for herself.

She twists and plunges her hands into the water again. "Think so." She yanks up with two more fluorescent jackets and holds them out for me. She's staring at me with an expression I can't fathom. "Seth. If you should make it out..."

"What?"

She shakes her head and starts fiddling with her life jacket. Then her hands drop to her sides as she looks at the ceiling. "Oh, shit. What are you doing, Kerry?"

"*What?*"

She frowns, mutters to herself, then flaps a hand at the window. "If we get another chance. To make all this stop..."

Metal squeals as the boat shifts again. Hallie's face appears over the edge, mouthing something I can't hear.

I look back at Kerry. "Spit it out, will you?"

"I found Jack. He's alive."

For a moment, I can't place the name. Exhaustion and fear, I guess. I have to repeat it to make an impression on my brain.

"Yes, Jack," she says. "At the safehouse. I was going to make him build the carbon capture thing again. He owes me. Or so I... Doesn't matter. If you get out. If he hasn't drowned. He's in Brent Cross, St Mary's Road. He could help you." Her eyes grow vague and unfocused. She turns to gaze through the side window at the Clock Tower. "Someone has to stop these people."

"SETH." Hallie screams as something thuds into the boat,

sending us reeling. With a metallic screech, the boat pulls free and shifts. We're thrown back as the boat's stern dips.

Kerry grips my arm. We lurch out of the cabin back on deck as Hallie falls to her knees at the bow.

"What the hell?" I glare at her. "We're coming now."

She gasps. "Jesus Christ, Seth, a bloody dinghy's just slammed into you. Didn't you hear me yelling?"

She's right. It's banked up on the stern, orange PVC bow pointing at the dark sky. The rear of the patrol boat sinks further as the weight of the dinghy takes hold.

"Could we use it?" Hallie's voice is jagged, but there's a spark of hope in it.

"I doubt it." Kerry has donned her lifejacket and is tying the chord at her side as she scrambles astern. "There's a breach in the hull. Either way, I don't have time to mess about with you. Carlo's out there."

I glance at Hallie as Kerry pauses for a moment, staring at the water rushing over the deck. Her shoulders lift and settle. Turning to face us, Kerry gives a tired smile. "Good luck."

She drops into the water.

# Chapter Thirty-Five

## Essie

### 26th November 2041 2.00pm

The leather chair creaks as Langford shifts Willow on his lap. I sit stiff on a hardwood chair opposite, staring at Jonah's gun on the desk between us. I can't bear to see Willow with his thick fingers curled around her tiny arms, her tear-streaked face a mask of confusion and fear.

Outside, the shouting continues. No guns have fired in a while. Caleb said they had to leave most of their weapons behind in the flood. Is that a good or a bad thing?

Someone is making a valiant attempt with a loudhailer, though: "Langford OUT… RESIST… STAND BACK FROM THE LEDGE. THE WATER'S SURGING."

Screams and rushing water ricochet below us. Thunder rumbles above. Then the whine of drones that makes my stomach churn. The dark room grows even darker.

"Sounds like your mates are having a tricky time down there." Langford chuckles. "Do they seem a little… *unprepared*…for this revolution to you?"

Sweat trickles down my temple. I shoot him a venomous look, but that was a mistake, because the sight of him clutching Willow winds up the nausea. My hands curl into fists. "With any luck, it'll surge again. Drown this vile place, and you with it."

"Not likely." His face smooths into indifference as he glances around the oak-panelled, stone-flagged office. "We're in the penthouse here. Four floors and more than a hundred feet up."

The office's only windows are too high to see if that's true. We rode in a featureless steel lift up from the basement level when he brought us here. Shoving me along a dark, green-carpeted corridor, he told me we were in the Houses of Parliament, like he was so impressed with himself for bringing me here he couldn't help it.

"Why don't you just kill me?" The brutality of my words hits home when Willow sobs, but the question remains.

"Do you want me to?" He peers over Willow's curls, eyes wide as though he's curious.

"You've got everything you want now."

He scoffs and glances at the windows. "Hardly."

"It's not like you haven't murdered before."

He screws up his lips, tips Willow off his lap and stands. When she tries to scramble towards me, he grabs her hair and yanks her upright.

She yelps. "Mummy."

"*Don't hurt her*!" I dive towards them, but back away when Langford snatches Jonah's gun from the desk. "Please don't." My voice is small, almost a whisper.

"I won't. *If…*"

"If what?"

"First." His eyes glint at me as he pivots the barrel towards the chair. "Down."

Every part of my skin burns with fury. I drop into the chair as if my legs are on rusty hinges.

"Good. Now, we can rehearse your part." At his last word, lightning flickers in the darkened windows, its glare bouncing off his head.

Bass thunder rumbles my insides. "The hell are you talking about?"

"You're going primetime." His perfectly aligned teeth gleam under the chandelier. "*How I learned to stop worrying and love Unity*, starring Essie Glass."

No words come while it sinks in. Then, "Fuck off."

"Charming."

"I'm not doing fucking propaganda for you, you prick.

What do you take me for?"

"What do you take *yourself* for, you arrogant bitch?" He yanks at Willow's hair again, making her hiss. His eyes narrow as they flash up and down me. "Look at you. Take just one honest look at yourself your whole life, Glass. You think you're staging a rebellion? Don't make me laugh. If you were any kind of revolutionary, I'd be dead already. Pitiful."

Despite his order, I leap to my feet. I won't sit for this crap. "*I'm* pitiful? A tinpot dictator is all you are. Squashing your fat neck into an old Eton tie doesn't make you a leader."

"What the fuck would you know? Leading this country, keeping the lights burning with this shit going on. It's more complex than you could imagine."

I thrust a finger at the window. "It's falling apart. On your watch. If history survives today, that's how you're going to be remembered. The man who murdered his way to power, lined his pockets, and let it happen. If I'm still around, I'll make sure of it."

He yanks Willow's hair again and shifts the gun away from her face to point at me. "History? I'd worry about your future. There's a hot pit in hell waiting for you, bitch." His eyes narrow. "You lied to me. When your friend was in pain, dying in that prison. You lied about the date, casual as you like. That takes a special kind of cold."

"How's your son, Alex?" My voice cracks like tinder. The gun stays on me, so I keep talking. "I saw him in the painting. You, your son, and father... Your poor wife. Hanging in that mansion of yours back home. You remember. When I was looking for Maya after you *murdered* her. My age, is he? Younger? Is he happy to let the planet suffocate while Daddy flounces around in Jags making deals to colonise the fucking moon?" I glance up at the window, where the sky lights up again. "I'm guessing he doesn't live in London. Or he does, and you don't give a shit he might be drowning."

His cheeks flood scarlet. "Shut the fuck up. You know nothing."

The memory of the family portrait flashes. "More than you think. That picture… Three generations of Langford men primed to beat the world into submission. If Junior's ashamed of you, that's gotta sting."

Langford's knuckles shine white around the gun. "You don't talk about my son."

"Why not? You ashamed of him, too? Or are you just too scared of *Daddy* to love him?"

The rage in his grey eyes dissolves, leaving ice that freezes my blood. The gun twitches as his grip tightens. "Fuck you, Glass."

A flash blinds me. Willow screams. Langford roars. An explosion distorts in my ears. Where's the bullet? Has it hit me, and I don't know it yet? Wouldn't it hurt more?

Willow cries out again, a wet, stricken sound.

On my knees, I force my eyes open. "WILLOW."

She's lying by the desk. Blood covers the right side of her face, welling through her clutched fingers. Oh Christ, he shot her. I scream and spring towards her, my knees scraping on the stone floor.

Nearby, Langford's feet splay outwards. He's motionless.

Willow's in my arms, sobbing, screaming like me. I grab her shoulders, pull back, and cup her face. She winces as I probe the wound on her cheek with desperate fingers. It's not deep, just bleeding a lot.

She twists away from me, vomits onto Langford's shoes and weeps. "It hurts."

"I know. You're okay. We're going to be okay." I rock her back and forth, shushing her.

Langford's foot twitches, and he groans something unintelligible. Sliding Willow off my lap, I scramble to his side. He's got a head wound too, but it looks more serious. A section of face by his nose has caved into a bloody mess.

Jonah's gun lies by his hip, the barrel split and peeled back lengthways like a banana skin. It must have misfired as he tried to shoot me. I attempt to pick it up, but it's burning hot, so I kick it away. It skitters into the far wall. Langford groans again and offers a wet cough which sends bloody bubbles out of the space that was his nose. His fingers twitch towards his waist. I thrust a hand in his back and come out with his gun. If he'd been less pissed off, he'd have had the sense to use it instead of Jonah's—and I'd be dead.

Langford's head lolls from side to side. He opens his eyes. Grabbing Willow's hand, I scoot back and point the gun at his face as he rises to sitting.

His eyes are bloodshot and hazy with hate. "You bitch." His voice gurgles. He spits blood. "You knew it would misfire."

"No." We back away. "The flood must have damaged it. I'm not sorry, though."

"I bet you're fucking not." He drags himself closer.

"Don't move." We're against the wall now, facing the tiny windows. More lightning flickers.

He raises shaky palms and gives a wet laugh, more blood boiling out of his mouth. "What now? I'm the fucking Prime Minister. Killing me would be suicide, and even you're not that dumb."

"Sit in that chair and shut up." I need to think.

But there's no time. Shouting in the corridor makes us all jump. Security forces. It's over. I push Willow behind me and hold my breath as the door slams open.

A young woman stumbles in. She's head to toe in filth, dark hair matted with mud and silt. A megaphone hangs in her hand. Her eyes glow white as she stares at me, and a tongue stud glints in the chandelier light.

"Ess! Oh my God, Ess. What the hell?" She runs into me, almost knocking me over. With a frown, she glances down at Willow.

"Hallie?" I pull her back and peer at her face, then nudge her aside. "Don't move, Langford."

Hallie whips around, falling backward into the wall as her eyes touch his ruined face. Her mouth opens, but nothing comes out.

"Yeah." I glance her way. "I've got the Prime Minister at gunpoint. So…"

She stares at him, me, the gun. Then explodes in manic

laughter. "Jesus Christ, Ess. Here I am looking for a balcony to address the crowd. Impressed with myself for getting this far. And you've shot the fucking Prime Minister."

"I didn't shoot him. He shot himself; and hurt Willow."

"Christ, is she okay?" She peers down at Willow again.

"I think she will be."

"Jesus, Ess. How…?"

I shake my head. "Long story. How did you get in here?"

"Whole place is deserted. I guess they evacuated when the pumps failed." She leans on the desk, her face pale around dark-rimmed eyes. "So here we are. The question is what now?"

I squint down at Langford, dimly aware of the distant chop of helicopter blades. An idea is sculpting itself in my mind. "Let's find that balcony."

# Chapter Thirty-Six

# Kerry

## 26th November 2041 2.30pm

Self-inflatable life rafts—you've got to love them. This one disentangled itself from the police boat when the dinghy hit us. Had to give the rope a good yank to free it. That alerted them something was afoot. Still, it was too late by then. Seth's face was a picture as he watched me ease away, the plastic paddle slicing through the choppy water. His mouth was moving, hands flapping.

It gave me little joy, but I have to find Carlo. I can't afford passengers with other agendas. Hallie, at least, wants me dead. Still, I hope they find a way out, maybe on this floating debris.

The air is rank with the fish-and-sewage smell of the river. The flood has swelled in the last half hour, rushing in with the tide. Thunder rumbles. God knows what happens if lightning strikes the water. Will we fry with the dying fish flopping around me?

The lowest buildings are nothing but rooftops now, crowded with filthy, bedraggled refugees. Helicopters circle overhead, occupants loud-hailing unheeded instructions for everyone to stay calm and follow the security forces' orders. But the security forces don't look calm. Shots fire as young men in uniform lose control. A body falls from a stone balcony and lands just shy of the raft, splashing bloody water in my face. Above, the helmeted head of a policeman pokes over the edge beside a rifle.

The crowd heaves to and fro in the water, but there's no single purpose. Voices tangle together, filled with anger, panic and grief. A young woman with a weeping burn on her cheek thrashes towards me with pleading eyes. I pivot the raft, so the opening of the tented cover swings away from her, and paddle on.

God forgive me.

I cast my eyes around the gloom, searching every visible face for Carlo's. When I scream for him, his is one of a hundred names in the air. Armed drones buzz overhead, but they sound wrong—tinny and undulating. They keep swooping down, then up, clicking. Maybe the storm has interfered with their navigation, or the rebels have hacked them.

I'm steering past the back of the Abbey now, the peak of its stone arch entrance just visible above the waterline. Spiky gothic towers loom out of the muddy mess like angels of death. Beyond it, bodies move between the crenelations that line the low roof of the Catholic church of St Margaret's. The bronze statue of Oliver Cromwell, just a bust in the flood, glowers across the road.

A shot fires up on the church roof, followed by a yell. A face appears in a crenel, silhouetted until the eyes pop wide.

"Mum. Jesus. MUM."

I squint through the rain, but I can't make out the features.

"KERRY TYLER."

I know that voice. "Carlo?"

He waves, but someone comes up behind him and grabs his arm. His face disappears from the battlements.

"CARLO!"

A lower flat roof abuts the main body of the church where Carlo sat. It's three feet above the water. I paddle towards it.

Thrusting a hand out, I grasp the blackened grey stone of the parapet and pull the raft onwards. It wobbles when I stand and turn my back to the wall. As I thrust up, the raft slides under me. I scramble backwards, searching for purchase on the wall, and push back enough to perch my bum and avoid falling into the water. With a grunt, I swing my legs and dive

303

back for the raft, catching hold of a trailing rope. It's long enough to tie around a merlon.

A yelp above makes me spin. Dark-jeaned legs dangle off the tiled, pitched roof facing me, knocking against a mullioned window. Above the legs and a bedraggled middle, Carlo is wild-eyed. He's bleeding from the temple, drops flying as he's kicked from behind. A police officer with thread-veined, slab-like cheeks looms over him, rifle aimed at his head.

"That's my son."

The officer scowls down at me. "Well, your son just killed a man." He nods down and to my left.

Ten feet away on the flat roof, a flak-jacketed body lies in disarray, one foot trapped beneath the torso. The head is turned away and he's not moving. Blood oozes from his crown.

"He slipped." Carlo's voice is brittle with panic. "I swear, he tried to grab me and lost his balance."

"Shut the fuck up." The officer twists his rifle, whipping it back down handle-first on Carlo's head.

Carlo whimpers, crumpling forward.

"STOP IT!" My chest constricts, bile rising in my throat.

The officer turns his tiny black eyes on me and curls his lip. Without looking away, he shoves Carlo. With a strangled yell, Carlo thumps to the floor.

"Carlo!" I rush to his side, glaring at the cop. "He's unarmed, you didn't have to do that." His shrug stokes my fury. "Do you know who I am? I work for Alex Langford. You know; the Prime Minister."

He hangs his legs over the side and launches off the slates, landing with an oof on his fat knees. "I don't give a shit who you work for. Your son threw my partner off the roof and now he's going to pay."

Through clenched teeth, Carlo says, "He fell. And you know it."

Rifle aimed at us on the floor, the cop backs away towards his partner. Tripping over an arm, he takes a shaky step to the other side of the body then leans down, feeling his partner's neck and chest. A choking sound comes out of his mouth.

Carlo nods, a sneer twisting his face. "Good. One less pig waving a gun."

"Carlo!" I grab his hand.

The cop stands, head cocked to one side, shoulders high. "What did you say?" He steps around his dead partner and raises the rifle's sight to his eye.

"No. Wait." I'm on my feet, holding out a shaky hand.

"Fuck you."

"No!" I spring as the rifle flashes. Fire hits my stomach. Pain so intense I can't breathe to scream. My hands clutch, my legs fold under me. Wet warmth spreads down from my belly button as I topple sideways.

"MUM." Carlo grabs my arm, then he's gone. "You fucking PIG." A roar almost as loud as the shot comes out of him as he reappears in front of me, lunging at the cop.

"No…" My voice won't work. The pain intensifies as I sit.

The rifle fires again, and I'm powerless to stop what comes next.

But Carlo keeps running. The cop missed him. Carlo crashes into him, propelling them both to the edge of the roof. The rifle clatters to the floor. They hang there, panting in each other's faces. Then Carlo thrusts his hands forward and his body back, hitting the deck.

Eyes wide, the cop flails his arms for a second, then disappears. A deep plop sounds as he hits the water.

*Like shit hitting the pan.*

"Mum." Carlo scrabbles up, grabbing the rifle, and limps towards me.

"Carlo, I'm—" But talking sends another fireball into my tummy.

"Shhh. It's okay." He's stroking my hair, tears streaming down his face. "We've got a doctor. Halima's at the Clock Tower. At least, that was the plan. Do you think you can walk?"

"Think so." My insides burn when I try to get up. The

305

world slips away into black.

"Mum." Carlo sobs. "Hold on to my neck." He puts his arm under my knees and lifts me as if I'm a child, though I'm almost as tall as he is. The drop into the raft is brutal, but I bite in the cry.

"We'll get you help, okay?" The muscles of his arms strain at his t-shirt as he paddles us away from the church.

"Carlo." My hands are stiff. I'm floating like I've had too much wine.

"Halima's not far."

"Carlo."

"No." Another sob. "You're going to be fine. No speeches, okay?"

"I love you."

He frowns at me and shakes his head, then returns to his frantic paddling.

"I'm sorry."

"Later, yeah? I'm busy right now."

The pain fades with my vision. Seconds later, it's merciful darkness.

***

"Jesus, Kerry."

I open my eyes, the sting of irritation giving way to a searing pain in my belly. Seth Fielding's eyes are wide with shock. I must look shit. One glance confirms it, my belly a mash of clots and oozing blood.

He got out, though. That's good.

Seth looks at my middle and grimaces. "What the hell happened to you?"

Somewhere further off, Carlo says, "Fucking cop shot her."

"Wh…" It's so hard to speak now. "…here?"

Seth and Carlo exchange glances. Behind them, the gothic hulk of the Clock Tower floats past.

Carlo leans closer. "They've got Langford."

"Who's…?"

Seth smiles, then shifts aside as Carlo puts a gentle hand on my back to lift me. I can't suppress the yelp of pain as I rise. It's the other crafts I see first. Hundreds of them bobbing on the water before the Houses of Parliament. Their filthy passengers in various states of injury and disarray. All wear a hollow air of aftershock. But it's different from the chaos before. It's quiet except for an expectant murmuring, a few sobs. Everyone is looking in the same direction: up at the parliament building in front of us. With dim eyes that long to close, I follow Seth's pointing finger. The water's still ten feet higher than it should be. Way above it and the old Speaker's house, over a three-foot parapet in the north corner, Essie's wrecked and shining face appears. She waves, her lips parting in the brightest smile I've ever seen her pull. She bends and lifts someone, holding them tight as dark curls sway for brief seconds, then disappear. Sobbing, Seth waves back.

Essie's face darkens as she reaches behind her and yanks an arm forward to the precipice. It's Langford, and he doesn't look like he's doing much better than me. My vision blurs, and I have to blink to right it. Langford's face is bloody, and it looks the wrong shape. His shoulders slump as the crowd erupts into cheers.

"ALEX LANGFORD IS A MURDERER." Essie's voice is amplified somehow, seeming to echo around me.

How is she doing that? She's like a goddess up there. It hurts to look at her, so I let my eyelids slide closed.

"Mum?"

My heart stings at the panic in his voice, but I'm falling, can't stop. I don't want to, but there's one more thing.

"Phone," I say.

It's so cold here that when the warm, black wave comes, I'm glad to ride it.

# Chapter Thirty-Seven

## Essie

### 26th November 2041 3.00pm

"Willow, wait inside. Turn your back and close your eyes, okay?" I squeeze her into a hug as tight as I dare. As she staggers through the wooden door, I close it behind her and raise the megaphone again. "He's killed hundreds, thousands, with his greed and brutality. He murdered my best friend, Maya." So many more, but the weight of her name is on my chest.

Langford's face pulls up around his wound in a sneer. "She was a stupid bitch."

As I deliver him a vicious shake, breath and bubbles of blood burst out of the hole in his face.

Hallie steps up behind him, pressing his gun into the back of his skull. "Shut up."

His eyes swivel towards her. "Killed some of yours, too, didn't I? Your brother, Francis. Your exhibitionist boyfriend."

Hallie's face freezes. Her knuckles turn white around the gun.

"Hallie..." I shake him again. "Shut up." Gripping the megaphone in my cramped, trembling fist, I peer down at the expectant crowd.

Everywhere is aftermath. Bodies float between makeshift rafts full of silent survivors. Some of them are people I recognise from Kim's camp, some strangers. Jez and Luisa cling together on a jagged fragment of broken boat. Among them, cops rip off their Unity badges and join the rebels.

Drones rendered useless by the flood skim and plunge, kicking up blades of filthy water and river stench. Bitter, black-smoked fires burn in the surrounding buildings, whether set by the rebels or caused by the flood I'm not sure. But their roar, and the irregular whine of the drones, fill my ears with distortion.

In the middle of it all, Seth's face is a glowing, steady presence. He mouths '*I love you*' and my eyes prickle with tears as I respond. I can't believe we made it this far.

Beside Seth, Carlo shakes Kerry, who seems out cold. He bows his head, then rummages in her pocket.

"Say something more," whispers Hallie.

My cheeks flare hot when I realise all gazes turn from the rafts up at me. "What?"

"I dunno, something. They'll be here soon to shoot us down. This is our last chance to speak the truth."

She's right. They abandoned the building for the flood, but now the worst is over, reinforcements will be on their way. Breathing hard, I stare down at the faces on the river. The megaphone lifts to my mouth, almost against my will. "They rig the system." The crowd jeers, then falls silent. "Rig it for themselves. They know we know it and they don't care. They've had hundreds of years at it. How many more different ways do they have to show us they don't care? What more proof do we need?" I pause to cough in the silence.

Is that a helicopter's whirr? They're coming.

"Go on, Ess," Hallie says in my ear.

I lift the megaphone. In my throat churn all the despair, the terror and helpless fury, that have bloomed since this nightmare began; since my family were killed, and the world's hate and greed took control. "Look at this place! Look what they've done. To *our* planet. Not theirs. It's for all of us. And all life on it." A murmuring grows below. "It's time to change. And it's down to us. There's plenty to go round, even now. We have resources. We have enough invention among us. I know because I've seen it for myself. So let's stop waiting for these bastards to give a shit. Because they never will." I stare at Langford, my lips twisting. "They had their chance. It's our turn."

Amid the cheers, Langford pulls away from my loosened grip and emits a wet chuckle. "You fucking idiot! People won't change. It's too much effort. How do you think I got to be in charge in the first place? Because your average prole can't be bothered." His voice is muffled and whistly, with air in the wrong places. He glares down at the people. "They haven't got the discipline. Or the intellect for such complexity. They'd rather suck on their pacifiers and let the grownups run things. Some of us were born to lead." He shrugs at my bitter laugh. "And if we accept the compensations that come with that, what do they care?"

"Compensations? Like murder, you mean?" Hallie makes a growling noise in her throat. "You *fucker*."

"Hallie…"

She shakes me off and lifts the gun, pulling back the slide and aiming at his ruined face.

Langford steps back from the parapet, forcing Hallie to twist towards it. "You haven't got the balls."

Below us, the crowd murmurs.

"Hallie, put down the gun. We'll deal with him later."

Hallie sobs, or maybe laughs. "There won't be a later, Ess. They're coming."

The helicopter blades are closer now. Their wind tickles my sweaty face.

Langford squints at Hallie. "Go on, then. Do it. Your street scum boyfriend would have by now. If I hadn't ripped a hole in his chest."

"No!" I push Hallie's hand off course.

Her arms jerk up and back as the gun flashes and recoils. The explosion distorts in my ears. Langford shrieks and grabs his head, blood flying above and behind. Clutching at the air, Hallie falls back. Her legs paddle as she collides with the parapet. Crying out, I grab for her, but my grip fails. Hallie takes a wheezing breath, and with a fervid grasp, catches hold of Langford. Seconds later, they're gone. A heavy splash is followed by more splattering, another shot. Hallie screams. Shouts erupt from the crowd.

"HALLIE." Nerves burning against hope, I peer over the edge to the water below.

Nothing.

Just the roiling, bloody water and shocked, wordless crowd bobbing on their fleet of rafts. I search for Seth, but he's not there.

"Hallie." I sink to my knees, weeping wildly. When hands grip my shoulders, I fight them off until I realise they're Seth's.

"Shhh. Ess." He rocks me back and forth, absorbing my grief, kissing my head over and over between sobs of his own. "It's okay. We're okay. I'm here."

Willow's cries join ours, her hands clutching. We cling to each other, we three, hopeless as the helicopter's roar slices the air above us.

# Chapter Thirty-Eight

## Willow

### 26th November 2066

For a long while, all I remembered was fractured, dim vignettes. To begin with, they were random and fleeting. Over the years, my mind has compiled them into some sort of order. The fragments arranged together, all pointing one way: towards that day, exactly a quarter of a century ago, when everything changed.

I remember sleeping in a shed with gaslight shadows. A kind man called Rook. Being locked in a strange house; another house, a posh one, with a black woman I later found out was Kerry Tyler. Crying for the want of Mum. The flash of a gun and burning. Crying in pain and terror in a dark wood corridor, then Dad running towards me, dripping wet and wild-eyed. All of us hugging on a stone balcony.

In the rear-view mirror, there's Boop, his green ears so long they drag on the parcel shelf. He's not the original Boop, of course. I lost him somewhere, while I was being dragged between houses and underground bunkers. When I realised, I wailed so hard they bought me a replacement and scuffed him up to look like the old one. I knew what they'd done, but I never let on. Boop II has been with me ever since. Silly, really, but I feel quite superstitious about his presence.

As the car eases me along, I stare out of the window. The new Riley units are much bigger than the early models. Various shades of natural green, their fronds blend in with the real trees and wild landscape much better, descending in richly foliaged terraces towards the black mirror of the solar panel road I'm travelling. So much of our countryside resembles this place, we take it for granted. Occasionally, I'm still ambushed by its beauty. And by the growing sweetness of the air.

Jack could have been a billionaire several times over, but he chose not to be, only conceding to our naming the carbon capture units for him, which I know still makes him squirm. Lucky for us that Brent Cross was spared the worst of the flood. And lucky they found Jack locked in that safehouse before he starved to death. He won't have it said, but without him, we wouldn't have got as far as we did as quickly. The Rileys have been our way back. Without them, it would have taken generations to clean the air.

For me, growing up was not easy—littered with frequent relocations, a lot of negotiations, and a great deal of work. By the time I was twelve, I'd seen more than one new city born, with gleaming, spiralling architecture cloaked in organic habitats. One compensation that everything fell apart so badly: it forced us to build again. We endured the floods, fires and storms inherited from the old ways. We still do, though in recent years they show signs of receding.

That awful day, so many innocents died in the flood. It was like the world had woken from a long, feverish sleep. Something changed. You could almost smell it mingling with the silt and damp.

Still, there were those who hated what we stood for, who threatened our safety. With Langford dead, Oliver Foster-Pugh was arrested, tried and imprisoned for crimes against humanity. To some, he became a martyr, an advocate for a traditional way of life. They defended it violently. The Redemption Charter grew militant, a self-fashioned resistance movement determined to restore feudal economics.

My childhood was punctuated with as much fear as hope. As the years passed, though, the resistance loosened its grip. It was a numbers game in the end: there were more of us than them. The tight security gave way to quieter protection. I could even make this journey alone, without my bodyguard

—today of all days.

As for the old cities, they still exist, though they're different now. They repaired London, though it never again reached its former glory. Newburgh, Northamptonshire is our capital now, and that's as it should be. It's central-ish, more accessible than London for most, and was the first new city built with Riley units integrated.

The sign for Balmford glides towards me, and my heart picks up speed. It's been months since I made it back here. Life in Newburgh is hectic. The Citizen Assembly takes up most of my waking hours. There's so much to learn. Still, I only serve for five years, so it has to come first.

But not today.

They've painted the gate of the vicarage since I was last here. It gleams white in the low, late-autumn sun.

Mum whips the door open, her face beaming, red and dusted with flour. "Wills." I don't have time to respond before she rushes me with a tight hug. "Thank you for coming," she whispers in my ear, then pulls back, her stroking finger finding the old wound on my cheek.

"Where else would I be?" I brush her grey-auburn hair back, revealing the scar around her eye. One of many she still carries, inside and out. Wounds inflicted by the cruel, old guard; wounds inflicted on herself.

Once, when I was old enough to ask about the marks on Mum's arms and wrists, she described them as her growth rings, like you find on a tree. She pointed at my scar and said I was special because I got my first growth ring when I was so young. At the time I couldn't make sense of it, but now I understand. Each of her own marks commemorated a moment of exquisite darkness for her. A point where she was so close to surrender the only thing left was to gouge it from her own flesh. Those moments came together that day, twenty-five years ago. They made her the person she needed to be. Or the person she always was but never understood.

She frowns and gives me a little smile, as though confused. "Come inside. Everyone's here."

In the kitchen, Brian has outdone himself. Eighty-one, but

314

he's still making legendary feasts. Meat rations are suspended on celebration days like today, so he's made his old signature— a golden-topped bobotie. The kitchen is aromatic with its spices.

He squeezes me into a bear hug, his scraggy beard scratching my cheek, then pulls back to cup my face. "Willow, my beautiful child."

"Child. I'm thirty next April."

"Ah, still a beauty, though. Zora's a lucky woman."

"Yeah. She knows." I roll my eyes and flap a hand at the table laden with sandwiches, chicken wings and rainbow-coloured cakes. "You've pulled a blinder, Bri."

"I had some help." He grins at a tanned, blond man standing at the stove, who winks back. "This is Kurt."

"Hi, Kurt." I raise my eyebrows at Bri as he blushes and chuckles.

"Hey, come here, errant daughter." Dad's leaning on the door frame, glass of wine in hand. "Give your old man a hug."

The sage-smelling aftershave on his neck brings a tangled wave of love and memory. Throughout the upheaval of my childhood—the many journeys, the strange beds, all Mum's half-heard speeches—Dad's scent was the one steady presence. I lost count of the times he carried me to bed in strange homes, hostels and camps, making up stories to help me sleep. There were times when Mum's absence was bitter. I think I understand now that she was doing it for me. Etched into the lines around her mouth, I see all the times she wanted to be the one telling me stories, the one tucking me into my covers.

"How's Newburgh?" Dad puts down his glass, grabs a clean one from the draining board, and fills it for me.

I take it and swig. "Busy. The Citizen Assembly meets again on Monday."

"No rest for the wicked, huh?"

"Says the defrocked cleric."

"I wasn't defrocked, I quit." He grabs Mum's waist as she wanders within reach. "For love."

"Unhand me, you fiend." Mum giggles and turns to me. "Come in the lounge. Everyone wants to say hi."

"Everyone?"

She holds up her hands. "What? Just a few people, is all."

My cheeks grow warm. "Mum, I told you I didn't want a fuss. I specifically said that."

"Everyone's proud of you. It's not every day a daughter of Balmford gets to write the Guardian's Tipping Point speech."

"I'm not the daughter of Balmford, you are. I'm a daughter of…everywhere."

She gulps her wine. "Well, like I said, it's just a few people." Inclining her head, she slips out the door.

I glance at Dad for back up, but he's no use. Just tops up my glass unnecessarily and gives me a nudge towards the door.

"I've still got to get back tonight," I call, following Mum down the hall to the lounge.

She's gone and done it. Expectant faces cram the room. Applause erupts when I enter. Mum has hung a silver banner with red lettering spelling out *Well done, Willow* over the mantelpiece.

There are a lot of heroes in the room. Jack's here, his grey beard curling into a smile as he stands. Jez's clapping echoes in the empty fireplace as his huge hands collide. He was the first one who came with the helicopter rescuers, security forces converted to the cause. Halima, too, who helped so many of the wounded the day of the flood. Jonah sits close to her, his long legs splayed over the rug. They made a hell of a team that day, Mum says, and she swears he saved her life, too. Idika is sitting on the arm of a chair by Martha, Hallie's mum, who smiles but looks frailer than ever. She's nearly eighty, but Mum says she lost her vitality after Hallie died. Son and daughter both killed by Alex Langford. How could she not?

Carlo is standing in the corner, stroking at a greying temple, a broad smile on his lips. I steer a course to his familiar face, my fellow Assembly member and best friend. "How did *you* escape Zora's edict to attend the speech?"

"I promised her I'd make sure you didn't get drunk."

"Good luck with that." I drain my glass. "If you wanted me sober, you should have stopped my mum organising this mass humiliation."

"No human could do that. Humiliation? Come on. The speech is incredible. You deserve the slaps on the back."

"This can't be an easy day for you."

He shrugs and looks at the wall. "It's okay. Well, it's not okay Mum died. But she did the right thing in the end, you know? I'm proud of her."

"She'd have been so proud of you." I squeeze his hand. "You shared those horrific documents with the world. Without them, I don't believe we'd have gained so much support."

"She took the pictures, not me."

"But you released them. Without knowing which side would win, you did it anyway. You could have been killed."

"Government plans for street militia and concentration camps. I don't know anyone who could have read those under the circumstances and stayed silent. Do you?"

"A few." I grin at him. "But most of them are in jail."

"O-kay." Dad claps his hands. "Two o'clock. Show time." He presses a button on the wall and a screen descends, to my relief covering the *Well Done, Willow* sign. When it lights up, a stage is set with the rainbow insignia of the Global Citizen Alliance. Colourful foliage lines a podium. Dad pats the space next to him on the threadbare red sofa, and Mum sits down the other side, squashing me in the middle. I suspect she's trying to trap me so I can't run away.

As we quieten, Zora appears through a door on-screen. She looks great in the scarlet dress I helped her choose. It makes her bum look great and accentuates her shining, black skin.

Zora adjusts the mic and takes in an expansive breath the way she does before a speech. "My fellow citizens, I am honoured to be here today to speak as your new Guardian. I'd like to begin by thanking my predecessor, Ash."

Dad leans over to me. "Punching above your weight,

317

aren't you?"

"Listen to my words, Father. You might learn something."

"The arrogance of youth."

Mum glares across at him. "Shhh."

Zora has moved on, her French accent delicious. "As you all know, each year we commemorate this day we call The Tipping Point. After that first day, a quarter of a century ago, when the world awoke from its self-destructive fugue." Zora pauses, focuses her earnest, long-lashed eyes on the camera. "We lost many lives that day in London. Over three hundred thousand souls sacrificed to the old world. Martyrs of the elite's war against nature. Many heroes died. The names we know, yes. Kim Vella, Piper Moran, Gabe Astor, Hallie Morris…"

Martha pulls in a shaky breath, and Idika squeezes her shoulder.

Mum wipes a hand over her eyes and whispers, "Maya Taheri."

On the screen, Zora says, "There were many more whose names you might not know. Those who helped others escape the flood, those who treated the wounded; who disarmed the guards and destroyed the drones; who helped uncover the truth."

Carlo looks at his hands. Probably thinking of Kerry.

Zora pauses, glances down at the podium, then back at us. "To them all, we owe an unpayable debt. And to all those who continued the fight after that day. As history tells us, it was not the last of the old guard. There were many battles still to fight, and much work left to do. To bring to justice those who would destroy us all; to establish the world's first Citizen Assembly, to create the global renewable energy grid, and appoint the world's first Earth Guardian. They could not have made a better choice than Essie Glass."

Mum's shoulder grows stiff next to mine. "Your idea of revenge, Wills? It's just a few people…"

I giggle and knock against her.

Zora hasn't finished with Mum yet: "Essie's story, her strength and determination, her abiding compassion, made

318

her the perfect counterpoint to the old ways. Little by little, we won the battles. Some we lost, of course. But thanks to Essie's tenure, we reached critical mass within the first five years. More nations set up Assemblies of their own. Riley units were made available globally and free. To this day, Jack Riley continues to work to improve the technology, so it integrates seamlessly with the natural world. It's a truly awe-inspiring sight.

"But today isn't just about the grand scheme. It's a day for family and friends. For love and joy and thankfulness. You've already heard enough from me. I have incredible speechwriters, but even they don't have the words to express the pride and gratitude we should all feel that we brought ourselves to the brink of destruction and repented just in time. So, enough talk. Please, everyone, enjoy."

The on-screen crowd erupts at the same time as our room. Mum squeezes me into a side-hug. "Amazing, love. I'm so proud."

Dad chuckles. "Incredible speechwriters."

My heart pounds and swells. "I didn't write that bit, you clown."

# Chapter Thirty-Nine

## Essie

### 26th November 2066

The sky glows orange with the setting sun as Jack steps down onto the front path. He's a little unsteady on his feet, but perhaps that's the wine.

"You sure you won't stay? Willow's going back to Newburgh tonight so we've a spare room in the vicarage."

"Thank you. But I'd better be getting home. Curie will be missing me."

"She's a cat, Jack. You know she doesn't give a damn about you, don't you?"

"I can dream." He chuckles, then his eyes crease down into sadness, lingering on my scar. "I'm sorry I got you involved. It was weak of me. I should have gone public with the prototype myself, not used a teenage girl to do it."

"You were scared. Rightly. They'd have killed you. And then where would we be now?"

His gaze drifts past me into the hallway as he rubs at the scar Langford gave him. "It was never sexual, my interest in you."

My face feels warm—honestly, at my age. "Whereas my interest in you…"

He blushes too as his eyes return to mine. "I'm serious. I just wanted to help you; didn't want you to…get in trouble."

He rolls his eyes and we giggle.

"I wouldn't change any of it. It's a while since I've been in trouble. I had a lifetime's worth back then."

"And now you have Seth."

"Now I have Seth."

He fiddles with a frond of stray ivy by the door frame. "He's never trusted me, has he? Not really."

"It's not that. He's just… You're different kinds of people. Man of faith versus man of science, I guess."

Hands in pockets, he stretches them out. "Faith in God? After all this?"

"Not God. Not for a long time, I think. Faith in people."

He looks away. "Well, I never had any of that."

"You see? Different kinds of people. And I need both kinds."

He cups my chin in a cold, soft hand. "Ess. You *are* both kinds." He turns away down the path.

Willow's arm squeezes my shoulders. Together we watch Jack fumble the gate closed and weave his way down the lane.

In the backyard, Seth's doing drunken handstands with Carlo. Everyone else has gone home. Willow flops onto the patio slabs and lolls against the wall.

"Someone's gonna get hurt." Her speech is slurred and languid.

I screw up my mouth and nod as I join her. "Probably. But I'm not going to be the one to stop them, are you?"

"Hell hath no fury like an interrupted midlife crisis."

"Quite right." I chuckle and hold up my half-full beer bottle to toast them.

"Mum, these are ace." Willow's clutching the scrappy sketches I made at the party. She holds up the one of her and Seth laughing together. "You should do more drawing. You have a real talent."

"Maybe I will." I drink in her flushed cheeks and sparkling eyes. "You know, when you were little, you were such an incredible climber."

"I remember. Dad called me monkey girl."

"Scared the life out of me more than once." I push back a frizzy curl from her cheek. "Look how high you've climbed now. I'm sorry."

"What for?"

"Everything you went through because of me." My fingers trace the ripples of her scar. "And then not being there as much as I should. I know it wasn't easy growing up as my daughter."

"Are you kidding? It was the best. I mean, apart from all the kidnapping and being shot by sociopathic politicians."

My laugh comes out with a dribble of beer. "I don't even know why I'm still drinking."

"Because." Willow grabs the bottle from me and takes a slug. "Today is a day for love and joy and thankfulness."

"Amazing speech, Wills."

Her gaze turns misty. "Amazing life."

"I…" a smile stretches my lips as I wrest the bottle back, "…will drink to that."

# THE END

# Fantastic Books
# Great Authors

darkstroke is
an imprint of
Crooked Cat Books

- Gripping Thrillers
- Cosy Mysteries
- Amazing Horrors
- Fascinating Historicals
- Exciting Fantasy
- Young Adult
- Non-Fiction

Discover us online
**www.darkstroke.com**

Find us on instagram:
**www.instagram.com/darkstrokebooks**

Printed by Amazon Italia Logistica S.r.l.
Torrazza Piemonte (TO), Italy